Underground People

LEWIS NKOSI

Underground People

ayebia
An Adinkra symbol meaning
Ntesie matemasie
A symbol of knowledge and wisdom

This edition published by Ayebia Clarke Publishing Limited
7 Syringa Walk
Banbury OX16 1FR
Oxfordshire
UK

This edition first published in 2005
First published in South Africa by Kwela Books, 2002
28 Wale Street, Cape Town 8001
P.O. Box 6525, Roggebaai 8012

British Library Cataloguing-in-Publication Data
A catalogue record of this book is available from the British Library.

Cover design by 24bit design
Cover artwork by Louw Venter
Cover author photo © David Clarke
Typeset by FiSH Books, London.
Printed and bound in Great Britain by Cox & Wyman Ltd., Reading, Berkshire.

ISBN 0-9547023-2-8

Available from www.ayebia.co.uk or email: info@ayebia.co.uk
Distributed by *TURNAROUND* at www.turnaround-uk.com.

For Astrid Starck
who worked like the devil in the
preparation of this manuscript

Prologue

DISAPPEARANCE, abduction, kidnapping: causing other human beings to disappear without a trace, leaving behind them empty air, blue and vivid with unanswered questions. This is the speciality of our century, our most typical crime, our most daring feat and distinct achievement in an epoch marked by a preference for refined torture and technical innovation. Men and women disappear. Any particular night the hapless family may retire to bed with its numbers intact, confident or maybe mildly fearful about the future; the following morning, suddenly alerted to misfortune, an anxious crowd has gathered in this family's doorway, asking questions, sharing confidences. Usually someone is explaining: a wife, a son, a brother, very often a wife. With a slightly trembling mouth and tears coursing down her cheeks, she supplies details of what essentially has become a familiar story. At least, this is what Cornelius, reading newspaper reports about these grisly happenings in his own country and about murder and mayhem in many other lands, had come to think.

Cornelius had read one such report about an incident in a Latin American country which had followed the usual pattern. The wife, a mother, had supplied the details to waiting newsmen: 'It was early this morning, before the light of dawn, that a group of armed men in plain clothes drove up to the gate in an unnumbered car,' the woman was quoted as saying. 'At the point of a gun, they ordered my husband to get dressed quickly and quietly, and then they ordered him to get into the back of the car, flanked by a man on either side. One of them,' the distraught woman had added as an afterthought, 'had features which seemed kindlier than the rest, but when I asked him why they were taking my husband away he pushed the butt of his rifle against my stomach and told me to get back into the house and keep my mouth shut if I knew what was good for me. Everything happened so quickly I didn't even have time to get scared. Then, just as quickly as they had come, they were gone without a trace!'

Here the woman was reported to have paused briefly in her narrative, bravely attempting a smile through her tears; then she had added a small detail which seemed to everyone a bit eccentric: 'Beg a pardon!' the woman was said to have quietly remarked, holding out a stub of something still burning. 'One of them left this cigarette behind. It's a Gauloise.'

Of course, a Gauloise, but the cigarette could have been any other brand, Cornelius had thought at the time. That, too – the bewildering variety and profusion of brand names with which our lives are surrounded – is another significant achievement of our century.

Taking all this into account, the nature of the risks involved, the startling prevalence of this kind of crime – 'illegality' used to be the preferred term among the various peoples' democracies – what happened to Cornelius Molapo early one October morning was not so remarkably different from the fate of many others in similar circumstances in Africa, South America, Asia and the Middle East, except perhaps in a few unimportant details. Nevertheless, small and unimportant as these differences may seem, they tended to deprive Molapo's own disappearance of the necessary pathos and drama often mentioned in respect of such cases, such as the unequal struggle against heavy odds, the drama of attempted escape, pistols being fired, crowds gathering in the street, mourning relatives.

For one thing, in Molapo's case there was no wife to wring her hands and mourn her husband's disappearance. Maureen Molapo had walked out of their Dube home after only three years of marriage, vowing never to return. Molapo lived in splendid isolation, without a wife, without parents or relatives in the neighbourhood. A tall, lean two metres, a citizen of what visiting foreign journalists like to call 'the sprawling black township' of Johannesburg, an incompetent teacher of languages and a dabbler in poetry and politics, Molapo himself was not cast in a particularly heroic mould.

In the past, in his capacity as a local chairman of the National Liberation Movement, he had often addressed small but wildly enthusiastic crowds in the open space outside the Orlando community hall. He would stand on not one but two soapboxes set side by side in order to steady his tall gangling frame. The theme of his speeches was nearly always the same: the deepening political crisis in the country and the necessity to prepare for armed struggle. Though this is the impression he might have given, Molapo was not a 'ranter' except when the occasion demanded it. Very often he spoke softly, caressingly, of what he described poetically as the gathering clouds of revolution, of the victory that was sure to follow, as if the end itself was not in doubt, only the means. With his eye always firmly fixed on historical precedence, he mentioned a possible bloodbath as a prelude to momentous changes, but more often than not when he spoke of the cleansing virtues of violence, pressing his point home with abundant quotations from Fanon, Bakunin and Che Guevara, it was usually late at night, and not in the public square but in the *shebeens* when his drinking cronies were already in a far more receptive mood, already preparing to cast themselves into any epic role that an overheated imagination can supply. To these men sobbing openly into their cups, Molapo was the grand poet of the struggle, the inimitable stage-manager of its *mise en scène*, the creator and panderer to their lusts for meaningful action.

Otherwise, their local Guevara was a gentle person who spoke in soft, casual, at times deeply ironic tones, in a voice resonant with unsung music as he touched on the nodal points at which love and revolution intersect, the points at which the incorrigibly private and the irrevocably public are finally reconciled. An intellectual who lived for the most part in the richly tapestried world of ideas, fond of books, music and painting, this is how many were later to remember Cornelius Molapo.

In his quieter role of 'township poet', his work had already been praised in local reviews and overseas journals, and it was said by those who knew about these things that his best poetry lacked only such distinction as normally eludes artists who, despite their obvious gifts, have little time in which to devote themselves entirely to their art, the implication being that they have more important things to think about. As Molapo himself had often said: 'I have other fish to fry' – perhaps too many, unfriendly wags were heard to add. That may have been so, but in recognition of his own amateur status, and showing a healthy scepticism about his own talent, Molapo had often quoted his favourite American novelist against himself. 'I try to serve God and Mammon,' he joked, 'and I don't know how God will come off!' To please him his friends laughed with him without having any idea what he was talking about. But they liked the man's self-mocking, irreverent spirit, his desperate irony and his flirtation with the edge.

Needless to say, this charitable view of Molapo was not one that was shared by his comrades in the struggle. Once when Molapo was groaning under an oversize hangover and was feeling particularly irritable, he had done a great deal of damage to his standing with his comrades within the Liberation Movement, first by urging action to men whose first instinct was caution, men moreover more disciplined than himself; then by concluding a long, very intemperate, very vituperative speech by quoting, not a Lenin or a Marx, but his favourite American novelist against his comrades, sourly remarking on his way out of the meeting: 'For Goodness' sake, comrades! Let us act now. After all, our Movement can never surprise us anymore except by doing something.'

Some members of the executive thought the allusion was to the thoroughly discredited theory of 'permanent revolution.' In a tiny room already wreathed in cigarette smoke there was immediate uproar: tables were thumped and heads were shaken, and in an effort to silence him everyone began shouting at once before they realised he had already left the room.

Nevertheless, despite periodic calls for disciplinary action to be taken against him, Molapo got away with only reprimands for his many misdemeanours; for the most part the leadership of the National Liberation Movement took a lenient view of his deviant behaviour. They regarded him indulgently as a harmless crank who loved speech-making because of the mellifluent music to which words can sometimes lend themselves. They had long ago decided that Molapo's value, if he had any value, lay in his ability to raise the consciousness of the masses. This was a polite way of saying he was something of a demagogue. So when they were in good humour the representatives of the Movement referred to him simply as 'Molapo the poet', with the emphasis on the poetry rather than his politics; but when they were in bad humour they dismissed him as that 'Dube windbag!'

All of which came to one thing: everyone knew Molapo was not dangerous; only his love of fine words made him seem so. That is why when, following the declaration of the state of emergency, the National Liberation Movement circulated a list of names of some two hundred persons who had mysteriously disappeared from their homes, many people expressed mild surprise that Molapo's name should have been among those feared held 'incommunicado' by the security police. When asked by various interested parties, the representative of the Movement was in no doubt about it. 'Held incommunicado!' he kept repeating. 'We suspect he's being held incommunicado. Definitely, must be held incommunicado!' For, next to habeas corpus, 'incommunicado' was this comrade's favourite legal term.

Molapo himself would have been most surprised to learn that he was missing had not a dossier been thrust into his hands by a representative of the National Liberation Movement, with the most telling details underlined in red ink, emphasising his unexplained disappearance, complete with attached newspaper clippings which contained published expressions of concern from various humanitarian organisations in Stockholm, Amsterdam, Paris, London and New York.

One of these, the London-based Human Rights International, it was learned, was so perturbed by the numbers of people being held that it was sending a man out to investigate – one Anthony Ferguson, 'a white South African, born and bred', as the Movement's representative later told Molapo. Of this man and his reputation, the Movement's representative spoke with extraordinary enthusiasm, describing him as 'a true son of the soil', a man whose teeth had been cut in the Latin American struggle for human rights. 'If he is as good as his reputation,' the Movement's representative had finally declared, 'he should be able to understand our struggle better than most!' Then he smiled and patted Molapo on the shoulder. 'So, tell me, *mfana*, how does it feel to be "missing"?'

'Am I missing?' Molapo said with surprise.

'Of course you're missing. Else why would someone from Human Rights International come all the way from London to look for you?'

Both Cornelius and the Movement's representative treated this as one of the best jokes they had ever heard. As Cornelius was leaving the room, both were in stitches of laughter; though once out of the room and in the street, Cornelius wondered what the joke had been truly about.

Chapter One

THE day Anthony Ferguson left London for South Africa it was snowing. Ten days before Christmas and there was a dark chill in the London air that not even the cheerful Christmas decorations in Oxford Street could entirely dispel. The women, it must be admitted, looked marvellous in their thick winter clothes, booted and furred, tousle-headed and snow-stormed. The pubs were full of them. They looked as English women do in the excitement of shopping for Christmas, collectively animated and radiant.

His brow deeply furrowed under the brim of a brown hat that fell limply over one watchful eye, Anthony Ferguson, the putative international civil servant, emerged regretfully from a Dean Street pub on to the wet pavements of Shaftesbury Avenue, leaning heavily on Tina's arm, a little drunk and giddy from the excitement of farewells and all the sombre warnings he had been compelled to soak up like a sponge in the past hour.

'Look here, old chap!' Stephen Mayfield, an old friend who had recently covered the Stonybrook shootings for a Fleet Street newspaper, started it. 'When you get out there, Anthony, don't for goodness' sake go blundering about the townships on your own like a first-rate idiot! This Stonybrook business hasn't blown over by any means. Chances are,' Stephen warned him, 'if the blacks don't stick a sharp blade into your guts those infernal *boers* from the special branch will squeeze your testes for you very slowly, very exquisitely.'

'Stephen, for goodness sake!' This was the part Ferguson hated. He swallowed the last of his drink before attempting to catch Tina's eye across the bar. At that very moment she was trying to extricate herself from a bunch of chaps who had come in from the Film Institute across the street. Their eyes met briefly and Tina blinked in that rapid way she always had of shutting and opening her eyes when she was in trouble with men. He and Tina were not lovers in the true sense of the word by any stretch of the imagination; from the very beginning their sleeping together had been more the result of a warm feeling of comradeship than any deeply felt passion. Tina worked as his assistant in the offices of the Human Rights International; she was not pretty but she was sexually attractive in that small, cuddly sort of way some girls have; and she was exceptionally intelligent.

With a quick nod of the head Tina tossed back her flaming red hair; and Anthony, smiling tensely, made a leaving gesture before turning his attention to the flushed Falstaffian face whose sardonic expression was beginning to exasperate him. 'I'm a South African, you know, Stephen,' Anthony resumed, watching Tina from the corner of one eye as she assiduously copied something into her small pocket book, while bent over her shoulder a shaggy-haired boy with bright green eyes observed the operation with an air of unrelenting supervision. When Anthony turned again to Stephen Mayfield a new feeling of anxiety and suppressed irritation, very odd for him, began to quicken his normal bland diplomatic tone. He could hear his own voice sounding distant yet unexpectedly raspy with emotion. 'Stephen, just remember one thing. I know more about that country than you'll ever find out in a lifetime of nocturnal visits,' he said.

Stephen laughed good-humouredly, then squinted deprecatingly at his friend: 'Alright! Alright!' He waved a long arm at Ferguson, his smile growing more expansive, more seraphic.

'Only tell me this. How long have you been away from there? Ten years? Fifteen?'

'Fifteen,' Anthony conceded.

'There you are!' Stephen chuckled triumphantly as if that clinched the argument. 'My dear boy, you have no idea how much South Africa has changed in all the years you've been away. What the country was fifteen years ago bears absolutely no relation to what it is today.'

Stephen shifted his bulky weight the better to see more of the incoming crowd. Anthony found it irritating the way Mayfield divided his attention between the person he was supposed to be talking to and strangers at the far end of the bar whom he watched carefully, sometimes even listening to their conversations. Perhaps it was the insatiable curiosity of the journalist, Anthony decided magnanimously.

'There's a war going on out there between black and white,' Stephen expounded, more for the benefit of impressionable eavesdroppers than for Anthony's instruction. 'And the moment you step off the plane everyone wants you to take sides in their beastly quarrel. My advice to you, Anthony, or anyone else going out there, is never get into an argument over the race thing. I mean that. Nerves can get frayed very quickly. Then you have those security chaps to worry about. They get up to some awfully nasty tricks, I can tell you. I shouldn't think they'd be delighted to learn you'd returned to your country as a representative of Human Rights International.'

'Stephen, for God's sake!' Anthony expostulated. 'I'm no greenhorn, you know! I've visited quite a lot of Latin American countries whose record of repression can yield pride of place to none in the world, including South Africa. I know how to take care of myself. Besides, I have a perfect alibi for going out there.'

'Your sister's marriage?' Stephen instantly became more alert than at any time since the start of their conversation, and it was not difficult to understand why. During a recent trip by Mayfield to South Africa, Anthony had given him his sister's

3

address and telephone number, together with some messages to pass on to a few family friends. Hazel, it was very clear afterwards, had made a great impact on Mayfield. Anthony could tell by the awed, breathless way his journalist friend had talked about Hazel on his return to London. It was the same way other men had talked about Hazel after they had come, even briefly, under her spell.

Ever since they were toddlers, growing up in the poor white suburb of Braamfontein under the indifferent eye of a shiftless father and the obsessed brooding devotion of a doting mother, he and Hazel had been so close that at twenty-one Anthony had fled the country – literally – in order, as he later told his closest friends, to escape Hazel's dominating, maybe destructive, influence. Anthony often spoke of his closeness to his sister as men sometimes speak of the pernicious influence of mothers and persistent lovers, with a faked bitterness which did not conceal his adoration.

She was extremely pretty, his sister, as he never tired of informing anyone who cared to listen. She was slim, thin-fleshed, very quick of movement; and for Ferguson this alacrity always gave the impression of someone who attached great value to engagements of no particular importance: to luncheons, dinner parties, cocktails and club dates to which she was forever hurrying and for which, paradoxically, she was forever late. To Anthony it seemed that his sister also possessed a certain quality, very natural to her but awe-inspiring to others, of seeming to be somehow imperishable, like some exotic flower of the *veld*. Her prodigious vitality, her storms of emotion, even her momentous foolishnesses – above all her colour, that whiteness of flesh which, as she dawdled in a city bar at noon or lolled about on the sands of the beach in the afternoon, caused her body to look as though it were perpetually being consumed by light – made the very notion of Hazel's mortality seem not only ludicrous but an almost scandalous proposition.

Anthony's fondest memory of his sister was of Hazel

dressed in immaculate white; lithe in her splendid coolness, a bright glow surrounding her foliage of blonde hair like a halo, yet managing even in that moment of apparent virginal purity to summon by gesture, by a faint twitch of the mouth, or simply by the shifting movement of her hips, a suggestion of the most urgent of all human desires. No wonder that, hard-boiled as he was reputed to be – as most journalists were supposed to be – on his return from South Africa, Stephen Mayfield seemed to be still reeling under the blows of what was an exceptionally novel encounter for him.

'So? Is that really going ahead? The marriage I mean?' Stephen said tensely, one eyebrow arched higher than the other. Hazel had perhaps idly mentioned to Mayfield what were then vague plans to get married, but watching Stephen's gross features contorted by an unusual betrayal of emotion, Anthony was glad to extract some malicious pleasure from his friend's momentary loss of equilibrium.

'Oh, yes,' he said cheerfully, gleefully. 'I'm afraid that is very definitely going ahead.' For a moment Anthony allowed his eye to follow desultorily an eruption into the bar of a new crowd of Christmas celebrants.

'But why wait all these years and then all of sudden decide –?' Stephen's voice trailed away inconclusively.

'Money, dear boy, money!' Anthony exclaimed. 'Brody's rolling in it.' To maximise his friend's continuing discomfort, Anthony felt obliged to elaborate on Brody's pecuniary virtues. He leaned confidingly towards Mayfield. 'He's made pots of money, I'm told, by the simple method of buying abandoned gold mines at throwaway prices and then turning them into profitable propositions by using the latest extraction methods in mining technology.'

Stephen looked sceptical. 'Your sister didn't strike me as exactly mercenary,' he objected with a scarcely concealed hostility.

'Perhaps.' Anthony was pleased to concede that much. After all, his sister was not exactly poor either. In her restless, undisciplined fashion, Hazel had already been everything under the sun you could care to name: a cinema usherette, a ballet dancer, a minor actress on the boards of the Johannesburg stage, but, finally, with a stupendous success which took everyone completely by surprise, she had gone on to become an extravagantly well-paid fashion model on more than three continents, the only career she still pursued in her own haphazard way with any serious interest. With a frequency which often amused, sometimes infuriated Anthony, it was hinted by gossip columnists in more than half a dozen cities that Hazel's lovers were as many as the sands, at the very least as numerous as the flock of fashion photographers, couturiers and fashion designers who pursued her at each stop on both sides of the Atlantic Ocean.

'All the same, my sister likes her comforts,' Anthony said. 'I'm afraid she has grown accustomed to a different kind of lifestyle from the one she and I were brought up to in old Braamfontein. Anyway, Steve my boy,' Anthony grinned mischievously, 'you had your chances and you blew them!' There was a sudden lull in the noise of the pub, a lull also in the conversation. When Tina came over to their side of the bar Stephen put his arm around her waist. 'Hello love! Having a good time?'

Tina laughed conspiratorially. 'One of those blokes over there has just offered me a free trip to the Riviera if I'm prepared to be a little nice to him. I said I'd seriously consider it, seeing my boyfriend is about to leave town for at least a month!'

'You disloyal thing!' Anthony grumbled. 'My back is not yet turned and you're already plotting how to get off with another man!' The boy with the green eyes was gazing hopefully at Tina above his glass of malt. Anthony said: 'I've got a good mind to walk over to that green-eyed twit and punch his prissy snout!'

'Come on!' Tina said, seizing Anthony by the arm. 'We've got to get out to the airport on time!'

As in most things, Tina had judged the moment of departure perfectly: her coming over to Anthony's side of the bar, then herding him gently but decisively towards the door, had the appearance of resolution which brooked no opposition from the many friends, including Stephen Mayfield, who were then left to discuss Ferguson's impending return to his 'beastly' homeland with an idle curiosity rather than any seriously engaged interest.

For many of the media people, the writers and painters who normally crowded into the Soho pub, South Africa was an embarrassment and a disgrace, an anomalous place where odd things went on. So many people had died there unnecessarily, they agreed, sometimes extending their concern to the tragic idea that so many more simply disappeared unaccounted for. But, quite extraordinarily, with so much going on there, it was the general opinion of the pub's habituées that South Africa as a subject of conversation was incredibly boring. South Africa and apartheid: everyone concerned with the 'beastly quarrel' was boring. The white South Africans who craved forgiveness or protested at being misunderstood by the 'civilised Western world' were a bore; and so were the blacks and their representatives who appeared with stupefying frequency on television to promote their causes in rhetorical voices rent between impotent rage and futile menace, as they solicited for support from the great 'Western democracies': they were also a bore.

Watching Anthony and Tina exit hastily into the swirling snow of Dean Street, Stephen Mayfield remarked wistfully to no-one in particular: 'I suppose there are worse places one might think of in which to spend a Christmas.' At that moment Mayfield was thinking not so much of Johannesburg or the heat of the African sun on the hot beaches of the south as he was of Ferguson's sister.

Anthony, too, was thinking of his sister. Only a month before, while Human Rights International, quite unbeknown to him, was mooting the idea of sending him out to South Africa, by some uncanny sixth sense Hazel had chosen to telephone out of the blue to inform him of her impending marriage to Mark Brody, a fifty-five-year-old business tycoon whom Anthony had met briefly once or twice on one of Brody's business trips to Europe. Ferguson was in his flat at the time, preparing to go out, when the call came. He paused, as he had done so many times before, with the instrument still in his hand, for the time being unable to make sense of whatever it was Hazel was saying. He was not elated by the news.

'Anthony, are you there?' her irritable voice came over the line. 'Can you hear me?' Anthony's spirit groaned metaphorically with frustration. How many times before had he sat exactly as he was sitting now, in this same chair, using perhaps not the same gestures as he was using now, but leaning back against the cushions, listening with alternate incredulity and annoyance, but mostly with amusement, to Hazel's voice as she related some South African gossip or reported some minor personal misfortune – always with that tone of voice usually reserved for the broadcast of news of disasters like earthquakes or crashing empires? Now he was listening to this same voice announcing a real disaster. She was getting married, she said, and she wanted him present at this event. 'A sort of a bridesman, darling!' She chuckled. Anthony reflected wryly at the time that Hazel's past failures with men had done nothing, apparently, to abate her enthusiasm for fresh romantic adventures. On the line from Johannesburg Hazel could sense her brother's bewilderment and despair.

She said: 'You don't seem very pleased at any rate.'

'Pleased?' Anthony expressed astonishment. 'Should I be?'

'Why not? Mark is a fine man,' his sister cooed on the telephone. 'You've often said so yourself.'

Anthony had no recollection of ever having made such a judgement for the simple reason that he had met Brody no more than twice; and his impression was of a dull, taciturn businessman with a passion for scrutinising ledger books and not much interest in anything else. Brody was said to be shrewd, hardworking and well acquainted with the foibles of the human heart; which meant, Anthony concluded, that he was something of a cynic.

'I don't remember ever having expressed an opinion about Brody,' he protested now.

'That's because you don't know him as well as I do,' Hazel countered, blithely shifting the argument. To this statement Ferguson had no response except to voice the wish that his sister could at least be more consistent. Strangely enough, it was Hazel who had been catty about Brody in the past. She had said: 'Oh, God, he's so dull, my Mark! My God, you don't know how boring he can be! Of all the men I have to see, I don't know why it should be him I let hang around me.'

Anthony could have told his sister why she let Brody hang around, as she put it, because in fact Brody did not hang around anybody. It was that simple. Of all Hazel's lovers he was the only one who let Hazel go her own way while he attended to the serious business of making money. Such an attitude had at first puzzled Hazel, then it had irritated her; perhaps that was why she was now marrying him.

Anthony said to her: 'So when is this wedding to take place?'

'We're planning it for New Year's Eve. I've told Mark to get you a ticket. Can you get away from London?'

He was tempted to refuse. 'Hazel, for fifteen years I've managed to stay clear of our beautiful country! To be honest, after the recent barbarities, I'm inclined to maintain my distance a little longer!' Only three months before, he had made a trip to Latin America and he was still nursing the emotional wounds from that. Also, unlike many South African friends, after fifteen years of living in Britain and Europe Anthony felt no desire to return to the country of his birth. He had no idea that even as they spoke, Human Rights International was making up his mind for him.

*

9

In the afternoon Anthony finished packing, assisted by Tina who held up each piece of clothing, and later books, papers and odds and ends, while she watched his face with her enormous brown, slightly troubled eyes, like one trying to guess at something which puzzled her. She spoke suddenly, as if to clear the air of a thing whose weight it was no longer possible to ignore. 'This man, Cornelius Molapo, what makes him so special to the National Liberation Movement? They've had scores of their members detained before. They've never made quite as much of a fuss as they've done over this one.'

Pausing with one brown dossier in his hand, Anthony looked surprised; he did not speak at once but stared at Tina with an expression of devotion mingled with speculative wonder. 'Absolutely amazing how you seem to know exactly what's on my mind!' he said finally. He waved the brown folder at her. 'You know, Molapo is exactly who I was thinking of this very minute. Quite amazing!' Anthony sat down on the edge of the sofa, gazing abstractedly at the ceiling of the living room. 'I was thinking exactly what you're thinking: how odd the NLM should want to focus so much attention on this particular case. As you rightly point out, others besides him have disappeared before. And yet this month alone we have had more than half a dozen press releases in which Molapo's case has been singled out for special attention by the NLM.

'And then there's the manner in which I am to make contact with the man in charge of Molapo's case. Someone by the name of Joe Bulane. A lawyer, apparently, among his other accomplishments. Very high up in the Movement. Holds a position in the central committee.' Ferguson paused, looking intently at Tina. 'And then there is all that cloak-and-dagger stuff; quite understandable, I suppose, in the circumstances, but I'm required by no means to contact this Joe Bulane directly but only through his legal partner, a white lawyer named Joe Wulitz.'

He started to laugh. Tina raised her eyebrows. 'What?'

'I was just thinking. It's remarkable how they all seem to

have the same name, Joe something-or-other. But you're absolutely right: what's so special about Cornelius Molapo?'

'Well?' Tina said. 'Who is he? Is there something more than we've been told?'

'As in most cases of this kind,' Anthony considered, 'we've stacks of information that is of absolutely no use to anybody. What I've read and what I've been told about Molapo would hardly make anyone's hair stand on end. Quite the contrary, in fact. He sounds quite a normal fellow, really, although I don't know quite what 'normal' means in South Africa any more. Wits University graduate. At the time of his disappearance was a school teacher at Orlando High. Married but separated from his wife. Typical illnesses of our times, I suppose. How much more regular can you get! Well, there's something else,' Anthony grinned, narrowing his eyes at Tina. 'The fellow reads Hegel before going off to bed. Phenomenology of Spirit, that sort of thing, before hitting the pillow!' With one finger Anthony tapped on the file. 'It's right here in one of the newspaper clippings. A profile written by some journalist friend of his who seems to know Molapo quite well. Fellow by the name of Joseph Poground. Obviously thought the fact worth mentioning.'

'Hegel! How delightful!' Tina shrieked. In a burst of appreciative mirth she tumbled playfully into Anthony's arms. 'How absolutely gorgeous! Hegel and marital problems! What could be more normal!'

'He also plays cricket!' Anthony announced.

'Cricket?' From the depths of her shiny eyes Tina gazed into Anthony's slightly sceptical ones. 'An African revolutionary who plays cricket!' Tina giggled. 'How extraordinary! Most unusual! Well, there must be more to this Molapo than cricket, that's all I can say!' She rose, and began clipping the bags shut. A dove sheltering from the snow under the eves of the mews flat began to croon. Tina paused. 'Well, what else?' she said.

'What do you mean, what else?'

'He must believe in something, this Molapo. What about his politics?'

'As far as his politics goes, he's no great shakes either. I went through his dossier very carefully. He was chairman of a small local branch of the NLM in a place called Dube township, but he was never elected to any high office. In fact, from what I've been told the NLM has no reason for holding him in particular.' Ferguson got up from the sofa and began pacing the room. After a while he stopped and sat down, pondering. 'Apparently he's always been a bit of pain in the ass for the Movement, something of an intellectual maverick. At one time or another he's been critical of at least some aspect of NLM policy. From what I can gather, Molapo is the sort of chap who's succeeded, on one occasion or another, in getting up just about everybody's nose.'

'Therefore,' Tina concluded, lawyerly, 'hardly someone the South African Government should want to get out of the way, I would've thought.'

'Exactly! The more trouble for the NLM the better. As a matter of fact, his credentials as a radical aren't that impressive either. From what is known about him, he's more popular in liberal white circles around the Johannesburg suburbs than in the black townships. And rightly so, given the sort of thing he likes to talk about. He delivers lectures on topics like "Love in the Afternoon: Diets of Courting Couples". What the heck do township people care about "The Impact of European Cuisine on African Courtship Patterns"?'

Anthony threw his hands up in the air. 'And this is the chap who suddenly vanishes like a puff of smoke. For six months he hasn't been seen anywhere. He hasn't turned up for his teaching duties and his wife from whom he's separated hasn't a clue what's become of him. Most surprising of all, given the history of what the NLM likes to refer to as Molapo's long history of 'disruptive activities', the organisation is now tearing its hair out trying to find him. Something doesn't quite add up somehow.'

12

Anthony rose from the sofa and Tina joined him. For a moment they stood together looking out of the window at the grey English sky. When the bags were finally packed, made secure and piled up on one side of the living room, Anthony suggested a last drink before leaving for the airport, but he made no move to pour it. Instead he returned to the window and for several minutes continued to gaze abstractedly across the square at the rain beating down on the bare, blackened trees. After numerous parties and countless cocktails, admittedly not all of them intended to celebrate his imminent return to his 'beastly' homeland, Anthony seemed suddenly dazed, out of touch with his surroundings. His face wore a drawn, slightly perplexed expression as he talked aimlessly of some unattended duties at the office, his regret at errands not done and the appointments not kept.

'A journey like this,' he finally gave way to his anxieties, the slight tic on the left eye becoming more pronounced, 'it needs very thorough preparation. Each name, each address, each file must be in its proper place. The funny thing is,' he confided in a dismal voice which to Tina sounded like a cry for help, 'I've made dozens of trips like this before for Human Rights International – any hotspot you can name in Latin America I've been there – but somehow I've never felt quite so unsure of myself as I do at this moment. After all, South Africa is still my home you know!'

'Or ought to be,' Tina said mockingly.

'Or ought to be.' Anthony agreed. 'So I ought to feel more confident than I do at the moment. If the truth be told, I've never been more at a loss about anything as I am about this mission.'

The plea – although plea for what exactly Tina could not make out – was unmistakable in the woeful expression on the austerely rigid, though quite handsome face. At other times that face possessed, for many women who misread weakness for strength, an irresistible charm and magnetism. Observing it closely, not for the first time out of bed, Tina accepted with a

13

miserable gnawing feeling that it somehow reminded her of those young Greek gods, immeasurably flawed, even doomed, enmeshed in the threads of Fate from whose net there was no escape. Impulsively, she put her arms around him: 'Oh, dear Anthony, it's quite simple, really. You're very nervous, anxious. Wouldn't anybody be? Fifteen years is a long time to have been away from your disreputable country!' She made a gesture which included in its compass not only the disreputable country, but its renowned tawny-coloured veld which for Anthony was only a backdrop to an ugly urban childhood. For Tina it provided a setting for romantic tales of the colonial days of empire that she had read as a child; the adventures of gold and diamond explorers which included, as they surely had to, chronicles of violent encounters between the white and the native tribes; and so it had gone on, to the most recent stories of strife, perennial shootings and disappearances. For Tina, there was an exoticness attached to this land.

Anthony wandered away from the window to the cabinet where he at last poured some drinks. 'I can deal with my official duties quite adequately, of course,' he continued, following a thread of his thoughts but still somehow managing to sound as if he needed reassurance. 'After all, no-one has the right to expect miracles. You go out there, you follow certain leads, you make the necessary connections. If your luck holds out, something turns up and you follow through with the necessary representations to the authorities.'

'Well, then,' Tina said, smiling encouragingly, 'try to relax. Enjoy the trip and try to find some time to spend with the family.'

'That's just the trouble,' Anthony sighed. 'It's the family side I am not so sure I can cope with.' He allowed a rock of ice to tinkle slowly against the glass as though the sound would succeed in lulling his troubled thoughts.

Tina was aware of a man walking a tightrope of self definition without any clear idea what words were proper to use. She let him talk, even though at times he seemed to be circling around the same ideas. For a long time he spoke of his sister, first hesitantly, then as if a spring had suddenly broken loose and released something within him. When at last he came to a pause his own face reflected what he saw on Tina's face: that wearied expression which came suddenly over people's faces when discussion had turned suddenly to topics of great misfortune like death, injury or illness. Or apartheid, Anthony thought ruefully. 'Sorry, Tina. I suppose I am going on a bit.'

'It's all right.' Tina said, kissing him. Then, as at the Dean Street pub, she moved decisively. 'Only it's time to go or you'll miss the plane.'

At Gatwick Airport the conditions were 'hellish', as Tina had warned they would be, with airport ground staff trying to cope with pre-Christmas holiday crowds. People came up from buses and trains, their eyes shining brightly in the dull light of the airport lounge, but it was sharper than the grey light of the damp December evening outside which held the threat of more snow. Everywhere in the airport lounge, from the check-in desks to the two upper shopping levels, people, luggage, earthbound airport workers, filled the space with the same dense quiet noise of moving crowds at airports the world over. The scene was one of utter confusion: clusters of Americans rolling their suitcases on castors as if dragging behind them their very lives; groups of Africans, refugees from collapsing economies, chaperoning vast trolleys which were sagging beneath tons of hi-fi equipment and other luxury goods; Indians, Spaniards, Italians, Germans in sudden loud possession of their mother-tongues wailed, shrieked and jabbered incomprehensibly.

Tina and Anthony were caught up in this crowd; they were shoved and jostled until, the relentless chores of checking in completed, they managed to extricate themselves temporarily from one crowd only to be absorbed into another; but finally, Anthony clutching passport, ticket and boarding card, they found themselves in front of Passport Control; and for Anthony Ferguson, the drama of departure was yielding at last to the miserable prospect of another drama of arrival. And this woman who had given him so much unstinting support would not be there to see him through the days which were to come. Hugging under her arms, as she had done on so many other occasions, newspapers and magazines that she hoped Anthony would have time to read between London and Johannesburg, Tina collected herself. Now she thrust these into Anthony's hands while they performed the usual ritual of separating couples, accompanied by mumbled exhortations to write or take care. 'Anthony, you'll be careful, won't you? I mean of those dreadful security chaps!' They kissed briefly.

Tina watched him move away from her with a detached sense of a sudden temporary loss until, just before he disappeared from view, he turned, as she had known he would, and waved. What she had not anticipated were the words, mischievously misplaced and unexpected, shouted at the top of his lungs:

'TINA, MOLAPO ALSO DANCES THE JITTERBUG!'

Chapter Two

IT was not the jitterbug that Cornelius Molapo used to dance, but the step was near enough to resemble it; a kind of township jive in which Molapo, legs bent at the knees and his arms flapping like the wings of a flamingo, shuffled ceaselessly without any need for a partner, for what good would a partner have been to him! He would not have noticed one anyway since his eyes were usually tightly shut while he danced – only the mouth was always partly open and it gave his whole face an expression of the most intense pleasure imaginable. After Molapo's disappearance, even the headmaster of his school, a close friend and a drinking companion of many leisure hours, referred to Molapo's style of dancing as a significant detail in the argument against any suggestion that he could possibly be in police custody. 'Anybody who can dance the "Flamingo" like that is not likely to be caught napping by these police dogs!' was Greg Mtimkulu's emotional comment.

Nevertheless, notwithstanding his confident assertions, after a tour of inspection of Molapo's house the headmaster had been alarmed. What Mtimkulu reported he had found in that empty house, his vivid descriptions of the chaos and destruction, and the incipient decay encountered in each one of those small rooms; his recollections of the wreckage 'as if a demolition squad had been at work', as he put it, have now passed forever into history, having been reported in minute detail by sensation-seeking newspapers and the so-called revolutionary press. Finally Mtimkulu's witness was to take up a small but important section of the wide-ranging report published by Human Rights International under the provocative but irrefutably even-handed title: 'State Crimes: East and West.'

The headmaster's descriptions were lent a special poignancy by the extraordinary attention he paid to certain particulars which a less careful observer might have missed. Even his keen nose for certain odours in that house, long kept airless, full of damp and rotting things, gave a special flavour to a description no more remarkable for the complete picture it provided than for its observation of those small instances of unidentified horror which even a trained intelligence might have missed. After a hastily called press conference over which Joe Bulane presided with quiet panache, the principal of Madubane High School was greatly praised for his thorough presentation. Mtimkulu claimed that after his inspection of Molapo's house, taking into account the amount of destruction which had been wreaked by persons unknown, he was forced to suspect foul play, even a murder, rather than a straightforward political detention. For was it not strange – he posed this question to members of the press in a most bemused, melancholy voice – that none of Molapo's close neighbours should have seen or heard anything when, as was presumed, the security forces had come to take him away? If they had come as usual, had come as it could be supposed, trampling on flower beds, overturning pushcarts and jerry-cans, smashing windows, breaking doors? But no: no-one had heard or seen anything.

In fact, not until a week later, Mtimkulu related, not until his school, alerted by Molapo's long, unexplained absence from teaching duties, had dispatched a pair of Molapo's pupils to investigate, did friends begin to suspect that he might have been among those who had disappeared during the security

18

clampdown, a suspicion later confirmed by a press release from the offices of the Movement. Even so the Movement had done no more than express a suspicion – 'a mere suspicion, mind,' Mtimkulu had emphasised – that Molapo might be amongst those thought to be held 'incommunicado' somewhere by the security police. Nothing was certain. To bring the briefing session to a conclusion, the Movement's representative had offered the view that only a full inquiry would confirm or dispel this suspicion.

Others, it is true, wished to look elsewhere for an explanation of Molapo's disappearance. Tongues wagged incessantly, some more maliciously than others. A few of those in the know pointed out that since his separation from his wife Molapo had become something of an enigmatic figure. An oddity, is how he was described by one of his township acquaintances. He was said to have taken to the bottle in a big way. He drank much too much and wandered late at night from one township to another. When he was home he was often confined to bed for days on end with a running fever – one of the reasons Mtimkulu had taken so long to investigate his absence from his teaching post. Even when he was well his neighbours had sometimes seen him walking down the dusty township road, his buttocks pressed tightly together, his arms swinging freely by his sides like a soldier in training, all the time smiling and talking to himself like someone who had seen a vision. Occasionally, he seemed to be reciting something – perhaps his poetry – to an invisible audience. So there was no knowing what he might have done to himself apart from what security might have done to him.

When two schoolboys were sent to Molapo's home to investigate they found all doors locked, and when they made enquiries next door the neighbours were as mystified as anyone else as to the schoolteacher's whereabouts. In over a week they had seen nothing of him. Even more mystifying was that they had noticed nothing which could have warranted suspicion. It was only then, finally, on a Saturday morning

19

when most township-dwellers were enjoying an extra hour or two in bed, that headmaster Mtimkulu decided to pay his own visit to Molapo's house, his purpose to conduct a discreet but extensive investigation.

A jolly, pot-bellied man of forty-two, the headmaster approached the house walking in a careless, confident stride, trampling over the unkempt flowerbeds, doing a circuit of inspection until he reached the front door, upon which he rapped fiercely. Receiving no response, Mtimkulu then went round to the back, where he hoisted himself up the forked trunk of a blasted peach tree and gazed in stupefaction through half-shuttered windows at the chaotic scene inside Molapo's bedroom. From this precarious position, feeling a bit like a peeping tom, the headmaster was able to observe the unmade bed, the spirit lamp which, after six days, perhaps more, still burned fitfully on the bedside table; the wardrobe completely wrecked and some of Molapo's clothes strewn across the floor; chairs overturned, a bookcase lying on its side, and all over the unswept floor books, papers and pamphlets lying about in scattered profusion. 'It looked as if a violent storm had swept through the house,' was Mtimkulu's comment to members of the press. He explained to curious journalists that, against his customary caution and better judgment, he had decided to force an entry into the house.

It was at this point that Mtimkulu's phenomenal powers of observation and description became a matter of extravagant admiration to those who heard him speak. Later records show that some of the details were of no use to the investigation itself but lent a certain colour to the cold official account. For example, Mtimkulu mentions that on entering the house he was obliged to step over a weather-beaten volume of a Charles Dickens novel which was lying on the floor with its spine broken. He says that for some odd reason, though he cannot explain why, the sight of a book with its spine broken, its binding destroyed and the pages falling out like the hair of a victim under police torture, alarmed him far more than the

20

discovery of bloodstains or bullet marks on the walls might have done. In his meticulous observation of detail not only does Mtimkulu mention the broken chairs, the overturned tables and the smashed crockery, the ransacked cupboards and the emptied drawers, the papers and pamphlets scattered all over the floor, but suddenly, in one of those off-the-cuff remarks which were to make him the darling of the news reporters, he insists that Molapo must have kept a chicken coop in one of the rooms.

A news reporter at the press conference, who thought he had had enough of Mtimkulu's vaudeville act, enquired rather aggressively: 'What makes you think he kept a chicken coop in one of the rooms? Did you find one?'

'Yes, sir! I did,' was Mtimkulu's unruffled reply. 'Otherwise I would not have mentioned it. A hen must have been laying eggs in there,' he insisted. 'When I entered the room I was met by a scene of horrendous destruction, worse than anything we human beings can do to one another. Well, perhaps no worse. As soon as I opened the door Molapo's normally overfed tomcat bounded past me. Locked in there for a week or more, the cat must have nearly starved to death, and in desperation must have finally attacked the hen in its coop and made a meal of it. What was left behind was a collection of bones and feathers still stained with dried-up blood. Talk about man's inhumanity to men!' At this odd flash of humour the amused reporters burst into applause and laughter.

The wry sense of humour for which Mtimkulu became celebrated was never more in evidence than during that appearance before the ladies and gentlemen of the press. The story of the chicken coop in particular made better headlines than Molapo's disappearance. In the absence of drinking water, he said, the eggs must have served the cat well. 'Normally,' Mtimkulu explained, in the manner of a prosecuting attorney reconstructing the scene of the murder, 'cats don't feed on chicken eggs but obviously, in desperate need of fluid, Molapo's tomcat found a way of smashing one egg after another until all of them – I counted at least six empty shells – had been consumed in the heat of that abandoned house.'

Finally, of course, there was the compelling strangeness of the burnished brass spirit lamp, the oil just about to run out but which after perhaps more than a week was still burning on the bedside table, the only item of furniture left undisturbed. He said that in daylight the light from that lamp gave to the room an eerie atmosphere that reminded him of a funeral wake in the small hours of morning. He remembered also that he was at first loathe to turn off that lamp but instead – and here is another eccentric detail – he climbed fully clothed on to Molapo's unmade bed, the better to reflect on the probable fate of his friend and colleague. After a few minutes his body warmed the sheets up and by now clutching only the faintest hope for his disappeared friend, Mtimkulu said he fell into a deep sleep. 'More like a coma than real sleep,' he said. The mention of this odd behaviour brought out another gust of astonished laughter from the journalists.

As a result of the complete failure to make sense of anything after these preliminary investigations, what had begun as a routine inquiry on the part of the school into another case of prolonged absenteeism by a member of staff soon settled down into a major search for the missing schoolteacher. The hunt moved into ever-widening circles which soon included Molapo's ageing parents, the mortuaries and the various police departments. In the city and in the countryside, close relatives, including his estranged wife, Maureen, were contacted; enquiries were made among his closest friends, but no-one had seen or had any knowledge of Molapo's whereabouts.

After that visit to Molapo's house Mtimkulu's search for his friend began to assume the nature of an obsessive mission. An agony of spirit came over him and his body underwent a tremendous transformation. He began to adopt a new posture, consistent with that of a man engaged in a time-consuming but

22

urgent quest. He moved constantly with his head bent forward, his shoulders drooping heavily as if he carried on his back an immense weight; indeed, had Molapo been his own son or brother, Mtimkulu's search could not have been more assiduous or single-minded in its concentration. After the break-in, the headmaster did not return to his own home for breakfast that morning. He showed up for lunch, then missed supper, not to return to the house until well after midnight. During the intervening hours he made the rounds of the shebeens where Molapo was known to spend weekends drinking and exchanging gossip with his soulmates. Very often in these low, insalubrious dives, where the headmaster now conferred in plaintive murmurs with other downcast friends, Molapo had been known to hold forth well into the small hours on what he was pleased to refer to as the country's deepening political crisis. Even now, as he expressed his deep anxiety about the fate of his disappeared colleague, the headmaster sometimes had the illusion that he could hear Molapo's scholarly voice sweeping across the smoky room, the inconsequential din of the shebeen crowd temporarily held in check by his grand passion until the poet in Molapo, perhaps in partnership with the teacher in him, or the teacher in partnership with the street preacher, worked his audience into a pitch of delirious excitement.

'We are no longer as once we were,' his voice rolled out. 'As a people, we are shrunk – no, reduced – by foreigners, to a fistful of dust, crushed into slouching, snivelling submission by the *boer* slave-master, like skunks driven into hiding holes and made unable to scale the heights for which God Almighty has set each generation of mankind!' They all remembered the words, enchanted, elated and blissful as though he were paying them a compliment; but they also remembered the laughter which followed and eventually the sense that perhaps he meant to goad them into expressing the rage which he knew always lay seething beneath the surface of their seemingly carefree existence.

But suppose the schoolteacher had disappeared forever, like so many others before him who had simply vanished into the voracious maw of the graves and the innumerable prison cells? Vanished in such a fashion. What then? Who was safe now from the rooting raping paranoia of power set loose upon the land? The headmaster's dogged, single-minded search, as instinctive as the peremptory needs of the flesh, was to lead him next to Nakeledi, a small dusty township in the north-east of Johannesburg where Maureen Molapo, long disowned by family for the disgraceful impiety of deserting a husband, was rumoured to occupy a small backyard room no bigger than the back of a hand.

Maureen had joined an army of young women who, for whatever reason – family, personal or criminal – simply disappear into the underground of South African cities. As far as Mtimkulu was concerned, the break-up of the marriage had been in itself a tragedy. It was, as everybody saw it, a sad ending to what had been the most ardent courtship ever witnessed in public in the streets of Mofolo, climaxing in the most spectacular township wedding Orlando had ever seen – an orgy of eating, drinking and dancing, claiming the slaughter of two animals, more than a dozen kegs of home-made brew and countless bottles of bootleg whisky, gin and brandy to wash it all down. Afterwards the inflaming music of the Sensational Jazz Maniacs sent a crowd of more than five hundred carousing celebrants into two days of unparalleled abandon.

And sitting in the middle of the wreckage which followed the failure of that marriage, Molapo gave his morose verdict: 'The gods were offended by that frivolity and the extravagance. They simply could not stand the foolish expenditure of money and energy.' His headmaster, a failed husband who in compensation had become a lover of all young lovers, a natural camp follower, had watched, mesmerised, the progress of that grand alliance. When he saw the marriage falter, founder and finally peter out into bitterest froth, Greg Mtimkulu was stunned, crushed by the sight of a distraught deserted husband;

24

so that even now, as he made his laborious progress, a little drunk and maudlin, first up one shadowy Nakeledi street and then another in search of Molapo's estranged wife, he was overcome by a profound depression at the thought of the crouching beast of failure which slouched at the heart of every human affection. Mtimkulu had worshipped the young couple; for Maureen, in particular, so evidently competent in the ministrations of all physical pleasures, he had always experienced that protective sentimentality by means of which male lust is able to sublimate its most incendiary cravings into respectful adoration.

After a few false turnings and deliberate misdirections by mischievous young urchins, Mtimkulu found the small house at the end of a dusty, ill-lit street, behind a shopping centre in which all lights had been extinguished. There was a fence and a gate and a small footpath which led to the back of the house. In that semi-darkness, under the shelter of a mulberry tree, a woman was taking a bath. Standing up, she scooped water from a tin drum and sluiced it down the shadowy length of her half-invisible body. The water made a soft splashing sound as she soaped and sponged herself to the kerosene tips of her breasts until, suddenly suspicious, she paused like a cautious antelope sniffing the wind, listening.

'Who is it?'

The headmaster wished that he could have observed unobserved that perfect ritual which brings the human evening to its ending: a body impaired by the day's labour being laved and cleansed for a night's rest. He responded in his wearied worldly voice: 'Greg,' he called out to her in darkness. Even to himself his voice sounded very far away.

'Greg!' There was a small pause, the barest interval. 'Greg Mtimkulu?' She laughed conspiratorially while her dark shadow moved almost imperceptibly under the branch of the tree; the leaves rustled like silk as the woman began to rub herself vigorously with a white towel. 'My God! Greg, what brings you here!' Her voice sounded bright and cheerful, and as usual, Maureen did not wait for answers to her own questions. 'Wait. I'm coming!' she said.

Emerging finally from under the shelter of the mulberry tree she came towards him walking in that long feline stride which had always cleared a path for her through a crowd of men. A tall woman, as slim as a bayonet, there was nevertheless a slide rather than a slash of steel in her walk which suggested the soft slither of a serpent. 'How are you, Greg?' She placed a hand on each shoulder, a greeting invested with so much affection that he felt himself uplifted – although not entirely – from his anguish. 'How are you, Mr Big Tree?' she joked, looking down at the diminutive man.

'I'm well, Mo. How are you?'

'Same as usual!' And she laughed, as if the question evoked a memory of some confederate mischief to which they had both been a part. 'Well, Mr Big Tree?'

'Mo, it's about Corny,' Mtimkulu began but had no idea how to proceed. A sigh of irritation like a tyre letting out air was Maureen's response to the mention of her husband's name.

'Oh, Corny! Is that what you have come all this way to talk about; Corny?'

Even without being able to see the expression on her face Mtimkulu could sense the tension in her voice, knotting like a clenched fist. He wished he had not come. Maureen let loose a string of derisive questions that came like a flurry of punches against a defenceless body. 'What's the matter with you people? You have plenty of time to waste? I thought even schoolmasters had hours of preparation to do for their teaching? No wonder the kids can't even spell their names when they leave school. You schoolmasters don't know what to do with your time anymore. Listen, please do me a favour!'

She did not invite Mtimkulu into the house. Instead they ended up sitting under the stars, talking for a long time. The headmaster, who was normally self-possessed and fairly immune to the charms of women suddenly felt vulnerable and strangely insecure under the onslaught of not just one but many subtle fragrances emanating from Maureen's freshly soaped body. For her eternal coolness and freshness, Maureen was a living legend, and water, it was said with some justification, was her element. Often sitting down with her long legs crossed she displayed crisp white or brightly coloured undergarments on a body which glowed with the enviable health of an athlete. Always she smelled, as she did now, not of artificial perfumes but of water and soap and her own subtle scent; and inhaling a breath of that scent in the hot night air Greg felt dangerously exposed. He sensed Maureen's palpitating young body only the stretch of an arm away from him, and he thought of its slimness and vitality, of fresh herbs and rain water, and his throat became dry. Aware of the need to escape early, he tried, unsuccessfully as it turned out, to be as brief as possible.

'Mo, Corny has been missing from his house and the school for close to two weeks now. Even his old people have no clue where he is. For all we know, he may be in police detention while I'm talking to you!'

'Corny detained!' Maureen laughed. 'What an idea!'

'It's no laughing matter, Mo! Hundreds of people have disappeared during this state of emergency.'

'I know,' Maureen admitted dutifully. Then huffily she added: 'Serious people, Greg, not silly pranksters like Corny!'

With his long experience of handling naughty young people, the headmaster decided to ignore Maureen's attack. 'Yesterday morning I went into the house to have a look around,' he said. 'I can't tell you what it looked like. Furniture overturned, books and documents scattered all over the floor. The place looked as if a hurricane had passed through it!'

In spite of her exaggerated show of indifference, Mtimkulu suddenly sensed in Maureen an undertow of anxiety which tugged at her well-guarded heart, something of that mysterious bond which unites man and wife even at the moment of a bitter, reproachful divorce was at work now; that

27

shared sense of mutual belonging, which is sometimes responsible for inexplicable displays of jealousy even when love has long since died, was twisting like a knife in Maureen's flat belly. She was not and could never be indifferent to her husband's fate. For a moment she remained profoundly quiet. Finally she asked: 'Has anyone thought of actually going to the police to make enquiries?'

'Not yet,' Greg confessed. 'As you know, among us the police are always a last resort in these matters.' In his slow, dogged manner, Mtimkulu explained: 'Under the state of emergency, the police are not obliged to tell us anything about the disappeared people. We first had to try everything on our own.'

'And you had the bright idea of coming to me?' Maureen laughed harshly. 'Listen, Greg. Corny and I haven't seen each other these last six months. Right now, I don't think he even knows where I'm staying. And frankly, I prefer to keep it that way.'

Maureen's studied indifference affected Mtimkulu more than he could have expected. There was a time, he remembered, when Maureen and Cornelius were inseparable, like twins. Separate, either seemed incomplete and lacking in poise, like a work of art that misses clear definition. For a few seconds, while they listened to township noises, both the man and the woman seemed to be occupied with their own thoughts and silence fell like a benediction on the pair. Around them the night was like a cloth, a black shawl wrapped around each. In that silence the headmaster was aware of the dull pressure of memory acting on him like the recollection of a long forgotten pain. Maureen, too, in her silent contemplation of the night, seemed oppressed by memories. In the past she had always thought that the headmaster, with his calm manner (though admittedly not free of the hint of the rake), should have been a priest rather than a schoolteacher; but perhaps ministering to wayward township pupils was the next best thing for a failed divine. Out of the corner of her eye she studied the morose figure and was moved by this man's friendship for Cornelius.

Sitting with his head bent slightly forward, one step down from where Maureen's long legs loomed in the darkness as she reclined on her elbows, the headmaster suddenly roused himself sufficiently to ask: 'Mo, tell me something. Don't you ever miss Corny even just a little bit?'

Maureen sounded surprised at the question but rallied quickly. 'Sure, I miss him sometimes,' she admitted without any effort at all. 'After all, Corny used to be a good husband, you know, and a good lover until he started hitting the bottle!' Maureen's voice lingered on the memory; then in a sudden burst of posthumous passion she giggled at the memory. 'Such a good lover, I tell you! Corny's hands were the best hands of any man I ever felt around my body. Honest-to-God, Mr Big Tree, that's the truth! When that man was being very good he played my body like a bowstring, like a musical instrument! And when he was under the pressure of his need, no place was safe from him in the house. I would be in the kitchen, cooking a meal . . . ' she laughed then and Mtimkulu thought he could hear the soft gurgle of Maureen's stomach and the pulse of his own blood went faster and faster. 'Anyway, that was before he fell in love with politics and the bottle. Honestly, you don't know what living with a man like that can do to a woman.'

Maureen's voice suddenly became outraged. 'I mean, how would you like having to go to bed every night with a freedom chatter!'

'Freedom Charter, Maureen!' the headmaster corrected her in a stiff, classroom manner. Then he added chastely, if somewhat distractedly: 'Anyway, the Freedom Charter is no part of my philosophy.'

'No? Of course not! I forget you're African Independence Party.'

Political programmes were the only subject on which Mtimkulu and Cornelius had strongly differed, but these political differences never permanently strained their relationship. When the Movement had finally split into two wings, the socialist and the nationalist wings, Cornelius had stayed with the revolutionary socialist tendency while Mtimkulu followed the path of nationalism.

'Mo, it's getting late, ' the schoolmaster finally announced; nevertheless, he procrastinated, looking at the long body of the young woman on the stone step. In the glow of the starlight Mtimkulu dimly perceived Maureen's knees gently swaying from side to side. They reminded him of the Junior Certificate girls he had seen through the window of his office lying flat on their backs on the curve of the grassy lawn, their knees raised just like Maureen's at this very moment, their dark half-formed breasts swelling slightly like dark plums under their half-unbuttoned blouses. His throat suddenly tightening with a craving for the flesh he was unable to ignore or alleviate, he rose heavily to his feet. His hunger, stirring a ferment of desires and urges long subdued by an exemplary self-discipline, would now have to be quelled by a brief visit to the shebeen on his way home. The headmaster reached out a friendly hand and touched Maureen's shoulder and felt her flesh yield just a little under his strong fingers.

'So long, Maureen!'

'So long, Greg,' Maureen did not rise with him. She continued to loll at his feet. 'So long, Mr Big Tree!' she sighed, rippling slightly. 'Come and see me sometimes,' she said indolently, 'when you're not looking for my husband.' Her laughter, slow and full of friendly humour, followed him all the way to the street.

Chapter Three

O N the long flight to Johannesburg Anthony was obliged to share the company of a big amiable fellow who introduced himself genially, first by slamming him on the shoulder, then grasping Anthony's small hand in his big hairy one and shaking it vigorously while repeating his own name several times: 'Murchison's my name! Tom Murchison!'

'Anthony Ferguson!' Anthony responded in return. Feeling stripped of any fixed identity as he stood in the aisle stashing Tina's reading material in the locker above his seat, he was pleased to hide behind the anonymity of his name. 'Glad to make your acquaintance, Mr Murchison.'

'The feeling is mutual!' Murchison's gaze became at once more contemplative, more meditative. 'Sit down, Mr Ferguson, sit down! Might as well make ourselves comfortable. Jo'burg is a long way from here!'

Instantly, Anthony felt trapped like a first offender who is forced to share a prison cell with a habitual criminal; but there was nothing else to do except reconcile himself to a long trip in which, he very quickly concluded, he was sure to become the unwilling auditor of Tom Murchison's tales of fortune and misfortune, his petty loves and hates, his grievances and his aspirations. Helplessly, with a rapidly sinking spirit, Anthony looked around the plane for a likely diversion but there was none that he could see. He knew he wouldn't sleep. He couldn't read. Usually on these sensitive assignments he never allowed himself too much in the way of alcohol. On the other hand, he thought hopefully, you could say this was a little more than an official trip; it was also a kind of return of a Prodigal Son to the bosom of the family, and as long as he was in said bosom he could be permitted a certain amount of self-indulgence. As soon as he landed at Jan Smuts Airport he would most certainly be taken care of. Hazel would be there waiting and would assuredly see to that!

While he was trying to make himself comfortable Ferguson listened to the other voices in the plane, trying to adjust his ear to accents among which he had grown up but which had progressively become fainter and fainter in his memory. After fifteen years of living abroad, the sensation of being surrounded entirely by white South Africans, listening only to the collective whine of nasal English accents and heavy Afrikaans ones, provoked a mild form of inner discomfort almost too physical to ignore. To this feeling of inner agitation another was added of which he had not at first been aware: a sudden attack of irrational guilt, as though his mission to South Africa on behalf of a human rights organisation was a form of treachery against his own country.

A powerful psychological mechanism, this kind of guilt, Anthony thought; it was this same guilt upon which the white laager mentality was built and which the white state was able to manipulate at will and to great effect; the sense of an inviolable solidarity among white people who saw themselves as having a collective destiny and feeling a collective threat. So even now he, who was on the side of the oppressed, was forced to experience this inner upset because of the secret knowledge that he was engaged in a covert mission to expose his country to international criticism and possible ridicule, while many of his fellow passengers talked only of returning home to their farms, to their children and their servants. Not surprisingly, in contrast to his own personal discomfiture, his countrymen displayed only calm

32

confidence, one might even say a kind of relief in returning home.

'British or South African?' Murchison began as soon as they had settled into their seats in a move so predictable that Ferguson almost groaned aloud with the sure conviction of having been here before.

'South African,' he replied. Suddenly, the plane lurched, dived, rose. Shooting straight up into the blue night sky it tilted on to its left wing, headed north; soon it would be west, then south. 'And you, Mr Murchison? British or South African?'

'South African,' Murchison beamed at the younger man as if to express the depth of his satisfaction at being one of the tribe. 'My people emigrated to South Africa after World War Two. I was only ten years old at the time. I consider myself lucky to be a South African,' Murchison explained. 'I'm proud of it!'

Ferguson thought this beginning rather ominous and resolved there and then to say as little as possible about himself to this patriotic emigrant. He had not, of course, reckoned with Murchison's own special need for communication. 'Been in the UK long, Mr Ferguson?'

Ferguson's spirits sank. 'Fifteen years.'

'Fifteen!' Murchison whistled. 'You don't say! You mean you can stay away from your country that long and suffer no pain?' Murchison continued to regard Ferguson with an expression of troubled amazement. 'What about your family? You've got parents back in South Africa, haven't you?'

'My mother and sister, yes. My father passed away some time ago.'

'And your mother and sister, they don't mind your defection?' Defection seemed an odd word, a bit too strong to use for what was, after all, only a temporary and voluntary exile, but Anthony let it pass without comment. After studying his travelling companion out of the corner of his eye, Anthony was surprised to note that in spite of Murchison's obesity the man did not, as is often the case, have a double chin. Instead, as if to compensate for this lack, he had a twin pair of cheeks, one pair above the other, and when he smiled the top pair had a tendency to climb towards his small reflective eyes, which gave to his face a humorous expression of amiable ferocity. It was clear Murchison expected from his travelling companion some kind of explanation.

'What kept you so long from your own country?'

'I went to Britain for my studies when I was still too young to tell the difference and when I completed my studies I saw no reason to hurry home.'

Like most people of his type Murchison seemed impervious to irony. 'So you stayed on? You have a good job in the UK?'

Anthony flinched momentarily. Though he had thoroughly prepared himself for such questions the first shots caught him by surprise. 'It's mostly clerical,' he said evasively. 'Otherwise it's not so bad as jobs go.' But luckily Murchison did not pursue the subject any further. Instead, he kept repeating his surprise like a refrain. 'Fifteen years! Fifteen years! For me that passeth understanding! I don't mind telling you, Ferguson, every time I'm obliged to go abroad I feel as if I'm being forced into exile.'

A stewardess, one of those freakishly pretty South African girls in whose faces and complexion the imprint of the country, its outdoor climate, its winds, rains and suns seem to have been burned forever, came and took their order for drinks. Murchison had a whisky and soda and Ferguson asked for gin and tonic. When the girl departed, leaving behind the smell of jasmine and eau-de-cologne, the two men watched her intently as she sashayed down the aisle of the plane, her marvellously rounded buttocks growing separate and independent with each step, suggesting something dull and Dutch, but also African, supple and graceful, a certain heathenish mobility of the body, as if responding to the subtle rhythms of the African tom-tom.

'Blimey!' Murchison exclaimed under his breath. He winked prodigiously, like an overgrown child. 'I'll tell you something, Ferguson. I have been to many places but they don't make them like that anywhere else!'

'She's very pretty,' Ferguson agreed.

'Pretty! She's sublime! Listen, Ferguson; when I go abroad and see what they call a pretty woman these days, I'm more than grateful for the home-grown product. I say to myself, the world has nothing more fair to show than what South Africa has to offer.'

Ferguson was beginning to find Murchison's spontaneous enthusiasms oppressive. To check the flow he said: 'Mr Murchison, pretty girls can be found in every land. No one country has the monopoly.'

'Not in every country. No, sir, in no country can you find such a one! I tell you, she is something special. Look at the complexion. Look at those cheekbones. Do you know how many different bloods have blended to produce that type? Dutch, German, English, French; you name it, she's got it running in her veins!'

'And maybe even a drop of the East!' Ferguson added irreverently to this improbable list. At this indiscretion Murchison first looked shocked and blood ran quickly to his face, then he swallowed; the expression on his face finally changed into one of uncomprehending sorrow, whether for the possibility that the girl might indeed be tainted, or for Anthony's rejection of the home rules of etiquette was unclear. For a few seconds he gazed at Ferguson as someone does in the face of an unexpected display of barbarity and cruelty. Maybe it was his response to plain bad manners. Anthony said: 'I'm sorry. That wasn't a tactful thing to say, was it ?'

'No! No!' Murchison quickly replied. 'You don't have to apologise to me. After all, such things have been known to happen.'

Murchison was being brave but he could not conceal his hurt. Ferguson's casual reference to racial admixture in the population had killed a budding relationship before it could even come to life; from now on, however hard they might try to patch things up, the cracks would remain exposed. To change the subject Murchison began to confide in his fellow passenger about his Yorkshire cousins. While over there, he said, he had been surprised to see the squalor in which his cousins still lived. 'Like a bunch of blackamoors, Mr Ferguson!' Though running a small retail business in Bradford the Yorkshire cousins led what by South African standards could only be described as a pretty cramped existence, plagued by debts, haunted by the spectre of bankruptcy and rising inflation.

Murchison's own side of the family which had emigrated to South Africa at the end of the war had become prosperous as operators of a medium-sized steel and iron foundry, producing castings for the mining industry. This enabled them to buy up two farms, to lead a life of relative ease, to travel and to see the world. As for Britain, Murchison shook his head regret- fully. 'My opinion, Ferguson, for what it's worth, is Britain has had it. Even my cousins, hard as it is to admit, in private they'll tell you so. In England people don't wish to apply themselves anymore! There's no vision, only feelings of defeat and despair. What happened to the Dunkirk spirit? It seems that the great British public has decided that life is not worth the candle!' Murchison seemed to love language and used it glibly with great enjoyment, relying on a ready stock of quotations and clichés from common literature and popular songs. Overcoming his disappointment with Ferguson's ill- conceived remark, he was on a roll. Pausing in the middle of his long denunciation, he studied the younger man, and when Anthony neither concurred nor disagreed that the Dunkirk spirit was gone, Murchison must have suspected dissent and began to argue his case with renewed eloquence. 'Okay, you tell me – you say you've lived over there for fifteen years. What hope is there for what used to be called Great Britain? Tell me honestly, Ferguson. What hope? Britain, I tell you, has had it. Britain is drawing her last breath, she is singing her swansong before the lights finally go out for good! The "Swinging Sixties", so-called, the Beatles, Carnaby Street, all of that: they're just a diversion, a little pride before the Fall. No-one seems to know it but the signs are there for anyone to see. The country is slowly going to the dogs. Britain no longer has what it takes. Things ain't what they used to be!'

Murchison had hit his stride and nothing could stop him now. Crouching forward oddly, like a beast suddenly roused from its lair, he rippled and ranted. 'And what about our new darkie friends then, eh?' Now leaning over the arm-rest separating the two seats he gazed intently at the younger man's face and winked. 'All those dark friends from every port of the globe? Black immigrants. Indians. Pakistanis. West Indians. What about our new British friends, then? There's no more talk of integration in Britain now, is there? No hi-happy-to-meet-you-feller and welcome to our happy overcrowded little island, no more of that now, is there! No sir! They used to call South Africans the polecats of the civilised world. Finally the boot is on the other foot and someone has found it pinches. Now the cry is "Blacks Go Home!"; "Rivers of Blood" speeches are the order of the day. Send them home! That's the latest cry from Her Majesty's public servants!'

Murchison hated Britain, he said. He hated the meanness, the smallness of ambition, the lack of courage, the lack of vision. He hated the moral presumption of those who wanted to tell South Africa how to solve her race problems. Britain should solve her own problems first; still, he was not entirely devoid of sensitivity. He noted Ferguson's non-committal silence. 'I know what you're thinking,' he said defensively. 'You think our own natives could be treated better than we treat them. I agree. There's room for improvement. But listen, Ferguson, you and I know better than to think you can buy the love of a native by giving him a few things a white man has. The native doesn't want to live like a white man. What he wants – and I agree with him – is to own the country. I know because if I were a native that's exactly what I'd want. It stands to reason.' The slight pause must have been intentional, then Murchison delivered his punchline like a seasoned actor.

'Only we can't let the natives have the country, Ferguson. For us that would be suicide! It's a terrible thing to admit but there it is. We can't allow it. So it's a question of them or us. And don't let anyone tell you otherwise.'

Anthony was shaken. In just over fifteen minutes Murchison, this big, hearty, boozy fellow who had warmly welcomed him into the seat next to him had turned into an ugly, belligerent, red-faced bull, ready to charge into the centre of what he had put down as an unthinking hostile world. His eyes had turned red; his ears burned as if they were on fire from either drink or the passion of his conviction. A thin bead of sweat silvered his upper lip. Only the arrival of the stewardess with a tray of fresh drinks calmed Murchison's raw nerves.

Ferguson dozed off into an uneasy, troubled sleep. While he dozed he dreamed. Sometimes these dreams were fragments of childhood memories. Even awake he seemed to be walking in his sleep, dreaming. His mother used to say: 'I have a great dreamer for a son.' Talking to Ma-Bezuidenhout over the fence she would ask the old woman in mock exasperation: 'So how would you like to have a dreamer for a son? A real dreamer, mind.' Now his dreams were few but recurrent. Dreams of departures and returns: trains, railway stations, airports, flights to foreign countries, ships steaming into ports. Sometimes his sister, sometimes his mother were waiting, as now, to receive him on their turbulent shores. Dreams of departures, dreams of arrivals, his own and others. He always remembered one return, his sister coming home from the Cape Town Ballet School for her winter vacation, a harsh, bitterly cold rainy winter. Though conveniently banished to 'learn something' at the school, Hazel had returned home that winter more thoroughly corrupted by her temporary exile than when she had first defied parental injunction not to haunt the Johannesburg youth dance clubs where, at sixteen, she had begun spending most of her

38

weekends in the company of slick ducktail boys of dubious plumage.

Hazel came home that winter to a Braamfontein already garlanded with the lights – reds and greens, blues and yellows – and the slumbering merry-go-rounds and painted caravans of the annual travelling fair. She arrived white and rain-stormed in the dying light, her slender, chaliced body, for all the ardours of a long journey, looking fresh, exquisitely articulated, a little tremulous. That winter, after the briefest of telegrams, she arrived in a green-and-yellow taxi, stepping lightly out into the working-class Johannesburg suburb and saying in her spoiled and nervous voice: 'Hello mother! Hello everybody! Where is Anthony? Mother, is Anthony home?' Anthony was in his second year at Wits and had come down early from the university to witness this homecoming, even to participate in it. Ferguson saw his mother smile and hug her daughter while the taxi driver struggled unassisted with the luggage to the front of the house, and out of pure mischief he was holding back before reaching the gate where his sister waited impatiently for one of their many cordial embraces.

Anthony remembered that winter more vividly than most because Hazel, who had won a scholarship at the Ballet Company, was more remarkably got up than usual. Apart from the unusual gear, the shoe covers of transparent white plastic material a little soiled by the mud of the journey, she was also wrapped up in expensive furs. No-one knew exactly where and how she had obtained those furs, but apparently Hazel gloried in the knowledge that not only would no-one ask where she had got them but the mother would be positively appalled at the possibility that Hazel might suddenly wish to volunteer such information.

From their father, now bed-ridden and slowly dying from lung cancer, there was nothing for her to fear. Long oblivious to the affairs of the Ferguson family, their father was now imprisoned forever within the implacable walls of his nightmare, fashioned by a life recklessly squandered on gambling and alcohol abuse.

So Hazel arrived home that cold grey winter afternoon, covered up in expensive furs, the source of which no-one was bold enough to enquire about. Years later Anthony wrote in his notebooks: 'We should have known, of course, that the furs and the jewellery were the first fruit of Hazel's use of men in what was to be a life-long career of wreckage and personal revenge against a society which had trapped her for most of her childhood in a life worse than a black person's – because a black person can at least provide an explanation for such intolerable penury and want.' So she came home that winter afternoon wearing her guileful smile, everything about her white and rain-stormed, her face unfathomable, bearing chiefly that smile which worked on the world like a pure devastation.

Anthony never forgot the way she looked that afternoon, alighting to be greeted by Mama Ferguson, at forty-two a little plump but pretty still, surprisingly dark and vivid in contrast to the daughter who stepped out of the cab and fluttered to the ground like thin flakes of snow.

Mama Ferguson stood uncertainly in the small gateway, staring with a small incline of the head as though puzzled by the apparition in front of her. After a while she moved forward but seemed doubtful still at what, after all, was not exactly anyone's idea of a daughter's homecoming from a ballet school but rather like that of a film star returning to the squalid surroundings of her childhood. The impression was created more by Hazel's appearance, by the extravagance of her gestures, all that funny fantasy and royalty of style (almost too theatrical to sustain) than by any fame she might have already acquired as a dancer with the Cape Town Ballet Company. It was that manner she had put on when she climbed down from the green-and-yellow taxi laden with pieces of luggage; the way, for instance, she persuaded the driver (for she must have persuaded him) to blow the hooter incessantly as soon as they reached the gate of the house so that the aroused and astounded neighbours came out of their homes to stand in their front yards staring hostilely at mother and daughter as they kissed and hugged while the cabby struggled with the luggage. Among the spectators was Willie Faulkner, the horticulturist, with his toothbrush moustache and gnarl-veined hands who, while Ferguson senior lay dying, had never bothered to call, had never stepped over the fence to offer any sympathy but preferred to read his American novels (including a curious work titled The Sound and the Fury that was translated into bad Afrikaans); he too had joined the others to stare at what was clearly a new phenomenon as homecomings go.

The daughter came forward then, the quality of purity given a surreal sharpness by the white furs, by the gleaming jewellery and plastic shoe covers, by the blonde hair winnowed in the July winter wind. The son watched them – the mother and daughter – quickly embrace, and then Hazel breaking off to laugh in that frail, nervous way of hers which was nevertheless washed with a tide of humour and vitality, her dangerous intensity kept well in check. In the moment of stillness between greetings and the next move, he heard his sister say very clearly: 'Where is Anthony, Mother?'

She was carrying one of her bags now, salvaged from the rest of her luggage, but when she saw him she swung it down and started to run. Anthony remembered from that dim past how he had also started to run. He had moved involuntarily, like a piece of paper blown by that ill wind which was whistling down from the mountains of yellow sand from the gold mines, between the shabby walls of the poor white dwellings; he had hastened forward then, but midway he and his sister had stopped simultaneously like two synchronised images on a movie screen and briefly gazed at each other's faces before resuming their run until, with a shriek, his sister flung herself into his arms. And Anthony caught her by the waist and felt the warm lissomeness of her limbs beneath the thick white furs, and pushing his fumbling hand inside her large fur coat felt the liquid flow of her thin, weightless body.

For a minute he held her away from himself in order to study her. Though his sister was smiling her lower lip was tensed; he had the impression that she was impatiently waiting for his judgement.

'Well?' she quizzed him, turning easily in his arms like the trained dancer that she was.

'Sis, you look absolutely, but absolutely wonderful!' he finally told her, laughing. 'I've never seen you look so well!'

She laughed happily then. 'Thank you. It's all that Cape Town sea air and exercise. Dancing is a great tonic, you know.' Then she gazed fondly at her brother. 'You don't look so bad yourself, prince,' she told him. 'As a matter of fact, shall I tell you something? You look quite delicious!' And a small cloud flitted across her face. 'Listen,' she said, reverting to her usual exaggerated gaiety, 'I want to hear all about these girls in your life! And, of course, I want to hear about your courses at the university. We'll have an orgy of talk, won't we, dearest?' And she added with a sudden desperate intensity: 'You're all I have, you know! That's why I'm so thrilled to be back!'

So on that first flight back to Johannesburg after fifteen years of living abroad Anthony slept, dreamt his dreams, woke and went to sleep again, and the next time he woke up the mood in the plane had subtly changed into one of random friendliness. A lot of drinking was going on. A couple of tall beautiful girls, magnificent in their smart travelling suits, kept walking by to the toilets, running a gauntlet of hot appraising eyes and flirtatious comments; and each journey from the back of the plane brought a trivia of undiminishing fragrance so that in time the different perfumes clung together communally in the body of the plane, raising the blood temperature to a new pitch.

Intimations of the south came to them even before the plane entered South African air-space. Perhaps it was the airline stewardess with her smell of jasmine and eau-de-cologne who suggested the rich, sensual density of that tragically divided country. The plane was flying over brown scrubland, flat and monotonous; in whimsical contrast to the dry truth of the land, the blonde stewardess, looking as if she had only just risen from a comfortable bed, came round distributing sweets.

After the plane had broken through the rim of cloud over Lake Tanganyika something seemed to change in the atmosphere itself. The light began to assume the soft diaphanous quality which invests the dawns and dusks of the South with their peculiar luminosity. Murchison had obviously consumed more than his fair share of alcohol. He slept heavily with his mouth open. When breakfast was served he excused himself and slept some more until the announcement came over the loudspeaker that the plane was approaching Jan Smuts Airport. Murchison scrambled to his feet and started rummaging wildly in the top racks. The stewardess ran quickly down the aisle and with icy politeness sternly warned Murchison to sit down until the plane had landed and to keep his safety belt on. Large and genial, Murchison grinned his apologies and staggered wildly, eventually attempting to support his weight on the surprised and disapproving stewardess. The plane lurched and dipped and the stewardess once more addressed Ferguson's flight companion: 'Sir, will you please sit down?'

'Surely, miss!' Murchison responded but continued to stand, still searching on the luggage racks. 'Why certainly, Miss! I'll be glad to sit down!' he said but remained standing, busily rummaging as if suddenly attacked by panic. Anthony was attacked by his own panic, for the plane was suddenly touching ground and tearing down the runway to the accompaniment of narcotic muzak; and with that he was being delivered finally into the bosom of his family and country.

Chapter Four

WHEN Cornelius Molapo was summoned to appear at a new secret address of the National Liberation Movement, he was surprised to find when he got there not an office but a dry goods shop in which an old Indian trader with dry leathery skin like parchment served behind a lengthy broken-down counter. Grey, bearded, wearing a long cotton shirt and trousers to match, the Indian looked to be seventy or thereabouts. He was all but blind, and, no doubt, hard of hearing as well; but for all his evident fragility there was a mocking resilience in the old man's voice, a certain wiry toughness which reminded Cornelius of a thin weasel. 'Yes? What can I do you for, man?' the old Indian began in his quaint English, and Cornelius at once felt trapped in the old man's obscure, mildly mocking gaze. 'I want to see Mr Joe Bulane.'

'You mean JB?' In some obscure way that was hard to place, Cornelius felt rebuked.

'Cornelius. Cornelius Molapo.' The old Indian pulled at the red circular lobes of his ears. 'Who? What did you say?'

And Cornelius noticed the black tufts of hair which peeked from the ears. All of a sudden he felt an unreasonable irritation. He had not wanted to come for this interview and he distrusted the mystery with which meetings with officials of the National Liberation Movement were currently surrounded. The whole thing smacked of conspiracy. And now this old fool who couldn't even hear properly: how was he to extract any useful information from him? A quick rage overtook him and, thrusting his face into the old man's face, he bawled out his name. 'I said, Cornelius Molapo! M-o-l-a-p-o! You understand?'

Grimacing, the old Indian drew back as though he had been slapped across the face: 'Okay! You don't have to shout! I can hear you!' Shuffling awkwardly in his badly fitting sandals the Indian withdrew behind folds of curtain into the back of the shop; a secret door was unhinged, and Cornelius could hear voices apparently engaged in hurried exchanges. Then the Indian reappeared, looking neither pleased nor displeased with Cornelius's credentials but bland and neutral. 'This way, my friend!' he beckoned and together they disappeared behind the massive folds of curtains. 'Mr. Bulane,' the Indian shouted at a figure who remained invisible as in a darkened theatre. 'Your friend!'

Cornelius was left standing at the top of a flight of steps leading down to the basement offices. It was dark below the stairs, but when a hand switched on a light he found himself face to face with a compact, dapper African with a small bullet-shaped head, very closely shaven, who held in his hand a piece of paper with Cornelius's name on it. The man seemed mildly amused by the new arrival who, in contrast to the other's amused self-assurance, looked uncertain and ill at ease.

'Good gracious, Corny!' the other suddenly chuckled, grasping Cornelius by the hand. 'How the devil did you find me?' JB's English, Cornelius quickly noted, was as affected as ever. He had always preferred an old-fashioned style, as though English from past eras lent distinction to expressions which would otherwise lack it. Apparently not expecting any reply to his own question, JB promptly led the way down a flight of steps, down the length of a dingy, airless passage, and, finally, into the office. Arriving there, JB seemed inordinately cheerful. 'Wonderful! Wonderful!' and he rubbed his hands together with inexplicable enthusiasm.

The office in which Cornelius now sat, facing his old university classmate, was no more than a cave really – cold, damp and cheerless, with a desk, two chairs, a safe but no filing cabinet. When Cornelius remarked on the absence of a filing cabinet, the other laughed in his usual engagingly boyish manner.

'A filing cabinet?' he asked, cocking his closely shaven head in amusement. 'But my dear fellow, we have nothing to put in the files! What on earth do we need a filing cabinet for? Anyway, what we do have is locked away in a safe in the Chase Manhattan Bank in Commissioner Street.'

'In an American bank?' Cornelius asked with some surprise.

'Why not?' the central committee man giggled engagingly, leaning his small, closely shaven head to one side. 'For a revolutionary movement such as ours an American bank is the safest place to leave anything of value. No-one would ever think of checking there.'

For a while their conversation seemed to hang suspended in a kind of hazy morning confusion. Somewhere at an indeterminate distance a clock was slowly chiming, stroke after stroke, the hour of ten.

'*A bad hour,*' Cornelius thought; for what had so often distressed him about that time of morning in Johannesburg was the sense, drawn from some inexhaustible silence at the centre of industrial chaos, of time standing still; the illusion that nothing was changing and nothing would ever change. It was an illusion, of course, but all the same, it was just this feeling of temporary disembodiment against which Cornelius now fought, struggling inwardly in silence, in an effort to regain the echo and pulse of his own existence against a tide of public indifference.

He knew it would soon pass and then the world would be restored to its former relations. And perhaps the man behind the desk would stop scribbling on a piece of paper and listen to what he, Cornelius, had to say. He was already in the middle of an explanation without having any clear idea of how or when he had begun. 'This separation, at any rate, was entirely unexpected,' Cornelius repeated, trying to rouse the other's interest in his latest domestic situation. A long unbroken silence followed this declaration, and Cornelius was about to resume when the man from the central committee, unexpectedly started to speak.

'Corny, my boy, I know how you feel about Maureen,' he began, shutting his eyes like a man in prayer. 'Believe me, I understand only too well how you feel; but Corny, boy, we must never permit ourselves to forget that in comparison with the exploitation and suffering of our people, personal problems are of no consequence. Of no consequence at all!' He repeated this with the heavy air of someone who had at last fathomed a profound truth. 'Only struggle will endow your life with meaning where before there was nothing but futility and "perpetual emptiness",' he said, applying a calculated quotation that offended the poet in Cornelius. Then he cheered up immensely: 'We have just the thing to counteract your malaise – an assignment!'

'Listen, JB,' he shouted. 'I don't care a damn about what you choose to call the "struggle". For me there are other things in life besides the struggle. And let me tell you something, JB, just now Maureen is the most important thing of all. More important than all your struggling masses put together.'

Cornelius hadn't meant to sound so reactionary but like a man bent on suicide he was aware of a new impulse in him lately, more pronounced since his separation from Maureen, which was driving him towards more extreme forms of public confession; these days he often spoke out of turn; frequently, it was to give voice to some misanthropic sentiment which he always uttered in a tone of self-righteous and obstinate indignation. Important figures within the Movement were beginning to remark on this change in Cornelius; his arguments, they duly noted, were beginning to show a surprising lack of proper ideological content. And it was some of these men who thought it was time Cornelius was sent to the front-line of duty. A spell with the resistance cadres in the bush, for instance, might prove a necessary corrective.

All the same, if the central committee man was at all surprised by the outburst from Cornelius he showed no signs of being offended. Instead, he smiled patronisingly at his old school mate, his upper lip, traced with a moustache, curling away into a sort of ironic twist. His smile was that of a priest hearing the sort of confession he had always expected to hear from one of his more wayward communicants. In the face of this relentless irony, Cornelius – a tall, slightly stooped figure with rounded shoulders and a small, sensitive mouth – began to show signs of nerves. When next he spoke his voice had a scratchy whine to it. He seemed to plead for sympathy.

'At any rate, JB, I was a fool not to see it coming,' he said. 'Maureen must have been terribly unhappy with her life to have left home the way she did. To be frank with you, JB, the whole thing has left me emotionally shattered. That's why I'm not sure I'm the right man for the job you have in mind.'

The man from the central committee merely bent his eyebrows together and kept his silence. He drummed on the desk with two fingers and seemed to be taking stock of a new situation that was proving unexpectedly difficult. Outside a cloud had burst over the city centre with an astounding suddenness; then, just as suddenly, it had stopped raining and the sun had broken through the clouds, hotter than ever before. JB was anxious to finish with the Tabanyane assignment, but Cornelius, stalling for time, continued to speak of other matters, chiefly of his estranged wife. 'I blame no-one but myself, of course, for what has happened. All the same, I can't pretend not to be broken by the experience. Honestly, JB, the way things are at the moment, I don't see how I can accept this assignment. Psychologically, I would be the weakest link in the chain of the Movement's general strategy.'

When JB seemed unimpressed Cornelius's voice assumed a tone of weary desperation: 'I need time to recuperate, JB.'

Again the man from the central committee said nothing. He merely stared at Cornelius with his small eyes; and Cornelius, remembering his past agitation for action, began to fidget uncomfortably in his seat. Silence hung heavily between the two men. Then quite suddenly Bulane broke into a shrill laugh: simultaneously he got up from the chair, and placing his hands on top of the desk he leaned forward toward Cornelius and talked to him as though he were addressing a meeting.

'Listen, Corny!' he said. 'You know as well as I do your marriage to Mo was doomed from the start. Mo, forgive my saying so, but Mo is a bitch! And what is more, you know it yourself. A beautiful woman, a most beautiful woman,' JB repeated, shutting his eyes, 'but a bitch all the same!' Abruptly, he opened his eyes and stared at Cornelius with what appeared to be a direct challenge.

'JB, you're wrong about Maureen,' Cornelius protested. 'She's not at all what you think. As a matter of fact, I happen to know that in many ways Maureen is quite a prude. A show-off, if you like, a tease – but a prude, all the same!'

Cornelius paused, swallowed painfully, for even though he would not admit it to himself, doubts came swarming to the surface of his mind like a host of stinging gnats. He was trying to convince himself as much as the other man but his feelings of certitude had begun to desert him. He said to JB: 'Oh, she likes to be surrounded by men, that I won't deny. She likes to be admired. All the same, Maureen, I can assure you, is the most conventional of women!' Even before he had looked up to see the cynical expression on the other's face he already knew he had succeeded in convincing neither himself nor the man from the central committee.

'Listen, Corny!' the man said. 'Who do you think you're kidding? You know very well what Mo is: a plain, tuppeny lying whore!' Cornelius jerked back his head as though slapped across the face; his fists clenched, a low moan issued from his half-closed lips and with his hands outstretched

49

across the desk he leaned forward towards Bulane as though to embrace his torturer.

'Why do you say these things, JB?'

'Because they are true.'

'How do you know?'

'Boy, do you want proof?' Proof, of course, was the last thing Cornelius wanted; like many husbands his whole life was built on an illusion and this illusion was designed to fulfil no other function save the propping up of a personality that was in the process of disintegration.

Self-delusion, lies, they were far more preferable to anything so costly as the truth; yet no matter how hard he tried, he finally acknowledged that the need to know in great and explicit sexual detail, how, when and with whom Maureen carried on when his back was turned had reached the point of a corrosive obsession. Fed on rumours in which names were mentioned but no evidence produced, Cornelius had begun to suspect that his mind was becoming unhinged. He brooded constantly over Maureen's comings and goings; at parties, suspecting her to be closeted in a room alone with a male friend, he burst in upon her – only to find her not, as he suspected, in the amorous arms of a lover, but gossiping with a woman friend. She knew he was spying on her and despised him for it, but though overwhelmed by shame Cornelius seemed incapable of letting up on his daily vigil. Insanely, pathologically jealous, he watched for tell-tale signs on her clothes, he foraged for clues in her handbags, he searched her naked skin for the evidence of a lover's bite or rough embrace; but if Maureen was carrying on, as everyone believed she did, she was careful not to leave traces of her secret love life. That was how it had been until – well, here was a man, an old friend, who seemed prepared to make the accusations Cornelius had heard only indirectly, in other places, from other mouths; here was a friend who seemed capable of presenting the evidence.

'Your wife sleeps around, Corny,' JB said in a calm,

disinterested voice. 'She has been doing so for years. You ask anyone who knows her. Marriage hasn't changed her. As soon as your back is turned she gets herself preened up like a damned slut and off she goes and slaps it around like a dog on heat. She even has men come to the house.'

'Who comes to the house?'

'The smart boys, Corny! The Jo'burg slickers. I've seen them with their zoot suits and two-toned Florsheim shoes.'

'JB, you're a liar!' Cornelius rose from his chair and the central committee man shut his eyes to mere slits, but through the slits he was watching Cornelius like an old woman keeping vigil behind a thin slat of Venetian blinds.

'Sit down, Corny, boy. Sit down! Your trouble has always been your temperament. You know I'm not lying. You're the only one, apparently, who doesn't know the facts.'

Cornelius pretended outrage. 'Facts?' he mocked. 'You mean rumours? Ugly, cowardly rumours! Is that what you call "facts"?'

JB's voice turned suddenly icy as he spoke the next words, uttered in a tone of brutal matter-of-factness that cut through Cornelius's attempt at sarcasm. 'Listen, boy, you ought to know I never talk from hearsay. I only talk from experience.'

Suddenly, Cornelius felt fear. 'What do you mean, JB?'

'What I mean is . . . ' JB shut his eyes again. Abruptly, he opened them wide and stared at Cornelius. 'I myself have had Maureen, Corny!'

Deep in his throat Cornelius uttered a sound like a group of Tabanyane women moaning collectively a funeral dirge. Bulane watched him in silence, his face reflecting neither sorrow nor contempt but boredom. As far as he was concerned what was now taking place was not entirely unexpected. As a matter of fact, he had assiduously prepared for it. Cruel and unpleasant though this kind of surgical operation always turned out to be, time and again it had proved indispensable. When it came to assigning men to their various tasks he had to see to it that they were duly toughened up, cleansed of

51

whatever sentimental slough prevented them from seeing their objectives clearly, without illusion. Private emotion, fantasy, romantic idealism, all these were enemies of the dedicated revolutionary. As JB now saw it, Cornelius's main weakness was his excessive sentimentality and a continuous display of cheap and worthless emotion.

'You don't mean that, JB?'

'I mean every word of it, Corny.'

Right from the start the man from the central committee had had his doubts about Cornelius; he had been critical of the Committee's choice of such a man, a schoolteacher softened by years of city life and good living, who also aspired (JB thought with furious amazement) to be a poet! That such a man should have been chosen to mastermind an important military operation was sheer madness. During a debate lasting five hours he had argued consistently against the choice of Cornelius as director of operations among the Tabanyane. 'Even though the Tabanyane mission is a propaganda exercise, from the start doomed to failure,' he had told the other members, 'in order to make the maximum impact we need a seasoned man to mastermind these operations.' JB had pointed to Cornelius's long career of disruptive activities within the Movement, his constant exposition of a kind of nationalism in the place of a broad international socialism; above all, he had pointed to his lack of stability, the failure of his marriage and his excessive drinking; he attacked these not on any moral grounds but on the risks of selecting a man for such an important operation who was for all intents and purposes a complete emotional wreck. But after much persuasion by other members of the Committee, he had been forced to conclude that intelligence and integrity, both of which Cornelius possessed to a remarkable degree, were a formidable combination in any man called upon to direct an operation of this kind.

There were other factors, of course, such as Cornelius's knowledge of the terrain, his undisputed familiarity with the

Tabanyane, his total grasp of the language and local customs. These were invaluable assets. But the doubts remained.

Looking at this man crumpled like a broken doll in the chair, JB felt again not only the old doubts but nausea, even disgust. In a sudden rage he got up from of his seat: 'I took Mo, Corny, not once, not twice, but many many times, you hear? Many, many times! I've even lost count how often; but one thing I can tell you, boy, she was good and willing!'

Suddenly the two men, old childhood friends, were engulfed in a cloud of violence, a darkness, the force of which shocked the central committee man, though he had waited long for this final cataclysm. Cornelius's bowels moved and quite involuntarily he farted, and Bulane spat in disgust. But like a man goaded beyond endurance, Cornelius had already sprung clear out of his chair: seizing the committee man by the throat, he squeezed it with all the force at his command. Taken by surprise, Bulane struggled to extricate himself. They fought silently in the small office, with a certain cold concentration, the only noise they made being occasional grunts and a briefly uttered curse. Bulane was stronger than his small size might have suggested and hours of guerrilla training in the bush began to tell against his opponent. Cornelius's hands were office hands, the hands of a lover; they were too soft to inflict pain. With the gradual loosening of his grip he began to substitute threats and curses for what he lacked in strength: 'JB, you are a liar! I'll teach you not to lie!'

The committee man shook him off like a man swatting a fly. Still cursing, he grabbed Cornelius by his shoulders and pushed him down, still struggling, into the chair. 'Sit down, Corny, boy, sit down. You should feel relieved you're free of a woman like that!' Spent, broken, Cornelius sat down and began to sob quietly. It seemed to him that everything he had ever valued, all that had given meaning and significance to his life, was now sullied, tarnished, and nothing could put the bright sparkle back again. A misery, a bitterness too great to control, shook him to the core of his being. Out of a deep and searing pain, a sense of humiliation too new and too fresh to wash away with tears, he wished quite simply to be dead rather than bear the scorn of a friend who had sexually known his wife. To be sitting here, in this gloomy office, taking orders from a man who was able to say quite frankly of the woman he loved, 'I've had Mo!'; the thing was unbearable!

He said: 'JB, you know I've always thought of you as a friend.'

JB grinned: 'Correction, Corny. Not a friend but a comrade. A comrade-in-arms. And don't you forget it, Corny, boy, because that's why you are here. Not to do a friend a favour but to perform your duties as a member of a revolutionary movement.'

A grave, uneasy silence followed JB's words. Cornelius was thinking with a sudden final fury of despair: I loved her once and I love her still, I should have known better than to surrender so much emotion into her keeping, I should have kept something in reserve, even if just a token of my own independence. But just as soon as he had thought this he realised quite simply that against Maureen's extraordinary personality, the inventive richness of her mind, her irresistible sexual aura, he had never had any chance at all. The battle was lost the very first time he saw her at a township wedding, sitting in a crowded room too small for all the guests, some of whom, he remembered, had had to be accommodated in a tent in the yard. He recalled Maureen sitting, transposed like a single note arrested in a confusion of sound and movement of young men in mail-order suits and jackets from England and America. These young men, worthy only of contempt, as Cornelius thought then, were busily pressing their claims on affected laughing girls, most of them members of the rising African middle class – and in the middle of all this, reclining in an unfamiliar pose against the shoulder of her elder sister, he remembered Maureen looking cool in the noonday heat; almost static, like a still life study, vividly dark – no, purple really, the mouth blacker than the rest of her face, eyes large, solid black set in pure white, and the breasts high and unsupported. He remembered, as if only yesterday, her white dress riding high above her straight long legs, which were vulgarly, loosely parted, the dress furrowing, corrugating around her hips, with that insufficiency of silk which exposed large acres of bare flesh, dark like ploughed up fields where the legs came together to form a triangular shape. Years later Cornelius still held this sexual image in his mind's eye, that first apparition for which, no matter how long he tried afterwards, he could never find any adequate poetic metaphor: the drama of that occasion, and also the paradoxical dignity of that moment when he walked into the room to behold Maureen smiling faintly, eyebrows arched questioningly while he, Cornelius, suddenly aware of his height and his conspicuous linen suit, nervously looked for a place to sit. Finding none he had stood in the middle of the room, looking foolish and not knowing exactly what to do with his hands, which were long and hanging limply by his sides. Their eyes met and he had a momentary illusion of ecstasy floating around him like white mist: then cessation. All motion seemed suspended for a second; then once again the universe began to tick like a gigantic clock.

'I loved her, JB!' he pleaded for the worthiness of the emotion. 'Loved her more than anything in the world. Can you understand that?'

'Certainly,' JB said. 'I understand more than you think. In South Africa everyone, apparently, has to find his own particular drug. Yours, Corny, I have no doubt, is love!'

'But without love,' Cornelius protested, 'what good is the political struggle?'

'Without freedom,' JB shouted angrily, 'what good is love?' Suddenly he laughed his bitter laugh. 'Love?' He paused and looked at Cornelius with distaste. 'Whoever heard of slaves falling in love?'

Cornelius shut his eyes, his head slumped back against the headrest of his chair. In spite of the angry sarcasm of the other, he was trying to hang on to a dream which had already broken.

In his private anguish he began to rock himself quietly, remembering at the wedding the unutterable thrill of the moment when a Kwela Jazz Band had struck its first note – Oh, Jonas Gwangwa! Oh, Hugh Masekela! – and Maureen, seated in the same place she had sat all afternoon – seemed to hear the music about the same time that Cornelius did. He saw her shift in her chair, the wide-brimmed hat slanted over one half-shut terrific eye, one free hand playing with the stem of an empty glass, the other inactive, hanging limply over her sister's shoulder. Observing him now, perhaps daring him to make the first move, her entire body seemed to awake slowly like a child roused from sleep: and yet she remained exactly as she had been before, frozen: and he, like a dumb piece of machinery, rose, began to move as though propelled forward towards her, but the notion that he had feet and was actually moving toward a woman he had never seen before was somehow incredible, astounding, a miracle whose only evidence was to see her face moving closer and closer toward him so that he felt like someone in the cockpit of a plane that was moving faster and inevitably toward an object, some obstacle, that was rising to meet it. But until he was standing in the middle of the room, partnerless, he did not know what had happened. The whole thing had come to pass with such astonishing alacrity! Then a *tsotsi* appeared our of nowhere, jerking himself like a flick-knife from the crowd, cutting him, beating him to Maureen. Foolishly, he watched the *tsots*i carry her away from him, leaving him standing in the middle of the room, miserable but not hopeless.

Cornelius felt a dim-witted desire to speak about Maureen, to explain, to confess, to render plain and self-evident the profound attraction that Maureen still held for him. He turned to the central committee man, who was now rummaging for something in the bottom drawer of his desk. 'JB, if only you had known the circumstances under which I first met Maureen!

If only you had seen her as I first saw her at that township wedding. There were so many people there, so many girls, pretty girls I tell you, but I can assure you not one of those girls could hold a candle to Maureen. Like a princess, a goddess, she dominated everything simply by being there. For days, for weeks afterwards, I couldn't get her out of my mind!'

The man abandoned whatever he was doing. 'Corny,' he said impatiently, 'are you still talking to me about Maureen?' His eyes were veiled with boredom and contempt.

'After what you've told me I suppose I should feel only disgust, but I don't. I can't, JB! I can't feel what I'm supposed to feel. Perhaps my love for her is a sickness. Perhaps all great love is a kind of sickness. At any rate, sex is much easier to handle.'

Bulane made no comment. 'Suppose,' Cornelius thought, allowing himself a momentary aberration, 'suppose JB has not been telling the truth?' It did not, however, take Cornelius very long to dispense with the essential fallacy of this supposition.

Remembering again Maureen's insatiable passion, remembering her extraordinary sexual ardour, the whipping frenzy of her sable body, as he entered it for the first time (it was in broad daylight in the kitchen of her mother's house in Dube while her parents and sister sat in the long lounge talking and maundering on as they waited fretfully for the tea that he and Maureen had volunteered to make but which had to wait, while they grappled amongst the pots and pans on the kitchen floor). Remembering all this, and the way she sometimes approached his working table when she wished to be made love to, roughly pushing chairs and tables out of the way, how could he doubt JB was telling the truth?

If only he could forget: forget that afternoon, the two of them struggling in elemental embrace on the smooth polished floor of the kitchen. For minutes after he had entered her he could feel her slip and roll while she coiled herself like a mamba around his maleness. But whether because of his anxiety that someone might walk in at precisely the moment the explosion came or because of Maureen's astonishing greed (her thrashing jerking movements as she drew him inside her) he never reached his climax. She was impossible. When she finally came he was drenched in the rain of her passion; she became then a trail lost in hot swampy jungles and dark misty forests, a sort of mystical kingdom at the core of a continent that remained inscrutable, very dark, very unconquerable.

'JB, I'm afraid I can't do it. I can't go to Tabanyane.' Bulane looked at Cornelius with neither surprise nor censure in his expression. 'I'm not your man, JB You must find someone else.'

The man seemed to have been waiting for just such a moment and seemed even relieved that it had finally come. With an abrupt movement of his body he pushed his chair back and opened the drawer of his desk from which he removed two glasses and a bottle of Mellowood brandy. Saying nothing, he carefully unwrapped the bottle and by a dull light that cast an ineffectual glow over their faces, the central committee man looked doubtfully at the two glasses, which were dirty from previous use. Shrugging his shoulders he poured a tiny drop of brandy in each glass, shook and rinsed them before emptying the contents on to the floor. Then he poured into each glass three fingers of brandy before passing one to Cornelius. Cornelius drank gratefully.

At last, JB spoke. He hardly looked at Cornelius as he made his brief, impersonal address. 'As you know, Corny, we've brought you into this thing right from the start because of your deep knowledge of the Tabanyane people, their customs, their language, and, of course, their terrain. Your familiarity with the people and their ways will be an invaluable asset in the execution of your mission. Naturally, I need not stress the importance of this operation, not only for the National Liberation Movement but for all the progressive forces in the country. For our friends abroad it will provide a real test as to our ability to mount and execute a revolutionary struggle.'

Nothing of what Bulane was saying seemed to penetrate Cornelius's mind. He drank, sniffled. The man seemed to go on and on; Cornelius tried to listen, then stopped altogether. Nausea returned: the feeling of hurt and betrayal by this very man who now had the audacity to speak to him of 'freedom' and 'liberation'. Cornelius suddenly interrupted: 'But JB, can you tell me something? How can the Movement survive with people like you at the top?'

Perhaps it was the mocking tone in Cornelius's voice which cut the committee man to the quick. For a moment, he seemed to lose his amiability. 'Listen, Comrade! The Movement will survive because it is more important than either you or me or anyone else! It is even more important than your damned sexual vanity! The trouble with you, Corny, is you've always thought of yourself as God's gift to women. Well, you're not God's gift to women, boy. The sooner you get that into your head the better!' The central committee man allowed himself a brief, distressful laugh, hollow and mirthless. 'And on top of it, you have these goddamn awful moral pretensions! Goddamn, boy, forget your bourgeois ideas about marital fidelity. The important thing is to enjoy sex when it is available, but for goodness' sake don't let's build up absurd romantic notions around what is after all a biological activity.' After this, as though they were both embarrassed by this outburst, they drank their brandy in silence.

From the top of his desk JB picked up some letters, looking first at one, then another; deliberately, he began to tear into them. While doing so he sipped with exaggerated delicacy at his brandy. And so did Cornelius. They drank till at last the central committee man showed signs of being affected by the undiluted brandy and the heat; his eyes, always veiled and sleepy, were now rimmed with red. A lone fly buzzed him constantly and he swiped at it with his free hand. 'Christ, Corny, I can remember you at "varsity, boy,"' he told Cornelius with a sudden spontaneous warmth and affection.

'Boy, you weren't so particular then about how many half-assed liberal white *bokkies* you took to bed, were you, boy! Atoning for the sins of their parents, you used to say; and you took full advantage of their guilt.'

'That was different, JB,' Cornelius protested.

'What was so different about it? White meat? Sure, it was different! More classy, more exciting than black meat! It came to you sprinkled with sweet-smelling toilet water. To hell with that! It was no different from any other form of exploitation.'

'I didn't mean that, JB'

'What did you mean then?'

'I meant, the exploitation was mutual. Believe me, JB, I got to know all those liberal white girls pretty well. Most of them, not all, had problems. Some had very very peculiar tastes, believe me!' For the first time since they had begun their talk Cornelius grinned obscenely at JB. 'In any case, as I soon found out, I was only a well-oiled prick for them to exploit until it was time to settle down with some nice Parktown boy who could join Daddy in business.'

'Boy, you're bitter! I didn't know you were so bitter! You have such a big chip on your shoulder. Bitterness will get you nowhere, my boy!'

Suddenly, JB dipped his bullet-shaped head behind the desk; for a minute or so he rifled through some papers in a drawer until he emerged with a time-yellowed photograph which he thrust into Cornelius's hands. Cornelius took the photograph and looked at it for some time. Then he looked at the man who had just given it to him with some surprise. Cornelius didn't know what to think of the enigma that was JB. In the photograph there was a girl with a mass of curly blonde hair: lithe but strongly built, she stood unsmiling, poised like a dancer on a wooded hillside in some anonymous country. Cornelius found himself staring past long eyelashes into enormous, icy blue eyes. Even in the photograph the girl looked dense with a ravishing kind of sexuality.

'A girl I left behind in Moscow,' JB said in a matter-of-fact voice that gave nothing away. 'For all practical purposes we were man and wife. I have a son by her.' He thrust another photograph at Cornelius which showed a handsome six-year-old coffee-coloured boy in Russian clothes. Half-Russian and half-Zulu, Cornelius thought; how astounding the twentieth century was turning out to be! Without being able to say exactly why, the blending of Russian and African blood disturbed while thrilling him. If he told his parents about this they would find the idea too far-fetched to believe and yet it was happening; depending on your own perspective the world was either becoming smaller or larger. JB said: 'When the time came to return to the country. I packed my bags and left. You see, Corny, the struggle is more important than our small domestic problems.' JB laughed a sharp, distressed little laugh, but this time Cornelius detected a scarcely concealed rage beneath the faked irony. His friend's eyes were red not so much from the undiluted brandy anymore as from some frustrated rage.

'Don't you miss them sometimes, JB?' Cornelius asked with genuine sympathy. JB seemed annoyed by Cornelius's troubled air of solicitation.

'Listen, boy,' he snapped. 'We've been talking too much, you and I. I've got work to do and so have you!'

From the drawer of his desk he pulled out maps, bus and train schedules which he spread out between himself and Cornelius, and with a show of intense businesslike concentration the two of them poured over these like two generals planning a difficult campaign. From time to time, JB interrupted himself to pass on information relating to what Cornelius would find on the ground in Tabanyane. 'Far from sitting on our hands, Corny, as you have so often implied in your speeches, the Movement is very active in Tabanyane, laying the groundwork, you'll find. I haven't told you, but there is a unit which is already in place in Malaita location commanded by a man named Thekwane, a graduate of military academies in Algeria, Egypt and the Soviet Union.

Very highly trained in handling all kinds of weapons. Though he will be operating independently, he'll give your men all the basic training they need in handling firearms, and you're expected to liaise with Thekwane on a number of important missions.' Bulane then went on to discuss in some detail the conflict in Tabanyane.

The dispute between the Government and the Tabanyane people had latterly developed many unforeseen complications but the main lines of the conflict had not departed significantly from the original source of the dispute. The trouble had started in the previous spring when the Government, faced with a shortage of development land, asked the paramount chief of the Tabanyane to cede part of the ancestral lands for industrial development. No ruler of the Tabanyane had ever been free to give this land away, even to his sons and other close relatives, without prior consultation with the tribe. This demand from the Pretoria Government was couched in the form of a harmless request, but was immediately rejected by the paramount chief, an elderly man then in his sixties. After a brief period of uncertainty, rumours began to spread that the Government was preparing to use force to evict the Tabanyane from their land. The elderly Seeiso, backed by his son Diliza, then a senior student of social anthropology at Oxford, started mobilising the tribe. An attempt by the native commissioners to hold a meeting in the Ancestral Place was called off when infuriated tribesmen overran the place, overturning tables and beating up Government messengers.

The Government response was swift and brutal. A huge police force was dispatched to the area, virtually occupying all of Tabanyane. Seeiso was deposed and his brother, a vain, authoritarian sub-chief, installed in his place; a state of emergency, followed by a reign of terror, was declared. A month after his deposition the gentle Seeiso, much loved by his subjects, died from a stroke, and the struggle between the new Paramount Chief Sekala and his people began in earnest. Beatings, assassinations and counter-terror became the order of the day in Tabanyane. A new clandestine movement of resistance sprang up, led by ordinary rural people and disaffected elders. It was this movement, growing spontaneously from the grievances of the people, which Cornelius was now being asked to take over and direct its operations from the caves of Thaba Situ. Not that members of the central committee entertained any illusions about the Movement's ability to extract victory, plain and simple, from such a campaign. On the other hand a protracted struggle against Paramount Chief Sekala and the Pretoria Government, clearly seen to be led by the cadres of the National Liberation Movement, would do much to enhance the reputation of the Movement across the entire country.

Sekala's victory, if he succeeded in crushing the Tabanyane resistance with the backing of his Pretoria masters, would be temporary, but the long-term objectives of the National Liberation Movement, which was to fan discontent all over the country, would be realised. The Movement itself could never be defeated, but would only grow more popular with every brutal attempt at suppression.

For more than thirty minutes JB worked deliberately, his brow beaded with sweat; he used red and blue markers to indicate positions. There were parallel lines across shades of dark brown indicating mountain passes where arms would flow down into Tabanyane from eastern and northern approaches through Mozambique and Swaziland. Friendly villages were ringed in red and those friendly to the Government were double-ringed in blue. Also prominently arrowed and ringed were Sekala's *kraals*, as were the army headquarters and police stations.

Bulane worked calmly, professionally, blue smoke curling away from his Havana cigar. 'As you will no doubt discover from the instructions contained in this envelope,' he said, thrusting a small packet into Cornelius's hands, 'each night during the operations, a friend of the Movement will be waiting by the telephone in a house outside Johannesburg, ready to receive and transmit messages from you. We've worked out an elaborate code, as you will notice. Above all, I must stress to you, Corny, under no circumstances must you try to contact us through normal channels.

'As you no doubt are aware, not even our rank and file members have been informed of the precise nature of the operation. If we're not telling our members we're certainly not anxious to inform the special branch.' JB giggled self-consciously like a schoolgirl at his own joke before continuing in a manner that was a strange mix of blandness and coyness: 'This is only a start, of course. We expect things to develop very quickly in the next month or two and then it will be time to issue statements – anonymously, of course – explaining to the people, courtesy of our tireless bourgeois press, the exact extent of our involvement in Tabanyane. Let me emphasise to you again, Corny, keep in the background. Leave the sensitive jobs to those of our boys trained to carry them out. Your duty as a representative of the Movement is to see to it that instructions are carried out to the letter and to keep us informed of developments.'

Though Cornelius had been somewhat relieved to learn that his own duties involved less risk to himself, he was none the less peeved that his tasks were to be on a less heroic scale, and would in fact be those of a glorified messenger, at best a party functionary, a political commissar; but he swallowed his pride. Still, something bothered him. 'JB,' Corny said sharply. 'We've discussed everything. Why I've been chosen to go to Tabanyane. The logistics and so on. What we haven't discussed is how I'm supposed just to disappear, go underground, as it were, without arousing suspicion. After all, I am a schoolteacher, a respected member of the community, how do I just suddenly disappear, simply vanish, without a huge hue and cry being raised everywhere to try and find me?'

'Very good! Very good!' JB chuckled. 'I was wondering when you were going to come to that.'

The man from the central committee spent another half-hour

going through the details of the plan. When it was all completed Cornelius was amazed at the apparent simplicity of the whole thing. He couldn't believe what he had heard. 'So I'm to be declared "missing"? As simple as that?'

'That's right, Corny, and you'd better get used to the idea.' JB giggled again. 'After all, there's a state of emergency in force and hundreds of able-bodied men, respectable citizens like you, Corny, go missing every day. As for you, I can tell you right now, I suspect the security boys are holding you "incommunicado" somewhere. As an influential organisation, though underground, it is our manifest duty to try and enlist every assistance, here at home and abroad, in order to establish precisely your whereabouts!' He burst out laughing.

'JB, this is crazy!' Cornelius exclaimed.

'Is it?' he asked drily. 'We've already prepared a statement and our lawyers are working on a habeas corpus right now. Anything else, Corny?'

Cornelius was still overcome and seemed a little dazed. Finally, he said: 'This messenger with whom I'm supposed to liaise, JB? What is his name?'

'She.'

'Okay. She. What's her name?'

'She's a friend of the Movement.'

'I should have thought so,' Cornelius observed with some sarcasm. 'But who is she? What's her name? Have I met her before?'

JB sighed. 'Corny, the less each one of us knows about what the other is doing the better. For the sake of everyone concerned. But if you insist on names, why let's just call her Jane.'

'Oh, yes! And Me: Tarzan!'

Bulane narrowed his eyes a bit. 'It's as good a name as any,' he said. 'Are you satisfied now?'

Cornelius was furious but he kept his anger under control. 'Is she white or black?'

'White, black, what's the difference?'

'JB, this is an extremely hazardous enterprise!' Cornelius protested.

'What's the matter boy? Getting cold feet?'

'I like working with people I can trust, that's all.'

'Listen, Corny!' JB said sharply. 'If you can't do the job, say so, but for goodness' sake, don't raise difficulties where none exists!'

Cornelius fell silent. Suddenly, he felt oppressed by the claustrophobic atmosphere of the small office, by the dank smell of the runny toilet and the stale odour of cigar smoke, and wished to be gone.

'Just one more thing, JB?' Cornelius approached the subject cautiously. 'Why did the Committee pick on me to mastermind this operation?'

Bulane laughed his brief distressed laugh, then grinning wildly at Cornelius, said: 'Corny, boy, we needed someone of your superb intelligence and delicacy. This is not the kind of operation we can entrust to a heavy-footed elephant. It needs a person of great sensitivity, that is, yourself! I'm sure you fit the bill to your bootstraps!'

'I should've known I'd never get a straight answer from you, JB,' Cornelius said, rising from the chair.

Bulane stood up abruptly and thrust a brown paper bag into Cornelius's hands. 'Here, take this! It's close to fifteen thousand. Just about. You might have to grease a few palms to get some doors opened in Tabanyane. Across the border too. Where are you off to from here?'

'Not very far from here,' Cornelius replied vaguely. 'As a matter of fact, I'm only going across the street.'

As Cornelius had expected JB's curiosity was immediately aroused. 'To the magistrates' courts?'

'Yes. Nothing to do with me. A little matter concerning my friend Jojozi.'

'Drunk and disorderly!' Bulane spat. 'Your journalist friends, Corny, all that *Drum* crew, they're always in court for the wrong reasons! They see too many Hollywood films.'

Cornelius was annoyed at the man's affectation of high-minded seriousness.

He said coldly. 'According to Jojozi none of them was drunk. A white woman reported seeing three natives enter a white man's flat, that was all. Police arrived. They found Leonard Mhlongo and George Sibisi sitting in Levi's lounge. There was a bottle of whisky on the table and some glasses. Jojozi had shut himself up in the toilet.' Bulane chuckled appreciatively. Cornelius said: 'The police took all three of them. Levi too. Separately, of course. I understand Levi has since been charged with illegally supplying natives with alcohol.'

'Who's this Levi?' JB asked suspiciously. 'A progressive?'

'I don't know exactly. Just an Englishman knocking about Johannesburg. He's worked at all kinds of jobs. Every now and then he writes some advertising copy. He travels a great deal. All over the country.'

'A bohemian?' JB said with distaste. 'A professional slummer!'

Cornelius said nothing because he knew Bulane expected no comment. Before parting, they shook hands. 'By the way,' JB said, smiling roguishly. 'I hear Diliza has a sister, a nurse who trained in Great Britain. Quite a devil with her hands, I'm told. Better look out, boy!' His laughter came up to Cornelius as though from the well of some dark theatre. Just as he was about to disappear into the folds of the curtains leading into Desai's shop, Cornelius turned and JB, still standing at the bottom of the steps, raised a fist in salute: 'Amandla! Power!'

'To the people!' Cornelius answered dully.

Chapter Five

CORNELIUS left JB's office by the way he had come: through Desai's shop, past its jumble of unsold merchandise lying in disorderly profusion behind the cobwebby windows, and then passed through the front door. Old Desai himself was not in his place behind the counter where he had been when Cornelius had first walked in; and yet, using his uncanny intuition, Cornelius was more than certain that somewhere behind the bales of cloth, standing watch like a sentry, old Desai was observing his departure with the same keen interest he had shown earlier when Cornelius had first presented himself at the shop. This feeling of being watched, of being appraised by a pair of anonymous eyes, was difficult to shake off even when Cornelius finally stood on the pavement outside the dusty, overcrowded shop, dully contemplating the street he must cross to gain the other side of the square.

Only a moment before, during the intensive discussion regarding the nuts and bolts of his Tabanyane mission, Cornelius had felt in absolute control of his mind: wry, sceptical and quite realistic about his chances of survival, but as soon as he had left JB's office doubts once more assailed him. Not only doubts, but panic! He felt distinctly ill. People walking by watched him curiously. Cornelius was sure they regarded him with suspicion. Perhaps he had already begun to show all the symptoms of someone harbouring a criminal intent. In his own eyes every step he now took proclaimed him a 'suspect', a 'terrorist' in the pay of revolutionary forces, which accounted for the sly, perverted interest which complete strangers walking by were now taking in him. He had become part of a vast underground network 'conspiring to overthrow the Government by violent means'. The aim alone, and certainly its execution, was punishable by long imprisonment, even death.

When Cornelius stopped walking everything cleared for a moment and the city rose above him; beyond the skyscrapers, gleaming in the brilliant sunshine, rose the mine dumps, mountains of yellow sand which were the chaff of extracted gold. He, too, Cornelius thought, was carrying gold, at least paper convertible into gold; fifteen thousand rands worth of paper currency! He could feel the lump of brown paper nudging like a tumour against his upper rib from the inside pocket of his jacket; the money that would help start a revolution.

He was in great need of a drink. The heat had become intolerable. So it had come to this. Every event which had led to his present plight came back to him now. From what had begun as a mysterious, even comic visit by the emissary of the Movement, it had come to this pass. Even without shutting his eyes, Cornelius could still remember clearly the arrival early one morning at his Dube home of the man who came with what sounded like a garbled message delivered in a sonorous voice. Though at first Cornelius had found it difficult to follow what he was saying, he had finally gathered the gist of the message, which was that he, Cornelius, had been selected by the central committee to travel to Tabanyane, there to direct operations on behalf of the National Liberation Movement in what had appeared to be a spontaneous uprising of the peasant population.

At first Cornelius had suspected a joke. From the beginning, the messenger whom the committee had chosen to deliver this message had acted in a manner calculated to raise all kinds of suspicion. He laughed a lot at his own jokes and looked more like a fugitive from the law than a political operator. He never sat still for more than a minute at a time. When Cornelius had tried to show him a seat near the centre of the room the visitor had declined the offer, preferring a shadowy corner of the small lounge where he could clearly see Cornelius's face but Cornelius could not see his. Throughout the conversation he was careful to keep his face in shadow except when he leaped up from time to time to peer anxiously through the window as though he feared a trap. From some of his rambling conversation Cornelius gathered an impression of a sad, much travelled man, who had seen and done a great many things; but somehow, to Cornelius's confusion, his manner of delivery belied his melancholy aspect. His voice was young, gay, vivacious. It had a light, playful quality, the kind his general aspect seemed to lack. A decrepit little man, judged by his appearance, was what Cornelius thought of him; a small African wearing a faded dark suit of uncertain cut and a homburg hat a size too big for his diminutive head. After a while, he had suspected the visitor of being from the special branch.

The man, who introduced himself simply as 'Comrade X', had no address, no past, no identity save this anonymous, much scarred, rat-like face and a head too small, Cornelius thought, for an honest man. Above all, the man talked an awful lot! His visitor babbled on – epigrams, quotable quotes, trite ideas dressed up as new; names – Dingane, Cetshwayo, Moshoeshoe, Marx, Lenin, Churchill and Roosevelt; they all poured forth from him in a bewildering stream of seemingly incoherent nonsense. And yet! And yet, Cornelius thought, he could discern in this lunatic, endless outpouring the glimmer of an idea, potent, dangerous and liberating all at once.

'Che!' the man told Cornelius at one stage. 'A great revolutionary! A brave man, and, I am given to understand, a good lover. Everything you could possibly need in a comrade, but unfortunately not good enough for us! His theories? For us they're useless! No, worse than useless, they're dangerous!'

The man sighed and looked away. There was a long pause before he began once more: 'The peasants, comrade Molapo, are stupid, conservative – they prefer bread and butter to freedom. We cannot leave the business of revolution to the shaky hand of the peasantry. Again and again they will betray us. In our situation the peasants are the most counter-revolutionary class!'

The man talked on, mostly nonsense – but nonsense, Cornelius noted, that was sometimes fused with something like revolutionary poetry. The man chain-smoked, he was miserably racked by coughs, he spat on the floor – to Cornelius's consternation – and wiped the spittle by stamping on it, shuffling his foot upon the wet spot as though he were testing the surface of the ice before skating.

'So many of us,' the emissary said, now smiling broadly at Cornelius, 'have been privileged to listen to you talking at meetings, comrade Molapo!' Again his lungs were racked by spasms of coughing. As if to show his contempt for his own poor health he went on to light the next cigarette; in the gloom of the room the matchstick flared, and temporarily the man's face was lit up in the glare, showing gaunt features, high cheekbones that were almost devoid of flesh, and sharp, penetrating eyes that seemed to look through everything. 'I believe I'm right when I say there are very few young men who know how to hold an audience in the palm of their hand as you do, comrade Molapo. A great gift that, comrade, I can assure you. I myself could never hold an audience's attention for longer than five minutes. That was my handicap. My great failure as a political worker. My talent, if I have any talent to speak of, is backroom planning. That's why you have never heard of me. People like us, comrade Molapo, have had to learn by long and painful experience to forego the limelight; to be self-effacing.'

Cornelius, who thought he detected sarcasm behind the other's self-deprecating manner, wished the stranger would quickly come to the point. That afternoon he had an important meeting to attend; then there was the Parktown Poetry Association Workshop at which Margot Silverman, a former classmate at Wits, had asked him to give a brief talk on 'The Cross-Currents Between Native Poetry and Native Music'. And though Cornelius did not expect a bunch of Parktown liberals to know very much about African cultural traditions, there was always a small chance that some old Jewish scholar, mouth twitching and almost blind with protracted research, would come loaded with the kind of information that Cornelius had never managed to get hold of himself. Discussion would then follow. Questions would be asked. He'd better look up a few sources.

'I suppose you're not very religious yourself?' The man asked, cutting through Cornelius's reverie. He was slightly taken aback by the question. What could this stranger, who for the most part talked of revolution, have to do with religion? The man must have noted the expression of perplexity on his face for he quickly explained: 'Believe me, Comrade, I ask with the most innocent of intentions. A simple curiosity, you might say. I myself believe in God when things are exceptionally bad! After all, if He's not there, there's no harm done, is there? There are times, of course, when things go very badly, as you'll soon learn during your mission to Tabanyane.'

Cornelius tried to protest that he knew nothing of the mission to which the stranger was alluding but the other didn't let him speak. He immediately coughed, spat, then wiped his mouth with a gaudy red handkerchief which he produced from the depths of the side-pocket of his shiny, conscientiously pressed dark pants.

'If I may say so, I speak from some limited experience of these matters. Operations of that sort are difficult to handle; skill with weapons, I need not explain, is no guarantee of easy victories. As you may imagine, there are always people to give orders to, certain jobs to be delegated to other shakier, clumsier hands; above all, there are always prideful hearts to placate at the end of the day. In the wilderness, faced with the

72

intractable laws of nature, attempting to manipulate the course of events with regard to time and destiny – you'll no doubt recall Marx's very perceptive remark to the effect that we do not make history just any way we want – some kind of belief then becomes necessary. Marxism, a belief in history, a faith in a god so long as He is on your side! Admittedly, it takes a certain innocence...!'

Abruptly, he stood up without finishing the sentence; quickly he crossed the floor to the window where he peered cautiously from behind a curtain and, satisfied with the lay of the land outside, he returned to his seat, smiling self-consciously at Cornelius. Impatient but still courteous, Cornelius said: 'I wonder, Comrade, if we might discuss the object of your visit?'

The man seemed disappointed in him. For a minute he stared uncomprehendingly, then suddenly he spoke again, flatly, without enthusiasm, almost sounding bored with what he had to say. 'Oh, that? Of course, you must wish to know what the Movement expects of you. Naturally, I realise you must be impatient. There's nothing much to tell, you know. I was simply asked to inform you of the central committee's decision – but I put it badly! I was asked to convey to you the committee's great and everlasting faith in your capacity to carry out the Tabanyane mission, and to express the hope that you'll grasp at this opportunity to serve your people at its great turning point in history.'

Cornelius waited for the man to explain, but the other suddenly laughed and coughed simultaneously. His breath was wheezing out of him, his eyes watering. 'History will not forgive us,' he recited from memory, quoting from one of Cornelius's many speeches on the subject, 'if we should fold our hands and do nothing to assist a section of our people which is most cruelly suppressed at this moment!'

Again the man laughed good-humouredly at Cornelius. 'As you yourself have so often put it, comrade Molapo, we cannot abandon the Tabanyane people to the tender mercies of the

South African Government. The committee, I think, agrees and I'm sure you'll be gratified to know we are at the point of linking arms with our revolutionary brothers and sisters in Tabanyane! With your assistance as go-between, with your direction as the man on the spot, I have no doubt...'

Again coughing interrupted him; he paused but with customary recklessness immediately lit another cigarette. Cornelius was about to ask who decided and why they had decided he was the most suitable candidate when the man suddenly fished out a piece of soiled, wrinkled paper from another sidepocket of his coat and smoothed it out before writing some squiggly lines for Cornelius. 'As you know, since being banned our Movement has decided to go underground. And you, Comrade, without a doubt, have become the most important member of the "Underground People!" In consequence I am requested to inform you that for any further explanation as to the execution of your mission you are to call at this secret address at your earliest convenience.'

After this announcement, delivered in a grave tone of voice, the emissary suddenly reverted to his former rhetorical style. 'Never let it be said,' he said with his eyes shut, once again quoting from one of Cornelius's most successful platform speeches, 'I repeat, let it never be said that we did not step forward when history summoned us to the barricades! Believe me, Comrade, in my innermost heart I wish I had the same opportunity as is now being handed to you to serve at the altar of history, truly to be a servant of the people at this most critical time!'

Cornelius was about to interrupt, to protest, when the man, this weird apparition which had come out of nowhere, was suddenly gone without so much as a 'Goodbye!', leaving his visitee staring dumbfounded at the open door and at the piece of paper in his hand.

Chapter Six

FOR days and weeks there was nothing to mitigate the merciless heat. The rainy season had come early and gone, leaving Tabanyane a bowl of hot dust. In the mornings before the shadows retreated from the relentless advance of the rising sun, police lieutenant Adam de Kock could smell the heat creeping up like a horrible beast behind the bush at the back of the crumbly corrugated-iron-roofed farmhouse, the parched dusty air fighting its way through the cracks and crevices into the bedroom in which he and his wife, Nellie, lay in their steamy bath of damp sweat, squirming and tossing, continuously frustrated in their quest for coolness.

Even before he was fully awake, grey-faced, heavy-lidded and impatiently rubbing sleep from his aching swollen eyes, De Kock was aware of the severe discomfort in his rumbling stomach, aware also of the dryness in his mouth, the thick chapped quality of his lips, and a tongue in his mouth which, when he rolled it gently against the front teeth, felt like rough sandpaper and tasted worse: the result, no doubt, of his excessive drinking the night before at the bar of the Meerdaal Hotel. A water pitcher was placed on the wash-stand in one corner of the room; cautiously moving first one leg, then the other, De Kock was able to step out of bed without waking his wife. Then, using both handles, he grasped at the water-pitcher and drank greedily in swift thirsty gulps, allowing the water to drip sloppily down the front of his night-shirt, soaking him through to the skin and refreshing him in the dense morning heat. Beyond the barred windows, which provided the most elementary protection against surprise attack by marauding guerrillas, was Malaita location. Sometimes in the mornings there was a mist in the flat bottom of the valley as far as the outskirts of the location, which caused the bronzed rust of the corrugated-iron *pondokkies* to look grey and silvery in the early morning sun, like a touched-up painting laid out for an exhibition.

Later the sun would mount higher and higher in the sky, the mist would rise and dissolve into fine motes of gleaming air; and under the vast canopy of sky would stand the immense cavalcade of the Tabanyane mountains, greyish and pale blue in the distance, a palisade of smooth and jutting rock, cutting off the white south from the hostile black north. Across the land, dotted against the curving horizon, lay white farms, and farther away, less easy to define, the native *kraals* and beyond them at last the Tabanyane mountains. Climbing up the mountain tracks, as De Kock had done many times on the trail of guerrilla fighters, he knew that a rider and horse could be lost for days up there on top of the mountains.

The land, the immense sky above it, always filled De Kock with an emotion he had never been able to analyse properly. It was not love exactly, not even a feeling of possession; it was more a feeling of wonder and awe, a religious emotion, a kind of ecstasy even, accompanied by an obscure conviction that God had put the white man here for a purpose. It was a thrilling conviction which sometimes subsided into a dim sensation like sexual pleasure. Nevertheless, drought had affected everyone's feeling about the land. Here in the valley below the mountain range, in the small white *dorp* of no more than eighteen hundred people the land ached with a feeble yearning for the rain that would not come. The sun rose and set. Sometimes wrongly sensing dampness in the air, the guinea-fowl sobbed out its false promise of rain, but lately there was dead silence in the scorched air, interrupted only by the periodic clatter of machine-gun fire in the foothills of the distant mountains.

Standing for ten minutes by the bedroom window De Kock gazed at the tormented land, at the fine dust which rose in the golden sunlight and blended with the mist which lingered. De Kock was already walking back to bed when he suddenly stopped dead in his tracks, as if arrested by an unexpected idea. The police lieutenant was a big man, not fat but with a bulky way of walking, of occupying whatever space was available, which made the room seem too small to contain that bulk. He did not really walk but lumbered. He did not stand but swayed. He leaned against walls, fumbled clumsily with objects.

His face was not handsome but was said to possess character by his admiring friends, and many women had once found him desirable but considered him less so as time went by. In stasis, sitting in a chair or behind the wheel of his disfigured DeSoto, he conveyed arrested power.

Too huge even for a man as big as De Kock, his head, with its closely-cropped faded blond hair, gave to the square flat features of his face the pugnacious look of a tough combative warrior. At that moment his face was half turned towards Nellie, who moaned and sniffled even in her sleep. The calico had slipped down, exposing a shrunken breast which looked pathetic in its unfulfilled earlier roseate promise.

Every now and then her limbs shuddered; impotently she gripped the edges of the sheet that covered a naked flank. In that brief spasm between sleep and wakefulness Nellie had sensed her husband's absence by her side and, sighing deeply, had moved gratefully into the empty space which the man had vacated. With a feeling of incredulous outrage De Kock noticed that even in sleep Nellie smiled her foolish, simpering smile. Then his outrage was replaced by real curiosity. He gazed at his wife in simple astonishment that he should have spent nearly a quarter of his lifetime with this absurd, impossible woman, at once frail and too strong for him, alternately docile and bullying; an ugly woman, really, hollow-chested and stringy-haired. By the thin early morning light he could see her profile, the eyes heavy-lidded in her bony face, the small sallow forehead with faint tired lines across it, the thin-lipped mouth whose casual harshness was softened by the ludicrous shadow of a smile.

While he gazed at her she moaned again, moving her lips as if talking to someone in her sleep. A blue vein throbbed slightly at her temple. Of course, he knew he was being unreasonable. Even in his most capricious moments, De Kock knew he was unreasonable about Nellie. After all, Nellie was not to blame for his pinched existence, for his wrecked ambition and crushed self-esteem. She herself had suffered more because she had suffered blindly, without hope or even a shred of dignity; even in sleep Nellie bore the marks of her own emotional impoverishment and defeat like a broken animal, sustained only by a sort of inhuman resignation that was as much of an affront to De Kock's fastidious pride as her surprisingly successful half-hearted attempts at bullying him.

She worked all day behind farm hands, shouting encouragement, curses or worse; in the house while the maid, Annie Lebua, cleaned, cooked and sewed, Nellie followed her around, doing much the same thing. She fell exhausted into bed at night, too drained to care when De Kock came home, as he had the night before, well after midnight, rocking unsteadily on his feet, Kristina Kemp still very much on his mind. He had entered the bedroom, to find Nellie in bed, fast asleep in the foetal position, her small hands clenched into tiny childish fists, a thin trickle of saliva silvering the side of her cheek. A quiver of pain, a jolt of anguish, had shot through De Kock's body, and in his wretched humiliation he had cursed himself, had cursed his wife, cursed the Englishman and his woman, and above all had cursed Kristina Kemp who even now in her *vervloekste* whoredom must be lying in the arms of another man.

For a minute De Kock had sat down on the edge of the bed,

trying to think. Slowly, one by one, the events of the day before came back to him, with the recollection of each accompanying mood, each separate moment encrusted with the memory of the pain and humiliation De Kock had suffered.

In his mind he went over each detail as a person might do when running the tip of his tongue over a chipped tooth, frightened of pain but drawn irresistibly to the exposed nerve. The day had started badly enough but nothing of what happened afterwards, including De Kock's awkward attempts and dismal failure to secure a bank loan from the *verdoemde* Englishman, could equal the misery and disappointment he felt at being stood up by Kristina Kemp, the blonde receptionist at the Meerdaal Hotel. Thinking about the girl in such scandalous proximity to his wife, even though she slept heavily like someone in a deep coma, caused De Kock a momentary twinge of guilt, as if his thoughts were loud enough to be overheard. In the few days following his humiliation it might be necessary to avoid the Meerdaal altogether because even the barman seemed to be armed with the secret knowledge of his humiliation, which added considerably to De Kock's bitterness. Perhaps more people knew of his being thrown over by the girl. If it were not yet the talk of the Meerdaal, it would soon become the only topic of conversation in the Oom Paul Bar.

The Meerdaal was a sprawling, semi-colonial, double-storey building set on the Main Street. Opposite was a petrol station with a single petrol pump; next to it was the red brick building of the Post Office and the Town Hall. In turn the Town Hall was linked by a courtyard to a stationery shop and a tiny *koffiehuis* in front of whose doors the owner had placed some wicker tables and chairs. Here, on a tolerably mild day the local burghers could be seen gossiping and refreshing themselves with endless cups of coffee and warm, lavishly buttered scones and buns.

As popular as the *koffiehuis* was, it could not compete on the same footing with the Meerdaal. It was always the

Meerdaal, especially Oom Paul's Bar with its comings and goings of commercial travellers and other birds of passage, which provided the focal point for the small farming community of white Tabanyane. And of course it was to the bar of the Meerdaal that, after being stood up by the girl Kristina Kemp and failing to secure a loan from the Englishman, that the chief of police had finally come to rest. From his fruitless searches for the girl he had returned to Oom Paul's long railbar, drink seeming then the only palliative; drink and a long spell of lonely reflection. While he downed beer after beer many things passed through De Kock's mind, many tentative solutions to problems which seemed to him intractable – thoughts of resigning from the police force, especially now that only a prolonged campaign against infiltrating guerrillas and rebellious tribesmen seemed the only prospect, thoughts of selling his farm and going abroad.

When De Kock had first acquired the farm with the aid of loans from the maize board and the bank, he had known the thrill of owning land as he drove through the fields; for a while the farm had made some returns. With part of the salary he earned as police commandant of the Tabanayane District, De Kock had increased the investment in the farm and introduced mechanised farming machinery where it was possible; he had poured fertilisers and more fertilisers on what was unalterably poor soil; at least, that is what all those who knew better about these things had told him often enough. Labour was getting more difficult to find, attracted to the bigger towns and cities by higher wages; his profit margin was too small to cope with the fluctuations of the market and the increasing costs of fertilisers and machinery, and his accumulated losses had become a millstone around De Kock's neck. And now the troubles with the natives.

He could move, of course – but where? So De Kock was compelled, finally, to reject each of these solutions with the stern realism of a man who knows when there is nowhere left to run. The girl alone had remained his solace, but now he was in doubt about her too, though he supposed something might have happened which would explain why she had failed to keep their usual rendezvous. The conclusion of his ruminations was that he should drive straight to the police station, check through the incoming reports, and then go down to the Meerdaal and have a pot of something with some of the farming lads; perhaps he would be able to pick up some gossip along the way.

With a sour, lurching feeling of nausea, De Kock remembered his encounter in the lounge of the Meerdaal with the greying, thin-faced Englishman who, after fifteen years of residence in the country, now controlled the lives and fortunes of many unfortunate farmers like himself. A fifty-year-old former Coldstream Guardsman – 'Mr JP Hamilton-Rose to you, De Kock!' – the Englishman had treated it all as a joke. 'I'll tell you what, De Kock, old chap. Stick to police work; leave farming to those with a knack for the damned business.' Fixing the part-time police-farmer with his penetrating gaze, the Englishman had added with obvious enjoyment: 'As my father used to say, farming, old chap, is not such an easy row to hoe. Financially, you'd need a lot of feather-bedding. In your case, De Kock, before you can even hope to break even you need an initial outlay beyond what any small investment banking outfit like ours can afford to offer at such a risk.' Then the Englishman had added insult to injury by deliberately punning on De Kock's name. 'You know, old cock, the days of small farms in this region are over. You need to expand and to expand; you need more capital expenditure per acre, more acres of land, more labour, more machinery, more fertilisers – more of everything, in fact, than a small chap like you or I is in a position to afford.'

'I know, Mr. Rose,' De Kock interrupted in a lowered voice, anxious to keep the subject of their conversation reasonably confidential. 'Only I was thinking...'

With his uncanny instinct for anticipating a request, the Englishman cut De Kock short: 'I know what you're thinking,

De Kock. If only you could get another swinging loan – but it's no use thinking of more loans, old chap. Try to be realistic. You couldn't offer any collateral. As far as we're concerned, you'd be a thoroughly bad risk. But I'll tell you what we may be able to do for you, and this is strictly between you and me. If you ever decide to sell – to cut your losses and run, so to speak – acting as appointed agents, my bank may be able to get you more than a reasonable price for your farm. That I can promise you.'

Passing into the gents of the Meerdaal bar later that evening, De Kock caught a glimpse of his face briefly reflected in the cracked, rusty mirror above the wash-basin in the sour-smelling urinal, and was greatly alarmed by what he saw: a sagging mass of puffed, pulpy flesh stared back at him. It was a sun-burned face he saw, grim, weary and deeply pitted like weather-bitten statuary; a grisly face, brick-red and unshaven, powdered with the fine dust of the veld; a face reflecting in its seams and heavily scored lines an accumulation of fatigue brought on by a treadmill of work, immoderate drinking and desperate whoring.

De Kock gazed directly into the eyes, dull slates, a little blood-shot; the expression he detected in the face was of a witless exhaustion, induced by persistent and unflagging effort with no perceptible success. He felt a wince of alarm at the sight of this mask of futility and frustration, which spoke as plainly as any medical report could have done of an imminent collapse. He saw reflected there a waning of physical strength hurried on by endless patrols in the bush, chasing after tribesmen who for the most part remained invisible and shadowy, rarely staking a stand to fight it out with security forces. The situation was rapidly getting worse, reports were being confirmed of infiltrations by better trained men who were careful to strike under the cover of darkness, leaving no trace as they easily carried their weapons and all they needed; reports, also, of arson, sabotage, and, more recently, firearms imported into the country from the north.

Looking at that face De Kock saw in it the blurred contours of fear – the most suppressed and unacknowledged fear, the dread of being ambushed and killed like Fritz and Brandewyn, who earlier that year had been cut down by gunfire while trying to investigate a report of suspicious movements by strange natives a mere ten kilometres from the centre of the white town.

Through it all, the fear, the frustration, the boredom and the rest of it, Kristina Kemp became for a while his sole consolation, the final straw at which he grasped gratefully with both hands. As one of the receptionists at the Meerdaal Hotel, Kristina had her day off every alternate Thursday and De Kock had contrived to take his own day off on the same day. Every Thursday he and the girl went on picnics on the banks of the Mokone River some fifty kilometres from Tabanyane, where despite the drought, the river flowed crisp and clear and it was possible to bathe nude among the bleached white rocks worn smooth by years of being washed by the waters of the Mokone River. In this sheltered spot, carefully selected for its natural beauty and seclusion, De Kock and the girl usually brought a basket of fried chicken and home-made bread which they washed down with ice-cold bottles of foaming beer. A brief rest under the shade of the willow trees, followed by another swim in the afternoon; then in the tall grass beyond the trees they would make love undisturbed. Afterwards the couple would drive back to Tabanyane with buoyant hearts in the soft dusk of a northern Transvaal evening, to the back room of the Meerdaal Hotel where, slightly drunk and amazed at his good fortune, De Kock would bury his face again in the white luxury of Kristina's breasts.

This time, however, things had gone badly wrong and seemed to confirm rumours he had vaguely heard that he was not the only man Kristina was exercising her fatal charms on; there was Gert Potgieter, for example, the wealthy Tabanyane farmer. At first, in his desperation, De Kock had chosen not to believe these rumours; he had even pretended to be reassured by the tearful protestations of the girl when he confronted her, but still the nagging doubt remained. Then, that Thursday Kristina had not turned up to meet him. In vain had De Kock waited in his DeSoto, carefully washed and polished for the occasion, which he had parked under the shade of the blue gum trees behind Joubert's Trading Store; waiting first half an hour, then an hour, and then another half-hour; and when he had waited a full two hours and Kristina had not shown up, in a furious temper De Kock had raced the car back to the Meerdaal, hoping either to find the girl there or to learn the reasons for her failure to meet him. No-one at the Meerdaal had any idea what had happened to her; it was her day off and they seemed to feel that she had a right to spend it any way she chose. Even Frank de Sousa, the Portuguese hotel manager, had no knowledge of Kristina's whereabouts, but that did not prevent him from expressing, in his cheerful manner, his confidence: 'Don't worry, lieutenant, I expect Kristina will be at her desk as usual tomorrow morning.'

'I'm not worried!' De Kock almost shouted. 'Who says I'm worried?' To prove his immunity to anxiety, De Kock jumped into his car and, leaving behind him a perplexed hotel manager, had driven fifteen kilometres across a broken track of dirt country road to the squatter's shack where Kristina's seventy-year-old widowed mother lived alone with her cats and dogs. The old woman was sitting like an ancient scarecrow under the shade of a Maroela tree when De Kock drove up in a choking swirl of dust.

At the sound of a car the dogs scrambled to their feet, barking and raising hell, while the old woman gazed at the lieutenant with her dead, unseeing eyes. She had never liked the policeman who made a plaything of her daughter. She did not answer De Kock's greetings when he stood before her, hat in hand, his anxious face streaked with sweat mingled with the dust of the veld. The old woman was no fool; she quickly caught the smell of an animal blindly searching for its mate. She cackled maliciously, showing her toothless gums.

'Where? Where?' she laughed at his endless questionings. 'Why not search the house? Search the whole *dorp* for all I care! And the native huts! Where? Where is she? Do I know where your whore keeps herself? Go and find her yourself!'

De Kock fled. Without any clear notion where he was headed or what he hoped to find, he drove around the country roads in a blind jealous rage. In his moment of distress, the girl with whose affection De Kock had merely toyed as a thing of no particular importance, suddenly seemed possessed of a value beyond any price. Now he recognised that warm, sensuous and generous beyond measure, she had given much and demanded very little. Not yet married herself, she never even mentioned the subject of marriage to him. De Kock had been inclined to think her stupid, as most men are likely to consider such a woman; but harassed by debts and forced to acknowledge the failure of his marriage, De Kock had unwittingly become more and more dependent on the girl. Kristina responded. She was that type. He had only to call for help for her to come running, like someone responding to the distressed cry of a drowning man. Except that she never seemed hurried. She came to him hesitantly, as if in a deep, walking sleep, as if blind-folded, proffering her body as she offered everything else, in a simple, silent trust that was an affront to the general view of what a modern woman should be. Her mouth was large and thick-lipped like a *kaffermeitjie's*; her breasts, heroic in scale, were still those of a young girl's, upright and thrusting; and in his rough callused hands, which in over forty years of hard living had known neither gentleness nor contrition, let alone how to caress a woman's flesh – hands which up to now had known only the meaning of struggle with the soil and even fiercer struggle with men in combat – Kristina's body felt like some mysterious object, smooth and pliable yet limitless in its capacity to yield pleasure. Tumbling out of her soft shifts and petticoats, the girl's breasts rolled and slipped, and sometimes, returning from a grinding patrol in the bush, De Kock found her in the afternoon lying in bed, her frizzy blonde hair wild and scattered over her pillow, her flesh tinted by the fading sunlight. Convinced she was some sort of miracle, De Kock would take her greedily while still half in uniform, still smelling of sweat, his face and hair still laced with the dust of the veld. Only later did it occur to him that it was he, rather than the girl, who remained in bondage while she was free to change her life, to become more completely herself.

Chapter Seven

A N hour before dawn, on a bend overlooking a deep
mountain gorge, the train to Tabanyane came to an abrupt
stop. The man awoke with a start. Outside the land was
invisible beyond the sombre bushes that huddled along the
edge of a cliff. The night was dark, black clouds stained with
yellowish tints from a half-hidden moon rolled eastwards,
promising a rain that would never come. Looking out of the
misty window into the dark countryside the man could feel the
profound silence of the African night like the weight of an
immense cloth drawn around everything. Here the silence was
punctured by the mutter of voices which soon erupted from
the other carriages. Before anyone had realised what was
happening the train had come to a complete standstill.

For the man the journey was cause for great anguish. From
Johannesburg he had shared the compartment with a woman
and her small baby, also a young married couple who were
visiting relatives in the Northern Transvaal and three other
men; but first the men, then the young couple and finally the
woman with her baby, had got off at various stations along the
route to the north.

Throughout the night the man had slept intermittently. Once
he had tried to read but his anxiety being too acute to allow
him to concentrate on such tranquil pleasures as reading a
book, he had given that up. He might have been grateful for

the company of a woman of course; these long train journeys were celebrated for the opportunity they afforded those who were in the mood for a momentary squeeze and cuddle atop the green leather bunks; and his sexual appetite, it now seemed to the man, went hand in hand with his state of nervous excitement; but in the interests of greater security he had finally decided against any foolish adventures.

From the other compartments there came, at regular intervals, noises of female voices in a state of cheerful alarm, as though forced to defend their virtue against a determined enemy. There were minor scuffles, there were muted protests, very muted; the man heard from the adjoining compartment soft shuffling sighs. Shutting his ears against the giggles and the passionate shrieks which had started to come at regular intervals, the man took solace by drinking steadily from the flask of brandy he had brought into the train at Johannesburg; and drinking, he passed from a state of agonising tension to a state of a grand euphoria, then to a state of passive calm and then back to his original state of fevered agitation, imagining any footsteps to be a prelude to his arrest; finally he slid into a state of deep depression.

At times the man felt so claustrophobic that the empty compartment seemed suddenly to have been transformed into a tiny cell, an interrogation room, with a single naked bulb overhead beaming its vapid yellow light straight into the eye. A natural hallucination, he thought, considering his present mission. After his fellow passengers had departed the air smelled of rancid sweat, of dank clothes and stuffy staleness, and the roar and clatter of the train grated like a file upon the nerves. Later the constant hum and clatter of the wheels, aided by the steady intake of alcohol, would produce its own lulling effect. Careful to conceal the guerrilla manual he had been reading, the man dozed, and dozing he dreamed. Once during the night he dreamed of his mother, a silent figure wearing ragged clothes and watching him accusingly from the bank of a river while he, a small frisky boy, cavorted in the stagnant pool of brown muddy water. Then, a little later, it was of a young woman that he dreamed, but strangely enough a young woman of no particular colour. She could have been black, she could have been white, but was probably a combination of both: Maureen and Margot rolled into one sack, the man had later punned lasciviously to himself. After all, dreams often played this game of concealment which left the possessor uncertain of what he possessed or what colour it was.

Naked as a young moon, her breasts as round as new cones, in the dream the young woman appeared to be more perfect than any girl he had ever known. And she was bathing in a stream so clear that he could see the white sand at the bottom; and along the bank of this river, so infinitely slow in its limpid flow, lush grass covered the ground like a thick carpet; and branches from the weeping willows trailed the ground like creatures in mourning.

The woman in the dream looked radiant in the morning sunshine. She was laughing, her naked arms were held out to him in a gesture of invitation. She seemed to be urging him to plunge in, not to stand hesitatingly on the sidelines of experience. When he failed to respond she began to shout and to gesticulate wildly but he could not hear what she was shouting. In the end she simply left him, walking swiftly through the tall grass until at a distance she appeared only as a pale figure wrapped in bright sunshine, already too far away to be heard or held in the flesh. The man awoke with his neck aching and felt such a tumescence of desire that his clothes could hardly contain it; at the same time he still felt mildly depressed, like someone who had lost something he could never regain.

All too suddenly there came from way down the corridor the sound of a familiar disturbance; the ticket examiner was making yet another of his rounds through the sleeping compartments, his demands for the production of tickets accompanied by the customary imprecations and threats.

'*Kom julle! Jou donderse kaffers! Gou jong!* Tickets!'

shouted a mean-eyed, corpulent figure in blue serge uniform and peak cap. The first time he had come round, shouting and scowling, the Movement's representative had looked upon him as yet another specimen of the mindlessly arrogant white rulers of the land, determined to spread terror and confusion in the third-class compartments; but later he was convinced that the white man was engaged in a sort of ritualistic sport in which shouting abuse at natives was a kind of theatre in which the victims also played their parts by pretending to be frightened. '*Hawu, baas*! What have we done now?' a man would say. And once, when straining against a door that would not open, the white man had farted and the passengers had laughed loudly and derisively and a man had spat in disgust but the white man took no offence.

Hours passed; farther and farther away from Johannesburg the train rolled on through the silent countryside, past the towns of the Northern Transvaal, until there was nothing to see but limitless stretches of dark plains reaching up to the sky at the edge of a dim horizon. An occasional string of lights in the night indicated the vague outlines of a town; otherwise the darkness closed in everywhere. Alone with his terrors the man felt strangely, profoundly isolated; he was travelling without a companion in a darkness dense and fathomless. Johannesburg, JB and the Movement seemed far behind him now. For a while he thought of his life, always so full of anxieties, of dreams unrealised; the suffering his broken marriage had caused him; Maureen and her shadowy life, and always, like a man pursued by devils, he thought of JB and the Movement. Gentle self-pity came to him like a salve to a nagging toothache. When he thought of Maureen he experienced such anguish and sense of loss that exile from the environment which had contained them both was a kind of deliverance. And Margot: he thought again with surprise of Margot, whose ultimate gift of herself, her body, had been to him one of the most generous acts of love he would like to remember, a suitable prelude to his departure for the northern regions of guerrilla warfare.

How good it would be to see Margot again one day, to feel the pulse of her blood in those small wrists held within the circle of his fingers!

The man suddenly noticed that the train had come to a stop in wild bush country with not a station in sight. He sprang up from his seat and rushed to the window. There was nothing but darkness out there, but something was surely wrong! No doubt about that! Immediately there were deep mumbles from protesting heads stuck halfway out of open windows. Questions were being asked to which no-one could supply answers. Why had the train stopped? Had the engine broken down or was there an obstacle on the line? So it was true, after all, that these engines were too old and had seen too much service! Alone in his compartment the man could not ignore the mounting hubbub. Tense, fearful but alert, he listened to the other voices getting increasingly edgy. Then all of a sudden there was a commotion. Flashlights flickered in the darkness; and before the representative of the Movement for National Liberation could comprehend what was happening the echo of boots upon gravel rang along the length of the entire train and angry swearing filled the air, shattering the night's precarious peace. Out of the morning darkness there emerged the indistinct shapes of men in heavy overcoats, with rifles and stun guns slung over their shoulders, crawling like insects into the stationary train. A feeling of intense dread descended upon the lonely representative; where had they come from at that time of morning? From what bush, what hole, had they crawled out? He could not explain it. He had no time to work out an explanation. Panic gripped him. But in an instant he was shaken from his apathy by the need to escape. The thought came suddenly to him.

Escape! Run!

Leaping towards the door of the compartment he saw that some of the soldiers were coming down the corridor with their guns held at the ready, their faces raw beneath their visored caps, the eyes glittering in the half-light. Some were members

91

of the police force with 'SAP' sewn on their uniforms. They were shouting, crashing the butts of their rifles against compartment doors. 'You think you can frighten us, *verdompte se kaffers*, shooting at the goddamn army trains!' One of the soldiers was beside himself with rage. 'Come on, open up you foul monkeys! Let's see your papers, all of you! Bloody goddamn terrorists!' Again the impulse to run for it nearly overcame the man but he thought: 'If I run they will surely open fire.' He heard shouting and a voice pleading with a controlled desperation: '*Wag my baas, asseblief tog!*' And the reply came back quick and sharply contemptuous: '*Wag jou ma! Ek sal jou moer!*'

'I'm ruined!' the man thought. 'If they catch me they'll surely hang me!' His heart gave a sudden lurch; and like a whirlpool churning his mind seethed with every small anxiety; above all, somewhere in the background there loomed the shadow of arrest and the hangman's noose. He could hear their heavy boots approaching his own compartment. Then he heard the thin clashing sound of metal rubbing against metal, the sound of guns against steel. Terror-stricken he retreated from the doorway and into his bunk. He was numb with fear. His stomach rumbled like the beginning of a volcanic eruption, and the man could smell the vile odour of his own fear and the rank stench of a person on the verge of losing control of his own functions. A phrase from an old English poem came back to him, something about the poor English sitting patiently by their watchful fires, ruminating on the morning's danger. He wanted to cry and laugh at the same time. Now he could only wait for them to come and get him.

Angry and agitated they came thrusting into the compart-ment: '*Ja, ja!* Open up, *jong!*' Tired, too, it seemed, their faces looked drawn and marked by tension, seams of young flesh folded at the corners of their eyes, their mouths drooping with venom. A young lieutenant stepped inside the door of the compartment and another lingered in the corridor. 'Come on, wake up kaffir! *Jy wil mos altyd slaap, ne?*' Trembling at the knees the man attempted to rise but felt the lack of support from his lower limbs as if he were being dragged under water by a mighty current. Another line of poetry came to him uninvited like a bubble of fear: 'How dread an army hath enrounded him!' The next thought that teased the edges of his mind was that he had been betrayed from the start, before he had even left Johannesburg.

Suddenly there were all over him, searching, prodding, their hands in the pockets of his coat, trousers, bags. They were so close he could smell their bodies and the violence they contained in the pores of their skin; they exuded a pungent, yeasty odour of sweat and gun oil. 'Papers, kaffir! Let's see your papers, and I'm warning you not to try anything!'

He held out his identity document but instead of taking it the young soldier raised two fists in the air and instinctively the Movement's representative raised his hands to his face to defend himself against the blows.

'*Ek sê*, what's up kaffir!' His fists were already bunched to strike out. 'Want to fight, kaffir?'

'No, *baas*!'

'What you raising your hands for then?'

This was another form of sport, only more violent than the ticket-examiner's. The blows were so many and came so fast that the man was unable to anticipate where they would fall; but the soldier was skilful enough not to cause any major damage; a lip was split, a cut to the nose and a slight cut above the eye was all the damage that could be seen but soon enough blood was pouring down over the man's shirt. Again the soldier raised two bunched up fists and again the Movement's representative raised his hands to protect his face.

'I see. You want some more! A fighter? You enjoy fighting?' The soldier lashed out again and caught the man's chin just as he was putting down his hands.

'Careful, Japie!' the older one in the corridor warned the young one. 'We're after terrorists, man, not just any kaffir!'

'Ja, but this kaffir is trying to fight me. He wants to put up a little fight, don't you kaffir! How about it? Want to have another try?'

This time the man steeled himself for another blow but kept his arms down. The boy grinned. 'No? You had enough?'

'Japie, come on, man!'

'I reckon we should search his bags all the same. I reckon they're all terrorists when you come right down to it! We should shoot them first and ask questions later!' Suddenly it was very warm in the carriage. Down the corridor a woman was screaming. The terrible sustained shriek of an animal between the jaws of a steel trap. Involuntarily the man shuddered.

'Sit down, kaffir!' Japie shouted. 'Sit! Don't stand up to me. You hear?' His eyes were like two bright arrows. While his hands fumbled among the man's luggage he kept up a flurry of questions. The man sat very still, very tense, wiping blood on the sleeve of his coat. 'Where do you come from, kaffir?'

'Johannesburg.'

'Johannesburg?' Japie whistled. 'What is rubbish like you doing in Johannesburg? I didn't know they allowed monkeys like you to get out of their cages and walk the streets of a big city like Johannesburg.'

The man wisely kept silent. 'And where are you going, may I ask?'

'Tabanyane.'

'To Tabanyane?' Japie's brows became knitted together like pincers, his tongue running along his bottom lip like a dog in the presence of a juicy bone. 'That's where they're having all that trouble with terrorists, *ne*? What business have you got in Tabanyane?'

'I was born in Tabanyane.'

'Born in Tabanyane? So you think you've got the right to return there to murder your own people?'

'I've never murdered anyone.'

'Shut your bloody mouth! And don't try to be bloody clever with me! And what work do you do?'

94

'I'm a teacher.'

'A teacher? Oh, that's why you think you're so clever! Let's see what you've got here!'

Sweat broke slowly on the man's brow. Hidden inside one of his canvas bags was the tattered copy of his much-thumbed guerrilla manual and a detailed map of Tabanyane. The guerrilla manual lay between the gaudy covers of a child's comic book: *The Further Adventures of Donald Duck*. Japie immediately caught sight of the comic book and started laughing.

'A grown man like you and you read comic books!' He caressed the book lovingly, with affectionate familiarity. 'I used to read these as a boy. Imagine, a grown up man like you!' But there was an unexpected tenderness in Japie's voice. 'It just goes to show,' he said but did not elaborate.

Just then the other soldier in the corridor shouted. '*Ag*, Japie, leave the poor kaffir alone! He's nothing but a school-teacher!'

'Who reads comic books!' Japie laughed.

'But that's no crime. Christ, man, there's a whole train to check! Besides, the *kommandant* is tired and wants to go to bed.'

Japie clenched his fists. 'That's the trouble with us! We never do a thorough job. Suppose this train is carrying terrorists, how do we find out without a thorough search?'

'Japie, *oupa,* you know as well as I do the real terrorists are out there in the bush. Leave schoolteachers to their comic books! As soon as it's light we'll go after them with guns and tracker dogs. Meanwhile, let's get a move on, man! The train is late enough as it is!'

The man couldn't believe his luck. Reluctantly Japie abandoned his quarry. Before stepping out of the compartment he adjusted his helmet like a pretty girl about to go out. 'Terrorists and murderers! Don't think we are not watching you! We are not stupid. We'll catch up with the likes of you! A little education and you think you're as good as white people, don't you?'

95

'Japie, come old man!'

'Better keep your nose clean in Tabanyane! Okay? Stick to your teaching and your comic books, no Karl Marx! Understand?'

'*Ja, baas!*'

'*Voetsek! Ja, baas!* We're watching you!'

Instantly, they were all off the train again; the whole thing had lasted a little less than twenty minutes but to the man it seemed an age had gone by since the police had boarded the train. He slumped back against the seat and tried to light a cigarette but his hands were trembling so violently that he broke two matchsticks without striking a light; his hands seemed incapable of holding anything. His face was swollen above the eye and a trickle of blood oozed slowly from the side of the mouth. When he looked at himself carefully in the mirror he saw that his mouth was only slightly cut and he dabbed at it with a handkerchief, saying to himself that the war had started sooner than he had expected. With a shrug he finally brought out his bottle of brandy and swallowed the remaining contents in a single gulp before tossing the bottle out into the dark countryside.

In the mist of dawn and before the Movement's representative was even aware of it the train had arrived in Tabanyane; the mountains of Taba Situ loomed suddenly over the iron-grey landscape. The man's eyes were full of sleep, his mouth tasted as if he had eaten ash, and he moved hastily towards the window to gaze out at what seemed at first sight an unfamiliar countryside. Tabanyane!

This then was home and yet he could scarcely recognise the place. In ten years so much had changed. New farm houses dotted the arid brown landscape where before there had been nothing but empty waste and pasture for grazing sheep; a new industrial complex, a cement factory, a huge granary with silos shooting up into the pale dawn sky, came suddenly into view from the western edge of the sleepy town. The town itself still lay hidden in the morning mist, with only the spire of the Dutch Reformed Church rising steeply from behind flat-topped buildings that dominated the eastern skyline. When the train came to a complete stop the man seized his single suitcase and plastic bags and walked quickly towards the exit. At that time of morning the station was still empty except for the sleepy-eyed station master and teams of African workers unloading bags of mail; the platform was covered with a film of fine frost which glistened in the pale morning light. The man tried as far as he was able to leave the station without attracting too much attention. He walked stiffly toward the exit, past the train driver and his engineer who dawdled on the footplate, their soot-blackened faces resembling gargoyles as they idly sipped coffee from huge mugs before shunting the train off to a sidetrack where it would be swept and swabbed to await another overnight journey back to Johannesburg. To gain the street the man had to go through the small wooden gate at the end of the platform, and through this gate was able to reach a small parking lot where he saw under the tall gum trees the old black Ford he had been instructed to expect, and behind the wheel of the Ford the figure of the youngish white priest, bare-headed and golden-haired in the sun, slumped over the wheel. The figure did not move until the man rapped, at first gently, then loudly on the window. Father James Stephen roused himself up from his uncomfortable position. Hastily he rolled down the window of the car.

'Mr Molapo?'

'Father Stephen?'

The two men chuckled slowly as though mightily surprised by their discovery of each other.

Chapter Eight

ANTHONY Ferguson had the first glimpse of his native land through the porthole of the aircraft, on a beautiful morning with the sun already high up in a sky so wide and majestic it seemed purposely enlarged. After the aircraft had come to a standstill, passengers had to wait some minutes while the ground crew brought up the steps to the exit doors and Ferguson had time enough to rearrange his feelings the way other passengers straightened items of clothing before disembarking, because, in a sudden moment of emotional recoil from the encounter with the land of his birth, he was disagreeably made aware that during all the hours of flying between London and Johannesburg, between the winter snow of one continent and the summer heat of another, he had succeeded only in postponing that moment when the prodigal must finally come to terms with the conflicting emotions of a return to his home. Through the porthole he watched black men wheeling the moveable steps into place, followed quickly by luggage trolleys, and in the excitement of arrival the other passengers were moving down the aisle of the plane while Ferguson drew back, wondering what he must do to preserve his acquired identity; how to belong without belonging, to accept his allegiance to that original experience of having been born in this place without having to submit to the demands of an unworthy commitment; that was for him now his single most important need. While he surrendered to his immediate emotional dilemmas, someone slapped him on the back and the shock of the physical blow – kindly meant no doubt – had the effect of recalling him from his mental exile.

It was Tom Murchison, naturally – gruff, drunk, and genial, grasping Ferguson's hand in a sort of posthumous farewell since what had only been a temporary bond between two men travelling together had long since dissolved into mutual incomprehension. But Murchison had his certainties, which was why he was cheerful. 'Well, Ferguson!' Murchison swayed dangerously, together with his hand luggage. 'It was a pleasure!' And somewhat mysteriously he added: 'An' I'll tell you what, Ferguson, never look a gift horse in the mouth!' Murchison whistled a tune as he left the plane: 'Oh, what a beautiful morning!' Anthony envied the man the more for his certainties.

Very soon he got up from his seat and followed the other passengers towards the exit. On the apron of the aircraft he paused to breathe in deeply the crisp Johannesburg air of his youth, feeling himself buoyed up suddenly by the gasping lightness of the altitude. In the airport bus to the terminal lounge he was flung about from side to side and then felt his heart tilt very slightly as he entered the immigration hall, for his restless eye was already searching the airport for signs of his sister. Hazel had promised to meet him, so walking towards the entrance, Anthony's heart was bumping awfully; the dream of a slummy Braamfontein childhood came flooding back unbidden, and with it came sensations so raw yet so tender, like moisture on the skin, and his sister and his mother flashed into consciousness like a twin image. Paying only the slightest attention to his surroundings now, he walked, or rather limped, behind the other passengers towards immigration control.

When he regained his faculties, the changes he saw all around him at Jan Smuts Airport did not surprise him at all. People had never ceased telling him – his sister, his friends – of the many material changes which had taken place in a country with a fast-growing economy; changes reflected in the personal styles of dress and domestic luxury; in the physical environment which now boasted expanded highways and gleaming new shopping centres. But these were not the changes which could have greatly exercised the mind of an international servant of a human rights organisation; for presently Anthony recognised that without even thinking about it his search for Cornelius Molapo had already begun right there in the airport lounge, at the very moment of arrival, during the long formalities with immigration and customs officials. While gazing with some awe at the trimly uniformed men around the airport, he was also aware of himself looking out for inadvertent signs in the faces of officialdom, something hidden in the folds of the skin around the eyes, their firmly clenched jaws and jutting chins, as if the mere expression on the faces of these representatives of state authority would betray the nature of the crime or in what garden the corpse was hidden.

Distracted, Anthony peered past the barrier, half-looking for Hazel while Molapo filled his mind. She stood behind a huge crowd of people waiting to welcome friends and relatives from the incoming flights. Impossible not to spot his sister at once, for in her uniform dress code of dazzling white Hazel would always stand out in a crowd, however vast. Walking swiftly towards his sister Anthony noted also the hard brilliance of the blue eyes as Hazel searched for the shape of her brother's person. In spite of his attempts at self-control, something leaped to his throat, a shifting lump which after so many years of living apart he wishfully thought he had learned how to control; and he found himself in that busy concourse already pushing people out of the way as he dashed forward past airport workers and luggage trolleys until Hazel also, suddenly catching sight of her brother, started to run, elbowing past crowds of idle bystanders, men and women who watched them resentfully as they dived past to storm into each other's arms.

In a wailing furious rage of happiness, brother and sister embraced. Anthony tasted the piquant freshness of his sister's mouth; clouds of perfume suddenly enveloped him like a breath of incense and a feeling of deep fatefulness overcame him. 'Oh, sweetheart! Oh, my love! My pet! Let me look at you!' Hazel was chanting wildly, her eyes very bright, very moist. 'I just can't believe you're here! My darling Anthony! Oh, I think I'm simply going to die of happiness!'

And they broke apart and studied each other gravely, more carefully, for perhaps a second or two before resuming the hugging and the kissing: 'Dearest heart, you look absolutely wonderful!' Hazel cried.

'A bit crumpled, wouldn't you say?' Anthony laughed, aware that after an overnight flight his linen suit must look crushed. But he was just as delighted with his sister and told her so. He gazed adoringly at her.

'You know, I'm not at all surprised so many picture editors are getting quite frantic to put you on the covers of their magazines. Princess, you look like pure gold!' And Hazel was pleased. To show it she leaned very hard against him and he felt her tiny pointed breasts squashed flat against his shirtfront and a feeling of joy mingled with deep apprehension got hold of him and shook him to the core of his being.

His sister suddenly exclaimed: 'Oh, but I don't look half so good as when I first went into the business.'

'I've gained a kilo since you last saw me in London.' Then, pirouetting smartly like the trained ballerina that she was, she tried to catch a glimpse of herself in the mirror opposite. 'I'm sure it's all the outrageous overeating I've been doing lately and – oh, dear! – some other unmentionable forms of self-indulgence!' She giggled suggestively. 'As you'll soon notice, everyone is spoiling me like mad before the wedding. For the last week or so I've done nothing but attend a round of cocktails, receptions and dinner parties. I'm getting as fat as a partridge, as you can see!'

She was exaggerating, of course; she was not fat at all. In

fact, she was as slim as a blade of grass and just as light; her voice was warmer now, he noticed, much richer, full of sweet feminine fibre; her skin, which had always been of an exceptionally fine texture, had developed an even keener, glossier tint that was a marvel of colour and sparkling good health. But soon a puzzled frown appeared on his sister's face as she looked around them. Realising why, Anthony chuckled: 'Oh, my luggage? The bags are over there!' He pointed to where, in his haste to embrace his sister, he had simply abandoned his luggage in the care of a black stranger. In the posture of someone left holding a baby, the stranger, an elderly black man in his sixties, had one small bag under his arm; he was holding another in his hand, and another was set beside him on the floor.

'Oh, the poor man!' Hazel laughed. 'Well, let's get your bags. Cynthia is waiting for you outside!'

It was Anthony's turn to look puzzled. 'Cynthia?'

Hazel giggled, 'Precious, that's my new sportscar! My wedding present from Mark. I call her Cynthia. She's a smashing blonde job. Very temperamental. I have to watch my foot on the pedal!'

'Oh, for a moment, I thought you had a grand welcoming committee out there.'

He hesitated, looking at his sister's feet, which were small and clad in casual but expensive leather, at the clean sweep of leg with its golden tint. Not understanding, Hazel laughed: 'Well, don't look so disappointed, pet. You didn't ask me to lay on any female reception for you. For the time being you will just have to be satisfied with your own sister. Incest is what it's called.' She winked devilishly. 'And it's supposed to be very good for you! And don't let anyone tell you otherwise.' While they went back to collect the luggage Anthony kept glancing at his sister with the same foreboding he had once experienced those many many years ago when all night long in the nearby fair the enclosed lions roared in their cages.

'How's mama?' he suddenly asked his sister as if to divert

attention from emotions too illicit to entertain. At the bottom of such an emotion, as he well knew, there was tendency towards hysteria.

'Oh, ma is just fine! Oh, my God, you should have seen her this morning. Such excitement, she couldn't have slept a wink all night! And up and about at the crack of dawn! This morning I could hear her ordering about the servants and practically turning the entire place into a lunatic asylum. Anyway, don't say you haven't been warned – Henrietta is full of beans and very much looking forward to welcoming her son home.'

While they got busy ferrying luggage to the car, Anthony was suddenly aware of people watching them curiously. He was sure it was on account of his sister that so many eyes followed them: something about her personality, always vibrant, the oscillating note in the voice, the vehement glitter of the eyes, they all combined to attract the attention of complete strangers. Of course, Hazel was aware of all this attention but, unlike women of more modest disposition, she was not embarrassed or ill at ease. On the contrary, she thrived on it. Taking in the scene around her, she became more theatrical. Two policemen in uniform, *keppies* over their eyes, were watching them with interest.

Not keen to attract any more attention to himself than he needed to, Anthony tried to avoid their eyes. Hazel wasn't helping: she had begun to flush with a kind of dramatic ecstasy, her body lively and sensuous, transformed into a wild egotistical animal. He dragged her along, one arm around her waist, another rolling along a suitcase.

While they loaded luggage into the car they chatted, finally lingering on the major forthcoming event – Hazel's wedding. Later, in the car, his sister tried to probe Anthony's feelings about being back in the country. 'It's odd, really,' Anthony said vaguely. He was thinking: after fifteen years of self-imposed exile during which mentally he had continuously moulded the country in his mind, its physical and political landscape changing according to the alterations of his own emotional states; after all the conflicting moods of anxiety and acute misgivings about the direction the country was taking; all of a sudden here he was now, simply plonked down before he was ready to work himself up into a state of complete panic or foolish ecstasy.

'*Agh, Tootsie*, give me time to catch my breath!' he laughed, thinking, I even have to relearn the language. 'I've only just stepped off the plane, you know. I need to find out what I think!'

'Will they give you enough time though, your lot, to find out? Darling, I hope you're not going to spend all your time while you're here, tearing across the country, trying to find your missing guerrilla fighter! Who is he anyway? Some underground communist terrorist?'

Ferguson wished he hadn't mentioned to Hazel that someone had gone missing and part of his job was to find him. 'I doubt it,' He replied blandly. 'In my file he is described as a moderate nationalist, a middle-roader, so to speak. He's said to play cricket and sometimes dances the jitterbug in his spare time.' Anthony chuckled.

'Darling, please be serious!' Hazel chided. After a moment's reflection she continued: 'It does no good, you know, all the fuss you people are making about the situation in the country! Everyone comes out here with their pet solutions. But it does no good. I'm absolutely sure when the time comes the natives will rise as one man and murder us in our beds. In the meantime,' she announced drily, 'I intend to enjoy myself while the carnival lasts!'

Anthony was thinking that his sister's views were pretty much those of almost any other white in the country. Only Hazel was more cynical than corrupt, amoral rather than immoral, if such distinctions mattered.

An avowed hedonist, she lived entirely in the present, awaiting Armageddon with caviar in one hand and a bottle of champagne in the other. Though Ferguson would not have admitted it, he found her attitude a relief. So much of his life was spent under the crushing weight of moral responsibility, worrying about man's inhumanity to man, that his sister's light moral baggage struck him somehow as an enviable form of travel. At least, the absence of cant he found endearing. Without knowing it he must have been smiling to himself because Hazel poked him in the ribs and said: 'Well, what on earth do you find so amusing?'

'My fellow passenger on the plane held views very similar to your own,' Anthony laughed. 'A fellow called Murchison.'

'Darling, nearly everyone holds views like mine except bleeding-heart liberals like you!'

She talked rapidly, squinting at the sun as she drove. Anthony watched the rise and fall of her straight slim thighs as she clutched and declutched the gears. As usual, she drove badly. Once, smiling wickedly, she squeezed past two huge trucks piled high with a load of fresh maize and in a nervous but excited voice she cried out: 'Close shave!' as the car shot past to come to a screeching halt in front of some traffic lights.

Anthony was immensely frightened. 'Hazel, for God's sake! You could drive more carefully! I didn't come back to die in Johannesburg!'

'No?' His sister grinned. 'But I'll tell you something. I'm so glad you're here, the only thing I could die of right now is happiness! In the meantime, darling, please don't be such a nag, I am a perfectly good driver as most people will tell you!'

And then all at once his sister's house rose up ahead of them in all its restored colonial splendour among firs and poplar trees that drooped slightly in the late December heat.

A monument to the free-spending spree of the wild 1890s when men panned their first Rand gold, the house was a true relic of Johannesburg's rakish past. It had once belonged to a colonial administrator, had served time as a bordello for inter-national millionaires, had been owned by gold prospectors and gamblers of every kind. Since then a succession of architects had worked their small personal changes into the original structure without substantially transforming it. A pool had been built on the front lawn and next to it, connecting to the house by a side entrance, a walled courtyard that became a dining room for summer luncheons and evening dinners.

Anthony had seen this house, its gleaming white exteriors and its opulent soft-hued interiors, in numerous photographs which Hazel had sent to him in London; but coming upon it so suddenly in its splendid actuality was somehow a shock and a wonder – how had his sister, a product of Johannesburg's poor white suburbs, become the wealthy owner of a turn-of-the-century palace? Hazel's meteoric climb to fame and fortune had been so spectacular that, even without Brody's millions, nothing which truly mattered to her was now beyond her means. And here they were at last, Hazel and her twin. Contemplating that sumptuous architectural indulgence, Anthony hugged his sister and exclaimed: 'Oh, Princess!' Together, without moving, they gazed at the white palace in a spirit of complete enchantment.

'Do you like it?'

'Do I like it!'

Just then Anthony caught sight of the handsome, greying woman who stood just inside the fence, clipping away at the already finely shaved hedge; and leaping down from the car he waved frantically and shouted: 'Mother!'

The pair of shears dropped from the woman's hands! 'Anthony!' she shouted back. Then: 'Jacob! Prince! Where are you all? My son is here! Oh! I think I'm going to faint.' His mother began to move forward but Anthony was faster, more agile, more impetuous.

Stocky and a little plump, like a Mediterranean widow with heavy, generous breasts, it was hard to believe that she had once been a small slim woman who rode fast cars with Jim Chandler on wild summer nights, but she still moved with the same jauntiness of earlier days. Anthony noted his mother's eyes, with small laughing crinkles at the corners, and an involuntary memory came back of the days when, after a late-night wandering, she would come in from the street looking sheepish. Then the fights started with his neglected father in their narrow bed.

Cooing like a dove, Henrietta hugged her son: 'Oh, to have my two children under one roof at this time!' she cried. 'This is going to be the happiest Christmas in years!' Again she called: 'Jacob! Prince! Rhoda! Agnes! Where the devil are they?'

Suddenly, the servants were all there, standing in line like a guard of honour; they were smiling awkwardly at the young white man about whom they had heard so much, whose photographs they had seen around the house but whom they had never seen in the flesh. They had heard the mother complain so often of the son's desertion that in their eyes Anthony Ferguson was very much the Prodigal Son who had finally returned home, and not a day too soon. One by one, they stepped forward to be introduced: Jacob, the elderly gardener in mud-stained clothes and gumboots, grinning splendidly from beneath his moth-eaten straw hat; Aunt Rhoda the cook, a fiftyish woman in starched white uniform; a pretty young girl called Agnes, the housemaid; and finally, Prince Modupe, tall, slim and regal and very much aware of it. This young man was Henrietta's chauffeur and something of a personal valet, the Young Pretender to the vacated Ferguson throne.

Right from the start Anthony could see his mother doted on Prince and spoiled him rotten; in return Prince worshipped his 'Old Lady' – as he ironically referred to Henrietta – and as far as he was concerned his elderly employer could do no wrong. Towards Hazel he was condescendingly indulgent. He was the only servant in the household who called Hazel by her first name. Now that the long expected son had returned from his wanderings Prince immediately saw that his star was about to be eclipsed – but only temporarily. Young Ferguson may be the man of the moment but Prince could afford to wait. He would be called upon to drive his 'Old Lady' around town, ready to offer his arm at the appropriate time as they mounted or descended the abundant stairs in the city's public places.

Guiding her firmly across the street or striding alongside her with armfuls of Christmas parcels, Prince looked like a courtier in attendance upon his ageing queen, and white shopkeepers smiled their admiration at him.

Yes, Prince could afford to wait. To show his magnanimity he now offered his hand to the new arrival: 'Welcome home, Mr. Ferguson!' he said graciously. 'Welcome!' This seemed to be a signal for all the servants to follow suit. 'Welcome home, Mr. Ferguson! Welcome home!'

Hazel smiled at her brother and her mother. 'Well, now that seems to be over,' she said and started up the garden path leading to the front door. Anthony followed the two Ferguson women inside the house, marvelling at its smooth stucco brickwork, its fan windows and magnificent spiral staircases. It was a thing of beauty beyond imagining, oddly quiet inside with a stillness that reminded you of the dim interiors of old cathedrals. Anthony was ushered into a living room filled with warm morning sunlight, a fresh breeze billowing the curtains apart. If somewhere in this Golden City war was disfiguring lives, it was not apparent within the confines of this living room, where Beethoven's 6th Symphony played and the servants crept about discreetly on softly-shod feet. Peace reigned everywhere.

A gigantic wedding party was planned for Mark and Hazel's wedding, following the ceremony in the Anglican church in town; already all over the place were signs of preparations for this momentous event. Boxes of glassware and crockery lay in confused profusion in a side room, tables and folding chairs were stacked on the back lawn, ready for use. In the living room, next to the Christmas tree, a notice board had been set up on which wedding and Christmas cards from well-wishers were pinned for display. Everywhere Anthony turned gave him the feeling that he was about to participate in a fabulous pageant. As if to add nature's voice to the celebratory tone of the place, Anthony could hear from a nearby shrubbery a whole choir of twittering chirruping birds in rehearsal for their own part in the grand performance.

Listening, Hazel became quite thoughtful. 'I travel a great deal, you know, but sometimes – just some odd afternoon or evening when I walk into my hotel room in Rome or New York – my heart suddenly does this awful lurch and I'm tempted to take the first plane out to get back to all this.'

Anthony nodded. 'I can see why,' he said drily. This land, this pleasant climate, offered opportunities for leading a life of uninterrupted leisure, with numerous badly-paid servants in attendance. And Anthony's major sin, according to the likes of Tom Murchson, was that he had thought it necessary to look the gift horse in the mouth. Hazel took her brother by the arm and showed him round the pleasantly appointed bedrooms furnished in Old Dutch style. She went on opening and shutting doors until they reached her bedroom on the second floor; here everything – the draperies, the furniture and the linen – seemed to have been chosen with both an eye to luxurious comfort and infinite delicacy of touch. There were mirrors which caught and reflected the light, and dark wood which drew and subdued the glare from bright colours. In a sudden quick movement Hazel pushed aside the folding double doors which opened to an adjoining room, a little less sumptuously furnished but no less comfortable than Hazel's own. 'This is Mark's bedroom for when he visits,' she declared.

Anthony was astonished. 'For when he visits? Are you not going to live together?

'Darling, you are so old-fashioned,' Hazel said complacently, batting her long eyelashes. 'Getting married doesn't mean we're going to change our lifestyles. Mark has his life. I have mine. The rest we can share.' She laughed a little at the absurdity of this statement. Apparently Brody had a small town house which he shared with his unmarried sister, but after the wedding he was to move into Hazel's palatial mansion – 'more or less', as his sister put it in her qualified way.

Anthony stared open-mouthed at his sister. 'But is that good for marriage vows?'

'It's a divine arrangement,' Hazel insisted. 'Absolute freedom is the first unwritten law of any good marriage. Besides, Mark prefers it this way.'

'I have no doubt; otherwise he wouldn't put up with it. Anyway,' Anthony chuckled pointedly, 'he must be the ideal husband for you, Hazel.'

'Darling, try not to be catty. Mark and I were made for each other, which is probably why we're getting married in the first place.'

'In order to live separately?'

'Sweetheart, you don't understand anything, do you? Living under the same roof, even sleeping in the same bed, doesn't necessarily mean closeness. The way I look at it, it's simply a way for one of the couple to enforce marital obedience. Neither Mark nor I cares for that sort of thing.' Slightly sceptical, Anthony remained silent, so Hazel felt compelled to continue: 'Mark and I suit each other down to the ground. Our marriage was made in heaven, as they say.'

While they hovered in Hazel's bedroom, admiring her exquisite taste, Anthony began to notice that the otherwise pure, almost painful delicacy of the bedroom had already been violated by his sister's tenancy; a touch of ribaldry, a note of vestal defloration was evoked by the sight of a white nylon nightdress with scarlet embroidery hung over the end rail of the bed; and contraceptive devices haphazardly pushed into containers – why so many? Anthony wondered. The sight of these intimate female accessories kindled in the brother vague intimations of harlotry and reckless incontinence, and a sort of strange, disembodied lust suffused the atmosphere in his sister's bedroom. But there was no time to dwell on such details. His sister took his arm again; hand in hand they walked down the corridor, past other, smaller bedrooms, past storerooms in which linen and cleaning appliances of all kinds were stored, finally into what, for the duration of his stay, was going to be Anthony's bedroom. Only a little less spacious than Hazel's own, it was flooded with abundant sunlight as they drew the curtains aside; French doors opened out onto a balcony with a view of the landscaped gardens. Anthony stood perfectly still at the window, examining his surroundings, which included his wayward sister. 'What do you think?' Hazel enquired. 'I thought since you have so much work to do you'd need a little more space to yourself.' She pointed at a desk and a cabinet of drawers in a corner of the room and with just a hint of irony added: 'While you're here you may consider this part of the house the Johannesburg bureau of Human Rights International, with a bedroom attached. I hope they appreciate the hospitality.'

'Hazel, this is heavenly!' Anthony gazed out at the poplar trees swaying slightly in the breeze; in the garden a small poodle was chasing sparrows but without much enthusiasm. They flitted here and there, waited until the dog, barking and snapping, got close before taking off in a cloud of feathers. Butterflies with gorgeously coloured wings fluttered about among the flowers and a resinous fragrance from the eucalyptus, burning under the noonday sun, drifted into the room on the cooling breeze. Anthony came back and sat down on the wide bed, looking at his sister with a new affectionate pride and wonder. She stood in front of him, her pale face suffused with unusual colour, an expression of radiant, voluptuous pleasure filling her eyes. Then quite casually she lifted the skirt of her dress and wrapped it round Anthony's face like a soft, shimmering, silken shawl. 'Tell me, honestly, sweet. Are you very happy to be here or not?'

Anthony was too moved to speak; instead he simply nodded his head. Then Hazel fell in a tumble on the bed. 'As for me, my darling Anthony, I'm simply delirious with happiness!' She announced. The dress had got caught up under a slim thigh, and a nameless fear clutched at Anthony's heart and he closed his eyes, attacked by a wave of dizziness.

'Darling, we're going to have a marvellous time, aren't

we?' Hazel whispered, putting an arm around her brother's neck. 'I want to take you everywhere! I want to show you off to all my friends. I know you'll love them, especially Leda.'

'Leda?' The name rang a bell but Anthony could not remember in what connection he had first heard it. 'Who is Leda?'

'My very best friend. I've often mentioned her in my letters. Sweetheart, don't you read my letters or what?'

'Yes, of course, I read all your letters.' Then all at once the penny dropped. Anthony remembered the name which had popped up with increasing frequency in his sister's letters, mentioned always with an especial fondness, as of someone who had played a significant role in Hazel's career by providing her with entrées to some of the best fashion houses in Paris, Rome, London and Milan. But Anthony had no recollection of the exact details.

'Ah, Leda,' Hazel sighed. 'Leda is wonderful! She's divine! She glows! There's no other way to put it. She is – how can I say? – exceptional! She is a Bernhardt heiress. Her family are in the shipping business in Bordeaux. Leda herself was born in Paris, and she's lived everywhere – Rome, London, New York – she's known everyone and done everything! She's a dream.'

'And you're in love with her.'

'Darling, everybody is in love with Leda.'

'Anyway, what's she doing hanging around Johannesburg?'

'Hanging around Johannesburg? My dear, she lives here. She married a Bremont,' Hazel explained, 'the racehorse owners and importers of pharmaceutical products. She met Gustave Bremont in Paris when she was going out with another South African student, name of Irving Danser, who she was very keen on. They were going to marry but Leda's parents objected to Danser's politics. By the way, Danser has caused a minor flap by suddenly turning up here after years of having absolutely no communication with Leda. But that is a story itself, ' Hazel said. 'Unfortunately, I don't think you will get to meet Gustave. He's never home for more than three months during the year, I don't think. Right now he's somewhere in Cap-Ferrat where he keeps another house.' As Hazel told the story, this Gustave had turned out to be the biggest peripatetic player of the casino tables, well-known in all the major gambling spots of Monte Carlo, London and Las Vegas. For the greater part of the year he was away somewhere, playing at the tables. 'And that leaves Leda with all the time in the world to get on with her own life just the way she wants,' Hazel said. 'And believe me, Leda has taught me a lot in the time I've known her.'

'Like what for example?' Anthony enquired with some scepticism.

'Oh, masses of things you wouldn't understand,' Hazel replied cryptically. 'How to live a life of refined pleasure, the way you can make yourself think only beautiful thoughts every day; above all, how to keep the body in perfect shape, like a beautifully tuned instrument, for the complete enjoyment of every pleasure.'

'Judging by the shape of your body,' Anthony laughed, casting a glance at his reclining sister, 'she's extremely successful.'

'It's all exercise, darling. Leda and I go to yoga classes at least twice a week. And we do some terrific erotic dances with the Fred Bellamy Studio. Wonderfully raunchy Asian dances, my dear, absolutely brazen and carnal. What Indian Hindus do in their temples! I'll show you some time. Everyone has to be *toute nue*, of course, and there's a lot of body-touching amidst clouds of incense and chanting to the sound of tambourines.'

'Really, Hazel, all this sounds like old-fashioned orgies to me, what they used to go in for on the West Coast of the United States. I didn't know this sort of thing happened in Johannesburg.'

'There are masses of things you don't know about Jo'burg, sweetheart! You've been away too long. As a matter of fact,' Hazel continued, 'Fred Bellamy did run a studio in Los Angeles way back in the late sixties and early seventies,

113

before coming out to South Africa. Anyway,' Hazel got up from the bed, 'I suppose you need a bit of rest after the long flight.' She ruffled Anthony's hair playfully. 'Maybe you want to have a quick bath. And then a little something to eat?'

'Yes, I think a bath will be nice, rather. The plane was a bit cramped,' Anthony laughed, thinking of Murchison sweating and pressing his greasy flesh against his side. In response to Hazel's puzzled look he said: 'I'm sorry, I was thinking of my fellow passenger. He was a bit oversized, you see, and he made the space between us seemed even more cramped than it would've been. He seemed to exude nothing but grease.'

'Ugh!' Hazel made a face. 'Oh, how horrible. Darling, you must always insist on having a seat next to a woman when you travel. The worst a woman can do is fall asleep on your shoulder and snore throughout your night flight! I'll have Agnes prepare a nice comfortable bath for you, shall I?' She picked up a small internal phone and gave instructions to someone. For the next few minutes the girl Agnes was in and out of the room, preparing a bath for Anthony, while brother and sister continued to sit around, gossiping about everything under the sun. Anthony was receiving at first hand some basic facts about the changes which were said to be taking place in many parts of the country: the easing of social apartheid in many public places; some city councils had permitted or were said to be contemplating permitting mixed bathing in public swimming pools; the Immorality Act had been suspended and mixed marriages were taking place with increasing frequency; there were the so-called 'grey' areas where black and white were living side by side. At the same time, vigilante groups, Anthony heard, were determined to take the law into their own hands to stop the gradual erosion of white privilege. This was accompanied by a frightening growth of private armies, even blacks were fighting one another in the black townships. 'We're all living in a state of absolute anarchy!' Hazel said. 'No-one knows what the future holds. Another Lebanon, most likely. I wouldn't wonder.' She threw her hands up into the air. 'Anyway, my darling, I say "Live now!"'

114

'And pay later!' Anthony said.

'And pay later! Why not?' She looked at her twin brother with a sober, calculating eye. For just a second their eyes met; Hazel reached out and touched her brother's lower lip with her tiny finger. Anthony felt again his heart lurch, as when a plane suddenly drops height. Hazel had a cold frozen smile on her lips that Anthony remembered from their childhood. The lips were suddenly dry, blanched, emptied of blood like the lips of someone thirsting for a tiny drop of water. 'Better get on with your bath, darling,' she spoke in a lowered voice, queer, grating and a bit breathless, as if her heart laboured under the weight of some intolerable pressure. Together they walked to the door. Anthony could smell the heat of the sun glancing off her hair and the hint of perfume from her bare neck and bare shoulders and off the gossamer clothes under which his sister's body burned like lighted brushwood. 'Oh, darling! Listen,' Hazel giggled.

'Ma's got in some wonderful bubbly stuff for your first breakfast home! Do me a favour. Get on with your bath quickly. Then come down for a bite of something. Don't keep the old girl waiting longer than necessary. I bet she's already feeling quite neglected, the poor dear. Afterwards, try to get some sleep. I have a nice little surprise for you this evening.'

Chapter Nine

ANOTHER dream, he thought. A dream, that's what it is; I'm dreaming. His mind struggled from the depths of an underground sleep into the freshness of an unfamiliar evening where objects, though the sun had set, had not yet lost their firm contours; and he tried to regain consciousness of his whereabouts, all the time vaguely thinking he was still in London, searching through the wide bay windows of what he thought was his London flat for the familiar sky that was as grey as iron, listening for familiar sounds and voices. In London his next door neighbour would be playing his favourite Mozart album, or perhaps Bach; but instead here he was hearing warm laughter from across the lawn; the sound of guitars and concertinas and a babble of raised African voices. Domestic servants, he thought. Agnes and her men friends. He was back in Africa. Then he heard the murmur of voices below the bedroom balcony like shifting sands, like the surf sigh of a distant ocean. And Ferguson got out of bed and began his preparation to join whatever jubilation was going on.

Hazel Ferguson was not someone who could let an opportunity like her brother's homecoming pass without arranging some sort of ritualistic get-together in which he would be exhibited to her friends like a prized trophy. Anthony had slept for the most part of the day but when he came down from his room in the evening his sister had her surprise for him as she

116

had promised. Several of her friends were already gathered in the living room and he was introduced before they were whisked away by his mother and his sister for consultations on the various preparations for Hazel's wedding.

A lively party it was, already animated by a wonderful spirit of Christmas cheer, and Anthony had his first opportunity to meet Hazel's fast set, among them a tall slim brunette, an actress who had returned from London a few months earlier to act in Johannesburg. She seemed to occupy an especially important place among Hazel's intimate friends. Janet Frazer: she looked and sounded like one of Chekhov's Three Sisters in a production that Anthony had once seen in London. On being introduced, Janet Frazer peered perplexedly at Ferguson. 'Hazel tells me that in the five years I have been living in London we were maybe only a few streets apart but in all that time our paths have never crossed. Isn't that funny? And Hazel is one of my very best friends!'

Janet's eyes were set far apart on a broad oval face, which gave it an expression of slight surprise when she looked at people; when they were not staring with wonder the eyes were narrowed to slits as if they hurt a little from late nights fending off too much cigar smoke in too many nightclubs and nefarious dens. Anthony agreed that it was a shame they hadn't met.

Another of Hazel's esteemed friends was a young interior decorator called Koos Martinus who looked and sounded like one of those proudly detribalised Afrikaners of whom there were an awful lot in the country lately, as Anthony was to notice; eager, fast-talking, rather purposefully cosmopolitan. Martinus's wife, the manager of a city boutique, was startlingly pretty as only Afrikaner girls can sometimes be: pretty, with a large, curved, petulant mouth and pensive brown eyes. Something about her looks reminded Anthony of the untamed *veld* and desert wastes of the interior, something hard and Dutch that, not unnaturally, he preferred to the smooth sophistication of her worldly husband. She was slim but strong, with long haunches like a well-bred horse, impressive in a solemn kind of way, shy yet provocatively earthy, painfully reticent but when drawn into conversation likely to unfold suddenly, as a quick responsive mountain flower after rain.

Other people were scattered about the room, some of them friends of Mark Brody: three or four elderly businessmen and their wives; a French boy who was a racing driver whom Hazel had scooped up from Brands Hatch to be included in her international collection. A more heterogeneous assemblage of individuals gathered under one roof would have been difficult to find anywhere. Brought together by no more compelling reason than their association with Hazel, they nevertheless happily mingled throughout the evening, forever dividing and coalescing, all the while making small talk and exchanging gossip.

Finally, there was, of course, Mark Brody himself, a small, plump figure, a little awkward in his shapeless, ill-fitting grey suit, but for all his clumsiness Brody looked immensely self-assured and powerful. Evident behind the awkwardness, some of which was no doubt put on for special effect, was a man of great strength and indomitable will. He moved from one group to another, his hands stuck deep in his pockets; silent, attentive, his small round mouth gave the impression of some-one soundlessly whistling a tune.

He spoke very little. He listened, he smiled with bridal chasteness at the risqué jokes. For a while, he and Anthony shared a sofa, Brody's knees firmly pressed together like a spinsterish schoolteacher, Anthony hunched and round-shouldered, while he listened distractedly to his future brother-in-law as Brody expressed gratitude at his willingness to come out to South Africa for the wedding. For some reason he seemed to regard Ferguson's presence as the seal of approval on an important business transaction, but he nevertheless seemed genuinely pleased that Anthony was there.

'Your sister was determined you should be present at the wedding,' he explained while he handed Ferguson his drink.

118

'There was some doubt whether you could be persuaded to return to the country after all the years you've been living abroad. You've been away a long time, haven't you? Almost an émigré, I would say.'

'I suppose so, yes. Fifteen years is rather a long time.'

Examining Brody's squat figure and his round, stolid face, Anthony kept thinking what an unlikely prospect Brody must have seemed to many people as the future husband of his vivacious sister. 'It's not that I haven't missed the country or anything like that,' Anthony started to explain, 'though I confess the politics was always something one could do without. It's just that, well, something has always seemed to come up at precisely the moment I was thinking of coming out for a visit. And always unexpectedly. Human Rights International, I'm afraid, exist from one crisis to the next: revolutions, wars, incarcerations, torture; that's what keeps us in business. Unexplained disappearances,' he added, thinking of Cornelius Molapo. 'But this time, I'm glad to say, everything suddenly came together in a happy conjunction. My sister's wedding was taking place at precisely the moment Human Rights International was considering sending a man out to South Africa to investigate human rights abuses in the country.'

'Human rights abuses?' Brody groaned slightly. He stared gloomily at his future brother-in-law. 'Just when we think we're doing better than at any other time in the history of this Government!'

'Well, Mark, that's not how people in many parts of the world see it.'

'They don't?' Mark Brody said with some surprise. 'Dismantling some of the apartheid laws at home? Pulling out of South West Africa and Angola? What more do we have to do to show the world that change is under way? Even as I'm talking to you, some individuals in the Government are proposing we should be holding talks with the underground opposition leaders. Shouldn't the new dispensation be given a little time to work?'

119

'Human Rights International has its own agenda to pursue laid down in its charter,' Ferguson responded. 'As far as the organisation is concerned, a state of emergency still exists in the country; many people remain incarcerated. Some missing people have yet to be accounted for. I'm sorry if this sounds like unnecessary meddling but that's why the HRI came into existence: to meddle in the affairs of world Governments when it's a question of human rights.'

People were drifting into the room, bringing plates of caviar and scrambled eggs; dishes of Japanese fish in ginger and garlic, and fat, succulent clams in pimento sauce. The party was getting livelier. As the flow of incoming guests continued, and Anthony felt, rather than heard, the chatter around him, he began to feel weirdly out of his depth; a spooky sensation of having been cast afloat in a world depressingly familiar and yet gruesomely mysterious took hold of him. He tried to listen simultaneously to several conversations going on around him.

Trying to pick up the thread of conversation where they had left it Brody turned to Ferguson: 'Of course, the situation is not normal,' he conceded. 'All the same, you have to admit the present Government is doing its best to bring about change through gradual reform. Not revolution, but reform. It's true a number of individuals are still in detention. But, after all, the guerrillas are still operating in the border areas of the Northern Transvaal. In this kind of situation the Government is surely obliged to retain some of its emergency powers.'

'Mark, no Government on earth has the right to abduct its citizens during the night and keep them under lock and key somewhere – God knows where – out of sight without a proper trial.'

'Of course! Of course! You're referring to your man, Molapo, I presume? But are you sure your man is under "lock and key", as you put it?'

Anthony had to admit he was not sure of anything. 'Which is why I have been sent out here to look into the matter,' he added reasonably.

'What if your disappeared man has simply gone underground to wage war against the country? He was one of the underground people, wasn't he, by the look of things?'

'The NLM have assured us they have no knowledge of Molapo's whereabouts. I have no reason to doubt their word. Surely they would know if he had gone underground?' All the same, Anthony suddenly had his doubts; someone had already mentioned the outbreak of a special dance style in the Northern Transvaal similar to the 'jitterbug' and the new step had broken out in the border areas where they'd never danced like that before. 'Everyone in Tabanyane is dancing it,' one of the party-goers had insisted, 'men, women and children, even grandmothers.'

It was easy to laugh off the suggestion of any possible link between Molapo and this outbreak in the bush of what was, after all, a fairly well-known dancing style. Nevertheless, Molapo was undeniably branded as the 'jitterbug king'. According to newspapers it was the first thing people remembered about him.

Brody had caught the unmistakable signs of Ferguson's uncertainty. He now tried to press his point home. 'Listen, Anthony. Things are moving so quickly here, outsiders are likely to get the wrong end of the stick.'

Anthony was about to protest but Brody lifted a pudgy hand in the air. 'Please, I know what you want to say. You were born here. You know the country as well as I do. But believe me, it's not quite that simple anymore. A lot more is going on under the surface than meets the eye.' Brody paused, looking sidelong at his future brother-in-law like a man trying to convince an unexpectedly obdurate adversary. He went on in a tone of quiet conviction. 'What were once unquestionably solid coalitions are rapidly dissolving. New alliances are being formed. And to tell you the truth, no-one knows where the country is headed.'

'I thought everyone knew,' Anthony said mischievously. 'At least, that's the impression the Government has always given to the world – of people who knew exactly where they were going. Maybe a little doubt after all is not such a bad thing.'

Their conversation was interrupted by the arrival of Leda Bremont in a chauffeur-driven Daimler. For a moment there was a wonderful hush in the room and then conversation resumed as if nothing had happened. Anthony had risen in anticipation but had no idea of what; and then Leda walked across the room to join the two men. Although no longer a young thing, she nonetheless conveyed an impression of unbridled, heedless youth, fresh skin and soft brown hair tumbling down to her bare shoulders. She put an arm around Ferguson: 'Anthony, I'm so glad to meet you at last. Hazel speaks so often of you, I almost feel I have known you all my life.' Her voice was soft and caressing, an underground voice with only the slightest hint of an accent. 'I feel the same about you,' Anthony lied gallantly. 'Hazel's letters are full of references to you. I sometimes have the impression that nothing happens in her life in which you don't play some part.'

'Oh, only a minor part,' Leda laughed. 'The truth of the matter is Hazel and I are what you might call kindred souls, doomed to follow the crooked ways of a heart that can find no restful place. Lost souls we are, *toutes perdues*, I'd say. At least, I am, wouldn't you say, Mark?'

The party, Anthony noticed, was changing, as parties always do: first there are the arrivals of the guests drifting in one by one, the introductions and getting to know each other; then there is the second stage when soulmates have found each other, alcohol is taking its effect and sharpens the appetite; later, during the last and third stage, after food has been served and the barn doors of lust are finally flung open, assignations are made and groups separate to re-form or re-group in various corners under more promising conditions. To Anthony it seemed that the second stage had now arrived.

Though informally served, the food was impressive, delivered to the guests in exquisite china and wine glasses that

122

looked as if they would bend at the slightest pressure. No doubt the servants had spent the day elbow deep in silver polish and ironing out the wrinkles from the linen. Angelhair pasta tangled with slivers of salmon, followed by melting slices of butterflied lamb and sautéd breast of guinea-fowl were being washed down with copious quantities of wine from the Cape and European vineyards. With the party moving slowly into its third phase, a certain abandon and accompanying indiscretion were becoming noticeable. During a lull in the conversation a booming voice, perhaps unaware of the likelihood of being overheard, said loudly: 'Well, Mark has made his bed, now he must lie in it, I'm afraid!' It was quite obvious Brody and Hazel were being discussed by some drunken sods and Anthony was angry and embarrassed but Brody himself, who must have heard the remark, remained cool and indifferent. Perhaps he had come to the same conclusion as the speaker but was far from being unhappy at the prospect of lying in the bed he had made.

Brody continued their earlier conversation imperturbably: 'Violence in the townships has been responsible for a financial haemorrhage of incredible proportions in the past few months. It's all very well for a few individuals to talk to African leaders in the Ivory Coast but isn't it high time we opened a dialogue with leaders of the National Liberation Movement!'

Money, the business of making money, was Johannesburg's sole reason for existence. It was so when it was founded, and it remained so now. Glancing across the windows at the distant city lights and the dim glitter of the stars above, Anthony thought that it would be all too easy to forget this if it weren't for the businessmen and their wives who would not let anyone forget it. The making of money and the losing of it, the indisputable power it bestowed upon those able to make it and conserve it and go on to make more of it; this was what drove these people and talking about it gave to the conversation an extraordinary charge.

'Anyway, Anthony,' Brody concluded, 'if you really want

to know what is going on try to have a word with Jocelyn Baird when he gets here. Jos is financial adviser to Daling National, and he knows an awful lot about the current political situation. Right now he's part of a team of businessmen which is holding a series of clandestine meetings with the leaders of the NLM.'

Out of the corner of his eye Anthony saw his sister approach. Hazel was picking her way delicately around the guests in that walk of contained energy of hers which always caused an involuntary shiver in men watching her for the first time. Moving about the room on velvet paws like a cat in Vanity Fair, Anthony thought to himself, smiling. She was wearing a shimmering lamé dress of gold and silver, and under the burning white light her face, her bare arms and shoulders, gleamed with a sort of pale, haughty glamour. Brody must have also noticed his fiancée's sinuous approach because, perhaps mindful of Hazel's dislike of political pow-wows, he began to repeat, quite unnecessarily, his expressions of sincere appreciation at Anthony's willingness to be present at the great wedding. 'You did us all an immense service,' Brody said. 'I need not tell you what your sister is like when she can't get her way!'

Then Hazel was upon them. 'I heard what you said just now, Mark!', she flashed her bright eyes. Brody blinked shyly like an owl behind his glasses. 'I was only trying to tell Anthony here how gratified we both are he was able to come out for the wedding.'

'I know,' Hazel said pleasantly. 'But you needn't give him the satisfaction of knowing how anxious we were for his presence! I think it's a disgrace the way he's tried to keep away from his own family and the country of his birth. Like a wandering Hottentot!' she added, cuddling up to her brother.

'Hazel, I see you at least twice a year during your many trips across Europe!' Anthony protested.

'You know that doesn't count,' his sister giggled. 'A quick supper with you in London, snatched en route to some old place somewhere, is not at all my idea of seeing my own brother!'

Presently, Henrietta, swathed in black satin and floating silk, came to join her children, pulling Anthony on to the sofa beside her, all the time murmuring sweet endearments. 'Oh, how happy you have made me! After all these years, my children under one roof!' It was clear that despite his physical presence his mother still found it difficult to believe he had actually come back, that he was not going to suddenly melt away like a jinn released inadvertently from some carefully sealed bottle. In that sudden warm intimacy in which they sat, side by side, arms linked, memories of the past came flooding back; childhood memories of his mother in the early evening dressed only in her slip, her face covered in thick layers of white cream like a painted warrior, carefully preparing herself before going out to the Sunday dances at the Maitland; returning home late and his father's menacing voice raised in outrage. Across a distance of years Anthony fancied he could still hear Henrietta's voice, defiant yet defensive, saying in hushed tones. 'Keep your voice down, Eric – you'll wake the children!' Later, when everything had failed, shamelessly and unscrupulously using her sexual weaponry to subdue and overwhelm his father, saying in her gin voice: 'Look at me, Eric! Why do you shut your eyes? What are you afraid of? Look, I'm still a damn sight more attractive than any of your cheap Braamfontein *hoere*!' Then later, thinking the children asleep, bending solicitously over him and Hazel, her skin breathing a mix of scents. It seemed to Anthony that he had never really known anything about this woman, who even now clung to his arm, murmuring with infinite tenderness: 'Oh, after all these years!

It was well after midnight when Jocelyn Baird and his wife Lucielle turned up at the party, as Mark Brody had promised they would. Judging by the ripple of interest as they walked into the room, many people were awaiting the arrival of this middle-aged couple with some anticipation. They were

125

immediately surrounded by a dozen or so intent faces. A large man with a genial face, Baird seemed to enjoy the attention he was receiving. Sweeping the room with an all-inclusive gaze, from time to time waving his hands in the air like a politician on the stumps, he did most of the talking. He had just returned from a trip to a neighbouring African state where a group of businessmen had met with the underground leaders of the NLM and many of the guests were trying to milk him for information as to what had transpired there. 'Right now,' Jocelyn turned to look at everyone in turn, 'I think we're going through what will be seen by future generations as a historic turning point in our country's affairs.' He was gently smiling, scanning the faces around him for signs of dissent.

'What do you mean, Jos?' someone asked, 'Are we going to see a breakthrough or not?'

'A breakthrough? Well – ' Baird hesitated. 'That's not the word we like to use. It's too much of a journalist's hand-me-down. What I can tell you is that we are holding intensive talks with leaders of the NLM in the hope of coming up with something concerning the shape of what would be a possible idea, supposing there is a will on the parts of both the NLM and the Government. I can also say that such an agreement would result in the release of Dabula Amanzi in exchange for the suspension of the armed struggle by the NLM. It's obviously too early to say what will happen next. Perhaps a termination of the state of emergency. Perhaps a preparation for a national assembly to draft a new constitution. However, there should be movement on several fronts sometime in the near future, perhaps in a matter of weeks, rather than months.'

'"Movement on several fronts",' the same voice now mocked Baird. '"Weeks rather than months!" Isn't that another journalistic hand-me-down?'

'As a matter of fact, a politician first used the phrase,' Jocelyn Baird smiled pleasantly, thinking of old Harold Wilson. 'Or was it the one about cutting down inflation at a stroke?' he ruminated pointlessly.

'But what do you mean by a movement on several fronts? After forty years of doctrinaire apartheid, what has suddenly happened to change some very obdurate minds?'

'It's simple,' Baird said. 'We can't afford apartheid. It's too costly. Any fool can see that. Look,' he was patient, like a teacher in a kindergarten. 'Two individuals are standing at a bus stop going to the same destination but one is white, one is black. So instead of one bus you have two buses to carry only two men at the cost of more fuel and more manpower.'

'And cost of woman-power,' Lucielle Baird interrupted. 'With a hyphen!' Wearing an evening dress with side pockets into which her hand seemed to be permanently stuck, Lucielle Baird was attractive without being pretty. A smile, sly, sceptical, seemed to hover always at the corner of her mouth. Lucielle and Jocelyn Baird made a formidable pair. She listened to him sometimes with a look of appalling disrespect, sometimes with a look of self-congratulatory achievement as if she were exhibiting a prized object. Now she called him by his family name but pronounced it like 'Bird'. 'Jos is a funny bird,' she punned. 'He has all these crazy ideas about drawing the natives into a market economy. He says the natives are natural capitalists. You only have to talk to him for a minute to get the idea that all our gardener needs is a few rands to make a killing on the Johannesburg Stock Exchange.'

Jocelyn Baird laughed uproariously at this idea. 'That's right!' he said approvingly. 'I have absolute faith in Kumalo's unappeasable longing for riches. A regular Dives Kumalo is! Do you know I went out to Nakeledi township to have a look at his fowl-run once. The man is expanding his business so much he is now breeding turkeys which he sells to a butchery in town packed in iceboxes. And to raise extra investment capital he works five days a week in my garden. But to get back to what I was saying.'

'Yes. You were trying to tell us that now we all have to travel in the same bus,' the businessman's wife got her word in at last. Travelling in the same bus seemed as bad a prospect as sharing an apartment block with Arabs.

'He means,' Lucielle Baird said very distinctly. 'Two bodies can sleep more cheaply in one bed for the price of one even if one body is black.'

'Well, yes,' Baird laughed. 'Provided you keep an eye on overproduction. After all, we are no longer terrified by the so-called *bloedvermenging*, are we? The collapse of the economy is a more terrifying prospect than blood mixing. The truth of the matter is, we are desperately short of money.'

They were back on the subject of money again. It was an obsession.

'That's right,' Mark concurred. 'That's what I've been trying to tell everyone here, Jos, that we're quite strapped for cash!'

'Again and again, we've been told, compared to the rest of Africa we have the strongest economy.'

'Not anymore,' Jocelyn said. 'Keeping down restless natives costs a great deal of money. Do you know that our defence budget rocketed from a mere sixty million dollars in 1960 to three billion dollars this year? Out of a population of only thirty-five million our armed forces have tripled from 11,500 professionals, 56,000 part-time soldiers and 10,000 national servicemen to 28,300 permanent force members and 157,000 part-time soldiers. A truly martial spirit has taken over the country! The point is: it's costing us a lot of money patrolling borders from the Atlantic Ocean to the Indian Ocean.'

'Can't we get the international banks to tide us over just this once?' someone bantered. 'After all, these days everybody in the Third World is living on credit.'

'The banks have got scared and have started calling in their short-term loans. And who could blame them? Up to now we have shown little inclination to put in place the necessary reforms; but all that may be changing.' Perhaps, perhaps. Change was in the air as the guests finally drifted off, silver and gold party dresses shimmering under an indifferent moon.

That night, waiting for sleep to come, Anthony Ferguson had

the strangest sensation of floating in a pool of darkness, of being stranded like a fish out of water. He was attacked by an uncomfortable feeling of complete displacement, like a person who after many years of wandering had returned home only to discover that his home was elsewhere. From a great distance came the sound of a guitar strummed African style by one of those itinerant troubadors who roam the South African cities. High, plangent, self-absorbed, the man's voice rode higher and higher above the strings of the guitar. Then as Anthony drifted to sleep he was vaguely aware of someone moving about in the dark, someone taking off her clothes by the starlight, someone bent over him, touching his face; no doubt yet another childhood dream. Ferguson slept until morning.

Chapter Ten

FOR the next few days leading up to Christmas, Ferguson lay low. For that is what he called it: lying low. All thoughts of Cornelius Molapo he simply pushed aside, individuals he must see, organisations he must consult, police stations he must visit; all that had simply been sidelined by a mind which, for a while beguiled and diverted, concentrated on the temporary pursuit of a life of pleasure and ease. He rose late and stayed up till the early hours. He breakfasted with his mother and sister and accompanied the two women to the market on their many shopping sprees for Christmas baubles and trinkets; but for the most part he was immured inside his sister's resplendent palace, behind high walls which were mounted with broken glass that was supposed to discourage unlawful entry by a growing army of daring Johannesburg burglars.

He rang Tina in London to tell her all about it. Jokingly, he likened his sister's house to a private retreat which had unexpectedly turned into a squatter's camp for the rich. Throughout the week, from morning to bedtime, Hazel's innumerable friends visited: young men sporting fashionable crewcuts and bronzed faces, who made their fortunes trading in illicit diamonds and marrying broken-down heiresses; and girls with shapely, sinewy limbs who, like his sister, were waiting to get married; or women who were already married and were now waiting to divorce their husbands; or else young women who had been jilted by well-known playboys and were currently seeking legal redress for breach of promise – but young women, at any rate, who were waiting for financial recompense in one form or another. And while doing so they were getting themselves ready for fresh adventures. These people came and went; they swam, they sat by the swimming pool gossiping; and from time to time, having nothing better to do and much time on his hands, Ferguson joined them and listened with a great deal of amusement to their tales of woe and misfortune.

'Honestly, you can't imagine what it's like!' he told Tina on the phone. 'Like living inside a foam bubble, the ones I used to blow as a child. Only this particular bubble is as big as my sister's gleaming white mansion. I suppose you could call it a kind of pleasure dome on the South African highveld.'

Amused, Tina said: 'What about Molapo then?'

'What about Molapo?'

'Well, I hope you'll find time enough to spare for the poor missing man.'

Of course, of course, Ferguson answered with more solemnity than usual; there was his mission to think about, certainly, but he had already decided that this Molapo business could wait at least until after Christmas. After all, he still had to reacquaint himself with the general situation in the country, take the pulse of the country' public affairs; he said he imagined his first task would be to arrange a meeting with leaders of the National Liberation Movement.

'Somebody called Joe Bulane,' he reminded Tina. 'Remember him?' Tina remembered. So what else? she asked. Then there would be consultations with individuals connected to humanitarian organisations after which, and only then, would he begin to approach Government bureaucrats and police departments. 'I know. I know,' Tina laughed. '*Quel boulot*!' Anthony was slightly annoyed by her tone of amused scepticism.

'After all, it was Brian Lomax himself who said – '

'I know what Brian Lomax said,' Tina interrupted. 'Go out to South Africa and have yourself a good time!' she bantered brutally. Brian Lomax was the director of Human Rights International who had advised everyone concerned with the Molapo affair to move with extreme care. Every legal precaution had to be taken, every precedent studied and taken note of before plunging into the choppy waters of South Africa's race laws.

Above all, people on the spot had to be fully consulted. That was what Lomax had said. So Ferguson now explained with some impatience that he was simply following instructions, laying the necessary groundwork before getting on with interviews with interior and justice ministry officials, and men in charge of the country's detention centres. There was a pause in their conversation.

'And meanwhile – ?' Tina wryly wondered.

'And meanwhile?' Ferguson could not resist a small chuckle. Meanwhile, in his sister's shining white castle he was feeling pleasantly trapped like a fly in jam, he said.

Meanwhile, in fact, he ate, slept, swam, and occasionally he read whatever official documents were placed in his way. In one of the guest rooms he had discovered a hand-printed edition of Conrad's *Under Western Eyes*, and, delighting in its improbable shady plots carried out by brutal secret agents and fugitive assassins, Ferguson had read the novel through in one sitting. But after a while, bored with his own company, bored also with Conrad's plotters and the jurists' reports and documents he felt obliged to read, Ferguson was persuaded to join the interminable round of cocktails by the pool.

There he sat on a deckchair at his sister's feet, listening desultorily to the doings of the Johannesburg jet set. His sister was obviously delighted to have a chance to exhibit him once again after his successful début at the party. Alluding vaguely – and quite misleadingly – to what she described as Anthony's work with United Nations refugees, his sister proudly introduced him to all and sundry; Molapo, the object of her

132

brother's visit, was of course not mentioned since Molapo was evidently not a refugee. Hazel's visitors listened politely to what they were told about the brother's presence in South Africa but quickly got bored. On the other hand, his long stay overseas was more intriguing. They wondered at the cause. Showing no sign of genuine enthusiasm, they asked him what he thought of the progress the country was making. After all, progress had been made and was being made. Or didn't he think so? Parliament had been enlarged with a separate chamber for 'Coloureds' and a separate chamber for Indian representatives, though the arrangements for the black majority remained a matter of heated controversy even among those who professed concern for the fate of the natives.

Most of these people looked harmless enough, quite sincere, in fact, even charming. One of the women who had smiled often at Anthony when things were being explained to him, a woman who appropriately enough bore the name of Belinda Lovemore, said to him just before diving like a porpoise into the sleek pool: 'Quite frankly, Anthony, I think compared with natives in other parts of Africa ours are doing extremely well. They have their own "homelands", don't they, where they can disport themselves as much as they like at their own pleasure? Only they don't seem to be able to get on with their own tribal chiefs! I wonder why?' Sedated, almost seduced by the sense of everything having been said before, Anthony felt the energy he had once brought to addressing atrocities in South America seeping away in the land of his birth.

However, by the end of the week guilt began to gnaw like a small worm on Ferguson's conscience. What if at this very moment, while he was being elaborately entertained by his sister, Molapo was languishing in some detention centre somewhere in the country? What if Molapo, sick, weak and blindfolded, was being starved, beaten and tortured, while the senior servant of Human Rights International slept in silken sheets and feasted on caviar, Bombay duck and oysters? Yielding finally to that impulse quite common among servants of large bureaucratic organisations, the desire to create order in the conduct of business – in this case to develop a more or less reliable method of setting about the search for Molapo – Anthony at last picked up the phone and rang the number of Joe Wulitz's office. 'Mr Wulitz? My name is Anthony Ferguson.'

'Ah, Mr Ferguson?' a light cheerful voice responded. 'Human Rights Corporation – sorry, of course, Human Rights International. Finally you got here! Excellent! Mr Bulane has been waiting to hear from you with the keenest anticipation, I can tell you! The keenest! Practically eating his heart out waiting for your call!' The lawyer chuckled agreeably. 'Anyway, welcome to Johannesburg, Mr Ferguson.'

When Ferguson pressed Wulitz for an early meeting with Bulane he agreed instantly to an appointment. A visit, he said, well, yes, yes, that would be most appropriate. Yes, this very afternoon, why waste any more time? An early meeting, just the thing to get everyone started off with this matter as soon as possible so that after Christmas inquiries could begin in earnest. Quite important in fact to inject a new sense of urgency into the search for the poor unfortunate man. 'The way our law is now constituted, Mr Ferguson, *habeas corpus* is simply out of the question, I'm afraid,' Wulitz said. 'Bulane tried it at the beginning but for cases of this kind *habeas corpus* doesn't exist in fact. As a result, my own hands are tied.' Several times Wulitz interrupted himself to consult with someone in his office before coming back on the line again. Anthony began to feel dizzy. 'These unexplained and frequent disappearances, Mr Ferguson, detention without trial... Ninety days incarceration without any charges being brought against the accused!... Well, frankly, we have reached a point in time when some form of outside intervention by humanitarian organisations may be necessary in order to internationalise the issue.'

Wulitz explained that Bulane was sure to come by the office in the early afternoon. They would then have a quick 'getting-to-know-you' chat over a Christmas drink in the office. 'You and Mr Bulane can then take it from there,' he said. Again there was a brief interruption while the lawyer seemed to be explaining something to someone in the office, perhaps to Joe Bulane himself, and then Wulitz's voice came back on the line: 'Would three o'clock suit you, Mr Ferguson?'

'Oh, absolutely, three o'clock is splendid!' Ferguson quickly responded, happy finally to bring the conversation to a conclusion because Wulitz's disembodied voice, though cheerful and friendly, was having an increasingly unsettling effect on him.

In his sister's house double preparations were now in progress: for Christmas and for the wedding. Extra help had been hired to scrub, clean and vacuum and set up banks of flowers and tents on the lawn; and 'meanwhile' – smiling with pleasurable irony at the thought of Tina – Anthony was happy to detach himself from this beaver scene in order to begin his first meetings with his contacts. On an afternoon when wispy clouds moved slowly across a ginger sky that precedes turbulent weather on the highveld, Ferguson allowed himself to be driven down to Wulitz's office in Mama Ferguson's car. For Prince the little excursion was welcome since his old lady was ensconced in preparations at the house and Prince was happiest behind the wheel touring city and suburb. After dropping young Mr Anthony at Wulitz's office he would no doubt profit from the interval of two hours to drive around the suburbs, checking on his many girlfriends and admirers. Justifying his enthusiasm to transport Ferguson, Prince explained: 'Sometimes Hazel is very, very reckless,' he said disapprovingly while holding the door open for her brother. 'And Christmas time everybody driving like mad. Better I drive you, Mr Anthony.'

In fact, they did not have too far to travel before they were caught up in something rather more tangled than a simple Christmas traffic jam. Just at the end of the driveway, as the car turned into the main road, Prince was halted by a religious procession which was moving slowly across a busy intersection; men, women and children strutting along and swinging their hips to a mixture of hymns, urban pop and country songs that built up to a complicated psalmody rarely heard in this neighbourhood. Every few seconds, indifferent to the chaos they were causing and heedless to the cacophony of automobile horns and vocal protests from frustrated white drivers, they paused to allow their leader, a tall, bearded, Christlike figure, to harangue the onlookers. Obviously enchanted by the spectacle, Prince stopped the car completely, switched off the engine, and smiled encouragingly at the last of the stragglers.

'They're Molema's crowd,' he explained to Anthony. 'At this time of year they're always remembering the Prophet who flew to heaven on the wings of a mighty black eagle.'

'Flew to heaven?' Anthony said doubtfully.

'Yes, Molema was a big prophet. He flew up to heaven on the wings of a big, big mighty eagle. In Tabanyane on Mount Taba Bosiu you can still see the big rock from where they say Molema jumped to heaven on the wings of a black eagle. That was a long time ago.'

'Broke his neck more likely I should've thought,' Ferguson said impatiently. 'I was under the impression tribal people don't believe much in heaven. When they die they go off to the land of the ancestors, don't they?'

Prince shook his head. 'These not tribal people. These Christian and African custom all mixed up together but definitely not tribal people. No bones, no flywhisks and all that monkey business! No, Mr Ferguson, this straight-forward religion. No less. No more! Even some white people in the countryside are members.'

When Ferguson reached Joe Wulitz's chambers he found a big crowd gathered outside the building only a few yards away from the entrance. Something horrible, a catastrophe, had happened, was his first thought. What struck him about this crowd of intermingled races was its stillness; a silent, sober, respectful throng of people who looked stunned. Ferguson was drawn to it, mesmerised. Occasionally, someone moved to get a better view. Some young people stood on the fenders of their cars. It appeared that someone was being carried off into a 'WHITES ONLY' ambulance and the general comportment of these spectators suggested that whoever was being carried away was already dead or would be dead before long. The scene reminded Ferguson of many things about life in South Africa that he had forgotten. Even as a child growing up under apartheid, one of the oddities which had impressed him about these occasions was how the smallest tragedy instinctively drew people of all races together. Here, too, they were suddenly caught up in a common net of feelings. Messengers on bicycles pulled up, exchanging greetings, and ended by donning the required expression of a grieving solidarity. Young whites from a pharmacy across the road came out to the street in their white overalls to join the ritual. From the hairdresser's shop nearby, women still in curlers had rushed to take in the scene. The pigeons above the crowd flew about playfully, indifferent to the human drama being played out in the street below; they whirled and scattered like chaff in the December sunshine. Soon the stretcher with the inert figure draped in white was wheeled into the back of the ambulance, the doors were shut, and watching with a clamped feeling briefly clutching at his heart, Ferguson saw that nearby an elderly woman, white and fashionably dressed, was quietly weeping while being assisted to take her place in the front seat of the vehicle. She was being comforted by the supporting arms of what appeared to be passing strangers.

Before he entered the building Ferguson heard a voice from the crowd pronouncing solemnly: 'Poor woman! To have someone die on you like that in the middle of a Johannesburg street. What a shame!' A woman's voice. For an instant, strained by a lingering sadness, the crowd remained motionless. But as soon as the ambulance began to pull away, it seemed as if they were rediscovering speech; and, like actors who had been temporarily playing parts on the stage and were now released, people began to slide back into their everyday black and white occupations. The messengers got on to their bikes and, shouting greetings to friends, pedalled away in different directions. For a moment, touched by the expression of spontaneous human sympathy, without waiting to learn the nature of the tragedy, Ferguson quickly entered the building, suddenly feeling profoundly grateful to be one of the living.

Wulitz's office was located in an old decaying building, dark inside even during daylight hours. There was no lift, only a narrow winding staircase leading up four floors, and Wulitz's office was at the very top. Reaching the fourth floor, Ferguson followed a darkly lit corridor flanked by walls with peeling plaster, past the litter of discarded paper and bundles of used-up documents packed away for pre-Christmas disposal; finally he reached a door with a brass plate on which was inscribed the legend: *Joe Wulitz: Advocate.* A vandal had sprayed in the word 'Devils' in front of 'Advocate' and, without knowing exactly why, Ferguson considered the insult a kind of indirect homage Wulitz might even enjoy. He knocked three times before the door was flung open by a dark-haired, whiskered man in his early forties – looking exactly like a Devil's Advocate – wearing brown corduroy trousers and a faded, open-neck yellow shirt with sleeves rolled up well above the elbows. Bleary-eyed, the face slightly puffed and wearing an air of fatigued puzzlement as if he had not slept for several days, this unsavoury figure recoiled at the sight of Anthony, as one in fear of a surprise attack. Then he stepped fully outside the door into the corridor. Ferguson introduced himself.

'Oh, Mr Ferguson!' the man said with a curious, rising intonation. 'I'm Joe Wulitz. We talked on the phone,' he remembered. They shook hands. 'Please, come right in, Mr Ferguson.' From Wulitz's main office the world outside was only a distant rumour, the hum of traffic, the clamour of voices, the blare of trumpets from a music shop – all that belonged to another region of the earth. The office was Wulitz's world, narrow, confined, sometimes even threatened, but possessing its own internal integrity and protection quite inviolate within its own parameters. For a second Wulitz gave Ferguson a frank appraisal; then as if slightly abashed by his own audacity, he smiled shyly at his visitor, drew up one of half a dozen chairs placed along the wall: 'Please, make yourself comfortable, Mr Ferguson.'

Wulitz asked about the flight: was it pleasant? Ferguson was tempted to mention his flight companion, Tom Murchison, but thought better of it. Was it overcrowded? Too many tourists visiting South Africa the 'Land of Sunshine?' Wulitz asked reproachfully. Where was Ferguson staying? Of course, of course: with the family. How stupid even to ask. 'Not at all,' Ferguson said helpfully. Sometimes the anonymity of an international hotel was preferable to the suffocating embrace of family. 'But to be honest, Mr Wulitz, putting up at my sister's house is rather like staying in those old French estate houses appropriately named *hotels particuliers*.'

Wulitz was curious. 'Your sister is extremely rich, isn't she? I think I've heard of her. A professional celebrity of some sort?'

'Former dancer and actress,' Ferguson replied. 'My sister models clothes when she can spare the time from her numerous other diversions.'

Wulitz listened intently. Ferguson noted on a side-table various beverages had been set up, surrounded by tumblers, glasses and tea cups, in what looked more like preparations for a social occasion than a planning session for the conducting of a search for a missing person. Wulitz got up from his chair, saying: 'I suppose we might as well begin by having our tea, shall we? Mr Bulane is in the next room. I'll tell him you are here.'

Though not exactly slim, Joe Wulitz was a man of extra-ordinary mobility; his movements were jerky and sudden, but just as quickly, unexpectedly, they would be arrested by some invisible peremptory force by which he himself seemed to be constantly surprised; he had a way of listening intensely to something going on somewhere else, as if an unidentifiable noise were bothering him; then, suddenly relaxing, his eyes twinkling like fireflies, he would offer one of his easily apologetic smiles.

Having poured tea, Wulitz suddenly sprang into action; he passed through a half-open door marked 'PRIVATE' and shouted: 'Joe, you have a visitor!'

The brief interval enabled Ferguson to take note of his surroundings. Wulitz's office was medium-sized and wood-panelled; from the main office a connecting door led into an inner chamber and kitchenette where his assistants, if he had any, as Ferguson supposed he must have, prepared his coffee and snacks. In the front office a big desk was piled high with documents, a heap of files in brown covers and a pyramid of scrolls ceremoniously tied with red and green ribbons. Most available space was taken up by bookshelves; bookshelves behind the huge desk, bookshelves on either side of the room, bookshelves along the back wall; the shelves held legal tomes, law reports, publications on jurisprudence and related practices in various countries; they included historical dissertations graphically illustrating countless instances of man's inhumanity to man. But placed reassuringly in the middle of the desk was a photograph of a younger version of Wulitz standing next to a pretty dark-haired woman. The woman's arms were wrapped around the shoulders of a teenage boy and girl who looked extremely unimpressed by the camerawork; less concerned with domestic joys were photographs and lithographs across two walls portraying the country in its various stages of development: Cecil Rhodes parleying with captains of industry on a sand dune outside Johannesburg; Milner, about to catch a train in Beaufort West, being seen off by men wearing dark suits and broad hats; and – surprisingly, given the rest of the company – Lenin stepping off a boat in Finland during his years of exile. Another early photograph captured members of an African delegation on arrival in London on a mission to petition Her

Majesty's Government against the establishment of the Union of South Africa on the grounds that the new constitution would exclude the black majority from the Government of the country.

When Wulitz re-entered the room he was carrying a tray with a Christmas cake and a pot of tea, but also had in tow a small, dapper African who wore a black suit with a jacket that was severely cut away at the back and whose cuffs were shorter than the sleeves of his shirt, so that the cufflinks gleamed when he put out his hand in greeting. He walked into the room in short, mincing steps like a bantam-weight boxer entering the ring. 'Mr Ferguson,' Wulitz said by way of introduction. 'Mr Joe Bulane.' The two men shook hands. Anthony took in Bulane's small, bullet-shaped head, very closely shaven, and the moustache which curled away into a sort of ironic twist on his upper lip.

'Delighted to meet you, Mr Ferguson, extremely delighted!' Bulane shut his eyes as though praying for an unexpected miracle to happen and then suddenly opened them wide. The eyes were tiny, shiny; yet behind the gleaming surface, they were strangely the *untermenschan* eyes of a vigilante; they studied the representative of Human Rights International with a kind of alarming precision. Bulane and Ferguson took their seats while Wulitz busied himself with tea.

'Mr Ferguson, I need not tell you,' Bulane began, 'your presence in the country in this difficult period of our struggle gives us great encouragement indeed.' And he cocked his closely shaven head to one side, as if the better to observe Anthony's lean clean-shaven jawline. Without waiting for response he continued: 'This is more than we had dared to expect, that you personally would take the trouble to come out here to give us the benefit of your aid and comfort. And, if I may say so, this proves to us only one thing: with humanitarian organisations like your own and men of your calibre at the helm, our miserable country is not going to be so easily forgotten after all. And you, Mr Ferguson, I am happy to see, you have not forgotten the country of your birth. Speaking for

141

myself and speaking in the name of the movement I'm privileged to serve, I would like to welcome you. We're most honoured by your presence in the office today.'

Against his own inclinations and despite his habitual resistance to such obvious flattery Ferguson found himself deeply moved by the seductive rhetoric. Not for the first time he was forced to acknowledge the corrupting power of flattery, its ability to tap into the need, deeply entrenched in most human beings, to be loved and admired, even if insincerely, so that Ferguson was able to say without lying: 'Really, the pleasure is all mine, Mr Bulane, though whether my coming out here will bring about the desired results is anyone's guess. For without wishing to be unduly pessimistic, I have to say that past experience with South African authorities makes a successful conclusion to this affair extremely difficult if not unlikely.'

But Bulane, it seemed, was prepared to be uncommonly gracious: 'Mr Ferguson, we can only try and fail.' Once again narrowing his eyes to minute slits he continued: 'You may not know this, Mr Ferguson, but in the past we have made repeated appeals to other international organisations to come to our aid in our protracted attempts to establish the whereabouts of our missing comrades but without notable success, I'm sorry to say. Yours, Mr Ferguson, is the first humanitarian organisation to respond positively to our desperate call for help.'

The ritual of introductions complete, Wulitz suggested that perhaps he might be permitted to serve the gentlemen tea? 'By all means, Joe!' Bulane promptly accepted. 'Mr Ferguson and I are entirely at your mercy.'

In Wulitz's office there was no sign of the usual 'tea boy' or 'tea lady' but this did not seem to hamper unduly Wulitz's preparations for what he was pleased to describe as a 'little end-of-the-year tea party' in honour of an important guest. He began serving tea to his two guests, offering them slices of rich Christmas cake.

Bulane and Wulitz were heavy smokers and soon the office was wreathed in cigarette smoke; for a while the aroma of tea, cake and tobacco was evocative of a truly Christmas festivity. In no time at all the three men had become noticeably relaxed, quite expansive in their attitude to one another. With an unerring instinct for spotting inconsistencies, Bulane soon remarked on the absence of Wulitz's office workers. 'And where is Jackson today?' he asked severely.

Wulitz gave Bulane his customary apologetic smile. 'Mr Mpho has taken time off to do some Christmas shopping,' he replied.

Bulane feigned surprise, even shock at the news: 'Christmas shopping?' he exclaimed. 'People are being rounded up, people are being detained and getting killed in detention and your Mr Mpho finds time to go Christmas shopping!' With forced incredulity Bulane laughed uproariously at his own sally. First Wulitz, then Ferguson, joined in in this small comedy.

Affecting displeasure Wulitz said curtly: 'A contented labour force is very hard to come by these days, Mr Bulane. One must do one's best for good labour relations.'

'Hear! Hear!' Bulane said, getting up from his chair. As though by some prior arrangement he approached the drinks table and started to preside over it, but not before he had made a show of soliciting Wulitz's consent. 'Shall I do the honours, Joe, as replacement for your absent major domo?'

'Most certainly,' Wulitz said. 'Go ahead.'

'What is your poison, Mr Ferguson?'

'What is on offer?'

'Sherry? Brandy? Some whisky? Queen Victoria's tears. Anything. There is a very good bottle of Cape Wine.'

'Sherry, I think, Mr Bulane, thank you.'

'Right-o! Coming up. And you, Joe. The usual?'

'Yes, I think I'll just have a snifter, if you don't mind.'

Bulane giggled like a schoolgirl. 'Why should I mind? All settled then?' He handed out drinks to the two men, then looked gloomy. 'I think I'll have a nib of KWV myself,' he announced, looking uncertainly from one bottle to another. He paused, poured, drank. 'Yes, KWV in memory of my dear old friend and comrade Cornelius Molapo, wherever he may be at this moment. 'Corny used to like his KWV,' he said reflectively. 'And that's a fact!! Even now I can hear his voice reciting his favourite *Rubaiyat of Omar Khayyàm* before he fetched himself a drink: "Come, fill the Cup...Lo! Some we loved, the loveliest and the best that Time and Fate of all their Vintage prest, have drunk their Cup a Round or two before, and one by one crept silently to Rest..." Oh, yes. That was Corny for you. A man of exceptional intelligence and political courage. What's more, a great poet of the masses. He would've made Mayakovsky weep like a child had he heard the way Molapo read his outdoor poetry.'

Ferguson tried to guess what Bulane meant by 'outdoor poetry'; perhaps poetry meant for public performance. At the same time he noted that Bulane was already speaking about Molapo in the past tense.

'Yes, a great poet! A man of many words, if you know what I mean,' he said expansively, while behind this bland façade he was thinking with repressed, furious rage: *just a windbag! A tin! A talkative empty vessel making a lot of useless noise!* He drank, swallowed, and pursued his thoughts: *a bad poet, in love with words but incapable of linking his poetry to historical process.* To Ferguson he said: 'I can't tell you, Mr Ferguson, how much Molapo is missed by the entire leadership.' And he thought: *I blame the leadership for allowing it to happen*; he remembered how hard he had fought against the idea of sending Molapo on the Tabanyane mission. Was it perhaps because of his mixed feelings about betraying him with Maureen that he couldn't bear to take him seriously? A bad choice in any case: *people like Molapo, always in love with adventure for its own sake, were a danger to the entire Movement, like loose wheels spinning off the main vehicle.*

Through the back window the sky was barely visible, pale blue and fragile in the diminishing light. While they drank, by way of making small talk, Wulitz said to Anthony: 'Mr Ferguson, I hope you don't come to the conclusion that all we South African lawyers do is drink sherry all day long. But this is a special occasion. It's a conjuncture of many factors which makes an afternoon like this possible. You've honoured us by your visit. And, as Mr Mpho took care to remind me before going off shopping, Christmas is Christmas!'

'Oh, I can understand Mr Mpho perfectly, believe me,' Ferguson said, laughing, thinking of the celebrations already under way at his sister's residence. 'I believe my sister and her friends hold the same opinion as Mr Mpho. Only in their case it all seems to have started nearly a month ago.'

He found the conversation intriguing but after a while Ferguson felt he was losing his bearings altogether. He no longer had any idea how to react to these constant shifts of mood, tone and content. He was beginning to feel dangerously exposed in his ignorance, like a tourist out of his depth, liable to react with light-hearted frivolity to expressions of unfathomable inner anguish, tempted to respond with a chuckle to serious statements explaining unsettling social conditions and circumstance; or else just as likely to react with misplaced earnestness to comments that were only intended as a jest. He was getting slightly giddy; ideas, suggestions, opinions and principles became blurred and confused, lost their focus; comedy and tragedy were joining in a single flow of indeterminate feeling. Probably the sherry doing its work.

'And think of poor Cornelius!' Joe Bulane suddenly looked quite distressed. 'Think what kind of Christmas he must be having in solitary confinement. Reduced to a diet of bread, water and tears! Truly, there is no justice in this world!'

'For all we know, Molapo may now be dead,' Wulitz pronounced with startling brutality.

'Certainly,' Bulane agreed. 'You know, Mr Ferguson, to tell you the truth, with us conflict has become second nature. "One lies here lapped in evils,"' Bulane quoted, '"watched over by beings that are worse than ogres, ghouls, and vampires. They must be driven away, destroyed utterly."'

After this outburst there was a moment of thoughtful silence during which time Bulane seemed to have become extremely morose, even angry, quietly mumbling something beyond proper expression while contemplating the possible fate of his comrade Cornelius Molapo. After a while he addressed himself to no-one in particular. 'But our struggle is not against occasional disappearances of individuals like Comrade Molapo. Our struggle is not concerned with merely fixing and adjusting the nuts and bolts of our miserable political institutions. No, what we wish to see eliminated in our country is the great social iniquity of a system resting on unrequited toil and unpitied suffering.'

'Hear! Hear!' Wulitz said. Again there was a lull in the exchanges while the three men reflected on the condition of the country. Finally, it was left to Ferguson to break the spell by asking: 'Mr Bulane, on several occasions this afternoon you have mentioned Mr Molapo, his possible suffering in detention; but how certain are you that he is actually being held in detention?'

Bulane looked surprised at the question. He and Wulitz looked at each other in complete astonishment. Then Bulane put down his glass, and shutting his eyes again as though in prayer, he brought the fingers of his two hands together at the tips. 'Of course, you're right to ask for confirmation. How do I know he is being detained at this very moment? In a normal civilised country this would be a normal question to ask. But this is not a normal civilised country, Mr Ferguson.' Bulane opened his eyes wide and stared balefully at Ferguson. 'There is a state of emergency in the country, Mr Ferguson. People simply disappear during the night and are never heard from again. Isn't that right, Joe?'

'Doubtless Mr Ferguson is aware of all this,' Wulitz said. He considered a little. 'You see, it's not simply the fact that, as we assume, Molapo is being held somewhere. It's also the possibility that he may be going through extreme forms of torture. A clumsy, unwieldy weapon torture is but in the hands of experts, Mr Ferguson, I can assure you torture can be refined into an exquisite instrument to induce suffering so extreme that by comparison dying can seem to the victim the most blessed state a human being can attain. Ask any of our chaps who have been inside. We have reports in our files which would shock you, not so much by the monstrosity of the machinery of terror they portray as by the essential attempt to reduce this terror to a form of everyday banality. So it is not even a question of discovering what these men are capable of doing to your body. After all, the Nazis cannot be bettered in what they attempted. What will shock you is not the extent to which these men are prepared to go to cow the opposition into submission, but the dulling of what should count as inner feelings. These are men who dispose of the evidence by burning the bodies of their victims and while doing so have a *braaivleis* alongside to celebrate the event. More sherry, Mr Ferguson?'

Ferguson shook his head. 'The information we received in our London office from the justice department was that a complete list has been published with the names of all the individuals who are being held. I have a copy of this list.'

'Just so,' Bulane said. 'But Molapo is not on that list, is he? One of our most beloved and trusted leaders disappears, goes missing, and no-one can find out where he is! Completely vanishes! His wife, his friends, his old parents, his neighbours, they're all asking what has happened to this man. No one is able to give an answer. In these circumstances, and given the general conditions in the country, what other conclusion are we expected to draw?'

'Nevertheless,' Ferguson persisted, feeling out of sorts, as if he were walking a precipice on the darkest of nights, traversing an invented territory of the mind. Perhaps it was the amount of sherry he had drunk, perhaps the December heat, perhaps Bulane's sweeping intransigence, the suppositions built into a system of self-sufficient proof, which had succeeded in undermining his whole sense of reality. 'Nevertheless,' Ferguson repeated, as if partly to himself, 'the situation, as I see it, Mr Bulane, is that we are going to conduct these inquiries on no firmer footing than a series of suppositions, however justified. What we have here is a grand hypothesis, your guess being as good as mine, nothing more, but nothing that permits us to accuse the Government of holding someone they deny having in their custody.'

Bulane got up from his chair. For a while he stood at the window, looking down at the busy street below. The city centre was filled with last-minute Christmas shoppers, probably Jackson Mpho among them. Under police surveillance black township residents would be having their last big fling of the year in a defiant show of an abiding faith in the validity of their often questioned existence. There would be much merry-making, but accompanied by the usual shootings, rape and murder.

Someone was bound to be detained before it was all over, taken into custody for a few days, then released with a fine. What could not be managed with such comparative efficiency was the fate of political detainees. Without turning round to face his companions Bulane spoke from his place at the window.

'He was my friend, faithful and just to me.' The effort to produce a sincere accompaniment to this sentiment proved too much and Bulane gave it up. Wulitz gave him a sickly smile. Of all the NLM leaders Wulitz had ever known Joe Bulane was not only the most widely read, he was also the one with the most endearing weakness for quotation, however inappropriate, and whatever the occasion. 'Mr Ferguson, all we have a right to ask of you is to do your best, that is all. Try to do the impossible, find Molapo and restore him to us.' Ferguson promised to do his best.

Hazel and Mark Brody were married at the Johannesburg Anglican Church on a bright sunny Christmas Eve morning as fresh as a young chorister's smile. Five hundred guests heard the Reverend Jack Thompson pronounce them man and wife.

148

An hour later they emerged from the church on to the pavement to be surrounded by a swarm of photographers, their flash bulbs popping ineffectually against the even stronger summer light. It was with an odd sensation that Anthony heard, for the first time, his sister called by a name other than the one with which she had been christened. 'Mrs Brody, would you mind turning a little this way, please? Mr Brody, would you please smile into the camera?'

Brody tried, of course, but the result was disappointing; his lips rounded up prettily, as was their wont; he looked as if he were whistling in astonishment at finding himself in such a strange predicament as to have been recently declared the husband to some young woman.

As was to be expected, the occasion belonged entirely to Hazel Ferguson, who looked to her twin brother at that moment as radiant as the morning, as if the personality itself was decked in the gloss and polish of the jewellery that sparkled in a diadem on her hair; it was a high moment of street theatre in which movement and colour conspired so wonderfully to produce a magical image of glamour and youth that, in addition to invited guests, crowds of passers-by stopped to applaud the production.

They clapped hands spontaneously when Hazel, in her ivory silk and crepe shuddered and settled like a gorgeous butterfly in front of the cameras. For an instant, beneath the shimmering image, Anthony sensed something lethal, readying itself to inject its poison. Then the bride and bridegroom, Anthony and his mother, got into an enormous Cadillac to be driven, followed by a cavalcade of cars, through the city centre to the suburban mansion where luncheon was served in the garden under the trees, the scent of flowers perfuming the dry summer air. Later the musicians played '*It Could Happen To You*' by special request; Anthony, slightly drunk from champagne and private misery, danced with the bride on the shaved back lawn and it was as though they had never left Antoine Restaurant and its tenebrous gloom, although that had been many, many years ago, Hazel humming under her breath 'It Could Happen To You... All I thought was...'

On the other side of the fence, celebrating the same wedding, some native boys were playing on their penny-whistles and dancing a new township jazz step resembling the black American 'jitterbug'.

Chapter Eleven

MOMENTARILY trapped in the folds of his soutane the Anglican priest struggled clumsily to extricate himself. On achieving success, he emerged, grinning from behind the wheel and stood facing Cornelius. He was a small man, quite young, perhaps no more than twenty-seven, ludicrously handsome like a young girl, all dimples, golden curls and flashing teeth, but for all his prettiness Rev James Stephens' personality was possessed of a certain hard-edged quality, a dangerous flash and glitter like Sheffield steel. The two men shook hands. Then they chuckled slowly as though mightily surprised by their discovery of each other. 'So you've come at last?' Stephens said.

'I've come at last,' Molapo echoed, grinning.

Under one arm Stephens carried a folder enclosing a newspaper that was full of news regarding the state of emergency that had just been declared in the country. Apart from the reports of the usual police raids and arrests of many individuals, in a separate column the newspaper carried brief biographies of those who were said to have definitely disappeared, or who, like Cornelius Molapo were said to be unaccounted for, feared to be held 'incommunicado' somewhere by the security police. Rev Stephens thrust this folder into Molapo's hand. Grinning again, he said: 'I had no idea you also write verse in your spare time, Mr Molapo.' The young priest laughed boyishly, appreciatively. Cornelius joined in the laughter.

'Oh, I do a lot of things in my spare time, Reverend,' he said. Then he glanced briefly at the paper, at the headline which proclaimed to the world: DUBE SCHOOL-TEACHER-POET DISAPPEARS. In the photograph accompanying the news, slightly blurred and stiffly formal, Molapo's own face stared mournfully back at him; it resembled the faces normally seen in the obituary sections of the newspapers or in posters of wanted criminals. It was his, of course, but it also seemed to belong to a complete stranger, an individual with an unsavoury past. The eyes looked shifty, the mouth was slightly open, suggesting someone surprised in a moment of wrong-doing. Cornelius was pierced by a strange sensation, like someone who picks up a newspaper one morning to read about his own funeral. JB had warned him, of course, about this small lie, calculated to further the revolutionary process, as he said, but seeing the concrete results in the form of newspaper headlines, Cornelius was seized by a mild panic. To conceal his disorientation he turned to the Reverend and continued with the joke. Laughing, he said: 'I'm also fairly good at cricket, Reverend, as most people who have watched me on the stumps will tell you.'

'Yes, well, the newspaper claims you're quite accomplished at dancing the jitterbug too.' This time Molapo and the priest guffawed as if they were two old friends who were meeting after a long separation. Molapo even performed a little soft shuffle, legs bent at the knees, to demonstrate his skills.

'My, my!' the priest chuckled. 'My dear Mr Molapo, what a splendid show! Really, quite splendid!' Stephens' enthusiasm and goodwill seemed to know no bounds. And yet Cornelius sensed beneath his *bonhomie* a reservoir of unease. He had noticed this from the start, while they were shaking hands. Cornelius had the impression that the English priest was carefully studying him, taking his measure as it were. Perhaps the priest had had too many brushes with the authorities recently to feel entirely comfortable with any new contacts with political operatives. But Cornelius had no reason to complain since he was doing the same, secretly observing the young priest, sizing him up. In fact, from now on, Molapo's own survival would depend very much on a faculty of exceptional vigilance; it would depend on a detailed observation of people with whom he had to deal; he had to remember the minutest aspects of their appearance and behaviour, however trivial; he had to remember not only the sound of their voices or the shape of their bodies or the odd expression on their faces, but also such things as whether they shined their shoes in the morning or properly knotted their ties; and he had to observe how they held a cigarette between their fingers, even the way they chewed their food. For example, without even being aware of doing it, he had already quickly noted that among his many other peculiarities, the Rev Stephens laughed only with his mouth; his lapis lazuli eyes remained serious, unsmiling, fixed on Cornelius's face as though he suspected it of harbouring many indecipherable secrets. In the end Cornelius felt obliged to apologise – for what, he did not know exactly – but about something, anything!

'I'm sorry, Father, it had to be this early in the morning,' he finally said.

'Not at all,' Stephens replied, perhaps too quickly. 'Really, no need to apologise. Besides, it's the best time to arrive in Tabanyane if you do not want to arouse too much interest.'

Under the gaze of the priest Cornelius still felt ill at ease, unable to defend himself from the implacable hieratic gaze; he also wondered what sort of appearance he must present to Rev Stephens because, although he had made a feeble attempt to clean up after the beating he had received on the train, there were still bruises and weals on the left side of his face, a blood encrusted cut still showed on his lower lip and a huge bump on his forehead; mementoes of the recent encounter with the forces of law and order. The memory of the assault on the train caused Molapo to wince at the knowledge of how closely violence stalked him.

Stephens was leaning against the side of his beaten Ford, chewing a blade of grass like a young calf. Tall, thin, and stooping slightly, Cornelius reluctantly permitted himself to be appraised. He could scarcely tell what the other man was thinking but he would make a few guesses. The priest was probably saying to himself: so this is the guerrilla leader they have sent us from Johannesburg! Not a very impressive-looking specimen, is he? A man of fragile frame, tall, gangling, eyes already weakened by too much book-reading and sheltering ineffectually behind dark sunshades. Not likely to stand up to the rigours of life in the bush. The way Cornelius imagined the other was looking at him was simply because this was how he had begun to judge himself. But if this was indeed what the priest was thinking he was doing his best to hide his feelings behind a mask of affable good manners. 'I trust your journey was not very arduous, Mr Molapo?'

Cornelius cleared his throat, then explained: 'Fifty kilometres from Tabanyane we ran into an army unit, Father. They stopped the truck and searched it inch by inch, then they searched all the passengers. As you can see,' Cornelius fingered the lump on his forehead, 'they were not very gentle".'

Stephens' eyes grew wide: 'Is that the result of their work?'

'I'm afraid so, Father.' On one of the telegraph posts nearby a vulture stared disdainfully at the man and the priest. Cornelius gave a full account of the incident on the train and when he concluded his report the Anglican priest looked appalled. 'What an inauspicious start to your mission,' was Stephens' gloomy comment, but after a brief reflection, he seemed to brighten up a bit, to relax, and he said: 'Since you are here now we can only assume that they found nothing suspicious to pin on you?'

'That is correct, Father.'

Stephens paused to consider. Then in a voice full of foreboding he went on: 'It's the first time I've heard of such random checks on passenger trains. This is a very serious matter and extremely worrying. We must lose no time in letting our field workers know of these latest measures by the security forces.' As if this decision had galvanised him into action Stephens opened the boot of the car. 'Give me your bag, please, Mr Molapo.' Cornelius handed him his bag, and Stephens shoved it into the boot of the car before locking it; walking round to the other side of the car he held the passenger door open for Cornelius to get in. 'Mr Molapo, please!'

But Cornelius did not immediately get into the car. For a brief spell he stood as though arrested by a force stronger than his will, gazing with the thrill of a first encounter with the landscape of his childhood, his ear cocked to catch the tiniest sounds from the countryside, the awakening cries of birds in the nearby trees, of cattle lowing in the distant pastures. True, much had changed since his last visit, but much also remained the same. Rising over the distant hills to the east the sun had the same old dusty glow, a vague nimbus of light which had affected him powerfully as a young boy herding cattle on the plains of Tabanyane; under the first shafts of morning sunlight the mountain range, vast, steep and rugged, stood sentry above the *dorp* as it had done since time immemorial – an immense backdrop separating Tabanyane from the rest of the world. Except for the train engine behind them chugging up and down the tracks the silence over the countryside was complete. So quiet, so profound was this calm that Cornelius had the sensation of having arrived at the end of the world.

That, of course, was exactly what Tabanyane was: the end of the world; a small dot on the map of Southern Africa, the last settlement between Johannesburg and the border; beyond there was only the bush and the hostile territory of the north. To many white South Africans, beyond the border was a mythical country, a kind of hell in which unfortunate black tribes had been obliged to dredge a living under the rule of bloodthirsty black dictators. Sometimes it was even less real than that; it was a landscape similar to that projected in films after an imagined nuclear disaster but never seen in reality or properly grasped psychologically. For such people only South Africa was real,

155

and Tabanyane was its outpost, its frontier; against a vast backcloth of breathtaking scenery, Tabanyane played out its trivial conflicts, the disputes over grazing land, the tribal raids and killing of farm animals in nearby white farms; and after cattle raids the search by district police which ended inevitably in random arrests and punitive cattle seizures to replace stolen white-owned stock. As long as Cornelius could remember there had been trouble between white farmers and the Tabanyane people who year after year watched helplessly while their best land was grabbed by the Land Commission and reallocated for white settlement. Now another, deadlier conflict had arisen, and for once the local police force seemed unable to contain, unaided, the spreading violence.

After Cornelius had finally got into the car, Stephens shut the door carefully, then walked round and got into the driver's side. For a second Cornelius could see nothing but the head with its blond curls bent low over the wheel while the young priest fumbled with the ignition. 'I'm afraid we'll have to get away from here as quickly as possible, Mr Molapo,' Stephens shouted above the noise of the engine. Then with a spasm the antique Ford jerked itself into motion; all the bodywork trembled mightily as it moved off in a swirl of dust, groaning and belching exhaust fumes. 'The fact is,' Stephens began to explain, 'at the moment the countryside is crawling with Chief Sekala's spies, all in Government pay apparently, who watch every coming and going in Tabanyane.'

'So I've heard,' Cornelius vaguely responded. The priest went on to describe the deteriorating security situation in Tabanyane; inter-tribal violence; increased insurgency and counter-insurgency attacks; there were details to fill the new man in on regarding the latest arrests, on armed clashes between Paramount Chief Sekala's 'home guards' and members of the resistance movement. But Cornelius was not listening really; suddenly overcome by fatigue, he felt the dead weight of all the sleepless hours on the train pressing down on his eyelids and eyeballs and he fought against a compulsive desire to shut his eyes and go to sleep.

'As if that were not enough,' Stephens went on without a pause, 'we also have Lt-Col De Kock's men to contend with day and night!'

'De Kock?'

'He's the head of the police force in the area,' Stephens explained. 'De Kock takes a particular interest in the latest arrivals from Johannesburg. You see, many of our people who have been to the city come back highly politicised and very conscious indeed of their political rights. While in Johannesburg they join trade unions, some even come into contact with the Movement, as you well know. This accounts for some of the significant successes your man Thekwane has been having in this area.'

'Of course, that's very gratifying news for us, Father.'

The Englishman shot Molapo a quick glance, as if to make sure there was no trace of irony in his response, but he could detect nothing behind Molapo's sunshades. For about forty-five minutes Stephens drove, if rattling over ditches and pot-holes at a hundred kilometres an hour could be described as driving. He drove with astonishing recklessness, scarcely paying attention to the gaping *dongas* on the side of the road or the cattle which appeared suddenly out of nowhere. While Stephens drove he talked. 'In the past few months the situation has deteriorated considerably here,' he said. 'Not a week passes without us getting some report of yet another incident. Violence has become a way of life. Beatings. Hut burnings. Rape. Murder. It's become routine.'

A donkey lay sprawled in the middle of the road, nonchalantly beating its tail on the sand and the Reverend Father had to make a quick detour over to the side of the road in order to avoid hitting the animal. At that stage brakes were out of the question. Another time a horse, a grey mare, shot across the winding road, giving Father Stephens only a poor second in which to pull the car up sharply in front of the animal. The horse whinnied, rearing up in the air. Stephens swore like a trooper. When the dust settled Cornelius saw again, with a stark sort of clarity, the mountains rising steeply and jaggedly above the early morning mist. It was with a feeling of a profound dread that he registered them, thinking of the secret passes through which his men would come down in order to launch strikes against Chief Sekala and the Government forces. Above the mist and the mountains the sky was a rinsed radiant blue, with the kind of immanent purity which only an African sky can have.

Ironically, though a native of the country, it was Cornelius who, utterly overwhelmed by the majesty of the landscape, showed himself to be something of a foreigner; on the other hand, the Anglican priest seemed so much part of the land-scape that there was nothing much to distinguish between him and the thorn-trees or the *khakibos* that was sprinkled about the hillside. Stephens had suddenly become silent and ruminative, his fair hair blowing gently in the breeze as he drove. The road twisted and turned, then rose sharply up the incline of a hill; when it had reached the summit Cornelius could see below them over on the other side, sunk deep into the navel of the valley, the white buildings of the Anglican mission; the mud-walled chapel with its white-painted wooden cross; behind it the clinic where a straggling queue of people was already beginning to form, and the school with its sandy playgrounds – empty, this being Saturday.

'There it is,' Stephens said as they began their descent. 'Not a very impressive place by most standards, I admit, but we do our best.'

'I'm sure you do a great deal more than your best, Father.'

Again suspecting irony, Stephens took a sharp glance at Cornelius, but again he could detect nothing. The priest's impulses were of the simplest. In the bush he lived among people constantly harassed by lawless elements; in Tabanyane danger and violence were the daily bread no-one had ever prayed for. He began to talk again of political conflict in his obsessive way. Rather pointedly he told Cornelius: 'Very often our people out here feel completely on their own, though of course we have seen a great deal of one-night-stand visitors, even from as far afield as the UK and the United States. People come out here with the obvious intention of building up their credentials. You know the type I'm talking about. They come out here and hop around taking snapshots of some burnt huts and then go back to hold press conferences calling for US troops to be sent in to sort us out.'

When Cornelius refused to be drawn Father Stephens went on undeterred: 'The great danger, of course, is that our people may be led to react to this situation without properly assessing some of the considerable risks inherent in it. What they'll need, Mr Molapo, is wise political guidance. I don't know how much you appreciate the full extent of the problem here, but since the late paramount chief died there has been an immense vacuum created in the leadership. Prince Diliza, I'm sorry to say, is perennially indisposed. A broken reed is what he seems to be, if I may put it that way. Quite frankly, the fellow seems completely demoralised, completely out of his depth.'

'I've heard that his sister enjoys considerable support among the people,' Molapo suggested in a not very subtle attempt to draw out the Anglican priest on the subject of the princess. It was well-known inside the Movement that the Reverend James Stephens was greatly taken with Princess Madi. JB had stressed the importance of this alliance between the princess and the church. Since Madi's return to Tabanyane, leaving behind in England a young English lord who had thought nothing of proposing marriage to an African woman despite the evident horror and despair of parents and relatives – perhaps he had anticipated the displeasure which was why he had proposed in the first place – the princess and the Anglican priest had become locked in one of those emotional relationships from which neither party knows how to break out without inflicting incalculable damage to the self, let alone to the other. All the more delicate and sensitive was the relationship for being complicit rather than explicit.

With her wry sense of humour Madi sometimes tried to laugh it off: 'With his golden curls and dimpled chin,' she told her closest friends, 'he reminds me so much of my Robert, my English ex-fiancé!'

When Madi's young English lord had proposed marriage and, not unexpectedly, met with outraged opposition from his ancient family, the besotted aristocrat tried patiently to explain to his mother that Madi was not just another African girl but a princess in her own right; that, but for her colour, there was nothing to hinder the marriage since they both belonged to the same class. In response to that ridiculous argument Robert's widowed mother observed scornfully: 'My dear, in their country they are all princes and princesses; for them distinctions of class don't mean anything!'

Nevertheless, the doomed Robert persisted; and after numerous councils of war with aunts and uncles, at last the grand dame yielded, but too late. It was Princess Madi, not the English lord, who backed out. She told her intimate friends: 'Marriage between Robert and me, I now realise, was of course out of the question from the very beginning. Robert's extended family, all his treasured uncles and aunts, to say nothing of his darling mama, would've made life intolerable. And I couldn't have given up my own family to live permanently in England.' Everyone recognised she was being brave, and while saying all this her full purple lips trembled slightly and tears welled up in her large brown eyes, for the belief in the impossibility of this marriage had done nothing to appease the periodic longing for the Englishman, at least for a temporary return to the bosom of that English class which, while rejecting her for her colour, had on many occasions contradictorily shown its gratitude for an alliance between this aristocratic class and the traditional rulers of Africa and Asia in the face of bourgeois ascendancy at home and proletariat revolutions abroad.

At any rate, JB's suggestion was now proving, if anything,

only too well-founded. At the first mention of Princess Madi's name the priest's eyes turned shiny liquid with admiration. 'A very remarkable woman, Mr Molapo! A very remarkable woman!' he enthused. 'Princess Madi is quite an exceptional personality with whom it has been my greatest privilege to work very closely. As you know, she is running our mission clinic single-handed. A doctor chap comes twice a week for medical check-ups and surgery but for the rest of the time it is very much Princess Madi's affair. The work she has been doing among the people has proved invaluable both from the point of view of the Church's standing and as part of our expression of solidarity with their resistance to tyranny in this part of the world.'

A very strange man this Stephens was: dedicated to the church, he had none of the tranquillity it presumably offered, and seemed haunted and troubled, with eyes which seemed always to be making an appeal for something to which the priest dared not give a name. Cornelius said: 'I'm looking forward very much to meeting the Princess, Father.'

'And so you shall,' Stephens promised. 'And so you shall.'

By any standards the princess was not a pretty woman but she was endowed with a strong personality, tempered by an overflow of natural affection which had quickly found favour among the best English families, some of whom still remembered seeing photographs of her great grandfather, the founder of the Modibo Seeiso dynasty, riding in a carriage with Her Imperial Majesty, Queen Victoria, near the end of her reign. Seeiso was every inch a king: silent, proud, remote. Seeiso was one of them; therefore, so was his daughter, but of course not quite. Madi's training as a nurse, it was generally assumed, was no more than a tactic frequently resorted to by the best families in order to form the character of a young girl; to give her, so to speak, something worthwhile to do while she waited for the right husband to come along.

At St Mary's Hospital where she had trained as a nurse the English girls deferred to Madi Seeiso, as did members of staff.

161

She was often chosen for the most important tasks. When Princess Antoinette of Belgium chose to come to the hospital for her confinement, it was Madi Seeiso – along with a carefully selected set of English girls – who assisted at the birth of the royal baby. The photographs which later appeared in the English newspapers showed an African girl, not very pretty but cheerful and personable, fondly holding a blond infant to the cameras while the happy mother looked on admiringly from her bed. Some time later the same African girl could be seen during her days off in the company of Lady Cavell, a well-known philanthropist and campaigner for obscure causes, exchanging gossip over cups of tea in the Dorchester. Still cheerful but now almost pretty in expensive silks and tulle, the same girl subsequently caused a flutter by turning up at Annabel's on the limp arm of Lord Beaumont, who had recently stirred an even greater flutter himself by announcing that he was using part of the family fortune to set up a foundation which would help to rescue Soviet dissidents – some cynics said from the misery of the East to the malady of the West. Such was the burden of memories which the princess kept stored up in her silted heart. Such was the nostalgia which tied her to Great Britain by an invisible string, such the commemorative joys of London which she now shared mostly with young Rev James Stephens in the solitude of the long nights at the foothills of the Tabanyane mountains.

After another twenty minutes Rev Stephens' old Ford threaded its way into the grounds of the Tabanyane Anglican Mission where a dormitory room had been set aside for the Movement's representative. The Tabanyane Anglican Mission combined the boarding school, the clinic where Princess Madi Seeiso was sole mistress, and the Anglican Church, which also contained the administrative offices where the Rev James Stephens held sway. Except on the special occasions when His Grace was expected to attend, the Bishop kept very much to his residence in Rustenburg. Being Saturday, it was a cleaning and gardening day for the boarders, mostly boys between the ages of fifteen and nineteen; the majority of them were armed with pails and mops for scouring dormitories and classrooms.

At the approach of Stephens' old Ford they set the cleaning paraphernalia down and saluted him with great pomp. The priest, who was accustomed to the routine was not greatly impressed. 'Mkgoti!' Stephens called out to a youth in rolled up khaki trousers. 'Go on, open the gate!' When the gates were rolled back Stephens drove through at his habitual reckless speed and came to a screeching stop in front of a quandrangle building which comprised, among other things, the guesthouse of the Anglican Mission. Assisted by the boy who carried the bags, Molapo and the priest climbed the staircase leading to the guestrooms. At the door of one, Stephens searched the pockets of his cassock for a bunch of keys, inserting one into the keyhole. 'Here you are, Mr Molapo,' Stephens announced, cheerfully throwing the door open. 'For a while this will be your hill station, your campsite, your pensione, wigwam, your pad!' Stephens laughed.

Having deposited his guest in his room the priest wasted no time in tearing across the grounds of the mission to the clinic to report to the princess. Molapo listened cautiously to the retreating footsteps of the Anglican priest until the door on the ground floor was banged shut before rushing up to the window through which he carefully checked his location, paying special attention to all means of quick exit in case of emergency. The guestroom in which he was installed for the duration of his stay at the Anglican mission before leaving for the mountains was on the top floor. It was a small room, extremely neat and quiet, and containing a single bed with a white bedspread, a wardrobe, a work table and two chairs. There were two windows, one overlooking the quadrangle, the other giving out on a view of fields rolling away in undulating waves to the edge of a dense bush; and farther north the land first dipped down to some kind of wooded ravine before rising steeply to the foot of the Tabanyane mountains. The road by which Cornelius and the priest had driven to the mission was half concealed by the stretches of mealie fields with their dry, half shrunken stalks rising no taller than the height of a small child.

For a while, too exhausted even to fall asleep, Cornelius walked about the room like a somnambulist, trying to think about his immediate future. His instructions were clear enough; he had with him a list of people with whom he had to establish rapid contact: Thekwane and his combat unit for a start; then he had to meet the men drawn mostly from the Tabanyane Resistance Movement over whom, it was hoped, with the acquiescence of the elders of Tabanyane, especially the formidable Princess Madi, Cornelius was to exercise supervision. Other individuals he had also been advised to contact: obscure elders, clerks, land surveyors, commercial travellers, some of them extremely visible but for all that never suspected of belonging to the 'underground'. They included a car-park attendant in front of the Meerdaal Hotel who spoke excellent Afrikaans, the blind beggar on the steps of the Standard Bank, and many other seemingly unimportant individuals, a good example of people who were every day exposed to the public gaze but whom no-one ever noticed. They were people whom the NLM had found it useful to recruit, people now working either full-time or part-time for the Movement.

Then there was Madi Seeiso, of course. For the time being Cornelius wanted to devote his mind entirely to working out the best way to win Princess Madi's complete confidence. It was not going to be that easy.

From all that he had been told about the princess, from the scraps of gossip and innuendo, as well as what he judged to be hard facts, Cornelius tried to assemble a picture of Madi Seeiso which would guide his judgement as to the best approach; nevertheless, however much he tried he failed to grasp the true nature of the woman's personality. Each time he tried he was confronted by a mass of contradictory details, a confusing mixture of irrelevant facts and malicious gossip. To

164

sort these out would require time, certainly a face-to-face meeting. But it was clear to him that this was no time to begin his inquiry. After an all-night train journey to Tabanyane in which he had been subjected to assault and other forms of abuse he wasn't in good shape to do much hard thinking; his torpid mind kept slipping away to other less pressing matters: to thoughts of Maureen, to Margot Silverman and her enviably uncomplicated embrace of the world's suffering masses; to JB and the Movement. It was nearly noon and the world outside, remote and insensate, dozed under a blue sky. Shadows had almost disappeared and the blazing sun had driven the unmilked cows to seek shelter under the shade of the thorn trees. In the shimmer of late morning heat the colours seemed to have been drained out of familiar objects, leaving them bare and bone dry like X-ray skeletons. After stomping up and down the room Molapo peered through the window again and caught sight of a figure on the edge of a maize field urgently responding to the call of nature. The tableau was not without humour, for Cornelius noted that the man who was evacuating himself in unadorned nature seemed to be wearing some kind of black suit and, to top it all, something like a homburg hat. The man was crouched over a small ditch; and after emptying his bowels he used a piece of stone to clean himself rapidly; then hitching up his pants he stood for a while motionless, gazing at the far horizon with an air of hopelessness, Molapo thought. Under the eaves of the guesthouse roof an invisible bird warbled suddenly with amazing sweetness, as if applauding man's perennial surrender to the call of nature. For some time Molapo remained standing by the window; then resumed his walk about the little room like a fly trapped in a glass jar.

Recently his waking hours had been marked by incredible fluctuations of moods, from states of unprecedented lightness and release, states close to joyous intoxication or religious ecstasy on the one hand, to feelings of profound depression on the other. Voices long forgotten, speaking alternately in tones of urgent warning or in cadences of cautious friendliness, seductive voices or stern voices, came to him at odd hours of day or night, in sleep or wakefulness. Among his mother's people, the Zulus of northern Natal, it would have been decided that he was about to become a recipient of some rare spiritual insights from ancestral spirits, *amadlozi*. These states were followed by moments of complete stillness when he felt like a man waiting for a sign. Such a moment was now. In some dusty cobweb-covered volume he had once read: 'To attain a state of lucidity... one must make one's way through many underground passages.' A foolish passage, scribbled perhaps in a momentary loss of nerves by a friendless monk. Was this then his own 'underground passage', or merely one more station along a tortuous route toward an impossible goal? Cornelius sensed again that inattentive wandering of the mind which had attacked him during that first lap of the journey out of Tabanyane station; he heard again in his inner ear, like the return of a recurrent nightmare, the ceaseless drone of the car engine and the endless flow of words from that talkative priest, and felt a kind of relief that he had been left alone for the time being.

Overcome by fatigue, Cornelius extracted from his shoulder-bag a torn copy of the *Phenomenology*, and stripping down to his underpants he lay on the small bed and for a few minutes read several passages at random; he read without pleasure, slowly, like a man in a trance, already on the edge of self-forgetfulness, ready to enter that night in which every cow is black.

Half walking and half-running, the Reverend James Stephens arrived at the clinic in a flurry of excitement, nearly out of breath, obviously in a state of great agitation. 'Well, Princess, the man is here at last!' he announced. 'He got off the train this morning. I don't know what to make of him yet but – ' Stephens stopped, breathing quickly and looking expectant, as if waiting for applause. But in this he was disappointed.

Madi Seeiso did not look up. She was bent over a wounded man; a tall woman, slightly plump but well-proportioned, she was favoured with an enormous rump that was the joy and secret erotic dream of every schoolboy in the district. Watching how, when she walked, one buttock went up when the other descended, young boys and grown men longed to run their hands over the princess's behind; shamelessly they wove elaborate fantasies around it and apparently even the priest was not immune to Princess Madi's earthly charms. Indeed, on the subject of Princess Madi's alluring shape, as in the appreciation of the finer points of feminine beauty and perfection in general, Father Stephens saw no reason not to concur with general African male opinion. After all, it was the Reverend Father's boast to have acquired over the years an African perspective with regard to the enjoyment of physical beauty. In support of this claim, he often contrasted Madi Seeiso's well-rounded shape favourably with the contourless bodies of the white women among whom he often claimed it was his eternal regret to have grown up.

On this particular morning he seemed insensible to the Princess's very considerable charms, however.

'I was there when the train got in,' he continued. 'It seems there was a small incident on the train but apart from that everything apparently worked as smooth as clockwork!' Flushed with heat and excitement, Stephens was trying very hard to calm himself but without any noticeable success. He seemed to want to tell more than the words were capable of communicating. But what? Impatience, anger, perhaps also a faint hope that somehow history was at last being shaped by human will. Many well-read people, intelligent, thoughtful people, were now in the habit of talking grandly about the 'end of history', but as Father Stephens had often told his friends back in England, one of the big attractions of living in South Africa was just this feeling of always living close to the pulse of historical events, always having to adjust to great shocks, like an army which must know when to move into positions vacated by the enemy but also when to retreat when its own positions are threatened.

Madi did not seem very excited at the news, in fact seemed scarcely to have heard Stephens. When the princess continued to maintain her silence, the priest experienced one of his rare irritations with the inexhaustible equanimity of Africans. He wanted to grasp the princess by the shoulder and shake her into a state of full consciousness. He wanted to seize her face and turn it towards himself and say, 'Look here, Princess, at least they've sent us a man to take charge of the great campaign against Sekala! It means that even the National Movement is taking our struggle seriously!', and in his state of thwarted desire, speech was Rev Stephens' only release; filled with uncheckable zeal he resumed his harangue with undiminished ardour. He spoke of the arrival of Cornelius Molapo as the three wise men might have spoken of the arrival of the Messiah: 'He is sleeping now,' he explained to the princess. 'Getting some rest, I dare say, after the night's ordeal on the train. Naturally, I advised him to keep indoors until we know the lie of the land.' With a great illuminated smile the priest finished off with a flash of impish humour. 'Your Highness will be glad to know I carried out your instructions to the letter. Even Thekwane, the man you love to hate, has agreed to attend tonight's meeting. As for Phiri, I know we can count on the man to keep his word without fail. He loves war, or at least, he loves fighting Sekala, as some of us love a wedding party.'

Only then did the princess raise herself to her full height, at the same time turning round to face the priest. 'James, just look at your collar,' she said reproachfully. 'Try and straighten your dress a bit. You look an awful mess.'

Stephens laughed, perhaps with relief at even this small acknowledgement, like a young girl who has just been told that her knickers are showing. 'So I do indeed,' he said amicably. Without further comment the princess resumed her work. In her starched white uniform and cap, surrounded by bottles of sharp-smelling drugs and ointments, the princess was bent over a man whose wound she was dressing, her hands swift, strong, capable yet gentle, the healing hands of a woman whose outward show of firmness contained a vast reservoir of inner compassion. Indifferent to the man's howl of pain she dabbed ointments into the wound; she put on lint, then bandages; and all the while Princess Madi Seeiso, graduate of St Mary's Hospital, Paddington, London, was thinking with part of her mind what to do with the school-teacher before he disappeared entirely into the bush, or fell, as sometimes happened, into the hands of De Kock's forces of law and order. After a prolonged silence she turned to Stephens: 'Is this Molapo bunking with you then or what?' the princess enquired.

'He's occupying one of the guestrooms in the boys' dormitories,' Stephens replied, trying to straighten his collar as he had just been advised to do. 'I thought that was the plan. Mind you,' he quickly added, looking apprehensively at the princess, 'the mission would prefer him to move on to somewhere more discreet as quickly as possible.'

Madi was amused by Stephens' nervous agitation. Smiling, she said: 'You mean you'd rather not get too involved? I suppose that's natural. Everyone is anxious not to get too involved. Guerrilla fighters bring nothing but trouble wherever they stay.'

Stephens became unusually defensive. 'Well, it's a big risk the mission is taking, or rather which I am taking. You must understand that the bishop is not being informed about any of this, which doesn't make my sleep any easier. You know the man's concern for strict rectitude as far as the laws of the country are concerned. If it ever came out that we're harbouring a guerrilla – ' Rev Stephens was interrupted by an uproar.

'Nurse! Nurse!' A man's agonised cry came. 'Help me, O Royal Daughter of the Departed Lion!'

All faces turned quickly to where the man who had so unceremoniously cried out lay in a heap of physical pain, his limbs trembling as if touched by a cold breeze.

In the middle of the night Sekala's men had broken into a circle of huts on the fringes of Malaita location; they had dragged the men out, systematically breaking their bones or chopping off their fingers with sharpened *pangas* before killing them or leaving them for dead. This man, whose face was now twisted into a coil of agony, was a survivor of the massacre.

'What is it now?' the princess called out without moving.

'My leg! Oh, Royal One! Help me! I think my leg is leaving me altogether!' An orderly tried to lift his leg into a more comfortable position.

'Have courage, *Nthate*! Your leg will not leave you just yet. The doctor will soon be here to look at it.' The princess did not leave the bedside of the man whose wound she was dressing. The clinic had started to operate as a kind of field hospital: the surgery was full of wounded fighters, casualties of the now all too frequent night skirmishes with security forces and Sekala's bandits. At noon it was stiflingly hot in the white-painted ward and the smell of medicine stung the nostrils like the caustic bite of metal; frightened and isolated from their families, the sick and the injured men worried about the visits from the security branch who would surely want to know how they came by their injuries. For this reason as much as for lack of space, those who had been attended to, those who could walk or be carried away by relatives, were dispatched as quickly as possible. The rhythm of this day was the same as any other; sweating, tired out with effort, the princess absent-mindedly patted a wound she had been dressing and she felt the wounded man wince with pain.

Her mind still on the Movement's representative, she cast a quick glance at the Rev Stephens and urged him impatiently: 'Go on, James, I'm listening. So what kind of a man is this Molapo?'

Before speaking, Stephens cast furtive glances around him. There was a lot he wished to tell the princess but a part of his mind worried about lack of privacy. Inside the large room of the clinic there was a constant movement of people trying to attract the attention of hard-pressed orderlies. There were screams of pain. Stephens would have preferred to discuss the details of what he had learned about the Movement's representative away from the unnerving environment of the wounded. Above all, the priest stood in great fear of a vast network of informers who were said to operate everywhere, even in the most unlikely places. Lift a stone anywhere, it was said, and beneath it you would find an informer. Madi Seeiso seemed to take no notice of the possible proximity of eaves-droppers, no doubt because she knew that, almost without exception, the people who came to the clinic for treatment were simple peasants who spoke no English; there was very little chance anyone would understand what they were talking about; the man in front of them might as well have been deaf for all he was able to glean from the conversation going on under his very nose.

'What kind of man is Molapo?' Stephens repeated Madi's question to himself. 'It's hard to say,' he replied cautiously, trying to evade the question; then laughing in his usual boyish manner, he added: 'Don't forget it was six in the morning when I picked him up at the station. I suppose at that hour it's too early really to make a proper judgement.'

There were times when, even in her best frame of mind, Madi Seeiso found Stephens' evasiveness exasperating. She supposed it had something to do with his middle-class English upbringing, the propensity not to call anything by its name where a euphemism would do; she could still remember how irritating she found reading English newspapers when, to avoid describing a public figure as drunk and disorderly, the newspapers resorted to formulae such as 'tired and emotional'. Brusquely she said: 'Come, come, James, even at that early hour of morning you must have exchanged more than the usual courtesies. At least, you must have talked with him long enough to form an impression.'

Something in her posture, crouching, covert, solicitous,

reassured Stephens and he told her everything he had learned about Molapo: the story of his stormy marital life, his immoderate drinking, his visionary poetry written to celebrate the secret corners of a heart defeated in love and in politics, his shifting moods of carnival play, dancing the jitterbug in the Orlando Halls and his celebrated game of cricket – all the titbits which Stephens had learned from the gossip column of the newspaper and from Molapo himself as they drove from the station that morning, but none of which he had been able to gather into a coherent unity of personality. 'A proud man,' at last Stephen felt at liberty to say of Molapo. 'Yes, a bit touchy I would say, quick to take offence, that was my first impression of him. He laughed too readily at my bad jokes, but a genial fellow all the same. Pretty well-informed about the current situation here.'

Her curiosity obviously provoked, the princess became meditative. Finally she said: 'Well, I hope this Molapo doesn't think he is here to give orders to country nincompoops! That's the first mistake they all make, to think us simple peasants. The Tabanyane Resistance Movement will co-operate with anyone prepared to join arms against that murderous rogue, my uncle Sekala, but we'll not be ordered around by individuals who come out here claiming to know what's best for us.'

Stephens, who liked to think of himself as one of the closest counsellors to the House of Seeiso, and in times of his most exalted states of mind even considered himself a member of the inner magic circle, was inclined to regard the princess as a bit impetuous and in need of his political and spiritual guidance. Sometimes he felt that Madi needed to exercise restraint in her zeal to preserve the initiative of the royal family. But the truth was that he was most critical of these weaknesses because, paradoxically, they were what most attracted him to her: Madi's perverse, almost juvenile peevishness, her rash defiance of the odds ranged against her. 'They have the arms, don't forget, Your Highness,' Stephens now gently pointed out to the princess. 'Against Sekala's bandits and the security forces, all armed to the teeth apparently, without the aid of the superior arms and training provided by the NLM the Tabanyane Resistance Movement can only offer token resistance.'

'Of that I'm only too aware, James. You needn't remind me all the time,' the princess retorted. Turning away from her patient for a moment she said to Stephens: 'The fact that we are weak doesn't mean we are ready to submit to become the convenient tools of the NLM in its struggles to achieve world revolution.'

A diehard conservative in everything but her people's right to land and self determination, for the princess 'restoration' of these rights, and not revolution, was the limit of Tabanyane ambition. She was not impressed with the National Liberation Movement's agenda of creating a new social order in which no-one would own anything and everything would be held in common. During a protracted secret meeting arranged to forge a working alliance between the Movement and the Tabanyane Resistance, one of Princess Madi's counsellors had asked Thekwane, the leader of the bush fighters: 'When you say everything will be held in common, do you mean as in the old days when King Seeiso held the land in trust for the entire nation? Or do you mean we must share everything, even our sleeping mats and blankets, including our wives in your new social heaven?'

Thekwane had laughed, treating the question as a joke. 'We must share everything, *Nthathe*! Everything. No-one must go without. The people shall share the wealth of the country!' These exchanges had not remained amicable for long, though. Recalling the debate, which later became too heated, the princess still smarted from what Thekwane, the underground leader, had shouted at her. He had described the alliance between the NLM and the Tabanyane Resistance Movement as 'a marriage of convenience'. She said to Stephens: 'Don't think I have forgotten what that man Thekwane said to me to

173

my face. He said, 'Your family and the class it represents remind us of a certain species of bird now considered extinct. That bird is called *i-dodo*.' That is what that man Thekwane said. At least he was frank with me but I hope this Molapo doesn't talk like that man Thekwane.'

'I doubt it,' Stephens laughed. 'He seemed to me more conciliatory and full of respect for the House of Seeiso.'

'You mean he is more diplomatic?' the princess corrected.

'Well, there's no harm in being diplomatic.' Then Stephens quickly added: 'As I understand it, the NLM has many tendencies of which the Marxist-Leninist is only one. Certainly, the nationalist wing is one of the strongest.'

'I hope so,' Madi said. 'I very much hope so!'

A man had quietly entered the clinic and now stood just inside the door. 'Here is Sam already,' the priest said, staring across the room. The doctor was a tall handsome man with a long square head and an unusually long nose for an African, upon which on any normal day hung a pair of steel-rimmed glasses behind which his eyes flashed like lanterns. He wore a darkish brown suit and a white coat, from one of whose pockets dangled a stethoscope. The doctor flexed the fingers of his hands as if readying himself for performing an operation; they were strong but supple hands. The doctor's only frailty of feature was a large mouth which had soft, sensuous corners.

'I'd better go.' Stephens smiled his quick, watchful smile. 'If I were you, I wouldn't worry too much about Molapo, Princess. Who knows, you and he may even like each other.'

Without knowing why Madi felt irritated by Stephens' tone. 'James, whose side are you on, I wonder?'

Stephens blushed like a young girl, his silky cheeks dimpling prettily. 'Yours, naturally, whatever your side is supposed to be,' he said, smiling. 'Of course, I am under the impression we're all on the same side, you and I, the Tabanyane Resistance Movement and the NLM. The Church stands by its commitment to defend, with whatever resources are at its disposal, the security and integrity of the Tabanyane people. That much we've always made clear even to the Government in Pretoria. What we are not committed to, by any means, is a policy of revolutionary violence – that much is known to all concerned, I think. See you tonight. Make sure to bring your soul with you!'

The princess started to say something but Stephens was already flouncing out of the room, pausing only to greet the doctor at the door.

'Morning, Sam!'

Chapter Twelve

WHAT Molapo did not know while trying to make himself comfortable in that little guestroom which resembled a clean, well-lit prison cell, was that on the other side of the Anglican mission, the princess was at that very moment completing her morning's work and getting ready to pay him a visit. What the princess called her 'normal day' was about to begin and she had decided this would include a quick call on the new arrival in Tabanyane. After making her rounds of clinic beds she handed over to a younger nurse and hurried over to her humble residence in the nurses' compound.

The simple thatched-roof cottage was separated from the nurses' home by a hedge, surrounded in turn by barbed wire, which insured a certain amount of security and privacy for the princess and her guests when she had occasion to entertain, which was not very often these days, what with the war and the constant call to duty, day and night. War meant an endless stream of casualties passing through the clinic and little free time for personal enjoyment. There were times when the princess, in a sudden rage of frustration, yearned for a return to the dives and clubs of European cities where she had spent her youth among the privileged. It was a temporary weakness, of course, a temptation she quickly stifled; for after all, she would quickly remind herself, her place was here among her own people. As a last resort, in moments of intense loneliness there was always the young Anglican priest to turn to for spiritual and intellectual comfort.

While she took a shower – the shower was one of the few luxuries Madi had insisted upon when she returned from Europe – she allowed her mind to dwell a little on the man the Movement had sent up from Johannesburg to take over the leadership of the Tabanyane campaign against Paramount Chief Sekala. Under normal circumstances the princess was known to be a woman of inquisitive mind, eager to meet people from all walks of life and to gather whatever scraps of information were there to be gleaned; with so much going on now, with the choking traffic in men and ideas moving through Tabanyane like water through a filter, Madi was in her element. To Stephens she had done her best to pretend no more than a mild interest in this Cornelius Molapo, but left to herself her eagerness to meet the Movement's representative became a pressing need. Molapo might be present at her 'little dinner party' later that evening but there would be other people to distract his attention, other people to distract her own attention, and long before she had emerged from her shower the princess had already decided she would not wait until the evening before making the acquaintance of this latest arrival in Tabanyane.

When, an hour later, Princess Madi entered the guestroom, making as little noise as possible, she found Molapo fast asleep on the narrow single bed from which a white bedspread had been carelessly removed. Completely naked except for a pair of trunks he lay on top of a blanket, his long thin legs spread out wide and ungainly over the edge of the narrow bed, his mouth slightly open and a thin trickle of saliva oozing down the side of his cheek. Although the window was open the room was stiflingly hot; the dense noonday heat had closed in around everything, it seemed to vibrate for a minute in the motionless air, making the princess feel her own skin growing pricklish with heat under her fresh underclothes, as if invisible insects were crawling up the small of her back. From under her arms and where her heavy breasts were gathered up into the cups of the soft cloth of her brassiere, droplets of sweat stole down the sides of her body. Molapo, drenched in sweat, seemed to float before her on a tide of noonday heat; the man lay unconscious, the discarded bedcovers trailing over the side and the bottom of the bed, and standing in the middle of the room the princess watched him with the stupid fascination of a young cow.

Molapo had been reading a book before he fell asleep; the book lay face down, abandoned, the pages half-crushed by its fall from the hands which had held it. Out of curiosity Madi bent down to pick up the much-thumbed volume; she stepped close to the window to read passages which were heavily underlined in pencil; she read without any understanding but with complete absorption, like a child discovering expressions of unique value. Obviously, the book contained a lot of nonsense; the writer talked a great deal about 'split identities', or about what he called the 'unity of identities' in which objects discovered their true characteristics in the qualities of their opposite numbers: 'So that to use the previous examples,' the writer argued, 'what tastes sweet is really, or inwardly in the thing, sour.'

Remembering the English lord she had left behind the princess wondered about this; who was the 'sweet' and who was the 'sour', she or Robert? But perhaps it did not matter. She read on: 'the function of "measure" is immoderation'; more obscure phrases and also casual remarks that were so obvious they did not seem to her to be profound truths at all. She read: 'Just as everything is useful to man, so man is useful too, and his vocation is to make himself a member of the group ... The extent to which he looks after his own interests must also be matched by the extent to which he serves others ... one hand washes the other.' In any case, that she could understand; it was an African expression. The Ngunis said: 'The cow licks the one that licks it in turn.' After a while, partly to announce her presence in the room and partly out of

178

disappointment with what she read, she let the book drop with a clatter from her hand but the noise, it seemed, was hardly sufficient to wake up the Movement's representative. So the princess coughed loudly.

When Cornelius opened one eye he saw a woman standing by the window, completely still, who appeared to have been looking out of the window into the grounds of the mission. Now her back was turned to the window and she stood facing him. The woman was tallish, plump but not fat, with thick black hair which was severely brushed back from a face which, while not pretty, was strongly featured and pleasant to look at; in profile, half-turned away from him, the curve of her jaw was impressive, the noonday light from the window glanced down from a small nose to the mouth which was full but with an expression of girlish petulance. For a wild moment, still drugged with sleep, Cornelius thought he must be dreaming but, when the woman finally moved to the centre of the room, looking down on him with an arch smile that was half mocking and half-serious, he saw that he was not, after all, dreaming. Now fully awake, he scrambled for the bed-covers with which he hastily wrapped the lower half of his body. 'How did you – ?'

'Get in here?' the woman smiled. 'That was simple. The door was open. I walked in. For a freedom fighter you take a very relaxed attitude to your own security.' She had a pleasant, bouncing voice, provocative, energetic, with a slight English lilt to her African English – the mocking tone might have been taken as an African form of irony or it might have been English, depending on the hearer.

'I didn't expect to have a visitor so soon,' Cornelius grumbled. 'I've only just got here.' Under the bedcover he began to slip on his trousers. He wished the woman would shift her position slightly to the left where she could block the light from the window. The glare of sunlight had a shattering impact on the eyeball. Because of the intense heat Molapo's mind was moving much slower than he could have wished; sleepiness made him irritable and the woman's presence in the room reminded him unhappily of another visit not so long ago when the Movement's emissary came to deliver a message at his Dube home. He could still remember the shabby dark suit one size too small for the man's body, and the big homburg hat a size too big for the small head. 'Please, make yourself at home,' he invited the woman in a tone that suggested the opposite.

The alien female began apologising in a bantering tone that suggested apologies were not part of her make-up: 'I'm sorry to have caught you . . . '

'With my pants down,' Cornelius interrupted. 'Well, you very nearly did. I wasn't expecting anyone, you see, at least until this afternoon.' Cornelius looked about the room like someone trying to get his bearings. 'It's so hot in here I decided to strip to my bare essentials.'

The princess waved a negligent hand in the air. 'Please, don't trouble yourself with such things. I've looked at many men before without any clothes on. Men of many races and colours. You could say I have had a lot of experience with naked men.'

For the first time in what seemed like ages Cornelius chuckled with real enjoyment. He said: 'You must be Princess Madi!'

'And you must be Teacher Molapo,' she replied. They shook hands but when Cornelius drew up one of the two chairs for his visitor the princess declined, saying: 'Thank you. I prefer to sit on the bed, if you don't mind. Why did you immediately say, you must be Princess Madi when I spoke of my having a lot of experience with naked men? Am I that notorious?'

'I was sure you were only alluding to your noble profession of caring for the sick and the maimed, Princess Madi.' Cornelius smiled, settling down in the chair the princess had just refused.

'Sick men, maimed men, naked men,' the princess cawed. 'They're all the same. They're like small frightened children who need a reassuring hand in the dark. And Tabanyane is very dark at the moment and full of sick, maimed and very naked men.'

From the courtyard below came the sound of voices, the older schoolboys on their way to the dining hall, singing songs of incredible gaiety and obscenity, as if for the youngsters the two qualities were inseparable: 'When I was young and my grandmother was alive, under the blanket my grandfather's *knobkerrie* was standing up!' they sang.

The princess smiled. 'Just listen to that!' And commented more disapprovingly: 'In Tabanyane, it seems, even a church mission is no Garden of Eden!' then she added reflectively: 'A whole generation is growing up which has never known any childhood, which has never been young. Truly, a generation of vipers, I call them!'

'They're war children,' Cornelius said. 'They've known only limited peace in one another's arms.'

The singing in the dining hall had increased in volume and obscenity; a particularly trilling voice, chaste, and as yet unbroken, rose above the rest, singing: 'When I was young and birds flew higher than a missile could hit, my uncle's youngest wife's was the only fur I was content to touch.'

The princess broke into laughter. 'I never knew vipers could sing so sweetly!' she said, leaning back on the bed and watching Cornelius with her amused brown eyes. In silence they listened to the schoolboys' repertoire of bawdy songs, Cornelius suddenly affected by a nostalgia for a world which was still innocent and fresh. Seizing on the motif of the song, he said: 'When I was young, I thought a church mission was something sanctified, a holy ground inhabited by saints who had already traversed the distance between our fallen state and the realm of celestial redemption. A kind of paradise on earth, you understand, in which it was possible to catch the odour of eternal salvation. I dare say children have a funny notion about these things.'

'And the adults?' As if trying to capture the dying cadences

181

of the obscene song, the princess leaned her head slightly toward the window. 'I used to know an old woman once who was so convinced that the Red Sea and River Jordan were in heaven that she stubbornly refused to believe poor Malik's forebears at the Arab shop in town came from a place on the banks of the Jordan. She thought anything which was in the Bible happened in the other world. These days young people know better than to give a second thought to our holy places and institutions. Only the other day Father Stephens was telling me one of the boys wanted to know if Jesus Christ ever had an erection when he was still a boy? Imagine wanting to know something like that.' Madi shook her head.

The princess shifted to the edge of the bed, and Cornelius noted that despite the abruptness of these movements she gave the impression of total intimacy with her surroundings. She was bright and alert, her eyes like brown pebbles on a river bed. She said: 'I suppose you know why I'm here?' Fingering her necklace, a large bead rolled uncertainly into the dark hollow between the rising swell of her enormous breasts.

Molapo was startled by the suddenness of the question. 'I expect you wish to acquaint yourself with the man who is to liaise between the forces of the National Liberation and Tabanyane Resistance Movements,' he answered quickly. 'They told me in Johannesburg your Tabanyane Resistance Movement will constitute the bulk of our mountain fighters, that you're in a position to provide guides and couriers, and that it would be easier if everything was done through your people rather than through our own organisation.'

'That is true,' the princess responded. Looking somewhat gratified by Cornelius's manner of putting things, she added: 'After all, our people have lived here all their lives and they know the terrain as well as can be expected of people born and bred in the area. Your "freedom fighters", Mr Molapo, are drifters, if you don't mind my saying so, who come and go. It's not our business of course how you wish to conduct your struggle against Pretoria, but now that you've decided to work closely with us instead of belittling our efforts at every turn, we naturally don't wish to see anything go wrong. I'm here to inform you that you can rely on us. And that is because more than anyone else in Tabanyane we have good reasons for fighting.'

'I'm sure you have,' Cornelius conceded. He felt a tremendous wish to smoke, then he sensed a tepid lust for the flesh of a woman, any woman, rising slowly inside him like a dangerous snake and knew it for what it was. Anxiety. Feeling his way cautiously forward he went on: 'You say we have belittled your efforts in the past. What makes you say that?'

'We read the papers, Mr Molapo. And some of the leaflets you have been putting out don't make pleasant reading for us.' Unexpectedly, the princess laughed. 'What did one of your leading figures call us? "A hopeless bunch of backward-looking traditionalists more interested in the restoration of the Tabanyane monarchy than in waging the national struggle for liberation!" That is what your man Thekwane said not so long ago.' Suddenly, Madi Seeiso became very grave, very sober. 'Well, I'm here to tell you, Mr Molapo, that had my late father Seeiso the Second not resisted to the bitter end Government attempts to grab the lands which belong to our people, had he not fought against Pretoria's attempts to set up a phoney Government of independence under my rogue uncle Sekala, and had he not created the first shield against wholesale attack on our people's rights and property, there would have been no resistance movement for your organisation to denounce. Our people don't understand your revolutionary slogans, Mr Molapo, but they do understand one thing. Land is the Mother and Father of our nation.'

Cornelius waited for the storm to sweep past; when next he spoke he had assumed an even graver tone than that of the princess, who sat quietly now in the middle of the bed, her hands resting on each side of her body with their palms lying flat on the sheet, the two of them evoking a picture of lovers in a half-finished quarrel. 'Your Royal Highness,' Cornelius began in the thoughtful, didactic voice he sometimes adopted with his pupils or at meetings when he expected applause. 'I don't know whether you are aware of the fact but the National Liberation Movement is a coalition of many diverse forces; it is a mixture of various political elements and factions with different shades of opinion, of people who are united only in their main objectives. That is why it is a national movement. It is not a political party. And what are these objectives I'm speaking of? For us the single most important is the overthrow of the Apartheid regime and the attainment for ourselves and our children of freedom, peace and justice. That is all. To put it another way, our organisation is a national front organisation, embracing all patriotic sons and daughters of the soil who share in this aim – the workers and owners of small businesses, the teachers, students, lawyers and tillers of the soil, and above all, our fighters. Together they constitute the main body of our democratic revolution. The contribution of the Tabanyane Resistance Movement to this common task, particularly under your guidance and leadership, is one that our Movement is happy to recognise as the noblest achievement of the organisation of which your late father was sole architect.'

Cornelius was now marching up and down in front of the princess, energetically waving his arms in the air as he delivered a harangue which was designed to convince the princess of the compatibility of interests between the Tabanyane Resistance and the National Liberation Movements. Mindful of the many risks to his mission should the princess not give him full support, he went on with his address with increased passion, like a man defending his very existence against the hordes at the gates. 'Our organisation, Princess Madi, is a peculiar organism, the result of peculiar historical circumstances. Its internal character reflects the different strands which are woven into its fabric as a national movement created to mobilise all our people. From time to time, many voices are heard within it, disruptive, irresponsible voices, which purport to speak in the name of the National Liberation Movement. We do not always necessarily agree with all such voices but our policy is not to carry out our squabbles in public.'

Looking at once sombre but strangely animated, the princess seemed to be digesting all that Molapo had been saying without making any comment. The only sign that she was reacting was the quickening in her breathing. Her ample bosom, astonishingly well-shaped, rose and fell as if she were an ardent young girl, eager to be inducted into the mysteries of the Liberation Movement. But when next she spoke, her voice cheerfully inquisitive and touched with cynicism, took Cornelius by surprise. 'And you, Mr Molapo,' she said suddenly. 'Where do you stand in all this?'

'Me?' Confused, Cornelius paused briefly to reflect. 'I stand by the 1949 Programme, Your Highness.'

The princess laughed. 'Forgive me, Mr Molapo, but I know nothing of your 1949 Programme. I know only what I read in the papers about your Movement, and of course I've met some of your emissaries sent to discuss with us a common front against the Government and that stooge uncle of mine, Chief Sekala. Except for this man Thekwane, your representatives all seem sober, well-spoken individuals, but Father Stephens has sometimes expressed surprise at the number of card-carrying communists in your organisation. I can also tell you that many of our people think you're all communists disguised as national liberators. They say you are all only interested in serving the interests of a foreign power. Are you a communist, Mr Molapo?'

In the courtyard below a young man's voice laughed, another began to sing an old war-song. Confused by the directness of the question, Molapo paused to listen; he was aware of irritation, aware also that Madi was studying him, eager to pick up clues that would bare the mystery of the Movement for National Liberation, but Cornelius chose to speak only of himself. 'Your Royal Highness, I don't know what communism is. I know only what the South African Government says it is. Those of us who demand justice, those

185

of us who clamour ceaselessly for equal pay for equal work; those of us who demand the implementation of the democratic principle of one person one vote; those of us who fight for the freedom of movement and association, and for a fair share of the land and the wealth which comes from this land; those of us who want all South Africans, black and white, to marry whom they like and to live where they like: those are the people the Government calls communists and they are the people the Government has banned, banished, imprisoned, tortured, murdered and maimed in the name of the suppression of communism. If asking for the security of limb and property, if asking for the right of our people to be fairly represented in the political institutions of our country and to have the security of employment is communism, then I am a communist.'

Molapo ceased. There was a slow hum in the air like a buzz of bees, a monotonous sing-song of boarding-school boys from below, and another chant, voiceless and eternal, from the movement of the earth. A wind had sprung up from the east; a rustle of dry leaves from the courtyard penetrated the room. Madi sat very quiet, her shoulders hunched forward, listening to the heartbeat of a subcontinent.

The light behind her sharply defined the contours of a face whose planes and curves acquired a sheen like dull gold in the failing light. Madi looked thoughtful, meditative, almost unhappy with her secret thoughts. Sensing her unease but not understanding its cause, Cornelius sat down beside her on the bed, taking both her hands into his. 'You must help us, Princess Madi. Believe me, we need your help.'

He went on rubbing her hands, then her arm, in a soft, comforting, caressing movement. Madi did not withdraw her hand. 'I will help you,' she said very gently. 'In any case that was decided long before you came. We'll provide you with whatever materials and men you require. But is that all the help you want?'

Cornelius was confused by the question but he was so

186

accustomed to acting on instinct that his immediate response was to say: 'No, Your Royal Highness! No, indeed not!' The princess made a slow languid movement with her heavy hips, the weight of her breasts almost tangible in the sighing shift of the petticoat beneath her uniform.

For a long time after that Cornelius and the princess sat in the dense heat of the afternoon exchanging stories, petty gossip and jests, getting to know each other, as the princess later put it. It was clear that she felt much more at ease with Cornelius than she had anticipated; she had become quite talkative. 'My father had wanted me to be a boy,' she confided. 'He wanted me to have the full experience of what it means to be a man. I suppose all fathers think their daughters are missing something by not being boys. But I think I made up for it in the end,' Madi laughed, showing her strong white teeth. 'My father and I became very close. Diliza was his greatest disappointment.'

Molapo became interested. 'Your brother?'

'Yes. From the very beginning Diliza had no interest in the affairs of the Tabanyane. He preferred chasing women. That was my father's regret. Mine too.' Suddenly Madi seemed overcome by a deep sadness.

In an attempt to cheer her up Cornelius said: 'I suppose one Seeiso at a time is enough for Tabanyane.'

'Perhaps,' she conceded grudgingly. 'Well, there are two Seeisos again,' she spoke almost angrily. 'My uncle and me. It's an impossible situation, of course, because as you say, only one Seeiso at a time can come out on top. Uncle Sekala Seeiso is a ruthless character, as you can imagine, but he's hampered by one thing: the fact that he is dealing with a woman. Most African men have no experience of dealing with women.' The princess paused, then smiling, she added: 'Except in bed, of course. My brother Diliza is also an expert on that. He's a fine example of how men have always dealt with women – only between the sheets. From the moment they are weaned from the breast boys are shoved off to join

187

their peers in the bush, herding cattle or trapping game. Other boys bring them up. After that, it's touch-and-go where women are concerned. Women are a mystery most African men live with without any understanding. It gives us an unfair advantage.'

'You may be right,' Cornelius conceded. 'I don't think I ever understood my wife. We had our differences, of course, like every other married couple, but I never thought anything of it. Then one day she just packed her things and left. No particular quarrel or anything. Just left. Recently, I went to pay her a visit where she's staying. And she explained it all to me.'

'Why she left you?'

'Yes. She said she wanted to live. "I wanted to grasp at life with both hands", is what she told me.'

'So what's so surprising about that?' Madi asked. 'Any woman can understand how your wife felt.'

'Fortunately not every wife packs her things and leaves home because of such feelings.'

'Oh, I didn't mean to rub salt into the wounds,' the princess said cautiously. 'In any case, all that is behind you now. Luckily, from now on your enemy wears trousers like you. Its name is Sekala Seeiso.' She talked about the Tabanyane struggle against Sekala and the Pretoria Government, and the men and women who waged it. She talked of her life, which she said was narrow compared to the life she had lived abroad, but work and struggle against Sekala's evil forces made it full, she told Cornelius. 'Imagine having to thank my uncle Sekala, that devil of a rogue, for having a little excitement in my life!'

When Molapo, standing in the middle of the room, paid a warm tribute to her determination and courage, the princess was visibly moved. Finally, she was ready to leave. Standing up, she embraced Molapo: 'We welcome you to Tabanyane like a long-lost brother. Don't forget, I expect you this evening.'

Chapter Thirteen

CORNELIUS had to wait for weeks before the first drop of arms on the bed of a dried up river. Before this event, time was filled by the routine of combat training, lectures, discussions, and reconnaissance work. Occasionally, Phiri led the fighters on secret missions against isolated targets in Sekala's stronghold, burning huts, looting, generally settling scores, as Phiri saw it; but for Cornelius, the first few months in the bush had been remarkable only for their uneventfulness. Time seemed to lose its normal rhythm. Molapo had quickly discovered that in the bush it was all too easy to lose track of days. Time was no particular object; minutes passed into hours, hours into days and weeks. In the end there would be death, of course, mercifully swift or prolonged, it was impossible to know beforehand; but at the end of six months, with the support given unstintingly by the princess and her cohorts, the Movement representative had succeeded in establishing a network of contacts, informers, and recruiting agents. Slowly at first, but later in bigger numbers, men were coming forward to join Cornelius Molapo's army of forest fighters.

As is usual in such undertakings the beginning was the most difficult. When Cornelius was still trying to establish his credentials with leading personalities in the Tabanyane Resistance, minor disagreements had sometimes arisen; during the planning stage of the operation each move was accompanied by a complicated set of negotiations and tactical manouevres in which the role of the princess or the priest was crucial in determining the outcome. The NLM might exercise a degree of control through the supply of arms and training, but most of the fighters regarded themselves first and foremost as members of the Tabanyane Resistance Movement, and Molapo only a hired commissar of the urban-based National Liberation Movement. They were encouraged in this attitude by none other than Sefale Phiri, Molapo's own field deputy who, however grateful for the superior training and support he had received from the National Liberation Movement, was barely able to conceal his resentment at being placed under Molapo's leadership. Phiri resented any outside interference in the affairs of Tabanyane and had to be periodically mollified by an invitation to the residence of the princess, where he was grandiosely entertained and elaborately consulted on matters of policy.

After her frequent clashes with Thekwane the princess seemed to have a very soft spot for Cornelius, in fact proved during the many disputes with Phiri Cornelius's most valuable ally. She seemed to take a particular delight in their clandestine meetings, travelling incognito in the bush, meeting by special arrangement at weddings or funerals. On one occasion their negotiations took place in the back pews of the Anglican church while the Rev Stephens was delivering a most inspired sermon on the casting out of demons. The demons Stephens was most concerned about, as he was quick to tell his congregation, were of course Apartheid demons! Bantustan demons! Cornelius and the princess listened with one ear while for the better part of an hour they plotted how to put Stephens' sermon into practical effect by arranging for a series of strikes against the forces of Sekala Seeiso. As time went on the need for intervention by the princess became happily infrequent. For Cornelius a new problem arose. Up there on the mountains, isolation now became more of a threat than friction. Cornelius was supposed to be in constant touch with

190

Thekwane, whose men had infested Malaita location like lice; but in spite of frequent consultations Cornelius sometimes had very little idea where Thekwane's men were planning their next strike. Later he found out that this was not unintentional on Thekwane's part.

At first cautious to a fault, Thekwane had tried to keep his dealings with Cornelius to a minimum. Certainly he had orders from the Movement's headquarters in Johannesburg to co-operate as much as possible with Molapo by training his forest fighters in the use of firearms without actually sacrificing the independence of his own combat unit, which was considered more professional and better ideologically motivated than the rabble peasant army of the Tabanyane Resistance Movement. Thekwane was to help Molapo build up the strength of his forest fighters to a battalion capable of engaging security forces for days if necessary, but headquarters had also decided that the less each combat unit knew about the others the better for security. To that end, the National Liberation Movement had evolved a complex structure of command in which the various combat units around the country operated independently, with scarcely any contacts among the men except through their leaders, though sometimes they combined forces in order to mount a major operation. Keeping combat units separate was intended to minimise the chances of capture through careless-ness or betrayal.

Every fortnight Thekwane, a robust man in his early forties with a long history of underground resistance behind him, accepted two or three men from the mountain for training. Cornelius and his deputy commander were the first to attend the training sessions. A crash course, Thekwane had called it, for their personal protection. Later, with more practice, they would perfect their skills; so in twos and threes and sometimes in fours – but never more than four at a time – the men came down from their mountain fastness to the depths of the forest where Thekwane waited in a small clearing, among trees whose tops were festooned with climbers like rigging on a ship. The

191

weather was always either too hot or too cold; mist and fog shrouded the forest trees and, moving slowly in the undergrowth, the men saw little sunshine; they shared habitation with baboons and brown hyenas and dangerous snakes and they slept within reach of their weapons. Strange birds populated the night with hoarse shrieking screams and calls. It was odd how these brave fighting men, nearly fearless in everything else, were more terrified of snakes than of humans. Thekwane once told Cornelius: 'It's not that the men are afraid of death. It's only that, well, a snake crawls on its belly and has eyes that can look backwards.' And Thekwane laughed crazily at his own outlandish explanation. He himself was, of course, fearless, except when confronted by things that flew in the air. Once Thekwane had to pause, AK-47 in hand, while perched on a piece of rock in the forest clearing; an eagle of pointedly martial bearing watched him steadily, awaiting his next move. For the rest of the training session Thekwane was visibly upset; he seemed to think the bird was an evil omen.

In the course of planning their campaign Cornelius had numerous secret meetings with Thekwane in a house in Malaita location, a small, uncomfortable shack in which a lonely old woman cooked meals for the underground commando leader on a smoky wood fire; she had no idea about his real work. In a room in which Thekwane also slept on the few nights when he kept indoors, a cot was placed discreetly behind a partition of shredded cloth and old blankets. No sign betrayed the presence of the 'Dubula High Command' in the tiny shack, but beneath it a shallow cellar had been dug out and behind the cot a small trap-door led to this hiding place, which was packed with medical supplies and lethal weapons and ammunition, from small arms to hand guns and Kalashnikov rifles; in the deepest part of this underground cave was hidden a chestful of machine guns, hand grenades, and even a rocket launcher. To this arsenal Cornelius had contributed his share from a consignment, from across the border. After the arrival of the consignment fighting began to gather momentum. The war of resistance was now waged at all hours of day and night, with sudden unexpected attacks in broad daylight on villages and isolated farms and finally in white Tabanyane itself.

During the first nine months, as the campaign escalated, the struggle between Phiri and Cornelius, at first open and uncharacteristically bitter, had subsided into a humorous, subtle play of difference between two men of widely dissimilar personalities and backgrounds. In the long stretches of boredom between adrenaline-charged hours of action, Cornelius filled the time by writing, reading and reflection. Writing – especially poetry – provided the means of entering into another world in which time itself seemed timeless. He wrote mostly in the evenings by candlelight while the men told stories and wove elaborate fantasies about the future; sometimes Cornelius listened, incredulous, to tales of past adventures, of numerous seductions, to the accounts of imaginary encounters with women of extravagantly varied gifts. In this surreal environment he wrote:

Time passes and we hang by the strap
Each leaf held by nature's safety pin
to the dying angled branch. Held there
while the minutes echo the day's losses
like a vast gigantic clock.

And perhaps thinking of his estranged wife Maureen he added:

I measure mine by your absence
Time gives out such small pellets
 I tell myself I wish to die like you
     in small doses
pecking at my own entrails.

In the bush, time seemed an illusion. It was incredible how many days you could lose in the wilderness, Cornelius thought.

Sometimes a whole week would simply vanish into a vast black hole of blank consciousness while you were waiting for an important piece of news. Up there on the mountains even the smallest sounds of insects and plant life created their own kind of music, a curious rhythm of deviant time scales. Bees and flies humming interminably over fallen fruit. Small sounds of seed-pods plopping open during the long hot nights. And yet it was crucially important to keep track of the succession of days and weeks of the social calendar; knowing what day of the week it was could be critical in determining when an attack should take place. There were commemorative days which the Movement liked to honour: Sharpeville Day, 16 June or Africa Freedom Day, all important landmarks in the guerrillas' calendar. High days and holidays often offered a clue for each of the two sides in the war to assess the greater or lesser likelihood of an attack. From the point of view of the mountain fighters, the enemy was likely to launch an attack in the knowledge that on a particular day villagers would be participating in an important church service, that they would be attending a funeral or helping at a wedding. Funerals and weddings normally took place on Saturdays or Sundays, and, once announced, whole villages within a radius of fifty kilometres would know who was likely to attend.

Thus Chief Sekala's men had launched an attack in broad daylight at the wedding of the daughter of old Ndulu, one of Sekala's staunchest opponents in his district. In the ensuing slaughter that left more than twenty celebrants dead, both bride and bridegroom were butchered, their hacked, blood-soaked bodies left sprawled across gleaming white linen, kegs of beer kicked over and pots of food smashed. In what was the ultimate act of revenge, Sekala spared the life of the father, old Ndulu, telling everyone he did so in order that the parent would live with the agonising memory of that day of carnage. After the massacre, weddings became fearful occasions in Tabanyane; instead of a cause for celebration a wedding became something to avoid unless attendance was mandatory. Cornelius remembered what soon became known as the 'Wedding Massacre' long after the event; not only because Sekala's savage brutality made a deep impression on him, but a day later, paying one of his secret visits to the town centre in order to make small purchases for his men up in the mountains – a pouch of tobacco, some cigarettes and packets of chewing gum – for the first time he had come face to face with the monster himself. Though Cornelius had had no clear idea what to expect, the suddenness of this encounter quite unsettled him.

Sekala Seeiso came into town riding at the head of a cavalcade of shiny Cadillacs which paused briefly in front of Joubert & Sons General Store. Surrounded by his bodyguards, Sekala stepped down from his limousine to enter the store, and suddenly the entire place looked like an armed camp. The Pretoria Government had recently allowed Sekala to create his own police force, armed with modern weapons, with permission to enforce his orders, and they did so with unchecked ruthlessness. Cornelius had seen Sekala's photographs in the newspapers of course; he had listened to numerous descriptions of the man by people who knew him or people who had come across him. Almost without exception these people remembered the encounter as a chilling experience. Madi Seeiso had concluded her description with what Cornelius had dismissed at the time as possibly an exaggerated caricature of the man. The princess had told Cornelius: 'The day you come across my uncle Sekala no-one will need to point him out to you! Try to imagine a monster six-foot-ten, with a face like a train locomotive or the front of Mount Taba Situ, and you have the exact image of my uncle. Children have been known to cry when he has but looked at them; an attempt at a smile from him is likely to send children running for shelter behind their mother's skirts. When he makes a joke he smiles so hard that his eyes seem to close up and vanish, bringing to perfection his exceptional ugliness!' Molapo's own reaction was not so different when he saw Sekala Seeiso for the first time.

Cornelius had just completed making his purchases when,

195

stepping out of the shop, he ran straight into the paramount chief. Sekala was entirely surrounded by men who moved in closely packed formation around his immense body. Somehow Cornelius had got in their way and he was sharply prodded in the ribs with rifle butts for this indiscretion. Though he was able to obtain only a momentary glimpse of Sekala's eyes before he was shoved aside, roughed up and more or less impaled against the wall by guns pointed at his stomach, that instant when he stared straight into the man's eyes stayed with him for a very long time. It was not that they looked cruel or violent, something for which the many tales of his brutality and lack of concern for his victims would have prepared him: it was simply the emptiness, the soulless, myopic gaze of those blank, unblinking eyes. His face was immense, flat, the mouth climbing upward to a nose whose nostrils flared like a hippo's. He wore a brown suit too small for his huge frame. What secondhand descriptions could never have prepared Cornelius for was the startling physical force the man conveyed; his presence carried with it an aura of catastrophic violence, a power of evil and destruction which surrounded his smallest gesture from the moment he stepped down from his Cadillac and walked across the street to the veranda of Joubert's store, where he paused to gratify the curiosity of the gaping crowd, by now thick and noisily excited, and including even white shoppers.

Sekala stood perfectly still, gazing at his supporters, who cheered enthusiastically, perhaps responding to the prudent need to show their loyalty in the presence of the informers who always marked the public appearances of the chief. Astonishingly, scattered amidst the noise of handclapping and applause, a few unexpected jeers erupted spontaneously from a section of the crowd. It must have been foolhardy in the extreme for those few brave voices to offend so openly against the great man. Seeiso himself and his bodyguards seemed slightly taken aback at first. Then Sekala, by now his eyes bulging and his lips twitching as if beyond his control, did something so startling that even his reputation for crudeness could not have led anyone to anticipate it. To brave jeers of 'Stooge! Collaborator! Killer! Murderer!' Sekala Seeiso opened his mouth in a terrible grin, more frightening than even a scowl or his terrible twitches could have been; he put his right hand between his trousers, grasped his genitals and made a crudely obscene gesture at the hostile element in the crowd, which was tantamount to saying 'Fuck You!' before disappearing into the shop. That was like a signal for some of his bodyguards to start laying into that section of the crowd where the jeers had been coming from. A bizarre sense of normality returned, but Cornelius never forgot the gesture.

In the bush the men slowly changed their characters, like objects left in the open air upon which rain, sun and air beat down and finally did their work of transformation; like pieces of cloth discarded among the forest trees changed their colour as a result of long exposure to the passing of the seasons. The faces of the younger men were growing older, the skin of their faces and hands was slowly pleating into tiny folds, the older ones had hardened even more; their muscles became like ropes and the sound of their voices grew smooth and worn from caution, from always having to keep them low for fear of betraying their whereabouts to strangers.

While they whispered and waged war, news filtered through of changes in Government policy: men were now free to come and go in the big cities without having to show the hated identity documents; black and white were now free to marry although the future of the progeny of such unions was in doubt because although white and black could sit on the same benches in the park, they could not yet go to school together. Always such scraps of information, reaching hard-pressed guerrillas on the mountains of Tabanyane, bore an element of fiction, even a form of skilful deception. In as much as they hinted at the imminent release of Dabula Amanzi they were scarcely to be believed.

197

Chapter Fourteen

CORNELIUS and the other ten men were bearing on their sore tired shoulders crates loaded with small arms that had been dropped by a tiny chartered plane on a dry river-bed behind a high plateau overlooking Tabanyane country. They were coming down a narrow mountain gorge between two steep rocks: below them a footpath ran into a mouth of the forest.

The trees were dark green, alive with bird chatter – but for that the silence was complete, everything as peaceful, as ghostly, as a graveyard. Descending further, the men came down the foot-path on soundless feet shod in plimsolls, careful not to dislodge the small rocks and shard that had been worn loose by herds of cattle and goats.

Then Cornelius felt his foot roll on a smooth round pebble, he slid forward, and the small arms in his crate rattled loudly. The man behind him hissed: '*Tishera!*', reminding Cornelius that although he was the squad leader the men no longer thought him formidable enough behind his dark intellectual glasses. Tired and broken by days of trek across wild country, his feet swollen and blistered, he had become to them more of a burden than a guardian: he limped, he tired easily and slowed them down. At night, in the grip of nightmares, he woke them up with screams, and hearing him cry out the men jumped from their sleep; they reached for their weapons, to realise a moment later that their leader had only been having a nightmare. Cursing, they settled down again and tried to go to sleep without success. Their slumber, which was at best fitful, had been disrupted; for the rest of the night they lay awake, wondering about the strange school-teacher sent out from Johannesburg to take on the formidable Chief Sekala, the Government's mouthpiece in Tabanyane. Phiri, the lynchpin between the Movement and the Tabanyane Resistance, was openly hostile, if not contemptuous. The Johannesburg school teacher, Phiri told anyone who would listen, was nothing but a woman; the school-teacher was soft, perhaps tainted with the corrupt ways of city living, and knew nothing of fighting.

As he slid forward, Cornelius had tottered and had finally come to teetering rest against the ledge of a great rock which jutted across the footpath, half-hidden by the trees.

'*Tishera!*' Phiri whispered fiercely, disapprovingly. Behind him the red disc of the sun was slipping rapidly behind the mountain range across which they had come and deep shadows already touched with chill were covering their side of the mountains. As Cornelius struggled to keep his balance, more dislodged rocks began to roll away down the steep incline of the mountain path.

'*Modimo!*' Phiri swore, pulling up in a dead halt, his big eyes turning round and round in his massive head. A man of peasant stock, Phiri was a squat figure with powerfully muscled thighs: below a pair of torn khaki shorts his knees were pressed firmly together like a young virgin's. He and Cornelius were probably not that far apart in age, but whereas Cornelius was of light brown skin, a fact which led Phiri to doubt not only Cornelius's African lineage but his ability to endure heat, rain and other hazards of nature, Phiri himself was the very opposite. Dark in complexion, with a big sloping forehead, a snub nose and a pair of very thick lips, many girls thought him handsome; there were just as many who thought him repulsively ugly; but one quality was not in dispute; it was generally agreed that Phiri was a man of monumental weight, by which people meant that he possessed a certain charisma, a spiritual force.

'*Tishera!*' Phiri repeated. There was a moment of acute embarrassment while the rest of the men waited for Cornelius to adjust the load on his frail shoulders. Picking himself up with immense dignity he began to haul the crate back to his shoulders, leaning against the flat surface of the rock to do so and then hitching himself up, an effort that cost him his breath; pain like a searing hot iron pressed against his lung.

'Perhaps *Tishera* would prefer to rest?' Phiri sneered.

'I'm all right,' Cornelius lied but his suffering, both spiritual and physical, was too obvious for the men not to notice it and, noticing it, Phiri's stern face at once softened into a smile of startling beauty and tenderness.

'Listen,' he said to Cornelius, 'it is not necessary to play the hero before us. We all know that a teacher like you is not accustomed to heavy labour.' Phiri turned to the others for approval or confirmation: from the rest of the men rose a collective murmur of general agreement which, to Cornelius's ears was indistinguishable from the breath of the wind against the dark green leaves spread like an umbrella above the mouth of the forest. Somewhere in the depths of the trees a bird sang with an inadmissible desire that made the men think of spring and young love; but beyond this they felt an ache for something they could not name, something remembered from childhood; something, at any rate, they would fight to regain. It brought them closer together against the falling evening. Soon it would be night.

'We'll all sit down for a while,' Phiri said laconically. Without waiting for confirmation from Cornelius the men at once began to lower their loads to the ground; perhaps they, too, were tired. They had been walking for hours across wild country, with only brief stops for rest and only one longer stop for a midday meal.

The place where the small twin-engine plane had dropped crates of arms was a narrow strip of dried up sandy river-bed that was not marked on the map. After the drop the plane had a clear run back across the border, but as Cornelius remembered it now it was the waiting that had been an ordeal, the agonising moments of tension and anxiety during which the men huddled together like wild animals, listening to the smallest sounds and watching an empty sky for the signs of a little bird that would float in across the unpatrolled border. The drop itself, under the control of an experienced wartime pilot, had been a swift and smooth affair; a few dives overhead and arms were bouncing over the sand pits and being quickly picked up by waiting men who melted into the bush. Then started the long trek across the passes; on the other side of a steep mountain, close to the warring Tabanyane kingdom, the men had prepared a hideout in the rocky mountain caves, with hidden storage facilities for arms and ammunition, and it was from here that Cornelius, acting on the orders of the central committee of the National Liberation Movement, directed operations against Paramount Chief Sekala.

Watching the men putting their loads down Cornelius was seized by an irrational fury. 'Phiri!' he shouted. 'Who says you're going to give orders in my place?'

Phiri was amazed: 'No-one! I'm only doing this for your benefit. Everyone can see you cannot walk another ten paces with that load. What's the good of carrying on in a state like that? No-one will be impressed! We can see you're no lion.'

'I say we'll walk!'

A man behind Phiri said: 'What is the teacher saying?'

'He says we'll walk!' This information was greeted with stunned silence. No-one seemed to understand the nature of the struggle between Phiri and Cornelius; all the men knew and could see with their own eyes was that the 'teacher' was greatly in need of rest; the man was obviously near collapse; Cornelius's refusal to accept his condition inspired contempt rather than sympathy. After a few seconds of silent bewilderment the man behind Phiri began to laugh. A second joined in the laugher. A third and a fourth followed suit. Before long, either from surprise or the need to relieve the tension of three days in the bush, everyone was laughing. Everyone, that is, except Phiri. Not only did Phiri seem flabbergasted by the teacher's stubbornness; he seemed outraged by Cornelius's rejection of a truce between the two of them.

'The comrade leader says we're to go on,' Phiri wryly commented. 'In a struggle such as ours comity is more important than strife. So we'll go on.'

The tension broken, everyone was smiling, including Cornelius. In the six months they had been in the bush together, Molapo had frequently noted the extreme formality of Phiri's language, especially during those moments when he was most irritable. Cornelius had even secretly conceived the idea, which he quickly discarded, of entering into the military logbook he carried some of the more colourful phrases and epigrams to which Phiri was particularly addicted; only caution, a feeling that such an exercise could serve to isolate him even more from the men, prevented him from pursuing his idea: he was already too acutely aware of a slight but uncomfortable distance between himself and the men. They walked the rest of the journey in silence.

Night falls very swiftly in Africa. Before you know it, there in a jungle of dark forest trees and wild undergrowth, among sudden crops of rocks and lazy forest streams, the world seems to melt away into sombre shadows in which only the smells are potent; the smells and sounds. Here and there a patch of blue sky, already sequinned with clusters of slow winking stars, shows behind a filigree of feathery leaves above the forest trees, but the rest is a massed darkness in which the bulked shapes of tree trunks rise like ghosts out of an immemorial African past. Sometimes a bird shrieks, an owl hoots, but save for the sound of insects it is the silence that is horrifying in its primordial muteness. Each time Cornelius had led the men back to the cave he had sensed their unease in the presence of unknown spirits who inhabited the forest groves of Taba Situ. Tonight it would be no different. As they made their descent, their feet soundless except for the thin crackling of dry twigs over which they tiptoed to their mountain hideout, the men walking in single file communicated the old fear before which centuries of Western science and missionary teachings seemed powerless. Holding the crates carefully on weary shoulders, and using ancient landmarks to guide their way across the rocks, they worked their way laboriously to their mountain fastness.

It took them more than forty-five minutes of speechless toil, except for occasional, whispered curses. Then suddenly, in the small light of a rising star, the mouth of the cave loomed on the far side of the mountain footpath. And then a surprise: just outside the mountain hideout, still glowing like a worm in the dank night air, a cigarette end lay on the ground before them. The men stared at it as if it were the shining eye of an evil reptile.

Chapter Fifteen

T HE abandoned cigarette took on a life of its own in the cold night air and the men stood gazing at it in stupefied horror. No-one spoke; no-one moved; though the boxes of arms were still mounted on their shoulders they made no effort to lower their loads to the ground.

Finally Cornelius slid his crate to the ground, picked up the cigarette butt and examined it. His face was ashen with worry, tiredness and effort, but no matter how long he studied it the cigarette yielded no useful information beyond what its eye, glowing mesmerisingly in the dark, had already provided, alerting the men to an unknown presence in the neighbourhood of the caves. Disturbed, the bats in the cave flew and flew, never going anywhere, like condemned creatures bound to never-ending duty. On a nearby tree, a short-sighted owl scanned the arrivals with indifference. Another quarrelsome bird was asking over and over, with increasing irritation: 'Who goes there? Who goes there?'

The men were now crowded around Cornelius, waiting for him to act. For a moment he turned to them with a puzzled face, as though he did not know what was expected of him; or if he knew what was expected, seemed to feel such an expectation to be an injustice. The bush itself seemed to be listening, waiting, challenging Cornelius to do something, to act. When, after what seemed like aeons, he recovered from the initial shock he acted at once, hurling himself at his task with the recklessness of those who suddenly find purpose in adversity.

He motioned to his men to put down their crates, then speaking in a barely audible whisper, he said: 'This cigarette, comrades, is a bad omen. It means that someone we don't know has been in this neighbourhood. Phiri and I will go into the cave and search it. The rest of you will stand guard at the entrance. Keep your eyes and ears open! Keep your weapons at the ready and keep your mouths shut! If you hear or see anything suspicious give us word. Phiri and I will come out and join you immediately.'

Then he motioned to Phiri to follow him, but just as Cornelius was wearily bending down to enter the cave Phiri shot in ahead of him: 'It is better that I go in first, Tishera! I know more about these rocky trails than a teacher who has spent too much time in the city. I, Phiri, have lived with danger all my life. So I go in first and you follow. All right, Tishera?' Cornelius silently cursed his deputy. Would this rivalry never cease? But he let him go in first.

The men outside were left leaderless, which was only one of many mistakes Cornelius was to make during the operation they had willy nilly embarked on. Left to themselves the men at once fell prey to acute anxieties. Tense, hostile and jittery, they huddled around the mouth of the rock, listening to the sounds of the bush and the strain on their nerves was worse than on the two men who had already entered the cave; for in a time of danger action is an antidote to fear while inactivity paralyses the brain.

Under the stars, a dense canopy of foliage on one side and the grim silence of a rock on the other, the men waited, huddled together against the unknown. The smallest movement in the bush, the scuttle of a lizard or the dart and slither of an unseen snake among the leaves on the floor of the forest, would cause them to jump and they automatically tightened their grip on their weapons. Seconds, minutes ticked away; the giant trees, their trunks solid and black against the sky, were massed like an enemy in formation against the men in combat jackets. Everything was strange. Creepy. Hostile. These men, who had trusted the wilderness as they trusted their own mothers, now that it possessed secrets from which they were excluded, felt towards it nothing but fear and distrust. It masked their enemy: for all their intent listening they could hear or see nothing but the usual cries and sudden flights of wild birds and animals who made the bush home. No human evidence was visible; nothing but this cigarette butt which, surprisingly, the teacher had thrown away without stamping out.

Twenty minutes were gone but to the men outside it seemed like an age. They became restless. Hardest to observe was the injunction not to speak, for this meant they could not talk away their fears and once fear exists it must be acknowledged, otherwise it hangs like a bird of evil intent around the neck of every man, feeding on his anxiety. As the minutes passed and there was no sign of either Cornelius or Phiri the tension began to tell; someone had to break the spell. It was Ngo who spoke first.

'I don't like it,' he said gravely. The rest of the men looked startled, as though a stranger had spoken their collective thoughts. 'In an age gone by, but not really so long ago that we cannot remember, when our fathers fought they tilted their spears against an enemy that could be seen, men with flesh and blood and bones like ourselves, not ghosts that, when they are challenged, melt into darkness! Look, here is a cigarette burning and we cannot say who brought it here; we can only say that someone brought it; and the cigarette looks at us, it winks, mocking us. Eh, *batho*!'

While Ngo spoke darkness seemed to cling to the very breath he drew as steam clings to the face of a man on a cold day. Ngo was a tall man, raw-boned and well-built, but like all the others, after many months in the bush, he looked tired, doubtful and apprehensive. All his life old Ngo had worked as a farm hand, moving from one white farm to the next in search of a security he never found until, after years of wasted toil, in angry desperation he joined the incipient rebellion against the Government. Young men had come from the big city of Johannesburg to preach revolution, and although some of their words were too vague and too abstract for an old farm hand to comprehend, Ngo had understood their hatred for the Government of the white chief in Pretoria and for Sekala, the usurper of the Tabanyane throne who now wanted to cede some of the ancestral lands to that same Government. When the killings started and some huts were burned, Ngo joined a group of hard-core fighters who were training in the bush. But for all the enthusiasm he had shown Ngo was sometimes assailed by doubts; for all his dedication and undoubted courage, he was still not sure he was doing the right thing.

'It is a bad omen, this cigarette glowing in the dark. Who is to say who left it here? Who is to say we are not watched at this very moment? I repeat, I do not like it!'

Red Ramusi could stand it no longer; suddenly he lost his temper. 'If you keep your mug shut, old man, the future may turn out better than you think. Not only for you but for all of us!' Red was younger, angrier, more confident: but even he needed reassurance. They called him 'Red' because of his beard, which was russet brown, the colour of a field mouse. From the very start of the guerrilla training he and Ngo had been locked in the eternal conflict between youth and age, between unauthenticated courage and cautious stoicism. There was never any peace between them, only sleep imposed a truce of sorts between the two men.

'Red!' Ngo spoke sharply but still managed to keep his voice just above a whisper. 'How many times must I tell you not to mock my words? Must I challenge you to a stick fight in order to knock some sense into your peacock head?'

'Old man,' Red said calmly, contempt not far away from his voice, 'we have enough problems fighting the white man and that dog of his, Chief Sekala, without also fighting among ourselves, especially at a time like this. But since you are so eager to fight, I'll tell you one thing, old man. We'll find a time and a place as soon as possible and I shall be glad to accept your challenge!'

'Thing of dung!' old Ngo hissed, his body hulking forward as though ready to attack. 'You think I am afraid of you? You little button at the tip of your mother's thing! I spit on you!' As he said this he jetted saliva as far as Red Ramusi's feet. Ramusi shot his own back at the other's feet. 'I do the same on you! You old shrunken penis of a baboon!'

'Comrades! Comrades!' Rathebe tried to calm them down. 'We're not here because we want to witness bloodshed between our fighters: we are here to wage a war of liberation. This display of temper will ill serve the cause for which we all pretend to fight!' Though they had been glad enough for the diversion that took their minds off the lurking danger, the rest of the men grunted their approval. Again, silence fell and there was nothing but the serenity of the bush to listen to and the drumming of the men's apprehensive hearts to remind them of their own fear. The cigarette butt that had been the cause of all the disquiet had quietly gone out.

High above the mountains a shooting star suddenly streaked across the heavens and plunged down the sky to burn itself into nothing. The men watched it anxiously, their faces upheld as though to receive a blessing. But they knew the star was no blessing; it was an ill omen. This cigarette thing was a curse; until they knew who had left it there and where he had gone afterwards the men would know no peace. Every now and again an individual would swear furiously at the thought of the danger in which they all stood.

And the other two, Phiri and Cornelius, where were they? The men's nerves were getting as raw as a piece of rusted wire with the suspense of waiting. They knew so well the disposition of the cave, its various niches and the inter-connecting passages that formed a network in the mountain, that even now they could follow with their eyes closed the movement of the two men from one part of the cave to another.

Their safe hideout consisted of not just one but at least three cells with connecting tunnels. As an example of nature's ingenuity it could scarcely be bettered. Not only was it warm and dry but one end of the cave was conveniently equipped with apertures like a ship's portholes which allowed the air to circulate freely in every part of the cavern. Each of the three main chambers served a separate function. The first, which was much smaller than the rest, was set aside for cooking quick meals on a pressure stove. The second, slightly bigger than the first, held a cache of arms and stores of tinned food, medical supplies, blankets, sleeping mats and rock climbing gear. The third, and the most commodious, was referred to as the common room. Here the men played draughts, listened to the radio, and those who were literate provided with what were considered appropriate books. They were mostly simplified biographies of great nationalist and revolutionary leaders, from Marx and Lenin to Mao, Nkrumah and Gandhi. These were supplemented by a diet of theoretical works in translation on socialism and capitalism and assorted social and political movements. Sometimes out of boredom Cornelius read his poetry, to which his poorly educated comrades listened desultorily, out of loyalty and respect, but clearly they under-stood and cared nothing for what was, to them, a string of incomprehensible words and phrases in a foreign language.

It was inside this cave now that another drama was taking place which the men outside could not have even imagined. Torches in hand and weapons drawn, Phiri and Cornelius had moved cautiously along one slippery passage on to a shelf of rock which formed a kind of platform before descending sharply, like a spiralling staircase, to second rock level. Here another labyrinthine corridor led finally to a large grotto, the so-called common-room. However, before Phiri and Cornelius could reach this chamber they caught their first whiff of fire, the scent of burning wood and smoke. Phiri stopped in his tracks and looked questioningly at Cornelius.

'The white man says there is no smoke without fire,'

Cornelius whispered whimsically. Cautiously, crawling on their hands and knees, they moved to within three yards of the main cell before they could get a clear view inside. What they saw appeared to be the flames of a dying fire casting a dull but eerie glow on the wall opposite. Phiri's eyes turned white in his head like two brightly polished buttons and he reeled them up; alarmed and short of breath, Cornelius pressed forward, the better to look over Phiri's shoulder. Even before they could properly come to terms with their own fear and panic they heard a noise, first only a faint stir which became a scuffle; there was something in the scuffle that became tantalisingly unreal in such a place.

'A herd of goats?' Phiri whispered. 'It can't be anything else!'

'And the fire?'

'Some herd boys, perhaps, trying to keep warm.'

'At this time of night?'

There was another scuffle, more ambiguous this time like two bodies struggling or rolling on the pebbled floor; this struggle was conducted in complete silence. The silence did not last long; soon the scuffle grew louder and more intemperate. There was one brief, quickly suppressed shriek, a woman howling in pain or lust, and then silence. During that split second, reading the meaning in each other's faces, Phiri and Cornelius jointly made the decision to dive into the cave.

Chapter Sixteen

IT was a cruel moment: two white bodies, fire-lit, heaving and struggling into an eternity of lust that seemed to toss them into the air and leave them suspended in front of the two black witnesses. The two men stared open-mouthed at the white man riding astride his woman, his hands gripping her shoulders, his narrow flanks folding and unfolding like a concertina. And soon enough the moment that Phiri and Cornelius had been waiting for was approaching; and determined to make the humiliation complete, the two black men sprang into the middle of the cave, weapons drawn. Caught suddenly in the bright beam of Cornelius's torch, the woman half rose beneath the body of the white man, her mouth open but managing to suppress a scream. The man rose, too, just as surprised, piteously sheltering his genitals behind his two cupped hands. Then suddenly remembering who he was he bawled out at the two black men: 'What the devil do you think you're doing here!' The woman rose to her feet, taking refuge behind the white man.

Imperiously Cornelius waved the gun at the man's face, suddenly excited by the knowledge of the power he held over him. 'Shut up!' he shouted, 'or I'll put a bullet between your eyes! This is not a joke.' He turned to his deputy: 'Phiri, pick up their garments. I'm sure the rest of the men would like to see what white people look like without their clothes on!'

Not so powerful-looking, eh, comrade leader!' Phiri chuckled.

'No. Not so powerful-looking.'

For once Phiri did as he was told without so much as a murmur. Smiling, he gathered up the couple's clothes, first the man's riding breeches and khaki shirt, then the woman's simple cotton dress and the underwear, a little grimed and soiled by dirt. He gathered them together into a small bundle which he pressed under his arm.

The white man was more outraged than surprised. 'Hey, you can't do that!' he cried. 'You can't take the madam and the *baas's* clothes. You got to give them back to us! Come on, look sharp now! You be a good boy and give me that gun and we'll say no more about it!'

With her shrewd but frightened eyes the woman was the first to lose faith in the white man's power to protect her; pathetically, without much conviction, she cowered behind his gigantic form; a man who only minutes before might have been an individual of absolute power and confidence, now suddenly reduced to a figure of absurdity and banality. On the other hand, as is usual with white males accustomed to command, the man hung on desperately to the tatters of his former authority. He would not let go of the idea that whatever the circumstances he was to be obeyed. 'You have no business barging in here like this!' he shouted. 'I have a good mind to give the pair of you quite a thrashing! Do you think you can frighten me with those toy guns! Hand us our clothes now if you don't want to make things any the worse for you than they already are!'

Once more Cornelius waved the gun imperiously, the symbol of his newly acquired authority. 'Go on!' he ordered. 'Move over there and shut your mouth or you'll soon be without a mouth to speak of! Up against the wall and quick!' The white man hesitated but something in Cornelius's manner told him he was not bluffing. Reluctantly, dragging the woman behind him, he moved up against the wall of the cave.

212

Cornelius handed the torch to Phiri. 'Keep it shining on them!' From the pocket of his bush jacket Cornelius whipped out his pen and notebook and got ready to write down a few details.

'Your names! And make it snappy! We haven't got all night!' The woman looked at the white man before she answered.

'Kristina,' she said quickly, carefully watching the gun in Phiri's hand. 'Kristina Miranda Kemp.' A brief attempt at a smile merely produced a shapeless twitch of the mouth, a revelation of a few irregular teeth. She turned away from Phiri to Cornelius, perhaps feeling a sudden surge of confidence in Cornelius who, unlike Phiri, spoke the white man's language like a white man. She said: 'Kristina Miranda Kemp! That's my name. Ask anybody.'

'Kristina?' Cornelius repeated. The girl nodded foolishly. He turned to the man who still waited, naked and outraged, praying for a miracle to occur.

'And you?'

Again the white man hesitated. He took a deep breath before he responded to this question, which clearly outraged him. 'What is this?' his voice was halfway between fear and a sneer. 'A process? Preliminary examinations?'

'Quick, quick man!' Cornelius shouted. 'Don't waste our time! Or do you want me to loosen your tongue for you?'

The man's lips were moving but no sound came out. 'This is preposterous,' he finally spluttered, making a fierce grimace. 'You can't ask me for my name!'

'Why not?'

'You know very well why not. I'm white. You're black. Listen, I can see you are someone with some education. You must be intelligent. A man in your position, you know very well you can't just go around asking white men...you can't...!' He gave up. He had wanted to explain so many things towards which he could only vaguely and uncertainly feel his way but found immense difficulty in putting into words; probably he was thinking that, faced with primitive and unreasonable men, such explanations were foolish besides

213

being futile; so he merely stood his ground and shouted defiantly. 'You can't ask me questions and you know why! I'm white and you're only a *kaffir*!'

Cornelius lost his temper. He stepped forward and slapped him soundly across the mouth. The white man's face turned the colour of beetroot as disbelief mingled with outrage.

'Now you'll please answer my questions!' The man's lower lip was torn and bleeding and he looked at his interlocutor with wary astonishment. Phiri, too, forced to see a side of Cornelius he had never permitted anyone to see before, looked startled but pleased.

'You'll hear about this!' the man shouted, still trusting to the power of his privilege. 'In this country you can't lay hands on a white man and get away with it. You'll hear about this!'

He spat blood. 'What are you? Terrorists or robbers? We have nothing to give you. Here, take my watch. That's all I have to give to you!' This was true; stripped of every piece of clothing, it was all that he still wore. He made ridiculous preparations to take off his watch and hand it over but Cornelius waved the watch impatiently aside.

'You're wasting my time! You'll answer exactly what I ask you. Attempts at bribery will get you nowhere.'

'Who's attempting to bribe you?'

'What do you think you're doing, offering me your watch!' The white man opened his mouth a crack but thought better of making another protest. Cornelius was getting impatient. 'Okay. Let's start again. Tell me your name.'

The white woman looked frightened. 'Please, Gert, they'll only be angry if you don't answer.' Absurdly, she was still holding her breasts, protecting them from the eyes of the two black men. The white man turned angrily upon her: 'You can tell them. Tell them who I am. Maybe they'll understand. Someone will hear about this. You can't treat white people like *kak* and think you can get away with it!'

'Your name, you bastard! Do you think this is a game?' Cornelius slapped him again.

The girl spoke at once. 'Gert Potgieter!' She spoke quickly, her voice filled with alarm. 'Gert Potgieter! That's what he is called. Ask anybody. He means no harm. Please let us go now!' She smiled weakly, looking from the black man to the white man. Without comment Cornelius noted the name down.

'And the address?'

This time it was Potgieter who spoke, perhaps to save his woman further humiliation. 'Bus drie en twintig. Rooiplaas.'

'What work?'

'I'm a farmer and you'll hear about this. You think you can treat a white man like this and get away with it!'

When Cornelius finished writing down the details he glanced at the girl, his pen poised to record more details. 'And you?'

'I'm only his girl,' the young woman said, as if this fact alone excused her from any direct involvement in any offence they may be accused of committing.

'So I see!' Cornelius said sarcastically. 'And you live where?'

'At the Meerdal Hotel. I work at the reception. I have to be back there by seven. That's when I go on duty. They'll be expecting me. Better to let us go.'

'Let you go! Sorry, that's out of the question.'

'What are you going to do with us?'

The question, posed in alarming innocence out of frayed nerves, caught Cornelius by surprise. Indeed, what was he going to do with these two white people? He had no idea. This was one of those situations in which guerrillas are forced to take hostages before they have actually decided what to do with them. They were going to be forced to hold on to these two, it now appeared, for fear of having their secret hideout betrayed prematurely; and to that extent Cornelius and his men would become hostages as much as this frightened white couple. Cornelius had already guessed that theirs was an illicit affair which they would prefer to have kept quiet. On the other hand, there was no telling what a pair of humiliated white people could do once they were out of danger. Recognising Cornelius's excruciating dilemma, Potgieter tried to exploit it

215

to maximum advantage. 'Listen,' he said. 'If you don't let us go they'll be looking everywhere. There's a lot of unrest around here as it is. The slightest suspicion and they'll be everywhere, looking for us. You don't want that to happen, do you?'

'Neither do you,' Cornelius said calmly.

'What?' Potgieter seemed surprised at Cornelius's surmise.

'You don't want them to start looking,' Cornelius said.

'How do you mean?'

'The girl. She's not your *vrou*, is she? What your wife will think of your sleeping around with single girls in a mountain cave, frankly I do not know, but I can guess she won't be very pleased, will she?'

For the first time the white man looked genuinely frightened, perhaps even more frightened than he had been by the guns pointed at him and the girl. He grinned slyly at Cornelius. 'Okay. Supposing you're right? Suppose I don't wish my *vrou* to know? What can you do? You can't hold us here forever.'

'I can order your execution if you don't watch your tongue.' The girl shuddered slightly and looked apprehensive.

'You can't be serious!' Potgieter objected. 'Kill us? What for? We've done no harm.'

'That remains to be seen.'

'We're innocent individuals.' Potgieter protested. 'Our only misfortune was to fall into the hands of murderers!'

'Shut up!'

'Gert, please!' the girl pleaded plaintively.

'Phiri!' Cornelius shouted. 'Ask the rest of the men to come in. I'd like them to see what we've got here!'

One by one the men came into the cave like children on a school tour being ushered into a chamber of horrors. Their manner was eager yet hesitant and uncertain; after all, not even in their weirdest dreams had they ever imagined they would one day see a white man and a white woman completely in the raw. Their faces, which were faintly illuminated by the flickering flames of the fire, reflected an intense inner excitement that nothing could dispel until they had pressed their faces close to the cowering uncovered secret: the sight before them of a naked white couple. Habit being stronger than curiosity, the men first drew back, embarrassed by what they saw, but soon enough they were pressing forward, smirking and elbowing each other out of the way. The young woman interested them especially. Her white breasts, which were heavy and sagging, seemed more potent now than they were when they had first been disclosed to view. In a kind of defiant despair she had ceased attempting to cover them up. Her fuzz of dark, copper coloured hairs clung like a clump of trees between the two hillocks of her fleshy white thighs.

'There's nothing wrong with her that a strong penis will not soon put right!' Ramusi laughed coarsely. On the other hand, the white man's penis, suddenly shrunken from fear and embarrassment and droopy below his distended belly, drew only hostile comment and laughter.

Cornelius, assuming his proper role as the Movement's representative, addressed the men in their own language. 'Comrades, you see here a white man and his woman. We found them coupling on the floor of the cave. As you can see, they're still naked, they still have the smell of two dogs on heat, but that has nothing to do with us. We are not interested in what the white man and his woman were doing, only what we should do with them. This man and his woman have been foolish enough to blunder into our hideout. What we should do with them is now the question. If we let them go they may betray our position. On the other hand, we cannot travel light and undetected if we take them along with us. Of course, we can always shoot them if it becomes necessary but that should be a last resort. We're not animals like they are. We do not enjoy killing for its own sake. So what are we to do with them? That is the question.'

For the first time the men seemed animated by a force they could neither understand nor withstand. Collectively they

217

pressed forward, growling, grinning, giggling; then suddenly, as though some unseen power had imposed order, they fell silent. Cornelius repeated gently, almost wheedling: 'So, comrades, what shall be do with them? He was still trying to think his way out of his predicament when a man came through the shadows and touched his shoulders. He turned round and recognised Matebesi's face, a squat man with thick choppy muscles and a broad chest, but for all his physical strength, Matebesi had always appeared to Cornelius a timid man, inaccessible and solitary, without much to say for himself. Now, like the rest of them, he seemed to have been transformed by the drama of the capture of hostages. His face in particular bore the animated expression of someone whose angle of vision upon the world had shifted radically in a matter of an hour.

'So, comrade *Tishera,*' Matebesi smiled with satisfaction. 'What do you think of it all? A strange sight, is it not, two white people coming up here to canoodle all night?'

'It shows they're also human, comrade!' Cornelius curtly interjected.

'And how!' Matebesi beamed. 'You do not need to remind me, comrade leader. I have seen it with my own eyes. All the humanity is there between the white man's legs!' Matebesi laughed, emitting his usual bad-smelling breath. 'And the woman! She has everything. Look at her round belly and the roundness of her buttocks!' Matebesi whistled admiringly. 'The breasts are like two full-grown mangoes. You wouldn't have thought they have things between their legs just like our women, eh comrade? Some of the men, I'm sure, would like to have a taste of the white woman's thing. I can see it in their eyes.'

'And you, comrade Matebesi?' Cornelius retorted sourly. 'Would you like to have a taste too?'

Matebesi hesitated. 'Well, comrade leader, to tell the truth...'

'Well? What is the truth, Matebesi?'

'I don't know. It's not what we are fighting for, is it?'

'I'm glad you remember that, comrade fighter. Sometimes I think all of you are inclined to forget why we are here!'

Matebesi felt rebuked. He frowned resentfully and went away, muttering. Cornelius was glad to be left alone with his thoughts; he still had to work out a way of disposing of the two white people and there wasn't much time left. In an hour he had to travel with a guide the fifteen miles to the nearest public telephone on the outskirts of the tiny *dorp* from where he would send a coded message to Johannesburg announcing the success of the arms drop. Meanwhile, Cornelius tried to concentrate. Certain vague options presented themselves but none had the clear outlines of an idea from which would flow a rational course of action. When fully considered, every plan had some snag in it or remained too fuzzy on the edges to promise successful exploitation. In his predicament Cornelius wanted to be able to predict, at least with something approaching certainty, what consequences might flow if one or other course of action were pursued. Pacing up and down within the narrow confines of the cave, Cornelius smiled grimly at the thought that he was now a prisoner of his own good fortune; without wishing to take hostages, hostages had come into his hands; but the smile was short-lived, soon to be replaced by an angry scowl. What romantic fools, he thought of the white man and his woman, to abandon the security of a domestic bedroom for a love tryst in the mountain caves so close to where all the fighting was going on! Apparently, they needed more than what mundane sex could provide: they also needed the thrill of danger while doing it. In a sudden unreasonable rage, Cornelius looked at the white man and his woman with something very close to repugnance, but all the same, letting the couple go now was out of the question: they would immediately rush to talk to the police, and they would describe the hideout with justifiably intimate detail; above all, they would describe their captors.

There was another man, however, who seemed even more

uneasy at the sudden turn of events. Ngo, the one-time farm hand, felt less than elation at the sight of his comrades baying at a pair of helpless white hostages. He waited nervously at the edge of the thwarted circle of gawking men until the shoving and the howling finally subsided; then he, too, as though moved by an emotion stronger than his own disgust, pressed closer and closer until he was able to see what he had not yet seen – the hulking white man, naked to his toes, armed with nothing more dangerous than his humble droopy genitals. And then he saw sheltering behind the giant white man, the white woman. The effect on him was astonishing! Nothing in his long dealing with white people in the small country farms around Tabanyane had prepared him for this sight.

Red Remusi was standing behind Ngo, in his teasing mischievous way carefully studying the other's reactions. 'So what do you think, old man? Quite a sight, eh? A white missus without any clothes on! They should let us take her in turns, that's what I say!' Red lifted his russet beard and laughed good-humouredly, his narrow eyes disappearing inside their sockets. Ngo spat and moved away to the side.

Someone heaped more wood on the fire and the white woman instinctively fell back in terror against the surface of the rock, her honeyed breasts leaping upward in an undulating movement; once again Ngo was forced to acknowledge the desperate vitality in her frightened blue eyes, the vivid incandescence of her flesh. A great agitation seized him. Like the other men Ngo had once secretly wondered what it was like to see a white woman in the nude; the hundred-and-one laws which made such an occurrence extremely unlikely had merely added fuel to his imagination; as a result, frequently on the white farms on which he worked, he found himself probing idly, almost unconsciously, for an opportunity during which, unseen, he might catch a glimpse of a naked white body. He felt no lust for such a body, only a vague desire to discover the difference between the body of a fragile white woman and that of the black women he had lain with.

That was in the past. Here he was now, faced with a new and utterly unexpected event: how was he to cope with this situation? Ngo was just about to turn away when he suddenly cast another glance, not at the woman but at the man, who stared defiantly at all of them, no longer caring to hide his nakedness. Ngo took another, closer look; then without any warning he uttered another cry that was halfway between rage and despair. 'Comrade *Tishera*, look! It's *Baas* Potgieter!'

Potgieter first looked startled at hearing his name called; he peered across the blazing fire at the huge black figure who had called him '*Baas*' so nicely – high time someone showed some respect around here, he thought. Then just as quickly he, too, recognised the black man, the crinkly dark hair mixed with grey, the thick lips with a lining of red, the dark enormous eyes that looked both frightened and defiant. Before Potgieter had time to remember the severe beating he had once administered to this particular black man, he found himself sudden galvanised by extravagant hope, a feeling of optimism quite new since his capture; in fact, he was so relieved to see at least one familiar face among his tormentors that he gave a cry at once joyful and incredulous. 'Ngo, jou *bliksem*!' He moved forward as though to shake the man by the hand. Then he stopped. 'What are you doing here with this lot? You are not one of them, are you? Good God, man, you used to be one of the best *kaffirs* I had on the farm!'

The woman froze at the use of the much-hated term of abuse but Potgieter was so happy at the sight of Ngo that he was oblivious to the language he was using to address the black man. 'Come Ngo, my boy! Tell them who I am!' he shouted. 'Tell them! Tell them who I am. Maybe they'll stop playing their silly games!'

Potgieter spoke too fast, his sense of relief at the sight of his ex-farmhand causing him to throw all caution to the wind. Once again he stepped forward but this time Phiri jumped in front of him. Without much ceremony the deputy leader shoved Potgieter back against the wall. 'Get back there!' Phiri yelled. 'You're not *"Baas"* here and there are no *"kaffirs"* here! You understand?' Pinned against the wall, Potgieter saw his last hope fade. Suddenly he screamed at the only vulnerable black man he saw: 'Ngo, tell them they're playing with fire!' he shouted furiously. 'Tell them who I am, Ngo!'

Cornelius stepped forward and stood next to his deputy. 'What seems to be the matter with him? Why is he getting so excited?'

'Ngo says he once worked for this white man,' Phiri said with disdain.

'Ngo, is this white man a friend of yours?' Cornelius enquired hopefully. Anything, any straw he could grasp to help get rid of the white man and his woman.

'I worked on his farm once,' Ngo admitted, recovering from his shock. Then as if finally released from his dream, he said: 'This was an evil white man. He used to beat his workers every day. If we didn't fill up with maize the allocated number of bags the white man was always there behind us with his *sjambok*!'

'Ngo, what are you saying!' Potgieter protested vigorously. 'Didn't I treat you like a prince? Meat rations every Sunday! Mashed potatoes on Wednesday!'

'Shut up!' Phiri shouted. 'You and your mashed potatoes!'

'He was an evil white man!' Ngo repeated.

The men seemed to wait for the next move. Their eyes were turned hopefully to the '*Tishera*' and against his will Cornelius found himself gradually yielding to a subtle collective pressure. 'The white man will be tried for his crimes of assault against the people. If there is any truth in what comrade Ngo says he will be properly punished!'

'Tried?' Potgieter was incredulous. 'You must be joking! This is no court and you can't try a white man!'

'My friend, I can assure you, this is no joke,' Cornelius told him calmly.

'Tried? What am I accused of?'

'Ill-treating your farm employees. You heard what the man said. Ngo will be your accuser. He'll provide the evidence.'

'My accuser?' Potgieter laughed scornfully, showing two rows of pearly white teeth beneath a thistle-brush moustache. 'And who is to be my judge?'

'These men here. They represent the people.'

'Represent the people?' Potgieter laughed again. 'A bunch of thugs, criminal outlaws – what people do they represent? This is a joke, I'm sure! Eh, you a black gentleman with a great sense of humour, aren't you?'

'Ngo,' Cornelius said sharply. 'Show this white man we're not joking!'

The white woman whimpered and shut her eyes. Ngo hesitated. 'One slap, comrade Ngo, will suffice to show the white man we're not joking!'

The men looked at Ngo expectantly. Red Ramusi became unusually excited. Ngo, in turn, looked at his former employer, red, naked, and somehow formidable in the shadow of the cave-fire; and something seemed to hold him back. 'I can't hit a white man, comrade leader!'

'What?' Cornelius almost shouted. 'What do you mean you can't hit a white man? Why not?'

Ngo squirmed. 'I don't know, comrade leader.'

'He's a man like you!' This time Cornelius shouted with angry frustration. 'And worse: he's a criminal!'

'Come on, Ngo! You're not afraid of a white man, are you?' Red Ramusi taunted him.

'You, Red,' Ngo glared. 'I'll thank you to shut your mouth!'

'Me he wants to fight!' Red laughed scornfully. 'That's what black people are like. They know nothing better than fighting one another. What about the white man?'

Suddenly driven by fury Ngo went up to Potgieter and gave him a hard slap across the mouth. Potgieter looked astonished. 'Ngo, you bastard!' Potgieter shrieked. 'Are you forgetting yourself? You'll be sorry for this!'

'Give him another, comrade Ngo!'

223

Ngo slapped Potgieter again. 'Ngo, you are a good boy!' Potgieter pleaded. 'Don't listen to these criminals! Laying your hand against a white man is a very serious crime in this country!' Ngo struck out again. Potgieter bunched his fists and took a deep breath; his cheeks were now puffed, his eyes looked the colour of slate, but each blow against the white man seemed to endow Ngo with new confidence. He was about to strike Potgieter for the fourth time when Cornelius called a halt.

'Ok that's enough!' Potgieter had a weal across his right cheek; a fine trickle blood was dripping down from the side of his mouth. 'I think "Baas" Potgieter can now see we are not joking,' Cornelius told Ngo.

Turning to Phiri, Cornelius told him: 'Give them their clothes.' Phiri flung a shirt and trousers at Potgieter who scrambled gratefully into them, managing at last to regain some of his lost dignity. When he had finished getting dressed, he ran his fingers briefly through his sandy-coloured hair which bristled in the dull light of the fire. 'Maybe he also wants a mirror to admire his pretty face?' Phiri sneered. Meanwhile he was trying to disentangle the woman's garments one by one, flinging each piece at her as he did so: first the pants which he handled with elegant distaste; then the bra, then the dress; the woman put on each item while the men watched with amused interest until she was fully dressed.

Having only seen her while naked Cornelius was now prepared to acknowledge how impressive the woman looked fully clothed. So this was how his own fantasies worked: backward to hidden mystery, to clothed bodies, to the fig leaf after the Fall. Her fearful eyes sparkled like huge jewel stones in a face that now seemed implausibly handsome, even pretty. A tormented face, to be sure, but suffering seemed to transform it into a mask of detached radiance. Pushed back from her face, her hair hung over each shoulder in long strands, and she rubbed her bare arms nervously as though her flesh were a precious ivory that needed constant polishing.

'Phiri, I want you to keep an eye on these two,' Cornelius instructed his deputy. 'See no harm is done to them but keep them under constant observation. You have enough men to relieve your watch during the night. In the meantime Dinkole and I will go to town as arranged.'

'Yes, comrade leader.'

'I estimate, if everything goes well, we'll be back here before dawn.'

'Yes, comrade leader. And comrade commander – ?'

'Yes, Phiri?'

'Suppose the white man wishes to relieve himself?'

The men laughed together. 'Go with him!' Cornelius answered without a smile.

'And if the woman?'

Cornelius stared at his deputy. That was a difference he had not thought about. Again the men laughed. 'Ask Ngo to go with her,' Cornelius told him. He turned to go. 'Comrade Dinkole, are you ready?'

'Yes, comrade leader!' Together the two men left the cave but once they left its immediate vicinity, it was Dinkole who led the way through the mountain forest, up and down the goat tracks of the hilly countryside which lay brooding like a man in a fever under the starless moonless after-midnight mist. They had walked, it seemed to Cornelius, for hours through dense forest, down mountain rock and finally along the rolling plains where grass was as tall as a man when Cornelius suddenly saw the glimmer of white lights which swam out of the darkness of the countryside. All of a sudden, there on the outskirts of the sleeping town, was the dusty sandy road and beside it the phone box. Leaving Dinkole by the roadside with strict instructions to keep a lookout for passing vehicles, Cornelius walked the short distance to the telephone box to make his call to a house in Johannesburg.

Chapter Seventeen

IN Johannesburg, in the small basement office hidden beneath the ground floor of the dry goods shop that Molapo had visited so long ago, highly placed members of the NLM waited anxiously for a coded telephone message indicating that the arms drop had been carried out successfully from across the border. For hours they had sat in the gloomy office, smoking listlessly and telling half-finished jokes: occasionally a man disappeared behind the door into the leaking lavatory and the rest, in order to kill time, drank Mellowood brandy from white paper cups. JB spoke first: he spoke with an infuriatingly pedantic precision.

'You realise, of course, that this mission was doomed to failure from the start?' Across from him, coatless and tieless, sat his three comrades. In marked contrast to his excited manner the others looked tired and gloomy. They seemed worn out by the strain of waiting for the news. And the news that would come would be no good, they all knew. Everything in the men's past had taught them to expect nothing but disaster from the frontline; but even so, despite their considerable experience, the cheerful cynicism of the bullet-headed man seemed for once more than they could stand. After a short, speculative silence, during which the blue smoke of cigarettes curled toward the low ceiling, the small man resumed his bleak analysis, his voice still surprisingly cheerful yet cold, as precise as it had been when he had started:

'Even assuming that Corny succeeds in arming the rebellious tribesmen,' he paused, looking at each one in turn with his small eyes, 'something we are by no means yet entitled to assume,' he emphasised, 'one thing is nearly certain: with its secret army of spies and traitors it is only a matter of time before the Government discovers the mission's hideout.'

At this bland summary of the facts his comrades looked fidgety and resentful but no-one spoke. Though outwardly unimpressive, the small man seemed to exercise over them a power and influence out of all proportion to his physical appearance. He also seemed to have at his command sources of information which were denied to his comrades. In some circles it was said that in Moscow and North Africa JB had learned not only to concoct Molotov cocktails and to throw grenades but that he had also studied in exhaustive detail revolutionary theory without which, as he had later informed Cornelius, 'true' revolutionary practice was well-nigh impossible. He was now one of the most important men on the central committee.

'Gentlemen,' JB began his summing up. 'what we are now witnessing are the gradual beginnings of yet another political disaster.' He laughed suddenly, taking the others entirely by surpirse. They looked at him in complete astonishment but the central committee man seemed unaware of the shock his burst of mirth had produced.

Half-hidden in the shadows of the dimly lit office one of the men said 'Was it really necessary to put our meagre resources at the disposal of the Tabanyane tribesmen at this stage of the struggle? Especially in view of the crushing defeat our forces can be expected to sustain?'

'No-one can pretend the committee was happy at the decision but action had to be taken,' JB said. 'You know as well as I do there were rumblings amongst rank and file. A few aventurous individuals, especially in the nationalist wing of the Movement, were daily calling for action, not least Cornelius Molapo. A decision had to be taken. We couldn't afford to be seen to be sitting on the sidelines while rebellion was taking shape among the Tabanyane.'

'Even though the failure of that mission was a dead certainty from the start?' the questioner insisted. As if he expected a missile to be hurled at him, JB ducked his head under the desk and started opening and shutting drawers irascibly. 'What are you talking about, Nsizwa? No revolution has ever been accomplished without initial failures. We have to move slowly and carefully, but we must be seen to be moving all the same. We cannot allow a bunch of adventurist bourgeois nationalists to seize control of the Liberation Movement because of our cautious inactivity.'

One of the three men sighed and shook his head. 'Poor Corny. This time his goose is surely cooked.' The others laughed.

The man from central committee became hilarious. 'Corny had it coming!' he chuckled. 'After all those public speeches, urging the Movement to get off its backside and give material support to the struggle he cannot now complain of having been unjustly treated. What better man to head the Tabanyane mission?'

The man who had made them all laugh became more thoughtful. 'The trouble with some of our chaps who are always calling for action is that they generally have somebody else in mind who is expected to take all the risks.'

Bulane seemed mildly depressed by his own analysis; he gazed with unveiled irony at his comrades, who looked stupefied by drink, whose faces also bore the characteristic anxiety of men who live by their nerves. Then surprising them in their half-sleep he began to giggle: 'I remember very well the morning Corny came here. It was in this very office, you know, that he came for his instructions, his marching orders as it were.' Mirth seized Bulane, shook him, and helplessly he lay his head on the desk behind which he sat, whooping with laughter. 'As I recall, he was only worried about his wife, Maureen, from whom he is separated. A very beautiful girl, but unfortunately for Corny, also a first-rate bitch!'

Suddenly the telephone rang. As if they had not been waiting for it to ring all along, the four men jumped up simultaneously in an exercise of complete chaos. The man from the central committee grabbed it first. 'What? Yes, yes, speaking. What news? What!'

Bulane reeled back with the phone in his hand. He turned to the others and repeated what the caller was reciting on the other end of the line: 'Now is the sun upon the highmost hill of this day's journey, and from nine till twelve is three long hours.'

But then, contrary to the arrangement, the voice on the other end of the line went on talking. Something unusual had clearly happened. To the others Bulane gave the bizarre impression of a man hanging suspended in the air, like one contemplating a long drop down a steep precipice. He placed his hand on the receiver and looked with disbelief at the three men now crowded around.

'Goddamn!' Bulane said. 'Corny has taken two white hostages!'

The men looked stunned by the news. They performed like a chorus on a musical stage.

'What?'

'Taken hostages?'

'Goddamn!'

'What the bloody hell!'

'How? Where?'

Bulane gave them a brief résumé of what he had been told over the telephone. Then he was silent for some time while the others started speaking noisily among themselves. A moment ago they had been waiting to hear about a drop of arms. This was a new turn of events. One thought this unexpected event would give them a fresh initiative in their operations against the Government forces. But another asked pertinently what form this initiative was going to take? 'What is the market for turning a couple of white hostages into hard currency?' he asked humorously. The most disturbing result of this news, however, was JB's sudden dejection at the information.

The humorous man said to Bulane: 'So, Corny took some hostages. This wasn't planned. It was a fluke. A mere chance. An accident. So what? What's the problem? I don't get it.'

Bulane was astonished. He turned to the man with a look of complete stupefaction. 'What's the problem? You don't see the problem, *mfana*? I would've thought the problem is only too obvious. What the hell are we going to do with two white hostages?'

'Don't we have a policy on hostage-taking?'

Bulane shut his eyes and opened them: 'It's never been the aim of the Movement to take hostages at this stage of the struggle. What good are white hostages to us?'

After a brief silence one said: 'Well, I suppose we can always exchange them for our people in jail. Use them as bargaining chips to get Dabula Amanzi and our comrades out of Robben Island. Sure, fly them out to a friendly country. Tanzania. Algeria or Egypt.'

Quite unexpectedly Bulane broke into one of his fits of laughter. He laughed so much he had to lay his head down on the desk again. Then, stopping, he whipped out a handkerchief from his pocket and dabbed at the tears in his eyes. 'Use them as bargaining chips! Fly our comrades out of the country to Algeria or Egypt! Let My People Go! What a joke! Now I've heard everything.'

Just as suddenly, JB took control of himself. He became sober. He stared at his comrade with affectionate disdain. 'Flight to Egypt, eh? Mnn! *Yebo, mfana*! I can see you watch too many Hollywood films. I don't know when you get the time. This is South Africa, not Hollywood. Flight to Egypt! Do you really expect these gorillas in Pretoria to sit down with us in some corner café and parley over the fate of two white hostages for an exchange of prisoners? You must be out of your coconut mind!'

The man was annoyed. 'Okay. So what do you suggest? Let them go?'

'Let them go? So they can run straight off to the Tabanyane

chief of police and reveal our secret mountain hideout? What are you talking about, *mfana*!'

In silence they listened to the tick-tock of the office clock and JB's fingers drumming on the desk. The man who had expressed the opinion that Corny's goose was cooked was the first to speak. 'I suppose they can't run around the countryside with two white hostages in tow. That's for sure. Corny can't let them go either. So there's only one way out. If the worst comes to the worst Corny could always execute them. Do you think he would have the stomach for that or do you think his philosophy of *ubuntu* would interfere with the decision?'

Another man laughed without amusement. 'That's right. Why not have them shot and let's be done with them!'

'That's out of the question and you know it,' JB said with some irritation. 'Can't execute unarmed civilians. Against NLM policy. A man poking his woman in a mountain hideout does not constitute a military target.' They all began laughing. It started with small titters and sniggers and grew into loud belly laughter until they were all rolling about in stitches. 'Oh, my goodness! What a day!' JB said, wiping tears from his eyes. 'If it comes to the worst we can always execute them! A white man poking his girlfriend in a mountain cave? God, what blood-thirsty savages you are! I suppose the UN Secretary-General will be so delighted he'll invite you all to New York for a dinner reception!'

One man who had been silent all along picked up his hat and coat. 'I have an idea,' he said. 'A very smart idea.'

'What idea?' they all shouted.

'Corny took the hostages, right? Against the Movement's known policy position. I say, let Corny deal with the hostages the way he sees fit. He took them. Let him dispose of them. Comrades, I'm afraid I have to go.'

For the third time, sitting in his office with the negotiator from Human Rights International, Dirk Prinsloo said: 'Mr Ferguson, I don't know how to tell you this without appearing to be rude but many people in this office are getting tired of your face. Believe me, we all have a tremendous amount of work to do here. Obviously, you and your organisation have much time on your hands and plenty of money to spare. I advise you to go back to London and find something else to do.'

Since their first meeting when Anthony Ferguson called on the Bureau Offices the head of the Special Branch had mellowed somewhat, tending to view the man from Human Rights International as a kind of crank with a need to cultivate a new image for himself and his employers. This was not the first time Sergeant Pinsloo had expressed mild surprise that Human Rights International had so much time and money it was prepared to send a man across thousands of ocean miles on a wild goose chase. Enquiries about Ferguson's status indicated he was born a South African and the only other explanation was that he came out primarily to spend Christmas with his family.

'I sincerely wish you a happy stay, Mr Ferguson,' Prinsloo said.

A big blond man with a closely cropped cranium and ears that were cabbage-shaped and thrust out as if made for listening, today Prinsloo was surrounded by numerous assistants who immensely enjoyed these periodic visits by the man from HRI for the moments of low comedy they afforded everyone. Prinsloo had assured his staff that whoever Molapo was he had never been in police custody: someone had obviously blundered or the London organisation had received false information or was the victim of a hoax, Prinsloo said; and now this innocent fool, he told them, was beating a path to the office in an attempt to secure the release of someone who had never been detained and whom the police had not the slightest inclination to detain. Briefing his staff, Prinsloo said this Molapo, it appeared, had been briefly under surveillance: the man was an empty loudmouth but someone who could be useful for leading security to more dangerous types in the NLM underground. When the essential lunacy of Ferguson's mission was explained everyone laughed; for it enabled everyone to relax and enjoy the long-running comedy to the very end.

'I'll tell you what, Mr Ferguson,' Prinsloo now concluded his remarks to his tiresome visitor. 'We have your address and phone number in Johannesburg. Why don't you go home and relax. If we hear anything about the whereabouts of this Molapo we will let you know. How about it?' Prinsloo said, seeing Ferguson out of his office.

Chapter Eighteen

THE fighters took turns sleeping and keeping an eye on the white man and his woman, and looking out for security scouts and trackers. From the point of view of maintaining discipline, the first few days were the most difficult; the men were excited, eager to establish contact, to get as near as possible to the white couple even when there was no legitimate reason for it. Cornelius or Phiri had to spend a precious amount of their time shooing the men off. In the long evenings, nervous and tired from long tracks in the bush, hungry for a little diversion, the men hovered around the couple; they watched and they commented. 'Comrade Tishera, look at the white man, how he shovels down his food like a hungry hyena! He must be missing his dinner!'

'Alright, Matebesi.' Cornelius took the man by the elbow and tried to talk quietly to him: 'Comrade, don't forget they also have feelings. How would you like to be stared at like an animal in a zoo while you're having something to eat?'

'In a zoo?' Matebesi who had lived in the bush all his life looked puzzled. 'What's a zoo, comrade leader?'

'You don't know what a zoo is? Never mind.' Cornelius sighed. 'Only try to leave the white people to eat in peace, comrade Matebesi.'

If Molapo's fighters sometimes lacked discipline, dealing with Gert Potgieter was not any easier. Convinced that he deserved better from fate than to fall into the hands of native savages, he adopted toward Cornelius and his men a lofty moral tone and toward the physical conditions of his confinement an attitude of superior outrage. At least, the woman Kristina Kemp showed greater humility. Not so much concerned with maintaining status, the woman wished only to survive; so she took whatever comforts were offered her with unfeigned gratitude. Potgieter, on the other hand, found his reduced status hard to accept. On the first night he had been most difficult about the blankets. When Phiri handed the white man a soiled moth-eaten blanket which had once been used to wrap a stolen piglet before being slaughtered for meat, Potgieter was enraged. He snatched the blanket, sniffed scornfully at it before throwing it aside. 'It stinks,' he shouted.

'Do you expect me and the madam to sleep in a blanket which has been used by a pig!'

'Yes! Yes!' Phiri shouted back. 'And you know why? Because you are no better than a pig yourself!'

They glared at one another. Then thinking better of it, Potgieter picked up the blanket and held it to his nose with a show of immense disgust.

'Suppose *ek kry 'n siekte*, eh? Suppose I catch a disease from all this filth? You never think of such things, because for the likes of you dirt is *mos* a natural thing.' All the same, in the end Potgieter had had to swallow his pride and take whatever was offered him to cover himself and the young woman. To keep warm, but more for the comfort that such contact can afford during the long cold nights on the mountains, Potgieter and the woman drew closer to each other, they shivered listening to the shrieks of wild birds and the howl of predatory animals in the nearby forest.

But what concerned Potgieter most was the gnawing anxiety of Hettie finding out about his secret life which would soon no longer be secret.

For the first few days Kristina was completely bewildered by what had happened. For long hours she lay awake, trying to think her way out of the loops of horror and threatening violence in which she was entangled.

Very often her mind became a complete blank, unable to retain its grip on reality. At such moments everything became fluid, time, minutes passed into hours, hours into days, nights flowed into day as easily as day flowed into night. She wept. She prayed silently. She moved about constantly in a kind of dream, following orders, doing what she was told to do except sleeping when she was told; she could go to sleep. Eating, evacuating herself behind a bush in mortified shame at being observed by the natives; slowly she began to feel she was losing control over her mind. Only fear became her reality, uncertainty about the future the dominant mood. Waiting. She was in constant fear of violation. During the long nights she lay awake, watchful, listening to footsteps, to the crash of wild animals in the forest undergrowth, to the soft whispers of men coming and going during the changing of the guards. When she got used to the men she was able to sleep but only fitfully.

Occasionally, during the days when she and Gert had nothing to do but wait on the pleasure of their captors, brooding, nervous and depressed, she found her mind wandering toward thoughts of suicide. Not yet seriously but idly contemplating the idea of it. For example, if the men should decide to take turns with her...!

One night she dreamed she was rolling about naked on the floor of the cave, being violated by a group of black men. Chanting and shrieking and stamping their feet to some fiendish war music, they formed a ring around her cringing crouching body, pawing it, pinching it, stroking, fondling, poking and tweaking it. When she woke up screaming she was shocked to discover this was no dream at all but reality – at least that part about sleeping in a cave surrounded by natives. For there they were dozing, talking, planning or playing their endless game of cards. They hated her for 'racketing', as they called it. Startled by her screams they jumped up, grabbing their guns, stepped quickly toward the hostages to see what was wrong. 'I was dreaming,' Kristina timidly whispered to Potgieter who had been equally roused by her screams.

'The madam was dreaming,' Potgieter quietly assured their disturbed captors. 'Bad dreams, ugly dreams, white nightmare,' he elaborated helpfully.

After a week of captivity it seemed like an age since she and Gert Potgieter, in a supreme moment of ecstasy, had been surprised by the guerrillas. Kristina remember with horror and shame how she had been observed completely naked by these natives now keeping guard on them. After what they had seen it was impossible to assert, without reserve, her personal superiority. She saw how they looked at her, how they bargained with their eyes for the turns they would take to violate her body but they had not yet put their hands on her. Molapo, the one who appeared to be their leader, who appeared to have some book knowledge, seemed reasonable enough. Of course, the more they were like you the more reasonable they appeared to be. She was aware of that. All the same, she couldn't help feeling safer with the one they called Molapo or 'Commander.'

Nothing seemed odder than watching him trying to create an impression of normality in the midst of chaos and turmoil. There he sat reading his books by candlelight; he wrote constantly in his notebooks; sometimes pretending to be asleep she watched him watching her with a troubled expression on his face like someone trying to work out a plan.

Apart from fear of violation the worst thing about her captivity was lack of privacy. Responding to the call of nature, emptying her bowls, urinating, even having a simple wash; having to perform such intimate bodily functions under guard, being watched by a black man with a gun, was terrible. One native had said to her: 'Don't try to run away, madam! If you try to run for it, *ek sal jou skiet, hoor jy*? I'll shoot you!' Calling her madam! Under different circumstances it might have caused her to laugh; but then under different circumstances it would have been fitting to be addressed as 'madam'!

Below the caves, under the shelter of the shady *mkuhlu* trees and wild seringa, amidst ironwood and the tangle of tree ferns, there was a small stream which fed into a tiny pool with clean pebbles at the bottom. She and Gert had often used this pool for bathing after every visit to the mountains before this catastrophe overtook them. It was the prettiest mountain stream you could ever imagine, cool, very clear; icy cold waters ran like balm over naked skin after love-making. From such a mountain stream you could drink its clean waters and live to be two-hundred-and-twenty. Later, after bathing, she and Gert would lie on the grass, their wet bodies drying slowly in the sun. A perfect spot for bathing after lovemaking. And now this! She thought she was being punished for her badness, for being a *hoer*, a whore, sleeping with two married men – one beside the river, the other in the mountains – playing Gert Potgieter against Adam de Kock. But which man was not married in Tabanyane? The young ones were away in the big towns along the Reef, making big money, living fast sophisticated lives, going to dances in the night clubs and dining out with knowledgeable city women. Well, she tried to have a little fun too; this was her life, no-one had got hurt until now.

After a while she had become too absorbed in observing what the men were doing to dwell on the plight in which she and Gert found themselves. During the long nights she watched the men sitting or talking in small groups, plotting, as she thought wildly, their destruction. '*Hulle sal ons doodmaak,*' she told Gert. Bats flew blindly in and out of the caves; the men shooed them off. Through it all Gert slept deeply, showing very little anxiety over their fate. She asked herself: how it was possible to show such lack of concern for one's own survival? Lack of imagination, she supposed; an inability to imagine danger and destruction of oneself. In his congenital optimism Gert was the opposite of Adam de Kock; it was what initially had attracted her to Gert Potgieter, his cheerful optimism; it even seemed to affect the way he made love – thoughtlessly, recklessly, jovially, without remorse.

Adam de Kock was the opposite. Greedy he was also, that was true, but he also worried about everything – his wife, the financial markets, the terrorist campaigns. In the end she found Adam de Kock's constant dread about the future was getting at her; his depression became her depressions, infectious, spoiling her enjoyment of life; it was beginning to unsettle her, to infect her with the same feeling of insecurity. Gert shored up her personality against a feeling of apprehensive drift and rootless anarchy.

All the same, now she felt that something was definitely wrong about Gert. His dislike of blacks was not normal. Since their capture Gert had not ceased to bait them! That was quite odd. His constant need, quite incomprehensible to her, for someone standing in such immediate danger of destruction, to provoke the unleashing of malevolent forces.

It was as if insulting their captors restored Gert Potgieter a measure of his depleted energy and pride, making him the powerful *boer* he had been before they had seized them, before they had deprived them of their liberty. He grumbled, he cursed; fetching wood or water under guard, sweeping the caves like Cannibal the slave, or picking wild fruit in the forest interior, he complained bitterly of being humiliated by darkies who were no better than baboons. 'Who are they to keep Gert prisoner?' he asked in a moment of incredulous rage. 'Savages armed with automatic weapons trying to bring about a new dark age in the most enlightened part of Africa!'

They listened to him with perfect indulgence. They seemed amused by his childish tantrums. 'Shut up, you!' the one they called Phiri sometimes shouted. Squat, snub-nosed, with well-muscled arms and legs, this Phiri moved with brisk, chaotic, but determined steps. He pushed Potgieter roughly against the wall of the cave. 'You're nothing but white trash, you! And a criminal. Using forced labour. How many workers did you torture on the farm? How many did you kill? I can take you outside just now and mess up your face if you're not careful with your tongue!'

Potgieter grinned, showing marvellously white even teeth surrounded by a thistle of brush moustache and wild beard. 'You would like that, wouldn't you, *jou bliksem*! Assaulting a white master. It gives you pleasure laying your filthy hands on someone superior to you, doesn't it? You wait until the security forces get here and you'll laugh from the other side of your mouth then. You'll shit, I tell you! You'll *kak*, my boy!'

That was too much. 'I told you to shut your mouth,' Phiri shouted.

Kristina was frantic with worry. She pleaded strongly with Gert to adopt a more conciliatory tone but he was oblivious to her pleas. Then when the natives appeared to have had enough they lashed out against the unarmed white man. They tied him up to a tree and slashed at him with birch, they whipped him with thong, they smacked and kicked him. It made no difference to Potgieter's level of abuse. Insult was his own insulation against loss of status; his loss of status and liberty. He was bleeding, he had a permanent blue eye by now, but he continued to curse and verbally abuse his captors as if the blows had done him no damage. 'Monkeys the lot of you! A bunch of terrorists – you call yourselves freedom fighters! What will you do with freedom when you get it? Chop up one another! Have a fine festival eating one another as you used to do before the white man came!' So it went on, day after day. The tall one they called Molapo was away a lot.

Rain came up the plateau from Mozambique, the dense foliage outside the caves drooped with raindrops that cling like pearls to the leaves before their collective weight made them run off. Snails emerged from the damp ground, leaving a wet smear like semen across the ground on which they dragged themselves. When the one they called Molapo finally returned from wherever he had been Gert whispered that some negotiations seemed to be going on pertaining to their possible release. But what if they were planning their executions instead, she asked? Gert said not to be silly; they wouldn't be that stupid. He didn't say why they wouldn't be that stupid; perhaps it was only to keep up their spirits.

Then suddenly there were more terrorists coming and going; sometimes they had injuries as if they were returning from an engagement of sort.

On their return they were angry and excitable as if they had been engaged in some devilment down in Tabanyane, also weary and hungry. At such times some of them had to be restrained from molesting her. 'We should take her by turns, the bloody bitch!' one of them said. Sometimes they brought back casualties, men with ugly wounds which needed dressing. Such men were too weak to make the journey down to the clinic on a litter. So a doctor chap or someone who looked like a doctor was brought up the mountain; a tall native wearing rimless glasses who performed emergency operations on the spot, after which the wounded men were transferred under cover of night down to the mission clinic in Tabanyane. At such times they showed less patience with their captives; on one such occasion when Gert Potgieter tried his smart talk he was severely beaten with a *sjambok*. 'Do you remember this fellow?' they asked, one of them twisting and bending the *sjambok* in his hands. 'What you use on the back of our people. Suppose we give you a taste of your own medicine, eh?' Their captors were in no mood for any more of Gert's insults.

Huddled by the fire, they held long meetings over which this fellow Molapo presided, it was usually after one of his many wanderings. There were also sudden unexpected departures, men seizing arms and taking off into the jungle trails with no warning, leaving only a handful of guards to keep watch over the hostages and the stores. Fighting was no doubt going on somewhere because when they returned again some of the men were wounded.

One man had half his knee shot off; that night terrible screams, groans and curses filled the caves. Kristina Kemp was called in to assist with the dressing; Kristina was pleased to do something, to be useful in some way, to forget about her misery even if it meant aiding her enemies. Gert hardly concealed his disgust; when they were separated from the men he laughed with unconcealed satisfaction. 'Serves them right, the stupid murderous buggers!' he muttered under his breath. 'What do they think they're playing at, carrying on like that? Tin soldiers. This is not the game they thought it was going to be. They are getting hit, no doubt about that. Soon they'll run out of ammo, you wait and see. Then they will be clobbered!'

Not too long after that Gert Potgieter suddenly went on hunger-strike. For two days he went without food. He had tried half-heartedly to persuade Kristina to join him but Kristina, a healthy country woman with the normal appetite of a horse, declined to join. 'I'm sorry, Gert. You probably feel let down but I don't think I can last more than a day without food. Why, even now I'm always desperately hungry.'

Gert was good about it, very understanding, she thought. 'Maybe you're right,' he said. 'One of us must try to remain strong and healthy.'

Molapo was furious when he heard of Gert's refusal to eat. He marched up to the white man in barely controlled rage. 'What's this I hear about you not taking your meals?'

'I'm on hunger-strike,' Gert grinned. 'Ever heard of a hunger-strike? It's what civilised people are forced to resort to when they are held unjustly against their will.'

'Like the hundreds of detainees your bloody Government keeps under lock and key without trial!' Molapo shouted. 'Who are you to preach morality to us?'

'Those are criminals you're talking about,' Gert answered impertinently. 'People suspected of being terrorists. Your lot. Underground people!'

'Listen,' Molapo shouted again. 'you bloody well take your meals or I'll see to it you're force fed. Anytime we could be required to move from here and when we trek you'll need all your strength, I can tell you!'

'That's your problem, isn't it?' Gert was smiling now. 'I'm within my rights, aren't I, refusing to eat I mean? Red Cross regulations. I'm a prisoner of war. POW. This is a war camp. If you have to move you'll have to carry me.'

'Or have you shot!' Molapo said, stomping off in a rage. As it turned out, even Gert could not keep it up longer than two days. After the second day he asked for just a morsel of something. 'Just a wee tiny bit, mate,' he pleaded with the cook on duty.

Potgieter's last act of desperation was an attempt at escape.

Very often, while some of the men were away, three or four were detailed to keep watch over the white hostages and the stores of food and ammunition. Always armed, sometimes the men were careless, playing draughts, smoking and chasing one another around. Sometimes they spent an awful amount of time admiring Kristina, teasing her; perhaps because it unfailingly infuriated Gert.

During the day the two were allowed out of the caves for fresh air and exercise. The men were always amused by Gert's attempts at showing off, doing press-ups, standing on his head, lifting home-made weights, 'pumping iron', as he called it, body-building. It was during one of these sessions that, pretending to somersault backwards, Gert went over a steep embankment and crashed into a clump of bushes. He started to run for it. 'Stop or we'll shoot!' one of the guards shouted as Gert took off. Shots rang above his head but he kept running, diving behind trees, zigzagging while the men gave chase. Unfortunately for him, Gert ran straight into a company of guerrillas returning to base. He was immediately captured. 'Nearly made it too,' he boasted when he was shoved back into the caves. For two days he had to remain 'indoors', as they called it, without being allowed out for the daily exercise.

Chapter Nineteen

IN spite of his troubles the morning drive to the police station made De Kock feel light and purposeful. The old DeSoto spun out a cloud of dust as it hit the sandy road and De Kock had to put up the windows to avoid being choked. The dirt road from the house, sometimes no more than a potholed track overgrown with weed, cut across the fields in which De Kock could see the stunted maize under the relentless sun slowly drying out.

The small bushes on the side of the road were also yellowed by the sun, the leaves flaking away; the mildest breeze stirred and rattled them, filling the air with a soft shushing sound. Already at work, bent double between the rows of the mealie crop, a dozen or so of De Kock's African workers could be seen hoeing or burning dry mealie stalks under the supervision of old Mpenda. Behind them, bulked against the wide blue of the sky the mountains always seemed too solid, yet at the same time unreal, like a huge painting on a massive canvas. They gave the illusion of something piled up by a human hand which could equally be dismantled by human hands when the time came.

However, the nearer you got to the foot of those mountains the quicker you realised how impossible that illusion was, the scale of the thing was so massive and imposing. And yet the knowledge did not depress De Kock as one would have thought: on the contrary, it gave his spirit a lift.

But could this same land swallow the missing girl so completely that it would leave no trace of a grave where at this very moment her body might be lying, her flesh rotting? At the thought of the girl De Kock's temporary mood of exaltation vanished like a drop of water in the burning sands of the Tabanyane *highveld*. By the time he reached the police station, yielding to what was now his habitual gloom, he was sensing the approach of yet another onslaught of real depression.

The Tabanyane police station was no more than a small armed camp set a little back from the main street. It consisted of corrugated iron sheds surrounded by barbed wire. The barbed wire was a later addition put in to reinforce the security of the station since the opening of the Tabanyane campaign. Each day a few grey Land Rovers covered with the dust of the *veld* could be seen parked in the small yard at the back of the station, ready to move into action at the summons by service radio or by telephone to one of the many trouble spots around the countryside. The radio service also linked the station with mobile patrols and crackled constantly with activity. The calls everyone dreaded came during the night, rousing a half-asleep duty officer who then had to track down the whereabouts of the armed patrols on the map before dispatching reinforcement if such reinforcement was required. The majority of the emergency calls reported incidents of arson and other forms of sabotage; actual shootings were few and far between and then, by the time the patrol arrived at the scene, the culprits had long vanished, melting into the bush at the first blink of the headlights from a patrolling Land Rover.

Any day of the week a passerby could look through the wide grilled windows of the flat square building squatting uneasily a few yards away from the pavement and see uniformed officers, black and white, their features set in concentration, writing their daily reports, stamping documents, hurriedly passing from one room into another. Most of their work was taken up with petty crime, the criminals invariably black, dragged in from police carriers still screaming protests of innocence.

Some were simple drunks picked up from the streets of Malaita location on suspicion of being about to foment trouble; there were also stompie-smokers found lying comatose behind Streyker's bakery, and recalcitrant workers who had been rounded up after running away from nearby farms or white households. According to current security doctrine they were all dangerous men, apparently potential recruits for the guerrilla movement; they were brought into the charge office in handcuffs like chained animals. Occasionally, a man was said to have committed a graver crime; he had answered back when reprimanded by an employer; or, worse still, had raised his hand against an unprotected housewife. Such cases were dealt with in an exemplary manner by *Magistraat* FD Nel, the presiding commissioner of the district, whose court adjoined the police station.

A hard-drinking man in his off-duty hours but God-fearing in the administration of justice, Nel was as old as Tabanyane itself. No-one could remember when he had not sat in judgment, rain or shine, over the case of some poor miscreant devil unlucky enough to have run foul of the intricately woven net of native law.

On arrival at the police station De Kock first went into his office where he read through the stack of letters at his desk, mostly unexciting official memos, reminders of unfinished business, notification of impending criminal trials and posted bail; one or two letters were from hire-purchase firms threatening to recover by distraint goods for which instalment payments had not been received for three successive months. More hurtful to De Kock's dignity was a letter, unnecessarily formal, from JP Hamilton-Rose, De Kock's bank manager, which the Englishman had failed to mention to De Kock during the brief encounter at the Meerdal. The letter warned De Kock that he had already signed cheques to an amount far in excess of funds held in his current account. The manager also thought it necessary to mention to the lieutenant (though quickly adding that De Kock probably needed no reminding,

246

being himself a law officer) that this was a criminal offence tantamount to drawing on an unauthorised bank loan.

De Kock was outraged by the officious tone of the letter; also by its dissembling, hypocritical ring typical of English doubletalk.

'Surely, a small overdraft – !' De Kock wanted to scream, when suddenly he heard worse screams of protest from prisoners being herded into the charge office by African constables Luke and Tsisi. De Kock could hear the two officers shouting curses and threats in their native language in a counterfeit of rage intended to impress their superiors but the blows were real enough, as De Kock was soon able to confirm when, still harrowed by his own anxieties and depression, he walked past bedraggled miserable forms, half-crouching and bleeding from many blows recently administered by the two overzealous black constables.

'Luke, Tsisi, cut it out!' De Kock shouted to them on his way to the duty room. 'And take this riff-raff out of here! I can't hear myself think!'

In the duty room Koos van Zyl was sitting by the telephone, laboriously copying out the day's report. Van Zyl did not look up when the lieutenant entered the room; his head bent low over the book into which he was making entries, grasping the pen like a pennant between his fingers, he went on writing painfully, his shiny blond hair gleaming like a bright yellow flame in the early morning sunshine. A heavily built young man in his early twenties with the steady, solemn manner of a neophyte priest, Van Zyl was thought a bit slow by his superiors but conscientious in his work and extremely reliable. His character was as regular as his features; there were scarcely any wrinkles, no bends or curves in it; even the girls were in despair, for Koos had reached the age of majority without experiencing what could in any way be described as lust for female flesh. De Kock had to cough twice before the boy interrupted his labour to look up with some astonishment at his superior officer. As though surprised in the middle of an indiscretion Van Zyl quickly jumped to his feet, his hands held respectfully behind his back, his heels pressed tightly alongside each other. *'Kolonel! Goeie môre!'*

'Môre, Koos!' Smiling sympathetically, De Kock waved the young constable to sit down. *'Sit maar, sit!'* As usual the duty room was spotlessly clean and smelled slightly of the sheep dip disinfectant which the prisoners used liberally to clean up the corridors. The windows were open, and De Kock was aware of the heat building up slowly outside, already turning into the infernal day he had guessed it was going to be the moment he got up. He strode across the room and paused to study a chart on the wall above the telephone. Near the chart there was a large map similar to the one the NLM had in their underground office in Johannesburg, like one of a pair showing important landmarks which were circled in red ink; there were also drawing pins stuck in several places of strategic importance. 'Everything all right, Koos?'

Van Zyl looked startled by the question. This was his normal reaction to any form of inquiry, however mildly expressed. 'Yes, sir. Only one telephone call during the night, sir. Constable Joubert's patrol thought they spotted some natives making their way down the mountain trail between Doodsnek and Karlstad. They drove out there to investigate but only found a group of native herdboys rounding up cattle for the morning dip.'

De Kock couldn't help a weary smile. It was always the same: a group of herdboys rounding up cattle for the morning dip until you got close enough for your carcass to be cleaved in two by a panga. 'Oh, *Kolonel, Mevrou* Potgieter also rang,' Van Zyl remembered.

'Again? What did she want?'

'She was shouting the devil and accusing us of not doing enough to find her husband.'

De Kock swore. 'Well, we can't be spending every blessed hour looking for Gert Potgieter! Next time she rings you tell her that. *Verstaan?* There is a guerrilla war going on here!'

For half an hour De Kock sat down at his desk, sorting requisition papers and making calls to Tabanyane and outlying districts; to Oom Krisjan Steenkamp, the Tabanyane station-master, to check what suspicious natives might have come into town by train; to Frans du Toit at the post office to get the lowdown on telegrammes, and on in- and out-going calls. After more than a half-a-dozen calls the only exciting piece of news De Kock had been able to acquire was that Greta Lienhardt was at last getting married to a boy from the Copperbelt in Zambia.

Hettie Meiring, who worked at Rina's Hairdressers, reported with great satisfaction that the wedding was set to take place in two weeks' time. 'That only shows,' Hettie said mysteriously, without any further explanation. As a result, De Kock was unsure whether Hettie's unusually terse comment concerned the boy's evident commitment or whether she disapproved of the haste with which the knot was being tied. Hettie said that after the wedding Greta and the boy would probably be going up to the Copperbelt to live. Quite unreasonably, De Kock felt mild annoyance at the tone of complacency he thought he detected in Hettie's voice. Listening to the sprightly, fun-loving widow of forty-five and a notorious match-maker, De Kock's irritation soon mastered him completely; acidly he told Hettie that getting married was not the solution to everything, you know; if anything, De Kock said, marriage can create more problems than staying single.

De Kock said what about all the strikes and the violence on the copper mines then? Hadn't Greta Lienhardt heard about striking miners on the bloody Copperbelt? For his own part, De Kock said, he would rather stay put where he was, with his own kind of war, in a place he knew, than running to bloody Zambia.

'Well, you're not the one the boy is proposing to marry, Adam, are you?' Hettie was laughing when she said this. You could hear her chuckling and passing on the comments to the other ladies under the hairdryers.

De Kock didn't appreciate the humour and told Hettie so

right away. God, De Kock was saying on the phone, isn't it just awful, isn't it bloody depressing, people planning for a future for which there was little prospect; young people getting married, children getting born, people fighting, dying for no reason at all? Where is the good, De Kock said. There was a small catch in his voice as he asked Hettie please to explain: where was the good? He knew he was working himself up into a tragic mood but he couldn't stop himself.

In the blazing sun the Tabanyane mountains shimmered like a mirage; not a wisp, not a tuft of cloud anywhere to suggest a break in the continuous drought. And the girl Kristina unaccountably missing. De Kock felt a surge of emotion constricting his throat and felt like sobbing outright but instead, as soon as he got off the 'phone, he shouted at Koos. 'Koos, I want you and Bert to check the fuel in all the vehicles before they leave the depot for patrol duty! Okay, Koos?'

'Right-o, *kolonel*!' Koos said, not raising his head from the pile of papers in front of him. Like a bloody village scribe, De Kock thought to himself as he moved towards the door. He was overwhelmed by bitterness; his saliva tasted like bile in his mouth. 'I'm off to the Meerdal if somebody wants me!' he shouted. 'You can get me there by telephone if something important comes up.' And De Kock strode out of the room, feeling angry and frustrated but not sure with whom.

Just as he was about to cross the floor of the waiting room in order to let himself out by one of the side exits a voice called out to him, 'Colonel!'; a smooth voice, gay, chirpy, a voice like fire, like a siren whispering news of catastrophe and imminent disaster, a voice De Kock thought had been silenced forever. Lieutenant Colonel De Kock stopped in mid-stride, and turning round, saw the decrepit little figure sitting on one of the wooden benches, wearing a faded darkish suit of an uncertain cut and a homburg hat a size too big for the dimunitive head. He immediately recognised the gaunt features and the high cheekbones, the sharp penetrating eyes beneath the sloppy brim of the hat. De Kock was astonished.

250

'What do you want here?' he asked in a low, excited voice, full of suppressed anger and reproach. 'I thought I told you never never to come back toTabanyane again?'

The man had been chain-smoking cigarette after cigarette before De Kock entered the waiting room, and though he was often seized by spasms of coughing, after squashing the last *stompie* under his foot he immediately lit the next one; for a while he gazed sceptically at the cigarette before thrusting it back between his distended lips. He coughed a lot; he spat into his gaudy handkerchief and crushed the gob of phlegm with vigour; he was obviously a sick man; he looked consumptive, badly undernourished. Not getting up from the seat the black man said in his smooth, pleasant voice: 'Ah, colonel, as Cain said – I believe it was Cain, wasn't it – who said it is far easier to get rid of my brother Abel than getting rid of a good old friend!'

'Cain said that?' De Kock asked with some surprise. Then quickly recovering his balance he bawled out at the insalubrious figure: 'Never mind about bloody Cain! I thought I told you to leave Tabanyane. You have no job, you have no permit to reside in the area, and you have proved to be of little use to us.' A yellowish substance trickled down from the man's gaping mouth, but he did nothing about it; he let the slime dribble down from his lips on to the floor before stepping on it and shuffling it with his foot. De Kock tried to avert his eyes from the spittle. 'If you insist on staying here I'll be forced to run you in like any bloody vagrant of no fixed abode,' he warned the other. *'Jy verstaan?* You understand me?'

'Colonel, is that how you return favours?' the black man asked pleasantly, seemingly unhurried and unperturbed.

'Favours!' De Kock exploded. 'What bloody favours? And don't mess up the floor with your bloody gobs of spittle. I'm asking you: what do you want?'

The man carefully lit another cigarette. De Kock had to wait a few seconds because he was immediately seized by another spasm of coughing, after which he produced from his

251

side-pocket a gaudy red handkerchief with which he collected the spume rather than wipe it off.

'Colonel De Kock,' he finally responded, 'I sent you so many messages, Lieutenant! Many many messages. You'd be surprised how many! I've forgotten myself how many. Did you not receive them? I wanted to pass on very important information to you but no-one came to meet me at the place and time indicated. Why? But never mind. Finally I thought I'd better come personally. As you can see, here I am!' The black man became extremely cheerful, and laughing, he drew from his inexhaustible stock of quotations, trite maxims, proverbs, aphorisms. Finally, he remarked to the police chief: 'You know how the saying goes, Colonel. If Muhammad won't go to the mountain the mountain must come to Muhammad!'

De Kock was enraged. 'Look here, you're no bloody mountain and I'm no damned Muhammad, you hear?' But instantly he dropped his voice to a whisper. 'I thought I told you never to come anywhere near the police station. That's the first rule you've broken. What do you want? Have you got something big to tell me or are you after more payment as usual? I can tell you right away the people at the top are not very pleased with the quality of the information they've been getting and they've paid you more than enough as it is!'

The black man got up and looked briefly through the small window of the waiting room into the backyard of the police station. A white constable with blond hair was supervising two black men who were preoccupied with putting petrol into some vehicles. One of the two black men finally straightened himself up and, wiping his hands on a soiled rag, paused to stare directly at the window of the waiting room. De Kock's visitor beat a quick retreat from his position at the window, and turning to De Kock he said: 'Colonel, your people have no-one but themselves to blame for the many mistakes they've made. If only they'd listened when I gave them some very important leads!' the black man sighed in mock despair. Assiduously he pulled the hat down over his face, nearly concealing the eyes altogether; then he resumed his seat on the bench so that the police chief and his visitor looked like two brothers with troubled consciences, attempting to exchange inconvenient information. Finally De Kock complained: 'Always the information you give us has proved worthless. Usually it's what everyone else already knows, what everybody down in the location is already talking about, or it's what the terrorists want us to pick up so that we can be led into a trap.'

'Ah, Colonel, you know better than anyone how good my intelligence is! What I tell your people is always topnotch, first-rate, what Churchill himself, with his exceptional command of the English language, would have called *nonpareil*. You know what the trouble is, Colonel? Trouble is your people never take me seriously when I pass on a hot tip. That is their trouble. Was there no blast at the power station last November as I warned them? Was there no sabotage of the railway line at Langeni? Was *baas* Bezuidenhout not ambushed on the road to the farm?'

'Yes. Always too late for us to make proper preparations. That's another thing security wants to talk to you about. They have their suspicions, for example, why you've never been able to lead us to where the terrorists have their bases. Frankly, that would be a thousand times more useful than your hot tips!'

'Believe me, Colonel, I'm working on that, but it's no easy matter, I can tell you. My informants get their information in a very roundabout way. They need to build enough confidence before they can take me to certain individuals they suspect to be connected to the underground. Then they always have to be paid.'

'*Jy praat 'n klomp kak, man*! Tell me one thing. Why have you come today?'

The black man first cast a furtive glance around the room. 'Colonel, believe me, there are many stories going the rounds in Malaita location.'

253

'Ah, stories,' De Kock breathed. 'Always stories. So what stories?'

'Faces have suddenly appeared in the location that no-one has ever seen there before. New faces. There is even a new dance which has hit town. Something like the old-fashioned American "jitterbug" dance. It is now the craze of the location. No-one knows how it came into town but some people say it has its links to the underground.'

De Kock finally lost his temper. 'Look here, I have better things to do than to waste my time listening to your "jitterbug" nonsense. I'll also tell you something else. A big "bug" is what you've got inside here!' De Kock pressed his finger against his own head.

'You see, Colonel? That's what I mean. You people never want to listen. Believe me, a lot more is going on down there in Malaita location than your boys in uniform seem to know about. I've heard stories which would turn your hair, Colonel.'

'Ah, stories again,' De Kock shook his head in despair. He wanted to be rid of this ridiculous black man as quickly as possible but feared to dismiss him without lending an ear to his nonsense just in case. 'Stories? What sort of stories?'

'There's talk, Colonel.'

'Talk? What talk?'

'Talk of a possible attack. Of course, it may all be idle gossip. All the same, who can tell?'

De Kock looked intently at the small black man who seemed to him to be a little desperate, haggard, his face unwashed, his clothes old and soiled with grease and cigarette ash on his sleeves; he said: 'Okay, come into my office.'

When they emerged half an hour later De Kock's face looked sick, his jowl hung lower than usual, and his eyes were haunted with shadows darker than those on the underside of the Tabanyane mountains. He walked with the black man as far as the door. 'I'll pass on what you've just told me to the proper authorities,' he said grimly, looking up and down the street. 'But you can be sure in a few days we'll have the whole of Malaita location turned upside down. I promise you that. Wait until Monday, you'll see. My men will go through Malaita location with a fine-toothed comb.'

Forty-five minutes later this information was in Thekwane's possession. As a result a decision was taken to act immediately.

Chapter Twenty

A T noon the main street in Tabanyane was already emptied of cars and shoppers and emptied of people whose duty it was to tend to the daily business of running the town: the main store, the dress shop at the corner of the small square, the post office, the insurance office across the street, they were all shut. The bank opened only in the mornings but the small library, perhaps in a desperate attempt to lure in more readers, stayed open all day until five o'clock. The hairdresser's and the barbershop also stayed opened in order to accommodate the clientele that was to able patronise such establishments only during the lunch hour. For all other practical purposes life came to a standstill at noon – the commercial life, that is – for another life immediately began that was more positive, more intimate, celebrating the leisure hours of the body. The coffeeshop, the Oom Paul Bar and the restaurant of the Meerdal Hotel became chockful of Tabanyane white citizens taking a break from the daily grind to make ends meet. It was at this hour that a black man often seen around Malaita location but very rarely in white Tabanyane took time off to reconnoitre the town. Hardly distinguishable from other black men, he kept walking up and down the less than two kilometres it took to cover the stretch of the main street from one end of town to the other, from the post office on the east to the police station on the western extreme, with the Meerdal

Hotel, the insurance office and the bank at the centre, and around the small dusty square, which was no more than a cleared space, the dress shop, the hairdresser's and the barber-shop; on the fringes were blackened trees whose trunks were stained with the pee of generations of urinating dogs. A dry heat, luminous in the midday glare, rose in the nearly motionless air, carrying motes of dust in shimmering waves.

When Adam de Kock stopped in front of the Meerdal he saw the black man walking close to the shop windows, pausing every now and then to admire the merchandise displayed in the shop windows. The man stopped suddenly. His attention seemed particularly drawn to a very lifelike mannequin, temporarily stripped of its fashionable clothing, its arms frozen in a gesture of supplication and surrender to window shoppers. A few white citizens had protested from time to time at the realistic representation of the human figure too obviously that of a white person, arranged in provocative posture and left nakedly exposed to lascivious eyes; to the town's stricter religious puritans, these briefly disrobed mannequins were seen as unnecessary stimulants to the not-so-dormant passions of male viewers, especially natives. Quite recently the town's *dominee* had vigorously protested to the city fathers.

In front of the shop window De Kock now saw the native pause to look at the stripped, life-size doll as he had known he would, then resume his leisurely pace, all the time whistling what to the policeman sounded like the music of the new dance tune about which he had just been told. All morning, it seemed to De Kock, he had been hearing this tune without being aware of it. He couldn't remember exactly where or when he had started to hear it but it was suddenly everywhere, in every street corner, behind closed shops and in backyard kitchens, where dark lips closed suddenly, pouting; it seemed that every black was whistling the tune. An hour later, when De Kock left the Meerdal for the second time that day he saw the same native walking close to the pavement, his straw hat pulled low over his eyes, wearing his indescribable pieces of clothing of no particular colour. This time De Kock accosted him. '*Wat soek jy hier*? What do you want?' he asked him.

'Me?'

'Yes, you. Who else am I talking to?'

'Why, nothing, *baas*.'

'So what are you loitering about here for?'

'Just looking, *my baas*, at the nice things.' The man pointed at the mannequin with outstretched arms.

De Kock was enraged. 'Well, I'm sick of having to look at your mug all day, you hear! I don't know what you are hanging around here for but I have seen you once too often already. Do you know I can run you in any time I like?'

'Run me in? What for? I've done nothing.'

'Don't try to be clever with me! I could run you in on suspicion. I could charge you with criminal intent. Loitering with intent to commit a crime! Is that what you want?'

'No, *baas*,' the man said but his voice gave nothing away; it was neither surly nor submissive, not even curious, only flat and neutral, as if the owner expected to be accosted in this manner every day of his life.

'Okay. You don't want to be put behind bars. So don't let me see you around here again.' It seemed to De Kock that the native, his face lit up suddenly by the warmth of compassionate understanding, was smiling condescendingly at him, and the colonel felt welling up within him a bitter rage of frustration; his throat felt dry and his cheeks were burning as if on fire. 'You think you so smart, wearing a straw hat like that,' he fumed, 'with so many holes like rats sleep in it!' Unexpectedly, the African chuckled with real enjoyment, which only increased De Kock's rage. 'You find this a joke?'

'Yes, *baas*. I mean, no *baas!*'

'Well, don't you try to be bloody funny with me, *jou skelm*! Look at yourself! You know what you look like? Like a bloody baboon!'

This time the native really guffawed. 'Ah, the *baas* is really funny, *nè*?' he offered tolerantly. 'Maybe the *baas* had a very bad morning?'

De Kock could no longer control himself. He raised his hand as if to strike him, then stopped himself in time. 'Go on! Take your *verdomde* carcass away from my sight before I run you in, *jou bliksem*! Just looking at you, you make me want to puke! *Loop! Voetsek*!'

'*Ja, baas*. Sorry, *baas*,' the man apologised, moving on. He walked off in an easy gait without a last look at De Kock. The white man watched him for a few seconds, not sure why this native should arouse such animosity within him. There were thousands like him walking the streets of Tabanyane every day of the week. De Kock's police duties made interest or curiosity in such natives understandable, but this one produced an effect on him which had something of the irrational about it; something about this native was not right somehow. He watched the black man strolling down the street toward Streyker's bakery, his gaze seemingly attracted to everything, however unimportant, as if each particle of dust held some alluringly, absorbing secret. Just before De Kock crossed the street he saw another native come round the corner to join the first one. When he looked back the second time he saw that together the two were holding a lengthy conversation, gesticulating and pointing out landmarks like two surveyors scouting new territory. His suspicions now fully aroused, De Kock had a good mind to go after the pair of them, perhaps detain them for questioning, for already he had begun to think of the two blacks as 'suspects', loitering with intent; only fear of making a fool of himself should the two blacks turn out to be harmless vagrants stopped him. Before long his thoughts began to drift to other matters; to Kristina Kemp and Gert Potgieter and their mysterious disappearance. While slowly making his way toward the police station, De Kock was going over mentally what De Souza, the hotel manager, had told him; De Souza had said that after an entire week, during which Kristina Kemp had failed to report for

259

work, the management had finally adopted the view that their employee was missing under very suspicious circumstances; that foul play was suspected, and they duly reported it officially to the police.

Thekwane and Molapo were leaning against the wall of Streyker's bakery shop, watching other black men lounging on the grass on the small lawn. As soon as they had exchanged greetings Thekwane launched into a fierce attack on the momentous decision about to be taken by the NLM. The word from Johannesburg was that the Movement was about to suspend the armed struggle in favour of extended negotiations with the Government on the future shape of the country. This could be their last combat mission, as Thekwane told Cornelius. 'Very soon,' he bitterly complained, 'we are going to be asked to sit down at table and sup with the same devil who has murdered hundreds of our innocent people and has made martyrs of many of our brave freedom fighters!' It was well known that behind the scenes the Movement was split between those who supported this new policy of compromise and those who, like Thekwane, suspected the Movement was about to be tricked into an irreversible policy of total surrender. Thekwane and his combat units, conveniently far away from the complexities of policy argument, had resolved to continue their military campaign regardless; they would act as if no changes of policy were imminent. For this minor insubordination Thekwane needed an excuse; so now he turned his beaming face to Molapo, his quick eyes twinkling with mischief: 'For some reason,' Thekwane said, smiling his crafty smile, 'we are not receiving the communiqués of the central committee which everyone is talking about. I blame bad channels of communication for this lamentable state of affairs. In the meantime, we see no reason not to proceed with the armed struggle as before. How about you, Corny? Very soon it will be time to return to civilian life, I suppose?'

'Not me, comrade T!' Molapo's resolute tone betrayed a

change in his normally vacillating character that took Thekwane by surprise. Much in Molapo's character had changed since joining the mountain fighters. Like a reluctant new recruit to a big public corporation he had found that over weeks and months he had grown with the job; now it seemed as if his very pulses had begun to beat with the steady rhythm of his mountain fighters; he had become one of them. He said to Thekwane: 'You forget I belong as much to the Tabanyane Resistance now as I belong to the NLM. Another thing. I am not a stranger here. I was born in Tabanyane. As long as that murderous scoundrel Sekala remains paramount chief of Tabanyane our struggle goes on much as before, with or without the NLM. In any case, as far as we are concerned, what is said to be going on in Johannesburg is all a matter of speculation, comrade T. As far as I know, the Movement has yet to come to a decision. Meanwhile – '

'Meanwhile,' Thekwane beamed, 'the struggle goes on.' Then he continued with fresh enthusiasm: 'Everything is set. Our people are split up into two combat units. The first, which I'm to lead personally, will hit the police station at seven o'clock exactly. We're moving in everything with us, including rocket-propelled grenades. The other unit will lay an ambush on the southern approach to the town which is the main conduit for reinforcement should the South African Defence Force decide to rush in personnel before we've made good our escape. Then we regroup and head, first twenty kilometres north, then backtrack and head south-east towards the border. As you know, we're counting on your detachment to draw some of the fire away from the centre of town – that is, if you should succeed in hitting your target as planned, before we hit ours.' Thekwane paused, looked questioningly at Cornelius. 'How's your end of the operation holding up?

'So far so good,' Cornelius reported. 'Our gear is already in place, all ready for action. Our combàtants are lying in wait less than a kilometre from the farm.' Molapo paused, watching a heavily built white man in police uniform strolling down the street in their direction. 'Excuse me comrade T, but isn't that De Kock, the police chief?' he asked in a tightly controlled voice.

Thekwane looked across the street. '*Ja*. That's him,' but Thekwane seemed quite unconcerned. 'Do you know that fool of a police chief had the cheek to say he can't stand to look at my face!'

Cornelius chuckled. 'To tell you the truth, neither can I, comrade T! You've run into him before?'

'A few minutes ago.' Thekwane seemed to be considering. 'The point is,' he went on imperturbably, 'that damn fool of a policeman doesn't know he's just about to have his head blown to kingdom come.'

A few paces away from where Thekwane and Molapo were standing a brightly coloured butterfly fluttered around a flower that looked limp, as if about to die from the heat. Quick, lively, slashing with its frothy, lathery wings, the butterfly rose, came back scattering vapours of light around the gaping flower but resisting all temptation to settle. Cornelius watched it; finally he turned to Thekwane. 'Jordaan is in town,' he said. 'He came in this morning accompanied by his five African assistants. Those black shits are no better than their boss. Maybe worse. They are the most notorious slave-drivers you're ever likely to come across. Cruel, vindictive, corrupt; even labourers' wives are open season to them! We have full dossiers on all five of them, including every atrocity they've ever committed. We even know the graves where their victims are buried.'

Thekwane seemed not to be listening to the words so much as he was closely watching Cornelius. For the first time since he had known him Thekwane suddenly noticed what an angry man Molapo was beneath what seemed to be an inexhaustibly playful humour; this was one of those revelations that come in a sudden flash of insight. There were rings around Molapo's eyes, as if he had not been sleeping much; his brown skin had darker patches around the mouth; his eyes seemed haunted by

262

an intense vision of two violently opposed forces and the inevitable conflict between them. 'Right now, Jordaan's truck is parked outside Joubert's General Store, loading supplies before returning to the farm this evening,' he reported to Thekwane. 'We've had them under surveillance all day. Jordaan is in there in the Meerdal Hotel, knocking them back with his cronies in the Oom Paul bar.' Molapo's eyes were fixed on the Meerdal Hotel, on the constant comings and goings of the weekend crowd. 'Like your police chief, what he doesn't know is that our men are lying in wait for his return less than a kilometre from his farm.'

'Corny, let's walk a bit,' Thekwane said, glaring beneath his moth-eaten straw hat. De Kock was slowly approaching from the opposite side of the street. 'See?' Thekwane said angrily, 'that fool of a police chief is coming our way.' As soon as they started to walk, he said to Molapo. 'I hope you realise, after the attack tonight there is going to be hell to pay all round. How are your escape hatches fixed?'

'Okay,' Molapo said. 'We have ropes in place on the north-ern face of the mountain. As soon as the job is done we'll be up on that mountain like a group of vervet monkeys. By seven o'clock when all hell breaks loose down here we should be in bed. We're planning on an early sleep.'

'Don't forget,' Thekwane warned, 'tomorrow morning, as soon as it is light, they'll be up those mountains looking for you.'

'Looking for you, you mean,' Molapo corrected.

'Okay, looking for all of us but the mountains is where they are going to go looking first. So you should be prepared because, comrade, they're going to bring in everything – helicopters, gunships, rockets, mortars, hunters and mustard gas, you name it. And if they find you up there they'll skin you alive!'

'We're aware of that, which is why tomorrow is removal day for us.' Cornelius then explained how it had been decided to abandon the mountain base for a while and disperse among the rural population until all the excitement had died down. As a prelude to the release of the two white hostages and abandoning the camp, in the past few days Cornelius had supervised the removal of the arms cache to the grounds of the Anglican mission; there they were secretly buried in the dead of night.

Thekwane asked in wonder. 'With the knowledge of that Anglican priest?' Thekwane had never thought much of Father Stephens' commitment to the struggle, or what he considered his self-appointed role as the Church's watchdog in the Tabanyane resistance. In fact, many of Thekwane's logistical problems, Molapo now realised, had stemmed from his distrust of religious personalities and the Tabanyane aristocrats. Thekwane's theology, Molapo thought wryly, had always got in the way.

'Well, as you know Father Stephens is a man of non-violence,' Molapo explained, 'but he was good enough to take his annual leave at the right time. He's down in the Cape. In his absence we've had to rely entirely on the co-operation of the princess which, I must say, has been excellent.'

'Glad to hear it,' Thekwane said sourly. Then he added: 'You were always sweet on your princess, weren't you? Tell me something. Has she been giving it to you on the side?' Suddenly they were more like dirty-minded schoolboys discussing past romantic assignations than two guerrilla leaders about to launch the biggest attack ever seen in Tabanyane. It helped to steady their nerves.

'Comrade T! What a question!' Molapo exclaimed innocently. 'It was all very fraternal.' Then he proceeded to give Thekwane a detailed picture of how they intended to make their escape from the mountains after releasing the hostages. Phiri, who knew the terrain like his own backyard, was going to lead them out on an escape route as small as a goat track at the back of the mountains, sometimes literally clinging by their toenails on the smooth surface of the rocks. 'First, we release the hostages and then, before the SADF gets up there, at the first light of dawn tomorrow we will be gone.' But he looked worried. 'Obviously, we would have been

better off without having to worry about the hostages,'
Molapo said. 'They have been our biggest headache. We've
had to decide whether to execute them out of hand or let them
go and run the risk of having the whereabouts of the camp
disclosed to the enemy. We finally decided to release them but
close down the camp altogether after today's action. Potgieter
will run to the police the moment he is released to lead them
back to where the camp is.'

After listening carefully to Molapo Thekwane summed up:
'If you ask me, you're making a big mistake to let Potgieter
go. After the clearly documented evidence of widescale use of
torture against his farm workers Potgieter deserves to be
executed. Let the girl go. White women don't have much to do
with all the crap that is going on in this country. But do away
with Potgieter. He deserves everything he gets.'

'Can't, comrade T. Against strict directives from headquarters. Non-military target.'

'Non-military target? Potgieter!' Thekwane was laughing
so hard he nearly fell on the pavement; his body was actually
sliding down the shopfront against which they were now
lounging. It took Molapo some time to realise that Thekwane
was not really laughing out of mirth but from an un-
controllable rage. 'Okay. So Potgieter is a non-military target,
what the Movement calls a soft target. So why do away with
Jordaan? There isn't that much difference between Potgieter
and Jordaan. They've both committed unbelievable atrocities
against farm workers.'

'Of course, that's how most people would look at it but
headquarters sees it differently. They have international
opinion to worry about. Giving the other side a major propaganda stick with which to beat us is what they worry about.
That people will say that they captured a couple of innocent
lovers in the bush and murdered them in cold blood! On the
other hand, Jourdan is a clear military target. He's one of the
leaders of the citizens' commando unit in Tabanyane. If our
people get him tonight they'll be celebrating in the Tabanyane

villages. True, after that there'll also be a lot of target-shooting by his commandos against anything black that moves.'

Finally, it was time to separate. Thekwane made the first move to go. 'Corny, we've done a lot of talking. We haven't got much time. Only four hours at the most.' They shook hands. 'Good luck, Corny!'

'Amandla!'

The plan was simplicity itself; perhaps that is why it worked so perfectly. Molapo had suggested to Phiri that the men should find boulders which they could place one on top of another across the road. They then hid in a ditch beside the road, not very far from the pile of rocks, screened from sight by a clump of trees. Behind the gentle swell of the hill they could see Jordaan's farmstead surrounded by its golden maize fields, the horses and the cattle grazing on the slopes; so peaceful was this scene that, far from being soothing, it produced the opposite effect. The men felt as though their nerves were pulled by invisible wires.

In the encroaching twilight before objects began to lose their shape entirely the men saw the approach of the slow-moving truck, its headlights stabbing at the giant trees along the dusty gravel road. The car seemed to take an age to get to where the men, clutching their automatic weapons and holding their breath, lay in waiting behind a bush which could so easily betray their presence. Like a giant cockroach the truck approached, its headlights blinking, swerving first to one side, then to the other; but as though equipped with sensitive antennae it finally halted directly in front of the clump of trees where the guerrillas were lying flat on their stomachs, hardly allowing themselves to breathe. Without switching the engine off, a large white man in khaki shorts, armed with a rifle, emerged from the truck's cabin followed by an unarmed African who, with a wide arc of his arm, indicated an area where he thought he had seen strange men walking about with short sticks. For a second the guerrillas, lying close together, hugging the earth, seemed to be mesmerised by the brightness and the pink glow of the skin in the glare of the headlights; then Phiri raised his hand for the men to open fire.

That was only the first attack of the night. When the attack on the police station happened it took white Tabanyane entirely by surprise.

After what had seemed an unusually quiet day, De Kock was sitting in the bar of the Meerdal Hotel when the fighters struck. No fighting had been reported in Chief Sekala's territory; no suspected guerrilla movements had come to the notice of De Kock's elaborate system of surveillance, to which hundreds of petty crooks and criminals owed their living; nothing save what the black man had told him that morning. But the man had given De Kock to understand that an attack could be expected in weeks rather than days. Malaita location, too, had been exceptionally quiet that day.

Then at seven o'clock five armed guerrillas walked past the police station, their weapons hidden under their coats; at the end of the main street they made a U-turn towards the police station, whistling a tune which was very popular with the 'jitterbug' dancers of Malaita location. At the time, African constables Leonard Tsisi, Joseph Luke and Bernard Gabela were sitting on the *stoep* outside the police station; Martin Scholtz, the senior officer in charge that night, was in the main office. Koos van Zyl and five other junior officers were lounging about in the common-room. Suddenly, without any warning, came gunfire from the street; bullets were flying, the sound of glass breaking.

Then came the grenades. While several officers dived for cover the grenades, at least four, only one of which failed to explode, were lobbed into the police station. The remaining three did sufficient damage, demolishing a whole section of the police station. The sound of the explosion could be heard about ten kilometres across town; it sent men scrambling for weapons while women switched off the lights and took cover with the children under beds. After the gunfire five officers were left dead on the scene, three black and two white, all blown to pieces; seven officers were badly injured, and their screams, coming from men trained to deal with violence, added to the eeriness of the atmosphere. Young Van Zyl, as if protected by the god of the slow and dim-witted, miraculously escaped and, contrary to Thekwane's express hopes, Adam de Kock was saved by his dereliction of duty.

Chapter Twenty-One

A NIGHTBIRD shrieked. Somewhere behind the caves a man hawked and spat, a tribe of monkeys, angry and disturbed, chattered wildly to a murmur of voices which suddenly filled the night air with speculation. Gert Potgieter, who in his dreams confused the bare stone of his captivity with the swinging hammock in which he sometimes slept on his farm, knew something was up the moment he was woken by the noise and saw the natives scurrying about, making preparations to leave. The commotion was more like a celebration than the twitter of excitement which normally accompanied the return of the guerrillas from one of their sabotage campaigns.

Rolling over on his side, Potgieter kept one eye on the natives while nudging the girl Kristina who slept beside him. She woke immediately and Gert whispered to her that he thought something was up. The natives were not going to sleep at all that night; they were all over the place, everywhere packing. It also seemed they were actually having a party, knocking back some of their bloody moonshine, and performing some of their favourite fancy steps which looked nothing like their traditional war dances. Even the tall one they called Molapo was at it. Quite absurd, if it weren't so alarming. Gert and Kristina watched with horrified fascination at this macabre dance. One native would hug another and they would whirl and twist and turn, bending their legs at the knees, gasping and sobbing like stricken devils. A right regular nightmare, Gert said it was.

But what to make of it all?

Gert suspected the bloody buggers might have achieved some minor successes against the security forces. It stood to reason. Let them be happy for a season, he thought, the bloody fools! Let them enjoy a few laughs before the tears. But definitely, he told Kristina under his breath, something was up. The terrorists were actually packing everything in their knapsacks and destroying what was left out. Of course, in the past few days there been a little of the same activity, some of the boxes – Gert thought maybe containing arms – had been moved out in the middle of the night to God knows where. Perhaps the natives were shifting after all. But if they were moving on where and how would they take the white hostages without being observed? Kristina Kemp, forever huddled up like a medieval martyr, had always feared the natives would order a summary execution but Gert knew better than that: natives wouldn't dare! Killing one another was one thing, they were always doing that down there in Malaita location. After a few cups, a few tins of their poisonous home-made brew, some insults bandied about rather freely over a woman and soon they were at each other's throats! It was their proud custom, fighting over the spoils; but killing a white man, well that was another matter.

Just before morning everything seemed to have quietened down a little. The natives were obviously taking a rest before a long trek in the bush but Gert was very much surprised when they started coming over to their side of the cave. Looking as if he had not shaved or combed his hair for over a week, the tall one said: 'Well, *baas* Potgieter?' Sneering a little. It was what Gert couldn't tolerate about this native, the way he always seemed to sneer when he addressed him, as if the bloody bugger knew more than a white man knew. Gert had never been able to tolerate an uppity native. Even the

270

violence, the beatings which Gert had sometimes received from the other fools, were preferable to the arrogant sneers of this one, who obviously thought himself better than a white man. Gert had once explained to Kristina that he could take a few slaps from a native quite calmly because when a native practised violence against a white man it only confirmed his hopeless inferiority; it showed he had no other means of asserting his equality except by resorting to violence against an unarmed white man. But this one, when he said in his mocking voice: 'Well, *baas* Potgieter?' Gert knew the man's form of address was meant to be ironic, even insolent, and he hated him for it.

'What is it?' Gert said in a truculent voice. 'Me and the madam are trying to get some sleep.'

'Oh, really? I beg your pardon then, *meneer* Potgieter,' the man sneered again. 'Awfully sorry to disturb Your Lordship. Anyway, don't let a little inconvenience like talking to me worry you. You'll soon get a lot of sleep, won't you? More than you'll ever want.'

Gert allowed an ugly thought to cross his mind. 'What do you mean we'll soon get a lot of sleep?'

'I'm afraid it's time to say goodbye, *meneer* Potgieter, sir.'

'Goodbye? You mean you're going to shoot us?' Kristina began to whimper. Gert felt sorry for the dear child. What she had gone through was almost beyond the capacity of one so young.

'Oh, no, no!' Molapo laughed. 'We're not that bloodthirsty, though there are some among us who think shooting *baas* Potgieter here would rid the world of a nasty piece of work. No, we're simply saying goodbye because we're leaving. When we're gone you can have as much sleep as you want. I'm sure no-one will disturb you except the stupid monkeys.'

Gert was amazed. At first he thought the man was joking, until he saw the others behind Molapo grinning, their knapsacks already hitched on to their backs, their caps pulled down over their eyes, and he realised they were serious. 'But you can't just leave us here like this!' Potgieter began to protest in quite a mindless way. He had not anticipated such a quiet, undramatic ending to his captivity. In spite of the hardships and the anxiety over their safety, captivity with his mistress lying next to him night after night had sometimes taken on the quality of a fairy tale. He and Kristina had sometimes woken up in the middle of the night to discover their bodies were unintentionally touching, their fingers intertwined. A return to Hettie, to the humdrum domesticity of daily farm management, suddenly opened up for Potgieter an appalling prospect. It inspired him with absolute horror. 'After all, we are your prisoners.' Absurdly, he pleaded with Molapo: 'You can't just abandon us.'

'Why not? We didn't bring you here. I'm sure Mrs Potgieter will be delighted to see you after the anxiety of so many days of fruitless search for a missing husband. As for you *juffrou* Miranda Kristina Kemp, in a way you have been a model prisoner. I'm sorry if we caused you a few inconveniences, that couldn't be helped. I hope you understand we were obliged to keep you here with us until certain tasks had been performed. We couldn't take chances, you see, over someone running straight off to the police to spill the beans about our military base. In a way, even though you did not know it, we have been more your hostages than you have been ours really. But for now, dear lovers, our revels are ended.'

The men were grinning, nodding their heads, pulling down caps over their eyes. 'Only request we'll have to make before parting,' Molapo told the hostages, 'we'll have to ask *meneer* Potgieter to make a donation of his clothes. Just in case he is tempted to run straight off to the police as soon as we leave here. At least this should give us enough time to be as far away as possible from here by the time *juffrou* Kemp is able to obtain a pair of trousers for him.' A howl of rage and curses broke out from Potgieter when the men began to strip him of his clothes, leaving him as naked as a pale dumpling to cover himself up with a blanket. Then, very suddenly, as if they had never been, the guerrillas were gone. 'Just like that!' Potgieter used to snap his fingers when he told the story afterwards.

Chapter Twenty-Two

THE news of the guerrilla attack in Tabanyane was carried in the late-night bulletins but, except for the known dead and the extent of the destruction, details were few. The police did not know who was behind the attacks. They had some ideas of course. They had leads. If Lieutenant-Colonel De Kock possessed some advance intelligence it would not have been wise for him to admit it for he would have been quickly accused of weakness and condemned for his inactivity. Already there were those asking questions about his where-abouts during the guerrilla attacks on the police station. Lieutenant-Colonel De Kock had been unable to give a satisfactory explanation. The Bureau of National Security issued what was described as a fairly comprehensive state-ment. The statement suggested that the Tabanyane Resistance Movement, linked to the late deposed Paramount Chief Modiba Seeiso, whose titular head was now his daughter, Princess Madi Seeiso, may have been involved, at least in the planning, of the terrorist attack. The movement was considered to be top on the list of villainous organisations suspected of being behind the outrage. Chief Sekala was of the same opinion. Nevertheless, and this was strongly emphasised, the Bureau could not rule out the hidden hand of the communist-led NLM, which was known to have built an elaborate guerrilla network in the area. The statement added that the most significant – also the most disturbing – element in these attacks was the discovery of the type of sophisticated weapons used: AK 47 rifles, hand grenades and other hand weapons. The statement concluded by stating that no-one with any knowledge of native politics could suppose that illiterate peasants could by themselves launch such a devastating attack.

Anthony Ferguson, his mother, his sister and brother-in-law were having a nightcap in one of the drawing rooms when the radio announced the attack. 'Good God!' Brody whistled without producing a sound from his sweetly rounded lips.

Hazel said curtly: 'Your underground pals, Anthony. Now they've taken a liking to hand grenades, it seems.'

His mother looked surprised by the sudden commotion around her. 'An attack?' Henrietta said wonderingly. 'Where?' She declared she had no idea where Tabanyane was. She said to Hazel: 'I wonder if the boys remembered to water my flowers in the west wing garden. I put in new plants yesterday morning.'

Anthony got up from his chair, saying: 'Excuse me, I'm going to have a word with Advocate Wulitz if I can reach him. Maybe he can arrange a meeting with his partner, someone called Joe Bulane. Maybe they'll know what this is all about. Supposing, of course, they're willing to share their secrets.'

When he got through to the lawyer's house Wulitz's voice sounded normal and relaxed, even voluptuous, as if he were in the middle of a pleasant meal or experience. 'Ah, Mr Ferguson!' Wulitz greeted him in his rising voice. 'How goes it with you? Oh, you heard the news? Same here. As a matter of fact, Joe Bulane is here and can talk to you himself, though I doubt he knows any more than I do what this is all about.'

On the phone Bulane's voice was strained, distant. Certain things, he said, could not be discussed on the 'phone, obviously. Perhaps a meeting could be arranged in the office as before, Bulane suggested. Tomorrow he would be out of the office for the whole day holding meetings. Obviously his organisation had to defend itself against false accusations. It was Saturday night. Monday was the earliest they could meet unless something urgent came up; on Monday at three o'clock as before. 'Your favourite hour, Tony,' Bulane said familiarly and chuckled; then he sighed and said: 'About this Tabanyane business, we had always warned the Government not to trade on the long-suffering attitude and patience of our people. They would not listen. And now this. Obviously, the chickens are coming home to roost.'

Anthony went to bed late and slept uneasily, wondering at the project of searching for a needle like Molapo in a haystack that was already burning. After weeks of frustrating visits to Government offices, security headquarters, police bureaux, and the untidy, cluttered offices of humanitarian organisations dealing with missing persons – mostly individuals assumed to be in police detention – Anthony had got no further than local workers in his search, though for obvious diplomatic reasons he had probably received better co-operation from Government officials than local activists could ever hope to get. However, for all the surly courtesy with which he had been received the search itself had proved fruitless. And now this latest news, dramatic as it was, did not promise to cast any new light on Anthony's inquiry except perhaps to render it slightly absurd. Perhaps this was the right moment to get in touch with head office and explain to Brian Lomax that it was time to end this particular mission.

The following day was a Sunday and from many pulpits around the country prayers were offered to the Almighty, less for peace than as a plea, asking God to help settle scores with the enemy; so the prayers sounded like a renewal of the Covenant at Blood River in 1838. For the entire day news of the attack on the Tabanyane police station was the running theme of radio broadcasts. In the columns of the Sunday newspapers it was a huge story with pictures accompanying the main report showing corpses being removed from the scene of destruction; pictures of the injured being helped into ambulances; of white faces, angry and bewildered, caught in the glare of flash bulbs. A separate story mentioned the assassination of one Robert Jordaan, a prominent farmer in the area, also well-known as the leader of a territorial commando unit among hard-pressed local farmers.

Then it was Monday, two days after the Tabanyane attack. Mark Brody and Hazel were sitting under an umbrella on the balcony, eating breakfast. On the ground floor the 'phone rang interminably. Anthony heard it while shaving. He walked down the staircase but when he reached it the 'phone was off the hook, dangling. On her way to collect the tray with breakfast things Liz stopped to say: 'Mr Anthony, the man was phoning and phoning and phoning. Is third time he phone this morning.'

'Who was on the phone, Liz?'

'Gentleman didn't say his name.'

Anthony picked up the phone but didn't speak into it immediately. With the palm of his hand over the mouthpiece he said to Liz: 'It's okay, you can go now, Liz.' And Liz went shuffling slowly up the stairs, humming her favourite church hymn under her breath. Swathed in her green working overalls, her broad back caught the patch of sunshine that spilled in through the huge glass windows; outside the birds were modulating their summer melodies in quick succession through every key known to bird and man; the servants in the morning enchantment of a new day were calling to one another under the trees, their voices invading and occupying every space; and mounting the last steps of the staircase to the balcony Liz disappeared into the shadow of the first landing, her shuffle absorbed by the sound of his sister's voice twittering against Brody's occasional murmur. Anthony spoke into the phone. 'Hello! Hello!' he waited, then spoke: 'Yes! Yes! Yes, this is he,' he said. 'Well, yes, I'm sorry to have kept you waiting. Yes, of course. Who? Colonel Prinsloo!' He repeated in complete astonishment. 'I don't understand. I should come over to your office. Is there – ' he was cut short

277

by the other. 'I'll understand when I get there? Oh, okay, okay. Yes, of course. Eleven o'clock exactly. I'll be there. Thank you for calling.' He put the phone back in its cradle and walked towards the stairs, stumbled, picked himself up, and began again to climb. Already the morning was pregnant with unanswered questions. Did Prinsloo have news of Molapo? Had they found Molapo locked up in some remote prison inadequately supervised and long-forgotten by the Bureau chiefs? His body drawn and quartered and finally discarded on some rubbish heap? Murdered by *tsotsis* or killed by police murder squads in some early dawn shoot-out. In his frustrated quest he found himself now irresistibly drawn to some creative fiction whose chief elements were woven out of popular romance and police thrillers.

'Anthony!' his sister called. 'Is that you? Come and eat your breakfast before it gets all cold.' On the lawns outside, in the nearby park and distant meadows, and on every treetop, the sun of early January lay like beaten gold on the velvet green. Through the window Anthony could see Solomon dredging the pool with methodical attention. When he reached the happy married couple his sister was lounging about on the cushions in the soft tissues of a coloured muslin dress while her husband, already dressed in his business suit, was turning the pages of the morning paper against the glare of the sun.

Hazel looked up: 'Morning, sweet. Had a good sleep?' He bent down to kiss her.

'Not really.' Anthony had to admit. Without explaining he turned to greet his brother-in-law: 'Good morning, Mark.' Brody peered at Anthony, groaning under the weight of the morning news.

'What's good about it?' he responded curtly, referring to the news that most preoccupied him. 'On the contrary, it's not such a nice morning, is it? Morning newspapers are full of Saturday's gruesome happenings.' He tossed the paper at Ferguson. 'After this I predict we'll see another big flight of capital out of the country.'

Anthony mentioned the call he had just received from the Security Bureau chief. In the morning papers there was an exciting turn to the unfolding story: a white couple, a man and a woman, who for ten days had been kept hostage by a gang of armed terrorists, had come forward to report how they had escaped after the white man had snatched a firearm from one of the gang; a fierce exchange of fire had then ensued; the lone white man had fought bravely against half-a-dozen armed terrorists, managing to escape with the young woman into the bush. The information they had given to the security forces regarding the existence of a guerrilla hideout up on the Tabanyane mountains, housing a veritable arsenal of firearms and grenades, would prove invaluable in tracking down the culprits. Army units had now been deployed over an area of over twenty square kilometres within which the criminal gangs were supposed to have taken shelter. It was only a matter of time before the terrorists were captured. After reading the paper Ferguson ate his breakfast silently, then said to Mark and Hazel: 'I expect Prinsloo will have a lot to say about the guerrilla attack when I see him today.'

'Maybe they've found your missing man,' Hazel said, 'eating grass in the country meadows and feeding on honey.'

As Anthony remembered the arrangement, the security chief was to telephone only if he had news of Molapo. Well, he had telephoned. Did this mean they had found Molapo at last? When he reached Prinsloo's office the sun was climbing steadily to its forenoon peak, beating down on naked flesh with the sharpness of white-hot steel, and along the suburban lanes the leaves sizzled in the motionless air. In front of the security building there were flowers in the small beds that Anthony had never noticed before; beneath the smell of motor oil and litter was the odour of garden flowers, festering and perishing in the summer heat.

At the reception the woman who usually signed Anthony in was at her post. Getting up from her seat, she smiled knowingly, and in spite of apparent effort seemed unable to control her mirth; a big smile fractured her rouged face and heavily lipsticked mouth as she came forward in a rush as though to embrace him. 'Oh, Mr Ferguson, come in! Come in!' She hustled him inside.

'Everyone is waiting for you! Mr Prinsloo will see you right away!'

Anthony could not help but remark on the sudden change of official attitude towards him. For once he did not have to wait for fifteen minutes while Prinsloo signed papers or spoke to people on the phone; for once he was not scowled at as soon as he appeared at the door or required to sign his name and then made to kick his heels for long minutes while he waited for the security chief to call him in; suddenly, quite on the contrary, he was being hurried through security checks and was immediately led into the inner sanctum.

It was true, as the woman had put it: everyone was there waiting for him. Half a dozen men of the special unit in plainclothes were waiting for him, smelling of soap and leather and hair lotion like scrubbed and well turned-out schoolboys attending an end of term ceremony; they waited, all the while smoking and drinking from mugs of steaming coffee. Colonel Prinsloo's young assistant, Sergeant Adriaan Berg, was the first to notice his presence in the room. He greeted the Human Rights International representative with exaggerated cheer in a tone that sounded much like an impertinent attempt at jolly intimacy. 'Ah, Mr Fergie!' Prinsloo's assistant hailed him but Ferguson noticed the repugnant snigger in the voice; taking their cue from young Officer Berg the rest of his audience laughed at Berg's sarcastic truncation of Ferguson's name to 'Fergie'. Berg had been smoking a cigarette which he now crushed into an ashtray as he hurriedly passed into the back room, saying to Ferguson: 'Colonel Prinsloo will no doubt be very glad to see you. I'll tell him you're here.'

Anthony was not offered a seat, but then everyone else was

standing up as though waiting for an unusual happening. What he had not expected was to find among the spectators a press photographer who was apparently waiting to take pictures. Not for the first time the thought crossed his mind that perhaps after all those weeks of effort his labours were about to be rewarded; by all appearances it seemed very likely that Molapo was about to be produced, the only explanation for the photographer's presence being that he was there to document the proceedings.

Prinsloo entered the room through the back door, walking with the steady tread of a platoon commander leading a death-march. With the exception of his visitor he was the only one not smiling, his mouth grim, stern and unyielding, the eyes gritty with an accumulation of intolerance. Long before entering the room the bureau chief had decided to assume a chafed expression, the look of a disappointed man about to reveal secrets which were better left in their wraps. But the men were not fooled; this was for a show, the best that had been put on for them in a long while.

'Well, Mister Ferguson!' Prinsloo breathed as though oppressed by the burden of what he was about to utter. He looked round the office at the others: at the woman in her white pumps and navy blue suit and dusty blonde hair, at the photographer with his parted hair and electric eyes already checking his equipment. Prinsloo wasted no time with greetings and other preliminaries.

'Ferguson, you are no doubt wondering why I telephoned you this morning, why I invited you to come and see me?'

'That is correct, Colonel,' Ferguson said uneasily but growing more curious. Then in an attempt to ease the tension, he said jokingly. 'Am I perhaps about to be deported, Colonel Prinsloo?'

'Deported? Why? A good South African like you, deported? Mister Ferguson, you have an overdeveloped taste for drama. No, you are not being deported. At least, not yet! Have another guess, Ferguson.'

This time Anthony thought he was sure why they had taken all the trouble. 'You found Molapo at last!' he exclaimed, looking from Prinsloo to the rest.

'That's right.' Prinsloo's eyes were like pincers; they gripped at the other's eyes, clutched at them. 'Yes, we've found Molapo!'

Involuntarily, Anthony moved forward, leaned his hands on the desk. 'I just can't believe it!' At a signal the photographer began snapping pictures of a stunned Anthony whose incredulous features were covered with an uncertain smile.

'This is not a joke, is it?' Anthony looked around at everyone in turn.

They all seem to be nodding in agreement.

'No, it's not a joke, Mister Ferguson, I can assure you! Molapo has been found.'

'But where? How? I mean, where was he being kept?' Anthony began rattling off one question after another without waiting for answers. 'What condition is he in? Would it be possible to see him?'

'Of course, we're going to make it possible for you to see him! But, oh, why so many questions, so quick, Ferguson! Where? What? How? A man like you with so much knowledge of the world should not be so easily excited. I can tell you, Molapo is quite well.' Prinsloo paused. 'Unfortunately. But as you'll soon find out, he wasn't kept by us.'

'So where was he found?'

'In the mountains apparently. All the time you have been badgering us to produce Molapo your man was living wild on the Tabanyane mountains.'

'Eating grass and honey,' Anthony said with bitter irony in spite of himself.

'Eating what, Ferguson?'

'Oh, just something my sister said this morning.' Anthony sat heavily on a chair without waiting for permission. 'She said Molapo was probably living on grass and eating honey.'

'Most likely,' Prinsloo said without any sign of humour,

'but that's no concern of ours. What concerns us, Ferguson, is that your man Molapo is one of the terrorists suspected of having attacked the Tabanyane police station over the weekend and most probably was involved in the murder of a white farmer as well. Only thanks to the unheard-of courage of two white individuals who for ten days have been held hostage by your criminal friends are we now in a position to map out the exact terrain where the gang has been operating from. These two white persons – a man and a woman – have come forward with vital information. At this very moment the Tabanyane police and security forces are following several leads. I imagine it will all come out on the radio and in the papers this afternoon. In the meantime police and army units in the area are closing in on what is thought to be Molapo's murder squad.'

Prinsloo paused. The others were listening intently, their eyes fixed on Anthony Ferguson who was looking distinctly unsettled by what he was being told. An air of suppressed expectation dominated the mood in the room. Noise from the street came thinly into Prinsloo's office, the sound of doors and windows being shut or opened, the clatter of footsteps from the outside passage, a car trying to start and stalling.

'Is there any evidence to link Cornelius Molapo to this operation?'

'Oh, yes. Security is not twiddling its thumbs, Ferguson. We have our informants. On the very day of the attack the Tabanyane police came into possession of a valuable piece of information which, had they acted on it in time, might have foiled the attack. In any case, from this informant we now have the names and the descriptions of the main actors involved. Your man Molapo is definitely one of the big fish, Mister Ferguson. A very big fish. Right now this criminal band has been spotted by army helicopters making its way down the mountain, most likely headed for the heavily forested region in the foothills of the Tabanyane mountains. Do you know what this means for you, Ferguson?'

283

Again Prinsloo's eyes were like nails being driven into flesh. Pleased to note the effect his words were producing on the representative of Human Rights International, Prinsloo continued his address in a voice distinguished more and more by a tone of exultation. 'This means, Ferguson, that I shall be compelled to hold you for questioning until we have clarified the real nature of your involvement with individuals who at the end of the day turn out to be enemies of the state; and what seems by now to have been your transparent attempts to put us off the trail of this murderous terrorist, Molapo.'

When after nearly four hours of questioning Anthony was eventually allowed to leave the police station it was almost three o'clock in the afternoon, barely time to keep the appointment with Bulane; Brian Lomax and the HRI board of management in London had been telephoned and various statements made. Anthony had succeeded in putting a call through to Mark Brody with the news of the latest complication but counselled his brother-in-law for the moment to keep the affair secret from his mother and sister.

There had been a further development sure to involve Anthony and Human Rights International. Perhaps in order to embarrass the organisation, the Bureau of National Security had come up with a plan which they hoped would provide an opportunity for HRI and their representative to perform an invaluable service in the interests of race relations and national security. Prinsloo stressed that in view of his entanglement in this affair he might consider it as a way of redeeming himself and the reputation of his organisation from its unwitting folly. It was now a matter of time before Molapo and his gang were rounded up and forced to surrender. Pretoria wanted the men to be captured alive so that they could be thoroughly interrogated. If they failed to surrender the army had orders to go in and shoot them on sight. The fear was that the men might try to resist.

'In that case, the army and police would have no choice but

to open fire on the group on contact.' Prinsloo said that in view of his considerable efforts to rescue Molapo, Ferguson might now wish to prevent his man from being executed by police gunfire through obduracy. Ferguson would be permitted to travel to Tabanyane, there to make contact with the men who were now virtually surrounded, and persuade them to lay down their arms and surrender peacefully at the police and army posts at the foothills of the mountain.

Anthony drove to Wulitz's office in a state of mental fog and emotional turmoil. His organisation had wasted money, time and energy lobbying for the release of a man who was all along leading a guerrilla unit on the Tabanyane mountains. Suddenly all the doubts people had expressed about Molapo, the sceptical questionings by the likes of Mark Brody, whose reservations Anthony had had to dismiss as politically inspired, now returned to mock him. He imagined Tina back in London, eyes popping and chuckling over the scandalous deception of Human Rights International ('The Old Shop'), or Stephen Mayfield and his chums bent over the front page of *The Times* across the bar of the Dean Street pub in Soho, ruefully shaking their heads over yet another example of liberal innocence, and Anthony felt a mounting rage that he was barely able to suppress when he reached Wulitz's office.

When Joe Bulane opened the door he appeared to be in a state of shock, but calm. Glumly he shook Anthony's hand but seemed unable to focus his eyes on the objects in front of him. 'Come in and sit down, Mr Ferguson,' Bulane invited the international servant of humanity and he himself went round to sit behind Joe Wulitz's desk. 'Jackson will bring us tea in a moment. Jackson!' Bulane called. 'Bring us some tea. And make it snappy!'

'Yes, comrade Bulane,' a voice answered from the back room. Ferguson thought: the famous Jackson who was out shopping for Christmas presents the last time I visited is back in harness. For a few minutes they reviewed recent events while Anthony wondered aloud about the role of the NLM in recent developments in Tabanyane. He avoided any mention of the humiliating interrogation he had already endured in Prinsloo's office; nor, as yet, had he made any mention of the plan to send him to Tabanyane to negotiate Molapo's surrender. He wanted to wait until the very end before unveiling the plan to the NLM representative. Bulane sighed, began drumming lightly on top of the desk. Then he started moving documents from one side to the other while waiting for Ferguson to come to the point of his visit.

'Well, Mr Bulane, what about this morning's news? I must confess, I'm entirely flabbergasted at the sudden turn of events!'

'Mr Ferguson, may I say that what has come to pass was not entirely unexpected. We've warned the Government again and again about the consequences of their policy. As a famous American leader once put it, the chickens are finally coming home to roost.'

'Yes. But what about Molapo?'

'What about Molapo?' Bulane echoed the question like someone repeating an unpleasant question to himself.

'Prinsloo says that Molapo was one of the two key leaders involved in the Tabanyane attacks.'

'How does Prinsloo know this?'

'Prinsloo provided details which lead me to believe that Molapo was indeed leading an operation in the area. Apparently white hostages were taken who were able to escape. It appears they have given the police a detailed report about the location, the men involved and the equipment.' Anthony paused to let the other react, but Bulane did not seem in a hurry to speak, so he continued. 'What the NLM does is, of course, none of our business but this involves a question of trust. From what we now know, my organisation was badly misled about Molapo. It is now obvious we were used as a cover for his going underground to wage war against a legally constituted authority. Molapo is not, as we thought in London, a victim of human rights violation. As it now turns out, he is a combatant in a bush war who has participated in, among other things, the assassination of a white farmer in Tabanyane.'

Bulane did not respond to this accusation; instead he began to fulminate against the barbaric treatment of farm workers by their white employers. 'Believe me, Mr Ferguson, Jordaan was an evil man who deserved all he got. We had a file on him a mile long detailing his routine use of torture on workers on his farm: how he made them work long hours without food and made them drink their own urine when they were thirsty. In fact, allegations have been made that Jordaan murdered some of his workers when they complained of ill-treatment and had them secretly buried on the farm.'

'That may be so, Mr Bulane,' Anthony protested. 'But so far as we are concerned, that is beside the point. We are not in the business of fighting liberation wars however unjust the system against which they are fought.'

Bulane stared at Ferguson with his small, speculative eyes; then he shut them in that familiar imitation of a man in prayer. The city noises coming dimly to them suggested the near midday chaos of external affairs, but inside the office an atmosphere of languor rested over the smallest movement the man was making and over the sound of Jackson rattling tea cups in the adjacent room. When Bulane opened his eyes he looked like a man too embarrassed to discuss a recent death in the family. 'Mr Ferguson, about Molapo, truly we're as much surprised by the turn of events as I expect you are. I know how much time and effort your organisation has devoted to the case. In fact, I can tell you, before coming to the office this morning my colleagues and I met briefly to discuss what has happened and, if the story is true, to consider what our response should be. As far as we are concerned – and for a long time his family was of the same opinion – Cornelius has been missing for some months, having disappeared from his home and place of employment

287

without any warning. All along we have been of the opinion that, like so many of our unfortunate people, he was being held incommunicado in some Government detention centre. Our basis of making an appeal to your humanitarian organisation, and to many others like your own, was based on anxiety about his whereabouts.'

Bulane leaned forward a bit, and seemed to regard Ferguson's sceptical face with new, studied interest. 'Therefore, this morning's news has come as a great surprise to all of us, a great surprise.' Again the man from the central committee shut his eyes. Then opening them suddenly he pressed the tips of the fingers of the two hands together and mildly observed: 'Of course, there may still be a fly in the ointment in the police story. About that, we shall have to wait and see.'

Surprised, Anthony said: 'A fly in the ointment? What exactly do you mean, Mr Bulane?'

'I am simply referring to the fact that this story is attributed to a police informer, with all that implies; a source in any case we cannot interview even if that were going to be of any assistance to us. In other words, what I'm saying is that the story of Cornelius's involvement in the so-called "Tabanyane massacre" may be a piece of calculated misinformation on the Government side.'

Anthony smiled. He felt almost elated at the simple recognition of a force, a habit, a trait, an affliction he had encountered before in Latin America; he was back in a territory with which he was all too familiar; of inscrutable political faces, of elaborate hoaxes, disinformation and counter-disinformation, of elusive motives and explanations that were more baffling than the mysteries they were supposed to explain. In trying to follow Bulane's thinking, Anthony felt like a man walking on sinking sands. He was trying very hard to concentrate. 'But what motive would the Government have for inventing such a story?'

'In order to embarrass us.'

'I don't understand. Surely, you can't deny the police

station was attacked and a white farmer assassinated in the area. There are pictures to prove it.'

'Pictures show there was an attack on the police station, certainly. What the pictures don't prove is that our people were involved, Mr Ferguson.'

Bulane twirled his small dapper moustache very slowly. 'I can see you don't grasp the point I'm trying to make, my friend. Simply the South African Government may be responsible for the attack on the police station to make it look like the work of the opposition.'

The two men stared at each other and Bulane drummed on his desk. Finally Anthony said: 'I can see, of course, that the stakes are very high for everyone in the next phase of the struggle for South Africa. In that case, I'm driven to ask: suppose some of your members are actually defying you? What then? Suppose Molapo and the other man – what's his name? – were actually involved in the operation?'

'Of course, of course! You're perfectly right, it's possible,' Bulane said almost impatiently. Again he shut his eyes very tightly as if it pained him to say what he was about to say. 'Mr Ferguson, I don't know how to say this. A movement like ours contains many individuals and tendencies, some pursuing private agendas. That is why we call ourselves a movement and not a party. I also have to admit that to our eternal regret, we have men and women in our midst, call them adventurers if you like, who in their very substantial achievements have been motivated by nothing more than the pursuit of private ambition and personal glory.'

'Excuse me, Mr Bulane. Are you trying to suggest that Molapo – ?'

'No, no, of course not!' The man from the central committee proceeded to answer Ferguson's unasked question. 'Far be it from me to make imputations of that kind against the character of my very best friend and comrade, Cornelius Molapo.'

He then dipped his head rapidly behind the desk, opening

and shutting drawers as if looking for some old photographs, then finding nothing to take out after all, produced a shrill laugh that took Anthony by surprise. 'We went to school together, you know, Corny and I. At varsity we were together like this!' He laced the middle and index fingers together. 'Like this! I also know his wife Maureen very intimately. I can only say I have been very close to both of them.'

Suddenly, Anthony knew, with his long experience of interviewing revolutionary figures, that a point had been reached when he must leave; the point at which the man, having nothing more to say or reluctant to commit himself any further, begins to reminisce about the past, about his family and his friends. Anthony stood up and shook hands with his host.

'One thing I can tell you, Mr Ferguson, we'll leave no stone unturned to find out if Cornelius or indeed any of our people were involved in these operations. And we'll let you know. We owe you, at least, that much.'

'Well, I may soon find out for myself,' Anthony said, getting up.

Bulane stared. 'What do you mean you may soon find out for yourself?'

'Oh, I didn't tell you, Mr Bulane, Prinsloo has arranged for me to travel to Tabanyane,' Ferguson said negligently, enjoying Bulane's look of surprise. 'Of course, it's natural they should want Molapo alive, not dead, and they think an intervention by an international organisation like ours may carry some weight with the guerrilla fighters. I have therefore been asked to travel to Tabanyane, to try and persuade Molapo and his men to lay down arms and surrender at the nearest army post.'

'I see.' Bulane became very thoughtful. 'Mr Ferguson, are you not afraid your organisation may be accused of acting as an instrument of the Pretoria Government?'

'It's a possibility I mentioned to my director on the phone this afternoon. But Prinsloo says that if Molapo and his men refuse to surrender the army will go in and shoot them like so many sitting partridges!'

For a long time Bulane was silent. When Anthony tried to put in a word Bulane deterred him by raising his hand to silence him. He went on drumming on his desk for some time, biting on the end of his pencil. Then as if recovering suddenly from his stupor he shot up from his chair and announced to Ferguson. 'In that case I'm going with you.'

'Going with me!' Anthony exclaimed.

'Yes. Cornelius may require some persuading. I tell you, it may require more than the good offices of Human Rights International to persuade Cornelius to surrender. I can do that.'

'You're a member of an underground organisation. You have no standing whatsoever with the Government, to say the very least. How do you propose to slip through the net?'

'Simple,' Bulane said. 'First as a native. And then as your servant.'

Chapter Twenty-Three

A T break of day, in the grey dark of dawn when light was slowly bringing into shape suburban houses and surrounding trees, and birds were commencing their chorus of warble and twitter, Anthony Ferguson and Joe Bulane drove to Tabanyane. On the phone, Brian Lomax had said: 'Hell, I don't know whether we are doing the right thing, Anthony. Taking sides in an armed struggle, I mean, for that is what it will look like. And then your men, even if they surrender they may hang anyway. Aren't we getting ourselves involved in something more complicated than we can handle?'

'Yes, I suppose so,' Anthony agreed. 'And yet if we can prevent a massacre?'

'I know, I know. The board of directors thinks so too... Well, you have the green light anyway. But keep us informed how things develop. The lines will be kept open day and night.'

Anthony picked up Bulane in a quiet Johannesburg side street as arranged. The car was parked unobtrusively in a driveway between two houses. Here and there dark shapes were beginning to emerge from the shadows, house servants and black people on their way to work. They walked with their heads bent in as though looking for something lost. At first, Anthony did not recognise the man from the central committee. Bulane was dressed in faded old khakis, somewhat soiled and torn and sprinkled with mud, and although this was the height of summer on the *highveld* and the sun would soon be scorchingly hot, he was swathed in a thick army coat that looked frayed and moth-eaten, like something which might have been bequeathed to an importunate servant by a jokey employer. His face was concealed behind dark glasses framed in red plastic which made him look like a friendly gargoyle. In spite of the sombreness of the occasion Anthony could not stop himself from laughing. Helpless, he leaned against the door of the car. 'Oh, Mr Bulane, what a sight to greet the plains of Tabanyane!'

Bulane peered shortsightedly at his fellow traveller: 'Perhaps you might start off by addressing me properly,' he said gravely.

'Yes, sir!' Anthony responded, unable to stop laughing.

'From now on,' Bulane said, 'I am not Mister Bulane. Just plain Bulane, your native boy.'

They entered the car, Anthony still giggling. 'Is this what a native is supposed to look like?'

'More or less. Before being spoiled by city living.' In the car they began to arrange themselves for the long drive to Tabanyane, but as soon as they set off Bulane launched into a solemn lecture about the meaning of the category of the native. 'You may laugh at the way I look, Ferguson,' Bulane said severely, 'but in Tabanyane this is what the *boer* will be most comfortable with if they bother to look. The native, Ferguson, is the most recent, the most preposterous Western invention; in fact, one could say the native never existed before the creation of the colony; the native is a figment of white imagination, a spook; that's why he or she will always play tricks with the minds of our white brothers and sisters in our country. If the native, so-called, exists he exists *by virtue of remaining outside vision*. The native genius, Ferguson, is to remain *invisible*, to be only one of many. And that's why De Kock and his men will look at me and they'll not see me under my native disguise. In broad daylight I'll slip through their fingers unnoticed. And then, of course, there is also the other important characteristic we should never forget. The *native* does not speak. The *native* is always *mute*. Once a *native* acquires speech he or she is done for, for he or she ceases to be a *native*. And that's when the so-called *native* risks imprisonment and risks being shot! So when we get to Tabanyane, you'll see, I will be silent.'

'Well, thanks for the lecture,' Anthony said, keeping his eyes on the road ahead. 'I wonder, can the native drive?'

Bulane scowled. 'Definitely not! You drive.'

Throughout the journey Bulane's mood fluctuated from manic euphoria to latent depression. He talked incessantly, obsessively, about Cornelius, about Cornelius's potential to be a great revolutionary leader 'such as was never seen in southern Africa before now'. He spoke of his great gifts as a public speaker, his capacity for incisive criticism: 'I can tell you, Ferguson, none of us has escaped lightly Cornelius Molapo's ever-lashing tongue.' Bulane considered a little. 'On the other hand, Corny's single great weakness is his essential romanticism, his lack of any sense of collective responsibility, a tendency to go it alone. Essentially, he is a loner!' Bulane seemed to consider his bill of accusations as somewhat incomplete, for he immediately added: 'And then Corny has sometimes shown a surprising lack of familiarity with some of the deepest currents of revolutionary thought.' Anthony was tempted to suggest that it was perhaps because of Molapo's lack of familiarity with the deepest currents of revolutionary theory that he had decided to take up arms and fight in Tabanyane, but desisted. In any case, it was difficult to know when to take Bulane seriously. Sometimes he seemed to be merely indulging in personal reflection. From time to time he looked out of the window at the vanishing landscape, at the bush, trees and cows grazing quietly on the *veld*, and then seemed to address himself to no-one in particular: 'There is, of course, Corny's well-known love of the bottle,' he said, smiling dreamily behind his red plastic glasses, 'but then I always say, let he who is without sin cast the first stone.'

At intervals they listened to the radio bulletins recounting the progress being made by army and police units tracking down what was described as dangerous terrorists. After the guerrilla attacks the defence and police forces had pinpointed an area in the mountainous region of Tabanyane where it was thought the fleeing guerrillas had taken cover. The area had now been completely encircled, the guerrillas were being given less than twelve hours in which to give themselves up; and unless Molapo and his men could be persuaded to put down their arms and surrender peacefully, they would probably be massacred by the forces of law and order. When, following the discussions with Brian Lomax, Anthony wondered aloud about his role in this mission, Bulane seemed, surprisingly, to have changed his opinion about the HRI intervention in the crisis. 'Believe me, Mr Ferguson, your coming along as a broker for peace can do nothing but good,' he said. After all, were human rights not at the heart of this stand-off between the army and the guerrillas? he asked. The man from the central committee emphasised that Ferguson's presence as a representative of an international organisation that had been so vitally concerned with Molapo's fate made it obligatory to see to it that now Molapo had been found alive he was not murdered in cold blood. Bulane thought that the presence on the spot of an international observer would most certainly act as a deterrent to the army from taking precipitate action, at least until every avenue had been pursued to lure the men down from their mountain hideout.

Having decided to go along with the rescue operation Anthony now found that he even looked forward to meeting Molapo, should such a meeting be possible. He was feeling distinctly light-hearted. 'Can it be,' he joked to Bulane, 'that I'm about to meet the object of my quest, the undisputed leader of the Tabanyane underground, King *Tokoloshe* himself?'

'After which your mission would've been accomplished, wouldn't you say, Mr Ferguson?' Bulane asked, giggling a little, his head cocked to one side.

'That, Mr Bulane, is another question,' Anthony muttered. 'Was there ever a mission to accomplish, I ask myself?'

The army and police had set up a command centre in the foothills of the mountains across the Mokone River. They had sealed all the mountain passes to the west and to the east and had placed troops on the back slopes of Tabanyane, completely encircling an area of about ten square kilometres. The single point of escape was a narrow goat track down a thin ledge across the face of the mountain, descending on to a narrow platform which led straight into the forest and into the arms of the waiting police and army detachments. On the plain at the base of the foothills a simple canvas tent had been set up, partly hooked to a baobab tree; beneath the canvas a working table was in place the top of which was cluttered with all manner of technical equipment, including a radio set and telephone, detailed maps of the area and photographs of some of the suspected guerrillas. Soldiers and armed policemen toting heavy automatic weapons and grenade launchers were lounging about everywhere, waiting for the order to go into action. Lieutenant-Colonel Adam de Kock was in charge of the civilian aspect of the operation while the army took care of the overall military strategy.

Very pointedly De Kock had refused to shake hands with the representative of Human Rights International when Anthony Ferguson and Joe Bulane, now partners in the cause of negotiated peace, presented themselves at the advance command centre. Without looking directly at Ferguson's black companion De Kock tossed back his head in Bulane's direction: 'And what is this? Is this the so-called interpreter you were supposed to bring with you?' Bulane gave a twitch of a smile and said nothing. 'Well, at least it can attempt a smile,' De Kock said.

He turned to Ferguson: 'Your people, Ferguson, have been spotted coming down the north-eastern side of the mountain, as we guessed they would. They're obviously headed for the forest creek about half a kilometre from Mostert. Apparently, they are hoping to make it across to Makapane.' De Kock paused, smiling pleasantly at Ferguson. 'But we are not going to let them. We'll cut them off before they can even get out of the creek,' De Kock explained cheerfully. He was in better spirits than at any other time since the counter-insurgency campaign began in late October. 'Your one chance of saving the lives of these men, Ferguson, is to get to them before we do and persuade them to lay down their arms. Come out of the forest peacefully, unarmed, with hands up in the air. We'll make all the necessary arrangements for you to reach them without interference. Then within a specified time we expect you to come out with or without them. If they refuse to surrender our orders are to go in and shoot them.' Ferguson and Bulane exchanged looks. 'That we will do with the greatest of pleasure,' De Kock finished.

Up on the mountain Cornelius Molapo, Sefale Phiri and the remnants of the Tabanyane Resistance fighters were trying to break out of the military encirclement by making their way down a steep and difficult mountain trail, across slippery rocks and narrow rock shelvings not broad enough to allow two people to walk across at a time, sometimes with a sheer drop of some two thousand metres on one side. While the men clambered down the face of the mountain, suddenly there appeared out of the dawn sky the first of the spotter aircraft, swooping down so low over the mountainside that the men prayed for a spectacular crash. Led by the redoubtable Phiri, who in his youth had herded goats on the Tabanyane mountains and boasted of knowing every nook and cranny of the dangerous terrain, the men had been walking for over an hour before they saw the first spotter aircraft. Instantly, they transformed themselves into hedgehogs, lying flat on their stomachs, and from this humble position hugging the ground like a loving friend, the men scanned the sky with an intensity that drained the eye of response to anything but the single speck of metal drifting across their immediate horizon. 'We ought to open fire at that damn 'copter before they spot us!' Phiri said with rage.

Molapo sucked at his teeth. 'Don't be a fool, Phiri! You want to let them know where to find us?' Each time the aircraft flew past the men would press themselves against the face of some rock, or if they were lucky enough to find shelter behind a clump of low shrubbery, they would crouch or lie flat on their stomachs until the aircraft had glided past. They could not pause even for a short time in their bid to escape from the area; until they reached the bottom of the mountain trail this particular route offered little opportunity for concealment. It was so narrow no horse could go up or down that way; a man sometimes had to limber himself up by grasping precariously on to a jutting rock or by seizing on the exposed root of a mountain shrub.

After the spotter planes there appeared a single helicopter, droning like an evil insect in a sky that was now tinged with the red of the rising sun. It flew so low the men could actually see from their place of hiding the faces of the people on board. It flew round and round, and Molapo was able to identify the rough-hewn features of the Tabanyane chief of police.

Looking down at the fleeing guerrillas from the air through the window of a police helicopter, Anthony thought the men resembled bed bugs creeping slowly across the wrinkled skin of a rock. They looked so small that at first you didn't think they were moving at all but were small, stationary brown objects stuck on the surface. But Adam de Kock's eye was too keen to miss anything. 'There they are, the murderous cowardly buggers!' he shouted with excitement. His massive bulk bouncing up and down within the confines of his seat, De Kock seemed to be about to perform a sedentary war dance. Far from taking offence at Ferguson's presence, when the police chief had been told by the men in Pretoria and Johannesburg that he would have to take along an international observer, he had become visibly animated. Finally, he had insisted that Ferguson should leave his native boy at the police post and accompany him on his half-hourly air surveillance of the area. Perhaps Colonel De Kock was only too pleased to display to his assumed adversary the undisputed efficiency of the police operation, tending to mistake in this area, as in many other aspects of life, technical for moral efficiency. In any case, De Kock's enthusiasm knew no bounds. 'First, we will cut them off!' he joked, punching the fist of one hand into the palm of the other. 'Then we'll move in and kill them! Who said that, Mr Ferguson? You get no marks for guessing correctly.'

'I don't know. A politician during the Roman Empire,' Anthony muttered. De Kock winked provocatively at the man from Human Rights International, who now sat hunched forward in his seat, staring down at the face of the mountain.

'Roman Empire?' De Kock grinned. 'That is bloody funny!'

Anthony had thought of the journey through the forest as an immensely stupid lark but once he and Bulane had crossed the waters of the small creek, picking their way over the pale smooth rocks that were used as stepping stones by villagers, he was suddenly overcome by dread. It seemed to him that danger, as his mother and his sister had repeatedly warned before his departure, lurked everywhere, that he could trust no-one, neither the police side nor the NLM. Behind Bulane and himself, concealed behind dense foliage and the heavy trunks of tenebrous trees and undergrowth, lay hidden De Kock's men, backed up by well-trained army auxiliaries with a barely concealed lust for action. In front of them, heading towards the creek, were guerrillas of the NLM or Tabanyane Resistance. The names mattered little. The two organisations worked in tandem; the people who led them were sometimes the same individuals, like Cornelius Molapo.

Anthony had the extraordinary sensation of being hemmed in on all sides by forces he did not understand. So little was known of the guerrilla force that was crawling down the secret gorges through the gaping dolomite rock and sandstone; not even their numbers were known. If Bulane had information about them he was not saying anything. In fact, in the past twenty minutes or so, Bulane had been very quiet. Perhaps, as the moment of a meeting with the guerrillas drew near, the burden of responsibility bore down more heavily on his shoulders than before. After they had crossed the small stream, the two men found themselves on a grassy patch of ground fringed by giant sycamore and ironwood; to the west of this small amphitheatre red bush-willows tangled around shady *mkuhlu* trees. 'What do you think, Mr Bulane?' Anthony enquired, casting around a piece of ground that looked like the original Garden of Eden.

Anthony had spoken only to hear his own voice, or perhaps to hear Bulane make some comment, but he need not have bothered. Bulane hardly had any opportunity to reply because they were suddenly aware that they were not alone in that neck of the woods. Emerging from behind a clump of trees, a group of armed men stepped forward quickly, without a rustle of leaves or creak of their boots, ready to encircle them. Presently, one of them, a very tall, lean man, seemed to recognise Joe Bulane. He put out his arm to halt the others.

Instantly, Anthony knew that in that hushed forest calm he was at last staring into the face of Cornelius Molapo, though this tall African wearing khaki trousers and olive green bush jacket had his eyes half-concealed behind very dark sunshades. Other black men, perhaps eight in all, carrying rucksacks and armed with automatic weapons, crowded quickly behind him and formed a kind of semi-circle. From numerous photographs he had poured over in his London

300

office, photographs that he had carried with him everywhere, Anthony knew with unsheakable conviction that at last he was face to face with Cornelius Molapo. The realisation filled him with confused emotions, with a feeling of yearning and thwarted intimacy. He was aware that the men were both curious and resentful of his presence. Bulane walked past him in an uncertain stride, then paused suddenly some twelve paces from the group. 'Power!' he saluted.

'Amandla!' the group replied listlessly, staring suspiciously at the two men. After the exhausting trek across the mountains it was obvious that they were dead tired and when their destination was so close, probably longed only to be allowed to proceed on to the plains of Tabanyane and into the villages. This meeting with Bulane gave them no pleasure.

'Corny boy, how good to see you!' Bulane exclaimed in his shrill giggling voice, moving forward to embrace the tall man. Then he hesitated. 'But what a way to meet!' Bulane cast a quick glance at the forest behind him. 'Shake hands, *mfana*. Corny, this whole place is completely surrounded by army and police. Right now it's touch and go! We had to get here as quickly as we could before those buggers started shooting at you. Corny, you and your men have walked straight into the arms of De Kock and the SADF. And, Corny, there is no time to lose. I advise you to put away your weapons and follow me. I'll explain later.'

Molapo made no comment. He was extremely calm, Ferguson noted, even detached. 'What do you want, JB?'

'What do I want? Corny, we are trying to save your skin.'

Molapo cast a suspicious glance at Anthony Ferguson. 'And who is this white man with you?'

'Why so many questions, Corny boy? What manners!' Bulane laughed, but he was nervous. 'As you can see, Corny, I've brought you a visitor. Mr Ferguson here is from Human Rights International. Remember? He came all the way from London to find you, Corny boy, when it was thought you were missing, perhaps in police custody.' Bulane permitted himself the luxury of a small giggle. 'Mr Ferguson is here to arrange for your evacuation.'

Cornelius stamped his boot on the soft soil of the forest. 'JB, this is no time for playing games. What's the purpose of all this?'

'Just a minute, Corny!' Bulane said sternly. 'Christ, Corny boy, you might at least begin by shaking hands with Mr Ferguson here after all the trouble he has taken over you. First he spends a lot of time looking for you when you're lost and nobody can find you. And now he is trying to save you from summary execution. Is this how you want to show your gratitude?' It was the old Bulane again, full of banter, even under the shadow of a possible tragedy.

Strangely enough, Bulane's little joke seemed to divert Molapo's attention for a moment. Briefly he turned to study Ferguson and he and Anthony stared at each other with curiosity. Anthony wanted to say something memorable, the first words of salutation between himself and his trophy, but he had no idea what to say to this desperately harassed man. As if to satisfy Anthony's curiosity Molapo slipped off his sunshades and Ferguson found himself staring into a pair of unblinking brown eyes glazed with fatigue; the long face, sharp cheekbones and bristle of a moustache. So this was his enigma in the flesh at last. How Tina would enjoy hearing about this ultimate encounter in an African forest between the falcon and the falconer.

'Mr Cornelius Molapo, I presume.' Ferguson could not resist the joke. Even Molapo must have appreciated the humour of the situation. But for Anthony it was a moment like no other in his career, rich in symbolism. Standing right there in front of him was his first major failure, his shame, his defeat: Molapo his demon. He and Molapo had been linked to each other from the moment Molapo's dossier, full of false information, had been bounced like a booby trap on to his London desk, and now they would be forever joined in an indeterminate future by this interminable search – a search for

302

what was not lost after all. What *was* lost forever for both of them was home and security; always a return to a home that was finally not home, for him to Johannesburg, for Molapo to Tabanyane. There by the small creek, in the forest undergrowth, Anthony Ferguson and his symbolic quarry shook hands.

'Glad to meet you, Mr Ferguson,' Molapo said in his slightly lilting voice. 'I'm sorry if we've put you to a great deal of trouble. Believe me, you're not the only one. A couple was left behind on top of those mountains.' Briefly, Molapo turned to look back at the mountains which had been home to him and his men for the past months. 'One man was left without his trousers,' Molapo continued, smiling a little in memory of Portgieter. 'It's the nature of the times we live in which are to blame.'

'Corny, we've got to get you out of here quick,' Bulane fretted. 'We don't have much time. They've given you less than forty-five minutes to give up and surrender your arms. As I said, the whole place is swarming with troops. They've even dropped men behind the mountains. Across that hill over there, on the east side of this forest, there's a whole squadron of the SADF waiting to take a shot at your ass.'

'What do they expect of us? To give up, just lie down and die?'

'Mr Molapo, if you and your men wish to avoid being executed out of hand...'

'They expect you to surrender, Corny. That's the deal. Give up your arms and come out with your hands in the air. They'll give you safe conduct.'

'Deal been struck!' Molapo repeated. 'Safe conduct. Willingly go into De Kock's jail and be tortured? Is that's what's called "safe conduct" these days?'

'You'll go to prison for some years, certainly. Maybe life,' Bulane pressed on. 'But that's better than being cut down by fire, isn't it? And who knows how long this regime will last? Meanwhile, Mr Ferguson's organisation and others like his will mobilise international public opinion. The main thing is you won't be hanged. There may even be a general amnesty for all political prisoners at some future date. Who knows?'

Cornelius considered this a little. 'JB, you sound more and more like a junior partner in some future political arrangement. Our answer to all that is: NO!'

'Corny, don't be a bloody fool!' Bulane shouted. ' I'm begging you, Corny. Give up your weapons. I repeat, you won't be able to get out of here alive if you do not surrender.'

'Neither will you, JB, get out of here, I mean. Remember how once upon a time, in a Johannesburg office, you persuaded me to come out here against my best inclinations. Well, you might say I've grown into the job, so to speak. I'm sticking with the people of Tabanyane until justice is done to them.'

'Corny, you're mad! What justice?'

'Until their expropriated lands are returned to them and that usurping traitor Sekala Seeiso is removed as paramount chief of Tabanyane.'

'Corny, you're out of your mind! You've lived up in the mountains too long. Come down to the deep valleys and the broad plains where real people live.'

'You're wrong, JB I've always lived with the people. Even before I became a combatant, that was my strength. It's my strength now. On the contrary, it's people like you, sitting in offices, taking decisions behind closed doors, who will always betray the people. But fortunately, you will not get another chance to do that. We will not let you.'

'Mr Molapo, can I talk to you for a moment?' Anthony said. 'It's true what Mr Bulane is saying. We don't have much time. There are men out there with fingers on the trigger, itching to open fire on you.'

'We are ready for them,' Molapo said. 'We've always been ready for them.' He turned toward his men. 'Ask these men.'

'Okay, Corny,' Bulane said impatiently. 'We've done all we

could. We drove all the way up here to get you out of the soup. You refuse to hear reason. It's your own funeral.'

'And yours too, JB'

'What do you mean?'

'Here's what we'll do. We'll let Mr Ferguson here go back to that fat ass of a police chief De Kock with a message to tell him we refuse to surrender. And you'll stay here with us when the shooting starts and defend the people's movement with your last drop of blood.'

'Corny, you're absolutely mad.'

'I'm not mad.' Molapo turned to Anthony; his automatic rifle was hanging from the shoulder by the strap, his finger hooked lightly on the trigger. 'Mr Ferguson, I think it's time for you to leave us. You'll please tell Colonel De Kock we have no desire to lay down arms. Our experience of South African conditions in jail and the men we have to deal with, whether it's De Kock or that murderous killer Sekala, is that laying down arms does not pay. So tell Adam de Kock we refuse to surrender. Tell De Kock he can go and suck his cock. Tell him we have no desire to go into a white man's jail. De Kock will have only our dead bodies to send to prison. Tell him that.'

'Mr Ferguson, perhaps we should now leave,' Bulane said. 'We've done all we could.'

'Not you, JB,' Cornelius said calmly. 'You stay right here with us and fight side by side with the people you helped to recruit. You know what they do in the army with officers who desert their troops. They shoot them, JB.'

Molapo raised his rifle to the height of his waist. Phiri and the other men waited in an atmosphere suddenly filled with tension. It must have dawned on Bulane that Cornelius was deadly in earnest, but his realisation that his life was in danger did not cause him to panic. On the contrary, he seemed to gather strength from his precarious grip on the situation. He became furious. 'You fool!' he shouted at Molapo. 'What on earth do you think you're playing at? You're tired of killing *boers*, now you want to murder your own comrades? My goodness, Corny! You call yourself a revolutionary. Good gracious, you're a bloody clown, Corny.' Perhaps in sudden desperation Bulane suddenly went off another tack: 'Oh, don't think you can fool me. I can see through all your posturing. You're out to settle scores. It's because of Maureen, isn't it? You want to take revenge because I once screwed your wife. Corny, I repeat, you're a joke! Anyway, what do you want? I'm getting out of here.'

Molapo turned to the young white man. 'Mr Ferguson, you travel around the world investigating human rights abuses. I think you have one more human rights abuse to witness before you return to England. You're about to witness an execution.'

Anthony had no idea who started the shooting first: Molapo, the guerrillas or De Kock's sharp-shooters, but suddenly the entire forest seemed to be ablaze with gunfire. Sheltering behind a giant fig tree in a clump of bushes, De Kock shouted in his booming voice: 'Ferguson, get out of the way! You'll get killed!' Anthony pressed his face down hard on the grass; in just a few seconds his shirt had become soaked with sweat; he felt an incredible desire to touch the limbs of his mother, to smooth the soft furrowed garments she sometimes wore at night, and to linger gently in the comfort of a mother's breast. It seemed to him he was losing his mind completely. Behind him where he lay face-down on the grass there was a sudden rustling movement from a cove that was covered with bracken and ferns. After what seemed a very long time he heard in the silence that followed the exchange of fire someone's footfall. Someone grasped him by the shoulder and lifted him to his feet. It was Colonel Adam de Kock. Anthony shook the man's hand off. 'Go away from here, Ferguson,' De Kock said. 'Go back to England. Go anywhere you like, but go away from here. Here you'll always get in the way. In South Africa the war has only just begun.'

And from the summit of an isolated yellowwood, a dove started to coo quite mindlessly.

Glossary

amadlozi:	ancestral spirits (pl in zulu)
amandla:	power, so amandla awethu is power to the people
baas:	master/boss
batho!	people!
bloedvermenging:	blood-mixing
boer:	white afrikaners/farmers
boere:	plural of boer
bokkies:	girls or chicks (as in young women)
braaivleis:	barbecue
dorp:	town
donga:	ditch
ek kry 'n siekte:	I am getting ill
ek sal jou skiet, hoor jy?:	I'll shoot you, your hear me?
ek sê:	I say
goeie môre:	good morning
Gou jong!:	hurry up!
hawu, baas!:	is that so master!
hoer:	whore
hoere:	plural of whore
hulle sal ons doodmaak:	they will kill us
Ja, ja! Open up, jong:	Yes, Yes! Open up, man
jou bliksem:	you bastard/you arsehole
jou skelm:	you sly old fox
juffrou:	madam/Mrs
jy praat 'n klomp kak:	you talk a load of shit
jy verstaan:	you understand
jy wil mos altyd slaap, ne?:	you lazy niggers always asleep
kaffermeitjie:	little kaffir girl
kaffir:	derogatory and racist term for a black person
kak:	excrement
keppies:	small caps/hats

khakibos:	stinkweed
knobkerrie:	wooden stick with large head used as a weapon
koffiehuis:	coffee house, café
Kom julle! Jou donderse kaffers!:	Come on! You bloody kaffirs!
kraal:	a hut or a pen or fold
maar:	can have two meanings depending on context. Can mean thin, as in a thin person, also means but or only just, as in 'just a little'
meneer:	sir
mevrou:	Mrs, or maam, when used as a term of respect for a woman
mfana:	boy (derogatory way of calling a black man)
mkgoti:	name of a person
modimo!:	Oh Lord!
mos:	only/just
nthate:	old man or dad a friend (a term of endearment)
oupa:	grandfather or grandpa
pangas:	machete
Parktown boy:	upper crust boy or upper-middle class
pondokkies:	little huts
shebeens:	illegal drinking dens
sjambok:	also spelt shambok – short, fat whip, (about four or five feet long) originally made of leather, but now of plastic or rubber. Used by police for riot control among other things
stoep:	veranda
stompie:	cigarette butt
tishera!:	name of a person
tsotsi:	crook/small time township gangster
ubuntu:	people/spirit of belonging to a community
untermenschan:	lesser person or person of little worth
veld:	bush or scrubland
verdoemde:	condemned
verdomde:	damned/bloody used as a swear word
verdompte se kaffers:	bloody kaffirs
verstaan:	understand or do I make myself clear?
vervloekste:	damned
voetsek!:	go away!
vrou:	wife
wag jou ma! ek sal jou moer!:	wait you mother! i'll whip you up!
wag my baas, asseblief tog!:	wait master please!
yebo:	yes/affirmative